CYPHER

Matt Ryland

NORTH SKY
PRESS

North Sky Press
Ravenna, Ohio

Publisher's Note: This is a work of fiction. Names, characters, places, and incidents are a product of the author's imagination. Locales and public names are sometimes used for atmospheric purposes. Any resemblance to actual people, living or dead, or to businesses, companies, events, institutions, or locales is completely coincidental.

Library of Congress Control Number: 2024918921

First Edition Published 2025
Printed in the United States of America

ISBN: 979-8-9912901-1-1 paperback

First Edition: 2025

For Mom,
for always believing in me even when I did not.
And for Dad,
for instilling in me perseverance.

CHAPTER ONE

Miami, Florida

It would be inaccurate to say she was dead already. But it was a certainty. He just hadn't pulled the trigger yet.

She was singing again. Something low. Melancholy. Brent Savage strained to discern the words of the song. He adjusted his earpiece, rooting it in place, but the result was the same. Gibberish. She was making up the lyrics as she went along. Louder now. Off-key. She was wearing her earbuds.

Still no visual on his mark. There was just an empty room, its glass door to the balcony open, curtains fluttering in the breeze. At this distance, his 10x night scope brought the room into sharp focus, its advanced electronics rendering the scene a sickly, eerie green.

Beads of sweat painted his face, their droplets pooling, succumbing to gravity, and forging a path of least resistance to the corner of his eye. The salt stung. But Savage ignored it. Pain was irrelevant. Even now, after remaining motionless for the last two hours, he refused to budge, his back burning in agony. He was a viper, poised to strike, and locked into the moment where nothing else mattered.

He had observed his mark come and go from the seventh-floor apartment for ten days. Learned her schedule. Studied her habits. Made note of her visitors and recorded their conversations. But mostly he watched.

Savage glanced at his watch. Twenty-three twenty-three hours Romeo. She should have been finishing her bath. As if on cue, the woman appeared again, gliding into his field of view like an actress in a Broadway play. Enter stage right.

Her name was Eliana. Eliana Bautista. Her clients knew her as Jade, though for two thousand dollars an hour, she would be whoever they wanted her to be. She was toweling the wet tangles of her hair as she made her way to the open door. She wore a short silken robe, loose and untethered. As she reached to draw the curtains, her robe parted, and Savage glimpsed the dark patch of hair hiding beneath her bare, smooth stomach. He blinked. Slowed his breathing. Discipline was to be maintained at all costs.

He was prepared to make the switch to infrared vision on his Viper/INF-1NS scope, but then she did something that took him by surprise—she hesitated. Instead of closing the curtains, she stared out the window, looking over the urban nightscape of downtown Miami. Even at two hundred and fifty yards, Savage could see the minute details of her heart-shaped face, see the orbs of her eyes blazing in the artificial light. Her eyes were unsettled, drifting without care across the horizon, while her song morphed into whispers, then humming.

My God, she's beautiful. Savage admonished himself for getting distracted, however briefly, and gave a systematic sweep of the studio apartment with his KS V Bullpup sniper rifle, his eye never leaving the scope. Antique bronze poster bed in the foreground, queen-size. Day-old laundry strewn on the floor. Metal nightstand with a glass top. Vanity. Utilitarian kitchen with white painted cabinets and stainless steel appliances in the background. Yesterday's dirty dishes piled in the double sink. Hello Kitty clock on the wall, two minutes slow.

He returned to his mark, his movement smooth and measured, instantly reacquiring her in the crosshairs. He froze. She was staring right at him.

Savage maintained his discipline. He was invisible. He had made sure of this. The sniper hide was deep within the room's shadows, away from the window. He'd hung a dark blanket for a backdrop to break up his silhouette, his clothes nothing less than a perfect match. Black grease paint obscured his face, assuring him of complete invisibility to the naked eye. Distance alone prevented her from seeing him. Still, her fixed gaze was disconcerting.

The woman sighed, brushed the towel across her throat, and daubed it down between her breasts before letting it drop to the floor. She turned and made her way to the bed. The curtains remained open. Perfect.

The sun had set hours ago, yet there had been no relief from the heat. The humidity was relentless, a huntress on the prowl from which there was no escape. He could hear the passing traffic below, the soft swoosh of their tires, interrupted only by the occasional distant blare of sirens. But silence wasn't necessary, nor a concern. Passersby below droned incessantly about their mundane lives, chattering like insignificant insects on the move, oblivious to their proximity to death's hand.

In the apartment, silence prevailed. The woman lay on the unmade bed, one arm draped over her head, the other resting on her stomach. Moments passed without movement. Savage wondered if she had fallen asleep but took note when she flipped open her robe, revealing her perfectly taut, athletic body.

Savage felt a slight elevation in his pulse rate but fought to maintain his focus. He wasn't immune to the sins of the flesh. Far from it. But his task was at hand. Nothing else mattered.

The woman sighed heavily, allowing her left hand to roam freely across her body, the tips of her fingers brushing lightly across her belly in small, circular motions.

This was new. Unexpected.

She stirred, her breathing more rapid, and as she let her hand slip to the recesses of her parted legs, she let out an audible moan.

Savage blinked, a trickle of sweat trailing down his back. His heart rate was on the rise again, and a troublesome tremor had worked its way to his hands. Something was wrong, but he ignored it.

He glanced at his watch. Twenty-three thirty hours. Time was up. Savage relieved the ache in his shoulders by easing into his shooting position. He took a deep breath and exhaled slowly. Tried it again. But the niggling sensation in the pit of his stomach remained.

It wasn't an easy shot. She lay fully reclined, her head partially obscured by the exterior wall. But it was doable. A broadside shot to the heart, like taking down a deer. Savage had her centered in the scope, but after considering the night's hot, humid air and slight ocean breeze, he adjusted his aim, holding three clicks over from the target.

Radio chatter crackled in his earpiece, breaking the thick silence.

"Cypher. You have a go."

Savage inhaled, allowing half of the air out. He increased trigger pressure, like a choreographed dance, muscle memory taking over. He stopped. Shook his head. Something wasn't adding up. New questions formed deep within the recesses of his mind, born amongst murky shadows, away from the bright lights of military discipline. Simple in logic, quick to form. Why? Why this mark? What threat did a high-end call girl from Miami represent that warranted eliminating her?

"You have a go, Cypher. I repeat: you're 'go' for target removal." Control knew he hadn't taken a shot. He was their eyes, their ears.

Savage remained motionless, the crosshairs of his scope steady. They had programmed him to follow orders, to follow protocol. To kill without question. And he was damn good at it. He had eliminated dozens of terrorists, drug lords, mob bosses, and enemy combatants. Yet with this nobody—this simple call girl—he hesitated.

"Cypher, do you read? I say you have a go. Take the target out."

After every radio break from Control, the audio returned to the studio apartment, where the woman was working her way to a crescendo. She extended her legs, her toes pointed like a ballerina. Her whole body was rigid, locked into the moment.

Savage activated his mic, then cleared his throat. "Control. This hit makes no sense. Why the call girl?"

There was a long pause. Dead air and static was his only reply. Precious seconds passed, devoured by indecision. Savage felt compelled to repeat the question. He didn't have to. Control severed the silence with an angry reply. Fever-pitched and taut like a rubber band about to snap.

"Cypher. Your target is the whore. The reasons don't matter. Got that? You will follow orders. Now take the goddamned shot!"

Savage clenched his jaw, his eyes narrowing ever so slightly. He recognized the voice. Understood the gravity of his direct order. He said nothing. He wiped the sweat from his palms and opened and closed his right hand to restore circulation. With his rifle secure on the tripod, he reacquired the target in the scope one last time.

The woman was still listening to her earphones; the white cord snaked between her breasts like a sleeping serpent. She was still trying to catch her breath, her arms draped above her head. It was a wonder she could hear the knock at the door. But the rap was loud and fired off in rapid succession. It startled her.

Savage watched her stand, hastily wrap herself in the robe, and pad across the tile floor to answer the door.

He felt the hair on the back of his neck stand on end. "Don't answer the door," he warned, somehow unaware he wasn't in the same room with her. He watched her give a cursory look through the peephole and open the door. She hadn't opened it halfway before the door imploded in on her.

"Fuck."

CHAPTER TWO

Somewhere near Denver, Colorado

The Control Center was pragmatic in design, from the ergonomics of the furniture to the state-of-the-art HDTV video screen wall that encompassed the room. Every switch, keyboard, and control console provided its operators with maximum efficiency. Despite these practical applications, the multimillion-dollar Control Center was likely to conjure up images of the Starship *Enterprise* of TV fame, a slick, newly painted Hollywood set that offered more flair than function. But in actuality, Control was the nerve center of Operation Darkwater, and the virtual brain for all its clandestine operations.

The room, though small, was circular and divided into three rings. Manning the inner ring were the handlers, the personnel assigned to keep in contact with the agents in the field. The hackers, code crackers, and cyber-warriors who gathered intel were tucked away in the middle ring. The outermost ring accommodated the think tank, the intel analysts who deciphered all the information and provided solutions.

But it was Deputy Director Theo Spearman who was in command, and upon entering Control at twenty-one thirty hours Tango, the room was all his. Short in stature and short on patience, Spearman knew well that many in the agency felt he suffered from a Napoleon complex. He didn't care. His authority was absolute.

There were more than a dozen agents on duty that night, the room abuzz with its typical crosstalk and radio chatter, and there was only one handler on station. Spearman wasted no time making a direct line to her console.

The reason the inner ring was sparsely populated that night wasn't lost on Spearman. He had made that call. He needed compartmentalization, and the only personnel assigned to tonight's hit were on a need-to-know basis. Or expendable.

"Cypher. You have a go."

Spearman didn't know the junior agent's name, but as he loomed over her, he stole a glance at her plastic ID tag. "What you got, Mendoza?"

"Nothing to note, sir. We have visual on a high-value target and have a go for a hit. But there seems to be a hitch, sir."

"Hitch? What kind of hitch?"

"I'm not sure, sir. Target acquired, but we're several minutes past go."

Spearman tittered. "What's the problem? We've got a closed window? Curtains?"

"No, sir. Window is still open. Asset sabotaged the AC unit, as ordered. He made sure building maintenance was out on another call, sir. He just seems…" Mendoza stopped and cleared her throat. Despite the icy, climate-controlled air in the center, beads of sweat sprouted from her pores like morning dew on a manicured lawn. "Distracted."

Spearman laughed again, though it was born out of disbelief. "Distracted? By what? A little splinter in his trigger finger? Jesus H. Christ! We can't afford to have a hitch, Agent."

Mendoza nodded.

"Who's the asset?"

"NT-Zero, sir. Cypher."

Spearman blinked and shifted his weight off the agent's chair. *What the hell? An NT?* He rubbed his hand absently across the crown of his thinning hair, paused, and then nodded.

"All right. Tell him again. Tell him to take the shot. He'll follow orders."

"You have a go, Cypher. I repeat: you're 'go' for target removal."

Silence.

"What the hell is going on?" Spearman nudged Mendoza. "I need visual. Hook me into his Viper scope."

Mendoza hesitated, saw the deputy director's piercing blue eyes, and then followed his orders. An overly exposed image bathed in green light filled the agent's widescreen monitor. The scope's reticles were visible, as was the nude woman lying on the bed, masturbating.

"Oh, ho! What have we got here?" Spearman laughed, shaking his head in mock disgust. "Now I've seen everything. A call girl that takes her work home with her."

Mendoza laughed along, but it rang hollow. She averted her gaze.

Spearman beckoned the duty officer over, amusement twinkling in his eyes. "You've got to see this, Blanton."

"What's up?" he asked.

Spearman turned to Mendoza. "Put it on screen."

Mendoza flushed. "Sir?"

"Put it on the big screen!" Spearman felt a burst of heat rush to his face. "On screen! On screen!" Impatient, he nudged the seated controller aside, striking the commands on the keyboard to send the live image to the enormous wall monitor. The dozen or so agents on duty welcomed it with a chorus of whistles and catcalls.

Blanton had just taken a sip of his coffee and it now sprayed from his mouth as if it had been blistering hot. "Holy shit! Is that what I think it is?"

Spearman nodded, then clapped Mendoza on the shoulder, securing her attention. "You were right, Agent. Our asset has been distracted. He's letting the little head do the thinking for the big head. By God! Can't say I blame him, either. That's a nice package. Too bad it's time to put it on ice." Spearman stabbed the F12 button on the keyboard, thus removing the overhead image, and returned it to their console; the impending hit would remain dark. "Remind this idiot he has a job to do."

Mendoza shifted her attention toward the deputy director, her brow furrowed in concentration. "Maybe there's a problem with the audio, sir."

Spearman didn't answer. Instead, he left the junior agent to wilt under the scrutiny of his burning stare.

Mendoza nodded smartly and returned to her monitor, adjusting her Bluetooth headset. "Cypher, do you read? I say you have a go. Take the target out."

Nothing. Just the faceless silence of white noise hummed through the intercom.

Spearman smashed his fist against the console. "Damn it!" Something had happened…something catastrophic. NTs always followed orders. They had no choice.

Blanton leaned toward the deputy director, scratching his ample belly through the straining buttons of his shirt. "What the hell? He slip a gear?"

"Good goddamned question. An NT, no less. Designation zero."

Blanton raised an eyebrow. "Prototype?"

Spearman nodded. "Where's Dr. Shepherd? He should have a line on this."

"On leave. Left for Cancun on Tuesday, I believe."

"Shit. Track him down, get him on the horn now. This is turning into a fucking soup sandwich!" Spearman plopped both hands down onto the console, scrutinizing the monitor as if it were a magic eight ball. "I need a fix on the asset and target, Mendoza, and I need it yesterday."

"Yes, sir." The junior agent tapped a few keys and maximized a 3D rendering of downtown Miami. Two red dots blinked in unison near the center of the screen. "The mark is in apartment 721, south side of the Idyll Tower. Cypher's blind is two blocks south, seventh floor of the Imperial Suites Hotel. Room 7013."

Spearman snapped his attention to Blanton. "I need a fix on our nearest assets in Miami. Check the branch office. I need immediate deployment to Idyll Tower and ETA."

"Yes, sir." Blanton tapped his Bluetooth headset and hurried away, disappearing into the jungle of video monitors and station consoles cluttering Control's inner two rings.

What the hell was going on? Spearman didn't like this. He had been meticulous in his planning, careful ad nauseam. He didn't like surprises.

That was, of course, when he got another. The asset broke radio silence, his voice steady, restrained. *"Control. This hit makes no sense. Why the call girl?"*

Spearman roared. He could feel himself flush with rage, as his face turned a nasty shade of red. He ripped the headset off Mendoza's ear and pressed it to his as he engaged the mic. "Cypher. Your target is the whore. The reasons don't matter. Got that? You will follow orders. Now take the goddamned shot!"

Static answered. Cold. Endless.

Spearman couldn't wait any longer. Too much was at stake. He had Mendoza patch him into the duty officer's headset. "Blanton. What have you got? Any word on Dr. Shepherd?"

"No, sir. We're still trying to track him down."

"Damn. Keep trying. How about our assets in the area?"

"Limited resources, sir. A lot of personnel are on leave for the Labor Day weekend. But we have two agents around the corner from Idyll Tower. ETA two minutes. Tops."

"Fine. It will have to do. Suits?"

"Plainclothes."

"This is getting better all the time. Excellent. Make it a drug hit. Hell. Make it a trick gone bad. Rough her up. I don't care. But they need to eliminate the target."

"Understood."

"And Blanton? I want you to get back on the horn to the station chief down there. Tell him we need a 'specials' team to carry out a hit on a new target, and we need it now! Tell him if there's any argument, he's going to feel my boot so far up his ass, he'll have to unlace it to eat. Any questions?"

"Just one, sir. Do we have a fix on the new target?"

Spearman laughed, shaking his head as if he were privy to some inside joke. "Room 7013. Imperial Suites Hotel. Tell them to exercise extreme caution."

CHAPTER THREE

Miami, Florida

Brent Savage had sensed it coming. Felt it. But it had still startled him.

The forced entry was sudden. Violent. And it threw the unsuspecting girl back several feet onto the floor, leaving her dazed and powerless. His scope bobbed for a moment, and by the time he recaptured her in his limited field of view, the intruder was on top of her.

He knew Spearman had ordered the hit, most likely as insurance against him not fulfilling his contract. But for a second, he entertained the idea that it was an overly zealous john wanting recompense. Indeed, a random hit by a third party would have gone a long way to solving his problems. But would Control consider his mission a success, his contract fulfilled, if the girl were dead? No. Savage knew it wasn't that simple. He had hesitated. Failed. And the beefy man with shaggy hair and a burly beard knocking down the door wasn't a john. He was a deep cover agent. For the call girl, the result would be the same: she would be dead.

"Cypher, we have an agent onsite. You are to stand down."

The assailant picked up the limp body of the girl, throwing her onto the bed before backhanding her across the face. In his earpiece, it sounded like a two-by-four cracking. The vicious blow should have knocked her out cold, but much to Savage's surprise, the stinging backhand served as a wake-up call. She groaned, a low guttural response, but as she regained consciousness, her cries turned into screams of terror. He cuffed her again, momentarily stunning her into silence and leaving her crumpled on the bed. Her hair lay draped across her face like a wet mop, her robe unfurled to reveal her bronzed body beneath.

"Cypher, you have orders to stand down. Agent onsite. I repeat...stand down."

Savage allowed air to trickle from his nose, controlling his breath like a deep-sea diver. He eased the crosshairs off the target, watching, contemplating. It wasn't too late to make things right. He could still fix this.

The assailant stood over the mark, a ravenous lion about to feast. Savage saw the man hesitate. Even in the emerald green of night vision, he could see his eyes slip across the contours of her body. This lit a fuse in Savage, hot and slow-burning. Still, he restrained himself. He knew the operative couldn't afford to escalate this beyond a quick hit and run, nor could he chance leaving any DNA. He would have to maintain discipline.

Savage was wrong. He watched in dismay as the assailant climbed on top of her, the bed groaning in complaint as he straddled her. He made a grab for her tangled hair but was stunned when she boxed him in the ears instead. The man roared, his ruddy face pinched in agony.

He lashed out and punched her. He cupped his hand over her mouth to keep her from screaming, but the woman bit him, her teeth tearing into his flesh. She kicked. She clawed. She wouldn't go down without a fight.

Savage clutched his rifle in a white-knuckled grip, his jaw clenched as he tried to tamp down the irrational anger inside of him. This wasn't necessary. The agent was reckless. Stupid. His lack of discipline was appalling. But there was something else bothering Savage, something beyond his understanding. This girl mattered.

He couldn't let it end at this man's hands. Not this way. Not her. Savage aligned the scope's reticles, a hair's breadth off target, aiming for the top of her thrashing head. The shot would be like hitting a moving grapefruit, center mass, from about two hundred and fifty yards. He wouldn't miss.

She was begging for help now, immense racking sobs overwhelming her as she tried to push the man away. He had given up on assaulting her. Her flailing hands were like a swarm of angry bees, and it was all he could do to swat them away. But he soon overpowered her, holding her at bay with his ape-like grip. As he crushed her throat, her cries turned to gurgles.

Savage pulled the trigger, practiced and smooth. The assailant's head exploded, his brain atomized into a cloud of pink mist and gray matter. He smiled.

"Agent down! I repeat—agent down!"

Savage ripped the earpiece out of his ear and tossed it into his gun bag. The last audible sounds from the apartment were the raspy coughs of the girl as she sucked in precious air.

He wasted no time breaking down his sniper rifle. He detached the suppressor, removed the barrel, and retrieved the bullet's spent casing. Then he quickly wiped down the weapon, grabbed the black canopy, and tossed his hood into the rifle bag. Forty seconds, no more. The hotel was free of his prints as he had wiped the place clean when he arrived ten days prior. It wouldn't be necessary to do so again, as he had worn gloves ever since.

Thunder rolled in the distance, its rumble low and plodding, the storm a reluctant bystander to the night's events. Savage slid the desk back into place, but as he finished, he received an audible warning from the surveillance device on his wrist. It was receiving signals from the perimeter sensors he had set up in the stairwells. West side: bloop…bloop, bloop. Eastside: *bloop, bloop…bloop.*

Savage stood erect and rechecked the device. He had heard right. Six bogies. Three from each stairwell. He was certain they weren't hotel guests returning from an evening of swimming at the hotel pool. Not at this time of night and not taking two different stairwells. But the tip-off was that no random group of hotel guests would take seven flights of stairs to return to their room. They would have taken the elevator. This was tactical. An assault team. And they were coming for him.

Savage felt his blood surge like a thoroughbred crashing through the starting gate. Hard. Jolting. And just like that, his senses came alive, hyperalert, his muscles tense and bristling with anticipation.

He grabbed his pistol from the inner pocket of his gun bag, a modified 9mm SIG P226 with a tactical light. He attached its suppressor, then slipped over to the door to spy through the peephole. Nothing. No movement. No sound. Just the steady thrum of the ice machine down at the end of the hall. As expected. He wouldn't see or hear anything from here on out. Not until it was too late.

Savage's mind raced. His only avenue of escape had been the two stairwells at the end of the hall and the elevator around the corner. He knew the elevator wasn't unguarded despite receiving no warnings from the sensor. It was likely that someone had sabotaged the elevator. Either way, it was a death trap. The only remaining option was the balcony door. Seven stories separated Savage from a safe escape.

Boom. He heard an explosion. Not far, yet muffled. They must have blown a transformer, as the entire building was now thrown under a veil of darkness. Silence.

Turning on the tactical light of his 9mm, he ran out onto the balcony, leaned over the rail, and took stock of the situation. He could see another balcony one floor below, but it was flush with the outer wall and impossible for him to drop to safely. He couldn't jump to the balcony one room over, either, as a privacy wall was erected between them.

Savage rushed back to the room and rummaged through the gun bag again, but he couldn't find another clip. He hadn't anticipated a firefight. Fifteen rounds in the SIG, going up against what was most likely a heavily armed six-man assault group. Not enough.

A couple of sputtering coughs sounded from the hallway, which Savage recognized as suppressed gunfire. They shot out the emergency lighting. He returned to the door, tactical light off, edging along the wall to look out of the peephole again. Nothing but darkness, its black wall impenetrable. But they were there. He could feel them hovering nearby. Waiting. He heard some light scratching near the doorframe, soft and barely discernible. Savage tilted his head toward the door, trying to place the sound.

Then he realized. They were setting C4 explosive charges to blow the door and storm the room. Savage didn't hesitate and made a break for the open door to the balcony. His fight-or-flight response propelled him like a rocket, but he only made it halfway to the balcony before the explosive charges blasted the door off its hinges, and the assault team breached the room.

Savage never looked back. His powerful legs drove him toward the balcony, his speed leaving him a blur. But as fast as he was, he couldn't outrun bullets.

They opened fire. *Pop. Pop. Pop.*

Lightning flashed, and with a monumental last lunge, Savage launched himself headfirst over the balcony's rail, disappearing into the dark void below.

CHAPTER FOUR

Through the pitch dark, Savage spotted the swimming pool and knew instantly that he'd calculated his trajectory correctly. Not that there was much he could have done to change it. This wasn't skydiving from five thousand feet, where he could manipulate the speed of descent by splaying his arms and legs. Nor could he change direction. It was up to gravity now.

It took him precisely two point one seconds to reach the point of impact. During that time, he somersaulted once, got his feet turned down, and his arms locked above his head. He entered the water pencil straight, landing at the deepest end of the swimming pool. That blind luck had saved his life. But colliding with anything at forty-four miles per hour—even water—had its consequences. He struck the bottom hard, his legs buckling, but they withstood the brunt of the impact like a car's shock absorbers. He felt his right knee wrench when he struck bottom, and he received a bloody nose, but those injuries were insignificant. It wasn't until Savage resurfaced and went to climb out of the pool that he noticed his left shoulder shuddered under the strain. Then he felt the searing pain and saw a swirl of blood clouding the water. They had shot him. The bullet looked as if it had passed through clean, but the surrounding muscle felt like a ball-peen hammer had struck him. He ignored it.

He pulled himself from the water. Staggered. Shook the cobwebs from his head.

A young Black couple was walking down the sidewalk along the hotel property, laughing and carrying on as if they didn't have a care in the world. They took little notice of Savage. Too drunk. But as he figured it, they were the only reason he wasn't being targeted by the assault team seven floors up. Witnesses were unacceptable.

Savage sprang into action and started down South Miami Avenue toward Idyll Tower. Despite his injuries, he fought through the pain and catapulted into a full sprint. He had to hurry. The call girl's life depended on it.

CHAPTER FIVE

Somewhere near Denver, Colorado

"He did what?" Spearman about fell out of his chair. "You've got to be kidding me!"

Rutledge swiveled in his chair and answered the chief directly. "The task force has eyes on him, sir. He made the jump from seven stories up. They think they may have hit him, but he definitely survived the fall. They're asking for permission to take him out."

Rutledge was the comm officer on duty and the point man to Miami's deep cover office for the Defense Clandestine Service, or DCS.

"I don't see how. They're not exactly in the fucking boonies. They're in downtown Miami. Are there any witnesses around?"

The comm officer relayed the question directly to the team leader onsite. "Affirmative, sir. The hotel property runs parallel to 7th Street. We got sporadic traffic. A couple of pedestrians, too."

"Then hell no! Can't risk it." Spearman tossed his hands in the air. A former Princeton graduate, the deputy director was certain he was the only buoy of reason in an ocean of idiots. It was arduous to keep them all on target.

"Team leader is urging pursuit, sir. The target is wounded. Fleeing on foot. He feels they still have the upper hand."

Spearman laughed and rested his left fist on his hip. "Of course he does, Agent. He's a fucking jarhead. They're not paid to think."

"Sir?"

"Of course not! Permission denied. How the hell are we going to explain a six-man 'specials' team running down the middle of South Miami Avenue in tactical gear and carrying fully automatic rifles? That would be like trying to place a hit on an ant with a shotgun. It might get the job done, but it will draw an awful lot of attention. Tell them to stand down."

"Yes, sir."

Spearman stood at Rutledge's console, studying the big screen wall monitor. A multitude of Miami's traffic cameras were on display, streaming live images in near real time. But Spearman didn't need them to track Cypher. He knew exactly where he was heading. "We don't need a shotgun to kill an ant, Mr. Rutledge. What we need is a well-placed magnifying glass. Laser-focused. Silent."

Rutledge unfolded his arms, wiping the sweat from his pronounced forehead with the back of his hand but offered no more.

Mendoza interrupted. "Sir? We can use the biosensor in his nanoport to triangulate his position via satellite. Very accurate, sir. Dials us into just a few meters."

"Fine. Get a fix. Monitor it. Rutledge? I want you to contact the remaining asset onsite to take out the call girl. She's our highest priority. When she dies, so does the intel."

"Yes, sir." He dispatched the orders immediately.

Spearman spied Blanton lumbering over to him, flush-faced and out of breath, a momentary distraction. "What about Cypher? He's still on the loose and much more dangerous than a stupid call girl."

Spearman huffed through his nose. "Yeah. He's dangerous. But he doesn't know why his target was the call girl. Eliminate her, and we will have accomplished mission priority. Then we can tie up the loose ends with him."

Spearman leaned over the comm officer, hovering. "What's the ETA for backup?"

Rutledge tapped a few keys on his console and spoke to the officer on the other line. "Ten minutes, sir."

"Tell them they have five! And warn the remaining asset he's about to have company. Tell him to make the hit on the girl and get the hell out of there."

Spearman snapped his attention back to Blanton, feeling pissy about the fact he was still standing around. "Have you tracked down Dr. Shepherd yet?"

"No, sir. That's what I wanted to talk to you about. We still can't get a hold of him. He's not answering his phone. We tried tracing the signal, but we've got nothing!"

"Maybe he's in flight. Turned the phone off."

Blanton shook his head. "Wouldn't matter. We should still be able to trace his phone signal. The only way to avoid detection would be to remove the battery."

Blood rushed to Spearman's face, a tick about to pop. "Fuck me." He rubbed the tension from his brow, massaging it as if it would work an idea loose.

The duty officer said nothing, knowing enough to keep his mouth shut.

Spearman shook his head in disbelief. "Listen up. I need you to check with Denver International. I need to know what plane he boarded, the time of departure, and his target destination. Put the full weight of the DIA behind it. And while you're at it, check Cancun for good measure. See if we can verify an arrival. I got a bad feeling about this."

"Yes, sir."

"And Blanton? Make yourself useful. Get me a goddamn Coke."

CHAPTER SIX

Miami, Florida

Eliana sputtered out a raw hacking cough as the return of sweet oxygen pushed back the shroud of tunnel vision from her eyes. She couldn't catch her breath, and she lay there for several minutes, unwilling to move. She thought she heard a rumble. Felt the floor vibrate. Thunder?

A bright pink light captured her attention from across the room. At first, it was nothing more than a fuzzy blur. But the image slowly came into focus. It was her Hello Kitty clock in the kitchen. She snapped her head to the left, then to the right. She was in her apartment. The heavy fog of disorientation was lifting.

She felt something wet and sticky on her face, like someone had splattered her with warm maple syrup. Eliana screamed and bolted upright as cold, stark realization set in. There, crumpled on the floor like a wet bag of dirty laundry, was the body of her assailant. A black, inky pool of blood had amassed around what used to be his head.

Eliana felt her stomach roil. Her first reaction was to make a mad dash to the bathroom, keep herself from making a mess—the murdered body on the white tiled floor notwithstanding. She retched before she took her first step. *"Oh Déu meu!" Oh my God!*

She collapsed to her knees as her body racked with convulsions. This wasn't happening. Not to her. Though her life as a call girl was nothing compared to that of a streetwalker, it was far from a life of ease. She had seen her share of violence. Personal and up close. One time, there had been a john who had beaten her so severely that she ended up with several broken ribs, a lost tooth, and a face so swollen she couldn't open her eyes for a week. One of her girlfriends had a cigarette put out on her face by a client simply because she giggled at him. Hell. She even saw an old man get stabbed during a holdup at a liquor store down on 3rd Avenue. But this was different. This was crazy. Somebody had broken into her apartment and tried to kill her! Eliana fought off a shiver, then wrapped her robe tightly around her.

Her mind raced, the images in her head flying by like the flickering windows of a passing metro train. This wasn't a random act of violence. The assailant had knocked on the door—*actually knocked*—so she would oblige and let him in. The assailant knew who she was—or at least what she was. Eliana shuddered. Threw up again. His intent wasn't only to rape her. He was going to kill her. She saw it in his eyes. But…he was dead. Shot! But by whom?

Eliana scampered to her feet, an abrupt spark of clarity slapping her back to sober like a splash of ice water to the face. Somebody had been watching her! Somebody shot the intruder. Or maybe they were shooting at her and missed. After all, there had been a serial killer on the loose in Miami. It had been all over the news. Two shootings in as many months, and she could have been the third victim! Worse, they might still come for her.

She hurried to the nightstand beside her bed, jerked open the drawer, and removed a loaded Smith & Wesson .357 Magnum. Its compact three-inch barrel made it easy to conceal in her purse, yet it still provided enough power to pack a punch. She had fired it a few times at the target range, enough to be comfortable but not proficient.

Alert to the point of high sensitivity, Eliana heard a hushed scuffle on the floor behind her and whipped around, her arm extended with the gun in hand. Standing in the doorway was the silhouette of a man, the stark light from the hallway washing out any facial features. But one thing stood out to Eliana. The man had a gun of his own, and it was pointed right at her. He said, "Put the fucking gun down."

She applied her other hand to the grip, steadying her aim. "Get out! I'm warning you. I'll scream!" Though she spoke perfect English, her accent betrayed her Catalan ancestry.

The man stepped forward and brought his free hand into view, as if to put her at ease. He spotted the dead body on the floor, her blood-splattered face. His eyes narrowed but offered nothing more. "No need," he said. "I'm a cop. But I'm going to need you to put down your gun."

Eliana eyed him. Hesitated. He wore khaki cargo shorts, a coral-colored t-shirt, and an unbuttoned white linen shirt. On his feet, he wore open-toed sandals. Though he didn't look the part of a police officer, a holster was peeking out from beneath his open shirt. She said nothing.

"I'm not a patrolman, if that's what you're wondering. Plainclothes."

She bit her lip and eased her grip on the pistol. Her hands were sweating now. Her heart pounding. "Where's your badge?"

The man chuckled, amused but not dissuaded. "I'm off duty."

"Really? Why are you in my apartment, then? Are all off-duty cops in the habit of just letting themselves into the homes of unsuspecting females? Or just you?"

His smirk widened into a shark-toothed grin. "I was going to say I heard gunshots…but that wasn't going to work, now, was it?" Before Eliana could answer, the stranger raced forward, closing the gap between them. He latched onto her wrist with his free hand, pushing the gun aside, and then pressed his 9mm Glock against her forehead. "You can't just wave a gun around, being all tough and shit. You have to be willing to use it," he said.

Eliana winced as he twisted her wrist to its breaking point. She dropped the gun.

The man had pale eyes, his skin flushed pink and freckled from the intense Floridian sun. Pearls of sweat dripped carelessly from his nose, his thin lips locked in a grimace. "Too late now."

"*Què*? No…wait! Why are you doing this?"

"Why do you think?"

Eliana looked at the dead man heaped on the floor like a sack of discarded meat. "It wasn't me! I didn't—"

"Save your breath. I couldn't give two shits whether *you* killed him. The fact is, you're a liability."

Eliana saw a flash of movement out of the corner of her eye and gasped. There was someone else in the room!

The stranger instinctually whirled around to face the unknown threat. He turned just in time to see a man donned in black slink out of the shadows, a panther about to strike. It was the last image he would ever see. The assassin put a suppressed 9mm SIG against his temple and dispatched him with a simple pull of the trigger. "You talk too much," he said.

Eliana screamed and stumbled back several steps as she tried to catch herself. "*Déu meu!* You shot him! Y-You actually shot him!"

The man studied her, his face chiseled granite. He offered nothing. Instead, he knelt by the man he had just killed, patted him down, then rifled through his pockets for anything useful.

"You shot him," she repeated, her face stripped of all color.

Lightning lit up the room like a disco strobe. Low, brooding thunder followed it, distant but moving nearer. "He would have shot you."

"But he's dead!"

"Yes. And you're not. I think you, of all people, would find that agreeable." The man confiscated a radio from the body, attached the earpiece, and then sorted through the contents of his wallet. "Credit cards. Two hundred and six dollars cash. Deep cover creds, including a fake passport. One sealed condom—expiration date last December. He'll need none of these things anymore." He pocketed the cash and tossed the wallet onto the dead man's chest.

"Deep cover? You mean he was a spy?"

"DCS. Defense Clandestine Service. Undercover agent."

Eliana swore her heart would bang through her chest, but she couldn't wait another second. Her life depended on it. She made a lunge for her gun lying on the floor, scooped it up, and cocked the hammer. By the time the man had turned his attention back to her, she had the gun's sights squarely pointed at his head.

He raised an eyebrow but otherwise seemed unfazed. He returned to his feet at a nightcrawler's pace, then turned to face her. He looked like he had just stepped out of a shower, his short dark hair spiked and his black jeans and matching tee sopping wet. This man was dangerous. She could see it in his eyes. Yes. The other assailants had crazed eyes and had meant her harm. There was no doubt about it. But this man's eyes were cold. Calculating.

"Who the hell are you?"

"My name is Brent Savage, and I'm the guy who just saved your life. You may do well to remember that before pulling the trigger."

Eliana shook her head and closed her eyes, if only momentarily. She couldn't afford to take them off this man. "Not your name. I want to know *what* you are. You're not a cop either."

"No. I'm not. I do wet work."

Somehow, Eliana didn't think he was talking about his wet clothes. "I don't understand. Wet work…like a hitman?"

"Assassin."

Again, Eliana shook her head. She felt a stabbing headache coming on. "You're a part of this…this DCS, too?"

He shook his head. "No. As far as the government is concerned, I don't exist. Completely off the books."

"You're lying. Why would you even be here?" She waved the gun toward the dead body Savage had pilfered the radio from. "To kill him?"

The man shook his head. "No. You."

Eliana felt her knees buckle. "Me? What?"

The man shushed her. He put his hand to his earpiece, privy to some unknown conversation she couldn't hear. "Eliana…we don't have time for this right now. We need to gather your things and get out of here."

Eliana stiffened and steadied the gun. "Don't come near me!"

The man ignored her protest. Took a step forward. "There are other men who will still do you harm…"

Her jaw dropped. "Wait a minute! You called me Eliana!"

"Would you prefer I call you Ms. Bautista? Or do you prefer Jade?"

"But I didn't tell you my name." Her eyes lit up. "I was right! Someone was watching me. It was you!" Eliana's mind flashed back to the horrific events of the night. She remembered the quiet moments before all this madness had started and all three levels of Hades broke loose. The most intimate moments of the night came rushing back to her as well, an unforgiving storm surge of memories. Her face burned at the thought.

The man neither denied nor confirmed her suspicion.

"It had to be you. You killed the man who attacked me. He was choking me. But I remember nothing after that. You shot him, didn't you?"

The would-be assassin took another step forward. "Ma'am…Eliana. I saved your life tonight. I'm still trying to do so. And I need you to trust me."

"Trust you? How could I possibly trust you? You were going to kill me!"

"But I didn't. Look. I know this doesn't make sense to you. It doesn't make sense to me either. Something is wrong. And I need to find out what it is."

He took one last step forward and was now within easy reach of her gun. "You were my mark. I was to watch, follow, and eventually kill you. But something isn't right. I don't know what it is. Perhaps I'm…I'm broken. I don't know. Maybe. But I know I no longer wish to kill you."

For the first time, Eliana noticed the man had a hole in his shirt and blood pooling near the opening. Someone had shot him. She gasped, then recoiled instinctively.

The stranger took advantage of her distraction and snatched the gun from her hand. The move was so quick that the lines of reality blurred, and before her mind could register what had happened, she was staring down the barrel of her own revolver. He held the pose for a moment longer, then let the gun drop, his finger catching the trigger guard. He twirled it twice and handed it back to her, butt first.

"I'm going to need all the help I can get. Do you know how to use that piece?"

Eliana took the gun back, her movements slow and guarded so as not to startle him. She nodded in agreement despite being disarmed twice in one night.

"Look, Eliana. I need you to trust me. I disobeyed orders tonight. Not only did I choose not to kill you, but I've killed others in the name of protecting you. That makes me a marked man. They *will* send more men. We are in immediate danger and need to get out of here. Now."

Eliana let her gun hand drop to her side. Her face crumpled, and tears spilled down her cheeks. "Why is this happening? Why are people trying to kill me?"

He folded his arms, albeit with deliberate care, then said, "That's a good question, Eliana. Why *are* they trying to kill you?"

"I—I don't know."

The man's stare cut through her like a diamond on glass. He said nothing, letting the full weight of his silence leave no doubt in her mind: he wasn't a fool.

"I'm sorry, *Senyor*. I don't know."

He arched an eyebrow. Shook his head. He marched over to the closet, threw open the doors, and tossed Eliana a pair of black capris and a camisole top. "Well, ma'am. Let's hope, for our sake, that you figure it out soon. It may be the only thing that keeps us alive."

CHAPTER SEVEN

Savage made it clear to her that there wasn't time for a shower. But he realized she couldn't go out in public with her face peppered with blood either, so he gave her a moment to take a quick sponge bath in the kitchen sink.

She mustn't have expected privacy. She certainly didn't ask for it. The woman loosened her robe and let it fall to the floor as if it were only a dirty tissue being tossed into the garbage. He appreciated her forgoing the false modesty. Savage looked away anyway and turned his attention to the hallway. No signs of trouble. Not *yet*. The radio remained silent.

Eliana threw herself into the clothes he had picked out for her, being careful not to look at the two mutilated bodies on the floor. She looked pale, like she would be sick again, but held it together.

In the meantime, Savage made a brief sweep of the back hallway and bathroom, took inventory, and returned to Eliana in the living room. He was gone for a mere ninety-three seconds. Not long at all. But time was a precious commodity—something they could ill afford to lose.

The orders being squawked into his radio's earpiece alerted him to impending trouble. Control was demanding backup for the field agents. Savage grabbed Eliana by the arm and pulled her after him. "We've got to go. We're about to have company."

Eliana tried to jerk her arm free, but he had a tremendous grip, and she couldn't escape. "No, wait! I need to get something!" She tried pulling away again, but his grip was inescapable. "*Si us plau.*" *Please.*

Savage saw the desperation in her eyes. Near panic. Against his better judgment, he let go. "We leave now or risk ending up like them," he said, gesturing to the two dead men sprawled out on the floor.

Eliana blanched but quickly gathered herself. She made a mad dash to the closet, found one of her spike-heeled, knee-high leather boots, and buried her arm deep into its recesses. Before long, she found what she was looking for—a two-gallon-sized Ziploc bag stuffed with what was easily twenty stacks of one-hundred-dollar bills.

Savage raised an eyebrow. She said nothing. Instead, she stuffed the money into her oversized knit bag and flung it over her shoulder.

There wasn't time for questions, so they made their escape from Idyll Tower.

They charged down the back stairwell, taking seven flights of knee-jolting jumps at breakneck speed. The girl surprised him. She did a respectable job of keeping up—no simple task, even when you considered his injuries. But his unique ability to regenerate damaged tissue at an extraordinary rate had his injuries already on the mend. He just needed to find a quiet place to settle down, to rest.

At the bottom of the stairs, Savage grew cautious. Slowed down. He eased open the emergency exit door to the rear parking lot. More agents could have waited in ambush, but he spotted nothing obvious. Satisfied, Savage slipped out the door with Eliana pressed behind him. The night's humidity smacked him in the face, the sky still threatening rain.

They needed transportation, and they needed it fast. It didn't take Savage long to spot the crotch rocket. A definite preference. A Yamaha YZF-R1. All black. One thousand cubic centimeters of pure adrenaline.

He made a beeline for the motorcycle. Gave it a quick once-over. The first thing he noticed was that there was no key. But there were two helmets. A custom rear pillion passenger seat as well. Apparently, the rocket jockey had a girlfriend. Shame he'd be calling a cab for her tonight.

Savage took in his surroundings, his mind working through the problem. He needed to hot-wire the motorcycle and spotted a solution right away. He hurried back to the exit door, took a firm grip on the exterior security light above, and applied sufficient force until it broke free from the crumbling stucco wall. The result was a fist-sized crater and a few exposed copper wires.

He returned to the motorcycle, where Eliana was still standing, her brow pinched with concern. "What are you doing?" Savage pulled a multi-tool from his leg pouch and made quick work of the wires still attached to the security light. He cut off a four-inch piece and stripped the ends. "I'm going to hot-wire this rocket. Just need to find the ignition wires." He ran his fingers behind the key ignition on the dash and quickly found three wires leading away and down to several plastic connectors. Then he unsnapped the coupling and jabbed his new jump wire into two open sockets. He heard the bike click on immediately. With a quick push of the starter button, the engine rumbled to life, deep and menacing. Savage climbed on.

"You mean you're going to steal this bike?" Eliana swatted at a fat moth pestering her, then pushed her damp hair out of her face.

"You got it. We need wheels, and we need them fast. This bike fits our needs on both counts."

She blinked, her mouth agape. "You can't just steal some poor guy's bike!"

"What? Hold on. I don't think you grasp the severity of our situation. There are people after us. People who mean to kill us. We need to get away from here."

"I know. I know. But I don't like it. It just feels…wrong."

Savage stared at her. She was rocking back and forth, shifting her weight from one side to the other as if she had to pee. Confused. Out of her element. Terrified.

Savage flushed. Felt the burn of frustration on the back of his neck. "It feels *wrong*? Take a good look at me, Eliana. Everything about me is wrong. I'm an assassin. I kill people for a living. And I'm damn good at it. Hell! Tonight alone, I've killed two people in the name of protecting you! Do you really think I give two fucks if I steal some young punk's sweet ride?"

Eliana stood there for a moment, clearly unsure of what to say. Then she shook her head.

Savage said no more. He extended his hand. This time, she took it without hesitation and climbed onto the back of the bike.

"Hold on."

The Yamaha's engines roared in protest as he slammed it into gear and launched the bike out of the parking lot and onto the road. Some burned rubber. A cloud of smoke. And they were gone.

CHAPTER EIGHT

Somewhere near Denver, Colorado

Silence consumed the Control Center. Only the faint hum of stale air circulating through the ducts above breathed life into the room. The enormous monitor on the wall was equally comatose, still plagued with darkness.

Theo Spearman and the rest of the night's staff waited in angst for confirmation. Near a dozen agents held their breath, lifeless statues lined all in a row, unwilling to move as if the mere twitch of a muscle would sever the fragile connection between superstition and mission success.

Spearman, of course, didn't believe in such hoo-ha. However, the lack of visual and audio contact with the backup team didn't sit well with him. Time was of the essence. The longer the wait, the greater the risk of them escaping.

"How much longer, Rutledge?"

"We have an agent onsite now, sir. Patching in video."

The monitor flickered and came to life, casting a faint green glow across the Control Center. Severe, deep shadows fell across the faces of the captivated audience.

"It's about time!"

On the jumbo screen, apartment 721 of Idyll Tower came into focus.

"Inform the agent to proceed with extreme caution. Target's location is unknown. Consider male armed and dangerous."

The image on the screen paused momentarily, as if the agent was weighing the information just relayed to him. He began moving again, entering the apartment with deliberate restraint. The entirety of the studio apartment opened up before them, slickly bathed in the artificial light of the agent's night vision goggles. There was audio as well, though the only sound transmitting was his shallow, measured breathing and the nondescript white noise of electronic feedback from the speakers. The Control Center was equally quiet—just the occasional random cough or nervous sniff.

Spearman squinted as if he could will the fuzzy, low-light image on the screen to sharpen. This didn't feel right. This mission was unraveling fast. It had felt that way from the beginning, starting with the call girl. No. That wasn't it. He had given orders on numerous occasions that targeted American civilians. Nothing new. As Deputy Director and Chief of Operations for Darkwater, he was privy to the how and why of every hit. Most of the time, he had a hand in mission planning. This time was no different. The orders were for the target to be observed around the clock for ten days. In addition, the agent was to have searched her apartment to ensure she didn't have hidden evidence that would implicate Senator Kelley—not that Spearman cared. As far as he was concerned, the Georgian senator was a blowhard—a promiscuous old fart who was incapable of keeping his zipper up and his mouth shut. Still, Spearman had received assurance that the agent had conducted a comprehensive search and found nothing. That's why he gave the green light to eliminate the girl. Only *he* didn't choose an NT assassin. Yes, NTs were considered fail-safe, but therein lay the rub. They were perfect. They *didn't* fail. And that seemed a bit of overkill to Spearman. She was a call girl, for Christ's sake! If you're a cop, you don't bring an RPG to a routine traffic stop. You bring the right weapon for the job. An NT wasn't the right weapon. What was worse, the weapon was now broken. The most prevalent question on Spearman's mind was whether his reinforcements arrived before Cypher did. He had his answer before long.

There on the floor next to the couch was the first of two dead bodies, a perfect black hole marking the center of his forehead. Just a few feet away lay another dead agent, this one missing his head completely.

"Goddammit! We're too late. Rutledge—inform the agent to keep his eyes peeled! Target is hostile and is an expert in close-quarters combat. He may still be onsite."

The image on the screen jumped, then blurred, as the uploading information was slow to process. The agent's point of view shifted rapidly as he scanned the room in anticipation of an impending attack. He was precise in his every move. He checked behind the couch, swung wide around the bed, and flashed his pistol's tactical light beneath each piece of furniture. He meticulously sliced the pie around every corner, securing each section of the room before moving on to the next.

The agent onsite saw a flash of movement from the corner of his eye and whipped around to face the immediate threat. It was the curtains billowing in the brisk breeze from the approaching storm. The balcony door was wide open.

The agent took a tentative step toward the curtain, and the image on the screen bobbled. Spearman assumed the agent was concerned about the targets hiding behind the curtain. But he knew it was unlikely. Cypher was too intelligent to remain behind and play hide and seek. Even so, caution was the better part of valor. "Talk to me, Mendoza. I need Cypher's position ASAP!"

"Still working on it, sir! Thirty seconds."

"Thirty seconds more than you have, Agent."

The area agent onsite continued to make his way toward the open door. Silence. The curtains ruffling in the wind were the only audible sound.

"Almost got it, sir. I've got the map syncing with the coordinates now."

"Spare me the promises, Mendoza. I need results."

The agent was so close to the curtains now that Spearman could make out the weave texture on the fabric. He was careful not to make a noise, not to cause a disturbance. But speed was required. He ripped open the curtain, flinging it far and wide.

Nothing. Just a wall. Not even a picture.

The agent swept the room again. Hurried. Careless. The image transmitted to the wall monitor smeared like chalk on a blackboard as he rushed the search. Then he paused. Thinking. He turned his attention to the open door and the balcony. It didn't take him long to clear the enclosed area. Small, restrictive. There was nowhere to hide. He even braved a cursory glance over the rail to ensure the target wasn't hanging by his fingertips out of sight. Satisfied, he slipped back inside the apartment, his tactical light cutting the darkness from the room's farthest corners like a surgeon's scalpel.

"Got it, sir! Target is offsite! I repeat, Cypher is offsite!" said Mendoza.

Spearman approached the console and leaned down to get a closer look. "Details, Mendoza. I need a location."

"He's across the river, sir. Heading north on South Miami Avenue."

"Track him. Get me an update on the girl."

"Sir?"

"God! Tell me we did something right! We bugged her, yes? Bugged her purse, bra, or high heels?" Spearman knew Mendoza had been Cypher's handler and had worked closely with him during the past week and a half. She would know.

Mendoza spun around in her chair, muted her mic, and cleared her throat. "Yes, sir. Cypher bugged the compact in her makeup kit. He said clothes would be unreliable. She would always wear a fresh set of clothes whenever she went out. New dress, bra, shoes. She might even change purses. But he figured she would always need her compact kit to touch up her face. At home or on a trick, she would always have it near her."

"Frankly, I don't care if he planted it in her diaphragm. As long as you can tell me where she's at now, Mendoza."

"The signal is showing local. It hasn't moved since the show began."

Spearman snorted, giddy like a teenage boy about to get laid. "You mean she's right there? In the apartment?"

"Not exactly, sir. Her compact case is in the apartment. If she were in a hurry, forced to escape, she probably wouldn't take the time to grab her makeup kit."

"She's there." Spearman slipped over to where the communications officer sat. "Rutledge—the agent onsite—what's his name?"

"Brooks, sir. Agent Brooks."

Spearman reached across Rutledge's console, crowding the man's personal space, and jabbed the transmit button. "Brooks. Deputy Director Spearman. We have reason to believe the girl is alone in the apartment. She's probably scared shitless. Hiding. What's down the short hall past the kitchen?"

Agent Brooks maintained radio discipline and navigated through the furniture and bodies on the floor, creeping down a small hallway toward a closed door. He stopped.

Spearman folded his arms and drummed his fingers across his side, trying to make heads or tails of the image on the screen. It was just a closed door. Then he heard running water. Recognized it in an instant. "Do you hear that?"

Rutledge tilted his head. Squinted. "Water?"

"She's taking a fucking shower!" Spearman flashed a two-bit grin. Pumped his fist. "We got her!"

"I don't get it. Why would she be taking a shower now?"

"She's a bloody mess. Two people were just blown away in her apartment, at least one of them in very close proximity."

"Yeah, I get that. But why the shower first? Why not scream for help? Call the police? How about running like hell?"

Spearman laughed and then rested his hands on his hips. "She's in shock. Not thinking straight." He pushed forward again, stealing mic control from Rutledge one last time. "You have a go, Brooks. You have a go to take the girl out."

The image on the big screen was static, just a close visual of an unremarkable door with simulated wood grain. The personnel in the control room fidgeted in their seats, their skin crawling with anticipation.

Brooks didn't delay. Just like ripping open the balcony curtains, he tried to be fast. The element of surprise wasn't just important; it was everything. But if he had taken a moment to think it through, to examine his surroundings, he would have noticed the long strip of duct tape sealing the opening at the bottom of the door. When he kicked in the door, he set off a well-choreographed trap, a nightmare that Brooks was ill-prepared to face.

A cascade of water rushed from the flooded bathroom and rolled across Brooks' feet, cold and sobering. In the same instance, the explosive force of the door being kicked open knocked over a box fan set precariously on an upside-down clothes basket. Its splash into the water elicited a scream from Agent Brooks, his peril realized as he retreated from the room, his arms flailing like a flopping fish. He knew he was dead. Only nothing happened.

Brooks audibly gasped and ripped the night vision goggles and camera from his head. He was muttering to himself, repeating incoherent curses and swearing off being a field agent forever.

"What the hell just happened?" asked Spearman, throwing his hands in the air. The giant monitor turned dark again, the audio now nothing more than a static hiss.

"Clearly, it was a trap," said Mendoza.

"That didn't work," added Rutledge.

"Didn't it? Give me video feedback," said Spearman. "Go back to just before the door got kicked open."

"Yes, sir." A few key taps later, Mendoza had pulled up the video feed just before Brooks' forced entry.

Spearman leaned in closer and dissected the image on the screen as events unfolded in real time. Just like when it happened, they could see nothing outside of Brooks' point of view. Eyes straight ahead. Closed door. Kicked. Bright light. Smeared images degrading into a vortex of jumpy, scrambled footage. The sound of Brooks screaming like a scorned puppy, running with his tail tucked between his legs.

Spearman paused, his brow creased in thought. "Run that back in its entirety again, but slow it down to a crawl when he kicks in the door."

Mendoza cued up the video again and ran it as ordered. "There! Stop!" Spearman ran forward. Pointed up at the big screen. "The fan."

A collective buzz rolled across the room. Spearman scowled. Usually, he was a stickler for discipline. But he overlooked it this time. He had a point to make, and all eyes were on him.

"I don't get it," someone interjected. "How in the hell did Brooks survive that?"

Rutledge raised an eyebrow. "Should have been electrocuted."

"Christ! Details, people! Look at the image! It's right in front of you!"

The room fell silent again. Nobody was brave enough to break the silence.

Except Mendoza. "The fan. It's not plugged in."

"Thank you!" Spearman laughed, snorting through his nose. "The damn question is why?"

Rutledge said, "He screwed up."

Mendoza didn't hesitate. She shook her head. "No. Not Cypher. He doesn't make mistakes. He did it on purpose."

Spearman stared at the junior officer, gauging the strength of her conviction by looking the woman in the eyes. Determined. Unflinching. "Rerun the video."

The video display lit up, and the events played out once more for all to see in monochromatic green. This time, everybody spotted the fan's electrical cord sailing through the air, limp and untethered. "Wait!" Spearman spotted something. "What the hell was that?"

"Sir?"

"On the mirror! Back it up two seconds. Rerun it. Freeze the image. No…right after the fan is knocked over. Yes. That's it! Stop! Right there!" Spearman was center stage again, pointing at the screen.

"Looks like something's written on the bathroom mirror? Lipstick?"

Spearman tilted his head, compensating for the skewed words. They were smeared and unintelligible. Hastily written. "Zoom in. Enhance."

A couple of taps on the keyboard and the image magnified and sharpened before their eyes.

You've been warned. Don't follow.

The words barely qualified as chicken scratching. Messy. Hurried. But their meaning was crystal clear.

Spearman cursed, then raked his fingers through his hair. He turned around just in time to have Blanton walk into the room and hand him a sweating can of Coke. "They only had diet. I figured that was better than nothing. So what's up? What did I miss?"

The deputy director snatched the Coke from his hand, considered it, and then tossed it back to Blanton, never making eye contact with him once. "Listen up, people. Nothing less than total success will be tolerated. I want every spare man we have brought in on this. I want a BOLO put out to Miami's finest. Tell them we have the primary suspect for the sniper serial killings on the run. Tell them he's armed and dangerous and likely traveling with his accomplice, Ms. Bautista. And I want the goddamn FBI notified pronto. Give 'em names, descriptions, photos, and bio workups. The whole nine yards!"

The Control Center exploded into action, agents swarming to their stations like sharks in a feeding frenzy.

"I want all transportation hubs monitored. Airports, metro stations, bus depots, and car rental companies. People, I want a net cast so wide that our targets won't be able to take a piss without being noticed." Spearman turned to Blanton. "I need to talk to the director. I'll be in my office if there are any updates. And Mendoza?"

The junior agent looked up from her console, disengaging herself from the task at hand. "Sir?"

"I want those coordinates for Cypher, and I want them now."

CHAPTER NINE

Kansas City, Kansas

Dr. Henry Shepherd slipped through the sliding glass doors just in time, his leather bag not nearly as lucky. If he had been paying attention instead of trying to read the overhead signs, he would have cleared them easily.

He had never been to Kansas City International Airport before, but the taxi driver had assured him that this was the terminal entrance for United Airlines. The driver's command of English was spotty at best, so Dr. Shepherd couldn't be sure. But he was relieved to find that the ticket counters weren't far at all. Everything was going according to plan.

He had spent the last eleven hours on a bus, wedged in a seat between a Chatty Cathy and her two-year-old son and a bloated high-school wrestling coach from Des Moines, who smelled of Fritos and sour milk. The doctor's stomach was still churning. But it was a small price to pay for his freedom.

He had calculated every detail of his escape. It was late now. Control should have realized that one of their NTs had malfunctioned. They would need to know why, of course. And they would want him to provide the answers. By the time they realized he wasn't on the flight to Mexico, he would already be halfway across the country. But the people at Darkwater were sharp, particularly the chief, Theo Spearman. He was an egomaniac, to be sure, but was equally stubborn and would be dogged in his pursuit. Worse, Control had eyes everywhere. So, Dr. Shepherd used that to his advantage.

He waited his turn, seventh in line. Usually, the concourse would have been empty at this time of night, but the Labor Day weekend was one of the busiest travel times of the year. To his delight, the line withered away, and before long Dr. Shepherd stood before the ticket agent. He had to play this just right. Fail now, and his entire plan would unravel. He cleared his throat, and the woman at the desk greeted him promptly.

"I'd like to buy a ticket to Venezuela, please."

"Certainly, sir. What is your destination city?"

"City?"

The ticket agent pressed a smile onto her face, her muscle memory kicking in. Her name was Brenda, according to her silver name tag, and she wore her company's obligatory black pants and blazer. Her hair and long glossy nails were coordinated: both red, both plastic. "Yes, sir. What is your final destination? Caracas? Maracaibo? Valencia?"

Dr. Shepherd scratched at his beard. "Which city do you recommend, Brenda?"

The agent opened her mouth to speak but then hesitated. Apparently, snarky wouldn't do. Friendly skies and all. "Is this trip for business or pleasure?"

Dr. Shepherd stifled a laugh. It was ludicrous to think of traveling to another country without a predetermined destination. He went along with it. "A little of both, actually. I'm a doctor and want to set up a clinic in Venezuela. I've always wanted to make a difference in this world. Help people in need and all. But I've never been there. I'm doing a little scouting, I suppose. How about Caracas? That sounds nice."

The agent was unamused. Perhaps disbelieving. She smiled anyway. "Certainly, sir." A flurry of tapping on her keyboard pulled up the information she needed. "We have Flight 5558 leaving for Caracas later this morning, through Houston, then Panama City. Departure time is five thirty at gate C68."

"Perfect."

The agent filtered through the requisite questions to get Dr. Shepherd booked on the next flight, including if he needed to check any luggage. He didn't. Just a small leather bag for carry-on. Another curiosity for somebody purchasing a one-way ticket to another country. A short while later, he handed Brenda his credit card and paid the fifteen hundred dollars before being sent on his way, ticket firmly in hand.

He headed straight for the nearest men's room. But he noticed the man over in the waiting area right away. Royals ball cap. Tweed jacket and faded wranglers. Slouching behind a *USA Today*, doing his best not to appear overly zealous. Could Brenda have already alerted airport security about his strange behavior? It didn't seem likely, but it was possible. Not good. The doctor wanted airport security cameras to record him purchasing a ticket. He wanted to make an impression on the airport personnel, to be memorable. He was convinced he had done so with Brenda. But he couldn't afford to be discovered. Not yet. Not until he was hours away from Kansas City.

He ducked into the men's room and was relieved to find it empty. Dr. Shepherd wasted little time pulling out the toiletries he would need to pull off the next part of his plan. The bathroom stall would suffice. He retrieved a compact mirror, set it on the toilet tank, adjusted its angle, and got to work.

First, he applied the Just for Men hair color, stripping ten years away with a few strokes of the applicator comb, though he had to double his efforts on the temples. He let the color sit while he removed a pair of scissors from his bag's side pouch and snipped away the tangle of whiskers from his face. The clippings fell harmlessly into the toilet, where Dr. Shepherd disposed of them with a simple pull of the flusher.

Time was slipping away fast. Dr. Shepherd grabbed his bag and returned to the counter with the basin sinks and mirrors. *What luck!* There was still nobody around. He dipped his head under the running water of the faucet, rinsed the color from his hair, and dabbed it dry with a wad of paper towels. He slathered on some shaving cream, shaved his remaining whiskers, and slicked his hair back. Dr. Shepherd scrutinized himself in the mirror. He smiled. It was his birthday today. Sixty years old. He had earned every gray hair, crow's feet, and worry line. But today he looked a full decade younger. Sharp. Confident. Ready to take on the world. Like Michael Douglas in the movie *Wall Street*.

Time to wrap it up. Dr. Shepherd stripped off his dress shirt, revealing a plain gray t-shirt beneath, baggy and sweat-stained. He tossed the button-down into the trash bin, along with his excess litter, grabbed his bag, and slung it onto his shoulder before leaving the relative safety of the restroom.

But it was of no concern. He no longer resembled the man who had entered the restroom mere minutes ago, and he breezed on by the tweed-jacket man without notice.

Dr. Shepherd took care not to look back. Instead, he kept his eyes forward, using the reflection in the glass of the exit doors to monitor his suspected pursuer. The man had lowered his newspaper to keep vigil over the restrooms but made no move to check things out for himself. Eventually, he would lose patience and try to track down the strange man who wanted to travel to Venezuela on a whim. But he would never find him. Dr. Shepherd wouldn't be on that flight, nor any other.

Instead, he paused by the exit door, only long enough to dispose of his boarding pass in a nearby trash receptacle. Then he kept on walking.

He had another bus to catch.

CHAPTER TEN

Somewhere near Denver, Colorado

The acrid smoke from his cigarette, blue and ghostlike, made its way toward the ceiling, spinning and twisting until it dissipated into a roiling haze. The nicotine was just the pick-me-up Theo Spearman needed, as were the obscene amounts of sugar found in his lukewarm Coke.

Two floors below the control room, deep underground in the confines of the Defense Clandestine Service's new headquarters, Spearman took a moment for himself.

This seemingly simple mission was FUBAR. *Fucked up beyond all recognition.* Maybe. But God knows Spearman wasn't about to concede defeat. He had put the necessary cogs of law enforcement into motion, both local and federal. He was still waiting for an update on Cypher's whereabouts. It appeared there was little else to do. But he knew better.

Spearman took a long drag from his cigarette, held it for a moment, and then exhaled through his nose. He tapped the cigarette against the ashtray, rounding the tip against its outer edge. He hesitated, then picked up the phone and made a call to DIA Director Victor Blackburn, the highest-ranking official over Operation Darkwater. Then again, it wasn't the sort of title you'd find on a business card. Darkwater was a program so black that even the national security advisor was unaware of its existence.

It was late now, twelve forty-five in Washington, but despite Blackburn being at his residence, he answered the phone on the third ring. That impressed Spearman. He said, "We have a problem."

"Theo?" The director's voice was thick, sluggish.

"Sorry to bother you at this late hour, sir, but one of our assets has left the reservation."

Blackburn paused a moment, as though sweeping the cobwebs from the furthest recesses of his mind. "No, no, Theo. You did the right thing by calling me. Besides, in our line of work, who sleeps? Right? Fire away."

"We had a priority-one hit scheduled tonight. Remember the call girl we marked in Miami?"

"The prostitute that Senator Kelley slept with? What was her name? She was Spanish, if I remember."

"Yeah. Catalan. Eliana Bautista. We had concerns that Senator Kelley shared more than a bed with our call girl. He's on the Foreign Committee of Clandestine Affairs, after all."

Blackburn yawned, then urged Theo to continue.

"We're convinced she had no hard evidence in her possession, but as you know, to make sure we didn't have a breach in security, we decided to eliminate her."

"Yeah, yeah. I understand all that, Theo. But what's the breakdown here?"

He didn't hesitate. Communication needed to be transparent. Two-way. "We had an NT agent balk at his orders. He failed to carry out the mission."

"An NT?"

"NT-Zero, sir. Code name Cypher."

"Is that even possible? I didn't think an NT *could* disobey orders."

"They can't. I think he's broken. Something is wrong, though we don't know what it is. Not yet. We tried to contact Dr. Shepherd. We need him to troubleshoot this thing from the inside. But he's on furlough, and we can't seem to find him. Right now, we're searching all of our public transportation resources with a fine-tooth comb. But no luck. Not yet."

"My God! We can't have an *NT* on the loose, Deputy. You need to fix this."

"Yes, sir. That's why I'm calling you. He's already killed several agents from the DCS branch office. He's proving most difficult to apprehend, sir. We've put out a BOLO with the local police and notified the FBI. Spoon-fed them a story about the Miami Sniper on the loose."

"Hmph. Ironic."

"Perhaps. I'd say effective. The media will eat this shit up. It will be all over the local news."

"Hold on a minute. Are you mad, Theo? We want to put a lid on this business with the senator. Not throw a spotlight on it."

"Sir…the NT is proving difficult to apprehend. We need to tighten the noose. Snare him before he does any actual harm. We can't afford to let him escape and get this whore to safety. Gets her to CNN."

Blackburn cleared his throat, his voice still thick with sleep. "Which you've nearly done all on your own, Deputy. What do you think will happen when the FBI—or God forbid, the police—finally capture them? They'll be on every news channel from here to LA."

"We can eliminate them. Take them out once they're in custody, before they can talk."

"And if they do?"

"I won't let that happen."

There was a pregnant pause on the other end of the line, and for a moment Spearman thought he had lost the director. But the familiar clink of ice being dropped into a rock glass, the unscrewing of a cap, and the melodious gurgle of liquor being poured with practiced ease reassured Spearman that he was still there. He knew the director to be a scotch man. Johnny Walker Blue. Spearman hated scotch.

"Sir?"

"Your confidence is admirable, Theo, and as usual it will be your undoing. But I admire your determination. So this is what you're going to do. You're going to plant a story that the Miami Sniper has an accomplice: the prostitute. She just murdered a cop while they were making their escape. We'll paint a backstory about her being a drug addict. Trades sex for her drug money…all that bullshit. Doesn't really matter. The story doesn't have to be perfect. Just plausible." Blackburn took a swig from his drink, the rattle of the ice distinct, deliberate. "There isn't a patrolman in Miami who won't be taking a shot at our little cop killer."

"Fine. But what about the NT?"

"No problem. Keep the story about him being the Miami Sniper. We'll make it work."

Spearman clenched his jaw. Felt his frustration rising like bile in the pit of his stomach. The man was long on commentary, short on solutions.

"No, sir. That's not what I meant. We might have a mole in the organization. Somebody who has access to Darkwater, specifically the NT program. Somebody in the know."

"Dr. Shepherd?"

"As I said, we can't locate him."

"You better."

Spearman gnashed his teeth, then massaged the tension from his temples. He took one last drag from his cigarette, then snuffed it out in the ashtray on the far corner of his desk. "We're working on it."

"Fine. Keep me updated. And Deputy?"

Spearman grunted as he stretched across his desk for his lighter and another cigarette. "Sir?"

"Tell me. Why in the hell did you choose an NT for just a simple hit, anyway?"

"That's what I've been trying to tell you. I didn't."

There was a long pause, followed by the rattle of ice in a glass. "Well, if I were you, Deputy, I think I'd stop worrying about where Dr. Shepherd is and instead try to figure out where it all started."

Alexandria, Virginia

Silence followed in the wake of the phone call, the steady pitter-patter of rain outside the only sound. Blackburn remained seated at his desk, his stare fixated on the droplets streaming down the windowpane in his den, each a crystal facet shimmering in the sterile lights of Wilkes Street. The house was still, his wife in a deep slumber upstairs, as it was one in the morning.

Blackburn shifted his attention to the center of his desk where a crystal carafe of scotch awaited him. He considered it carefully, as the tug of temptation was strong tonight. Still, he thought better of it and put the topper back into place. He nudged his rock glass to the center of the desk, picked up the receiver on the red phone, and stabbed a button to make his call. He didn't have to wait long for an answer.

"Victor. I trust you have news for me?"

"Mr. President. I believe we have a problem."

C H A P T E R   E L E V E N

Miami, Florida

The unassuming diner was small and lifeless. And, at this time of night, deserted. It certainly wouldn't have been Eliana's first choice. The name was Lively's. She had heard locals talk about it, but nothing noteworthy. It had a kitschy fifties decor with checkered tile floors and surf-green vinyl seats. There was even a dining counter graced with paper placemats and donuts under glass.

Eliana was not impressed. The diner was grubby. The floors were sticky, and the place reeked of burned coffee and week-old hamburger grease.

"What are we doing here?" Eliana chewed on her lip, looked at the door as it closed behind them. *"Estàs boig o simplement estúpid?"* *Are you crazy or just stupid?* "The police are looking for us."

The assassin had chosen the booth in the corner, ensuring his back was to the wall. His eyes moved around the room with calculated ease, never staying in one place for long. "Exactly. That's why we're going to sit tight for a while. Let things settle down out there."

"But we're just across the river. We stole a motorcycle, and we've traveled—what? Three blocks?"

"Point six miles."

Eliana glared at him and waited for an explanation, but he was in no hurry to answer. He was cautious. Deliberate. His face was nothing more than a block of ice. But his eyes...they crackled with fire. "They will take us out if we go out there right now. A BOLO will have been issued. There isn't a traffic cop, state troopie, or federal agent within fifty miles that won't be on the lookout for us."

She took a deep breath. This was all becoming a bit too much.

They put the conversation on hold when the waitress arrived, a young girl with a strong Haitian Creole accent. She sounded tired and disinterested in her job. She returned a moment later with two black coffees before heading off to change channels on the TV in the far corner of the room.

"Maybe we should turn ourselves in, *Senyor*. Tell the police what's going on. We'll explain everything. Tell them people are trying to kill us and…" Her words fell away, slowly dying on her lips. One look at the man sitting across from her, and she knew it was an impossibility. He would never surrender. *Couldn't*. Eliana closed her eyes. "I'm sorry. That was stupid. I know you can't do that. It's just that—I'm scared."

The man remained silent. Showed nothing. Instead, he sipped his coffee, nodded in approval, and eased back in his seat, his attention momentarily diverted to the sidewalk outside. She noticed he favored his right side whenever he moved, but then she remembered he'd been shot. A sudden dread coursed through her veins, fluid and icy cold. He was bleeding.

"We need to get you to a hospital."

The man looked at his shoulder as if he, too, had forgotten. An inky pool of wetness saturated his black t-shirt from a discreet puncture in the fabric. He made a circular motion with his shoulder, then tested it with a shrug. "I can't do that. Control knows that I've been shot. Hospitals will be the first place they look."

"But you're losing blood!" Eliana blanched. She didn't know this man. She wasn't emotionally invested. But he could grow weak, pass out. Even die. "You need a doctor, *Senyor*."

The man made a pinched face. Shook his head. "*Senyor*." He let the word rest heavy on his tongue as if he were tasting pâté for the first time. "My name is Brent Savage. Remember?"

Eliana sat for a moment, staring, her mouth agape. Was he for real?

"I'd appreciate it if you would stop calling me *Senyor*. It draws unnecessary attention to us. Call me by my first name or my last. It doesn't matter which."

She thought about this and considered his reasoning. It made sense, if for nothing more than making conversation less awkward. "OK. Savage."

Satisfied, he reached for the napkin dispenser on the table. "I appreciate your concern, Eliana, but no doctor. I'll just have to make do." He grabbed a handful of the brown paper napkins, reached down his collar, and stuffed the wad against the seeping bullet hole. "My body can heal itself, provided I can hole up long enough to get some rest. The bleeding has already slowed considerably."

"Wait. I don't understand. Self-heal?"

"We are all capable of self-healing. We have white blood cells to attack foreign invaders and use fevers to fight off infections. Our blood clots, allowing our wounds to scab over, protect our injuries while our tissue regenerates. I'm just more efficient at it."

Eliana sat back in the seat and threw up her hands. *This is crazy! What the hell does that even mean? More efficient!* Something wasn't adding up. She thought back to her apartment, the ease with which Savage dispatched the intruder. The terrific speed with which he disarmed her. It was almost too much to comprehend. "Are you some sort of superspy? A genetic mutant?"

"No."

"No, you're not a superspy, or no, you're not a genetic mutant?"

"Keep your voice down." Savage eyed the server in the far corner, obliviously watching the news. The short-order cook was busy flipping burgers. Even the diner's only other patron, the scruffy elderly man at the counter, was too busy eating his oatmeal to pay them attention. "No, I'm not some sort of failed science experiment, if that's what you mean. No. I'm not a spy. *What* I am is your only chance at survival. I don't say this lightly, and I'm not trying to impress you. The harsh reality is that neither of us will likely survive the night. Our only chance is for you to come clean and tell me why they want to eliminate you."

Eliana drew quiet, her mind racing as she tried to think of anything to say to appease him. "I'm sorry! I don't know why this is happening."

"Sure you do. You're a smart girl."

She shook her head, then looked away. "I don't! I'm just a—I'm just an escort!"

That raised an eyebrow. "Escort? You mean call girl."

She opened her mouth to speak but hesitated, her voice catching.

"Look, ma'am. I don't care if you call yourself a hooker, call girl, or an escort. Be a princess for all I care. But the United States government sees you as a threat. Now, you've either seen or heard something that puts this country's national security at the highest risk. They wouldn't have had me searching your apartment for intel if you hadn't." He ran his fingers through his hair. Scoffed. "What? You think they marked you because you're a prostitute?"

Eliana felt tears beginning to well. Her throat tightened, but she held firm. How dare he judge her! He was no better. Worse, in fact. *Un assassí.* A cold-blooded murderer. But for some reason, men always found it necessary to put her down. Shame her. She wouldn't give him the satisfaction. She took a breath, dug down deep, and found her voice. *"Que et fotin!" Fuck you.*

Eliana snatched her bag and stood up, intending to storm out. But he caught her arm and urged her to stay, not violently, but with deliberate concern. That stopped her. She looked at Savage, not shying from his gaze. "I'm a *person.*"

The man's eyes flickered, his brow pinched, just for an instant, but then disappeared. It was so insignificant that it may have gone unnoticed by anyone else. But Eliana had a way of reading people's faces, and it hadn't escaped her scrutiny.

He said, "You're right. You don't deserve that." He released his hold on her, gesturing for her to sit. "It won't happen again."

Eliana hesitated. She was confused. Scared. People were trying to kill her. This man claimed he was trying to help her. Yes, he was violent. Dangerous. She had seen that firsthand. But there was something about him that reached her—something that told her to take a chance. She slid back into the booth and folded her hands onto her lap.

The waitress returned to take their order, and the conversation was put on hold. They weren't hungry, so she left them their check for their coffees and went somewhere to find a counter to prop up. The awkward tension between Savage and Eliana should have dissipated, but it remained palpable long after the waitress had left. Silence remained in her wake, save for the TV whispering across the room or the occasional clank of a spoon against a bowl.

The man exhaled through his nose and eased back in the booth, the seat squeaking in protest. He was waiting again. Calm. Deliberate.

Eliana followed suit and leaned back. She said nothing at first, but her eyes wandered, like her thoughts, searching for an indeterminate point to focus on. When she finally spoke, the words seemed far away, thick and unobtainable. "You know, a few months ago, the Republican Party held their National Convention down here. *Crist!* It was a madhouse. The town was busting at the seams with politicians, celebrities, and hordes of media. With all the influx of visitors, it was good for local businesses. Clubs, restaurants, hotels. You name it. Business was good in my line of work, too. Too good. All except for the last day of the convention. My calendar was cleared of all appointments. All but one. That night, I was hired to escort—you know—entertain someone. Someone of political importance."

Savage leaned forward, resting his elbows on the off-kilter table. "Senator Kelley?"

Eliana heard him speak, even in the rolling fog of her memories. She eased her attention back to the man, finally allowing her eyes to meet his. "No."

Savage blinked and leaned back in the booth again. For the first time, he seemed confused. Out of place. "Then who? Did you recognize him?"

Eliana rolled her eyes. "Of course I recognized him. It was the President."

CHAPTER TWELVE

Somewhere near Denver, Colorado

Spearman stubbed out his cigarette, drained the rest of his Coke, then tossed the crushed can into the wastebasket. He patted himself down, looking for his car keys, before remembering he had left them on the wet bar behind the desk. *Wet bar. What crap!* Dry bar was more like it. He abhorred drinking. It muddled the mind. Impaired judgment. But it was necessary for visiting dignitaries who liked to feel self-important and see their needs catered to.

He grabbed the keys from the tray and was about to shut down his computer when his phone rang. "Spearman."

It was Blanton. "Sir? We have an update on Dr. Shepherd. We've received confirmation that he was at Kansas City International."

Kansas? Spearman exhaled through his nose and rubbed the fatigue from his eyes. "How long ago?"

"A little over an hour ago, sir. Our facial recognition software fingered him using the airport security cameras."

"Send it down to my terminal."

Spearman blasted through a string of passwords and pulled up the video feed from Control. The image's resolution was adequate, but the time-lapse video was choppy and monochrome. He saw a man at the United Airlines counter talking to the ticket agent. He was wearing a white dress shirt, khakis, and brown loafers. Rimless glasses, neatly trimmed beard. Spearman had complete confidence in the recognition software and didn't question the validity of the man's identity. Apparently, Shepherd had traveled to Kansas City before purchasing tickets to his alternate destination. *Clever.* "Do we know where he's heading?"

"Yes, sir. The idiot used his credit card. He purchased a ticket to Caracas, Venezuela. Fifteen hundred dollars and some change."

"Hm. Dr. Shepherd is a lot of things, Mr. Blanton, but an idiot isn't one of them. He's one of the smartest men I have ever met. But I'll admit—he isn't a field agent. He's bound to make mistakes." Spearman remained standing. Leaned in closer to the monitor. "How many tickets did he purchase?"

"Just the one, sir."

"Fine. When will we have the good doctor back in the fold?"

"Unknown, sir. We haven't been able to locate him. We've dispatched local field agents and have the help of airport security."

"Well, when does the flight leave?"

"Zero five thirty, sir."

Spearman glanced at his watch and then turned his attention back to the monitor, where Dr. Shepherd was being handed his credit card and plane ticket. *Just a couple of hours.* "He can't be far. Do we have a track on where he went after leaving the ticket counter?"

"Yes, sir. He went into a nearby men's room. An undercover NSA officer watched him go in. But he never saw him come back out."

"Hm. *Saw* is the operable word, Mr. Blanton. Since even airport security can likely check a bathroom stall, I have to assume they didn't find him in the men's room." Spearman paused, scratched his nose. "The video surveillance is clean? No sign of him leaving?"

"Affirmative, sir." There was a brief pause. Then Blanton cleared his throat. "I don't see how this plays out, sir. He's obviously left the reservation. He's already bought fucking tickets to Venezuela, and he thinks he's got off scot-free. I say we wait it out, post sentries at the departure gate. When he makes a break for it, we'll grab him."

Spearman said nothing, his mind working the problem. It was true Dr. Shepherd wasn't an agent and had no training in the field. But he *was* a bioengineer and the leading authority in nanotechnology. Hell. Dr. Shepherd developed the very technology that made the program even possible. Something told Spearman not to underestimate him.

"Any other witnesses, Blanton? What about the ticket agent? Does she remember Shepherd?"

"Yes, sir. She does. She said he acted peculiar and wanted to buy a ticket to Venezuela but didn't have a destination in mind. He just talked of opening a medical practice down there. She claims she was the one who suggested Caracas."

Spearman looked at the ceiling as he tried to corral his racing thoughts. *Fuck!* "Once you found Dr. Shepherd at Kansas City International, you didn't bother rerunning the facial recognition software, did you?"

"Well, no, sir. We didn't need to—when the FRS zeroed in on him at the airport in Kansas, we merely followed him into the bathroom with video surveillance. After that, we just kept an eye out for him. But I can assure you, sir. He didn't come out of that bathroom. Maybe he exited through some ductwork?"

"Goddamn it, Blanton! I want you to run the video surveillance through the FRS again. We know he went into the bathroom and isn't there now. We're missing something!"

Blanton stumbled over an explanation, his efforts to find an acceptable excuse inadequate. Spearman heard a hand fumbling over the phone's mouthpiece while Blanton barked out orders to the cyber-jockeys.

"Blanton?"

"We're working on it, sir. Running the program now."

"Today, Mr. Blanton. Today!"

"Got it, sir. Plugging you in now."

A new video popped up on the screen, approximately ten minutes after Dr. Shepherd was last seen entering the men's restroom. Instead, there was now a frozen image of another man on the screen. A man with dark, slicked-back hair, his face clean-shaven. He was in his early fifties, wearing a gray t-shirt and khaki pants. No glasses. Yet the facial recognition software had mapped out his face shape, measuring his eyes, nose, and jawline. There was a ninety-two percent probability that the new target was Dr. Shepherd.

"Son of a bitch! That's him. Get Kansas City on the phone ASAP. Tell them the target is no longer onsite. He walked out the front door as pretty as you please and has a two-hour head start!"

"We've got the station chief on the line now, sir."

"I want every taxi cab, bus depot, and car rental place cross-checked for purchases made by Dr. Shepherd. Check for witnesses. And damn it! Make sure you analyze every closed-circuit video recording with the FRS."

"Yes, sir. I'm on it."

Spearman powered down his computer and snatched his car keys from the desk. "One more thing, Blanton. Call the laboratory at CINS and see who's working late tonight. Tell them I'm on my way."

CHAPTER THIRTEEN

Aurora, Colorado

Colorado Institute of Nanotechnology Sciences (CINS)

Spearman rolled down his car window. The night air was invigorating, and he needed to recharge. Things had gotten too complicated. Too messy. And it was time to hit the reset button on his way of thinking. But the drive was short, and the roads deserted. Twenty-two minutes later, he was walking down the dimly lit corridors of CINS.

The institute's architecture was sleek and modern, with vaulted glass ceilings, vast, empty corridors, and polished floors so shiny they were like black obsidian. During the day, it was a bustling hive of activity for cancer research where scientists were discovering new ways to improve the delivery system of chemotherapy medicines. At night, it was a mausoleum devoid of life.

Spearman headed directly for the southeast corner of the building, entering a no-access zone for the general public. He passed security with his credentials, then walked into the eastside service elevator, inserted his key, and punched in the access code. Moments later, he found himself at the deepest level of CINS, where the government's real interests lay.

Three layers of security, comprising thumbprint imaging, voice recognition, and retinal scan, opened the hermetically sealed doors. Moments later, Spearman had full access to the project's NT labs, or the Kitchen, as the researchers liked to call it. The painted block walls of the government laboratory stood in direct contrast to the slick corporate-funded facilities upstairs. But looks were deceiving. The Kitchen was where the real science was cooked.

Spearman's visits to the lab were infrequent; when he went there, he usually conferred with Dr. Shepherd. Tonight, it would be anyone's guess.

There was a solitary beacon of light at the end of Corridor E, evidence somebody was manning the lab at this late hour. Then again, when Spearman demanded that somebody meet him there, he expected it to be carried out.

Spearman barged into the lab and headed straight for a woman who was working across the room, wearing a white lab coat. "I'm Deputy Director Theo Spearman. Chief Officer of Operation Darkwater. And you are?"

The young dark-haired woman of South Asian descent jumped and smiled sheepishly as she extended her hand. "Dr. Nikhila Misra. It's a pleasure to meet you, sir." The doctor placed the blood sample she was analyzing back into the centrifuge and turned it on.

Spearman noted she was working the night shift alone. That was either coincidence, or she had drawn the short end of the stick when the orders had come down to report to the lab. "Good to know, Doctor. What are your responsibilities here at the Kitchen?"

"I mostly assist Dr. Shepherd with the synapse mapping of the human brain. But my specialty is renewable energy development."

"Come again?"

"I'm designing nanotechnology that can provide its own energy supply."

"That's a fancy trick." He wasn't good at small talk. He never had much use for it. Spearman looked around the cramped laboratory. Noted its sparse furnishings. It had the obligatory equipment: microscopes, centrifuge machines, computer stations, examination tables, and a pharmaceutical dispensary. However, the room's focal point was the climate-controlled "recipe" room, an eclectic collection of small bottles and color-coded boxes displayed prominently behind glass walls.

"It isn't a trick, Mr. Spearman. Theoretically, I could harvest power directly from the host's bloodstream by utilizing the electrolytes found in the blood. Of course, that technology is still in the early stages of development. Our current nanotechnology is nuclear dependent, which, of course, has its own set of complications."

"Interesting, Doctor. Perhaps you *can* help me. We're having trouble with one of your NTs. He's had a breakdown, balked at orders, and left the reservation during a highly sensitive mission. We need to bring him in, fix the problem."

"Balked at orders? That's impossible."

"Yet here I am."

"Have you tried getting a hold of Dr. Shepherd?"

"Repeatedly. He's out of the country on some R&R, and we're unable to contact him. That's why I need your assistance."

"Oh, that's right. Cancun. He's talked about it for weeks. All right. OK. Which NT is giving you fits?"

"NT-Zero."

Dr. Misra raised an eyebrow. "Hm. A *Prime*." She paused for a moment, her mind churning through the new information. When she saw the perplexed look on the deputy director's face, she added casually, "Prototype, Mr. Spearman."

"Of course. Anything you can do to shed some light on the issue would be immensely helpful."

Dr. Misra walked over to the nearest computer terminal. She tapped a few keys and then started cross-searching multiple databases. "I could pull up Cypher's medical history. He has to come in for routine maintenance and have his upgrades installed before each mission. That's because we tailor the nanobots to meet the NT's specific mission needs."

"You're talking about the NTs being programmable."

"Yes. In a way. Some of what we do is upload mission-sensitive data or provide them with valuable resources, such as city maps, foreign languages, and names and locations of friendlies. We can do this by stimulating neurons in the medial temporal lobe. It's a matter of unraveling the neural code, really, and stimulating individual cells in the right sequence. But our real breakthrough was increasing the neuroplasticity of the brain. The nanobots encourage the growth of new neural pathways, making the brain more efficient. The NTs not only have better comprehension but also better problem-solving capabilities."

"As I said, Doctor, that's quite a trick." Spearman picked up a microscopic slide, pretended to look at it beneath the overhead light, and then set it back down. "A perfect assassin, wouldn't you say?"

Dr. Misra shrugged, forcing a nervous smile. "Well, at least a superior one, Mr. Spearman. The NTs have nanobots that carry nine billion oxygen and carbon dioxide molecules—over two hundred times more effective than a normal human red blood cell. Do you realize the enormous advantage that gives them? The NTs are capable of running full tilt for fifteen minutes without performance degradation. They can hold their breath for hours. They have superior strength, feel no pain, need little sleep, never get sick, and are remarkably adept at healing—even battle-grade wounds."

"Well, Dr. Misra…if your NTs are so wonderful, why the *fuck* do I have Cypher disobeying direct orders and running loose in Miami, killing people?"

The doctor took a step back, startled by his abrupt outburst. Her cheeks flushed, and she meekly folded her arms in front of her. "I'm not sure. I'll see what I can find out." She turned back to the computer terminal, tapped a few keys, and pulled up Cypher's debriefing history.

"What are we looking at?"

"Well, after every mission, the NTs come in for debriefings. We give them a physical, treat them if need be, and do a complete neurological workup."

"Do you see anything unusual?"

"Hm. Not really. Most of Cypher's debriefings occurred at our Brown Mountain facility in North Carolina—which makes sense. We service most of our NTs out of there. But you see here? The last two debriefings? They took place right here at CINS."

"Who was the attending physician? I'd like to speak with them."

Dr. Misra clicked the mouse over the corresponding link. "Oh…well…that would be Dr. Shepherd. Both times."

Spearman squinted. "Is that proper protocol?"

"It's not typical. No. But it's not exactly against protocol, either. He's the Head of Research, after all."

"I understand that. But why the sudden change? Why have Cypher come back to CINS when most of his debriefings occurred at Brown Mountain? Something has changed, Doctor, and I need to know why. Were some bizarre nanobots introduced into Cypher's system? Something that would cause him to malfunction?"

Dr. Misra shook her head, reluctant to continue the search—not because she felt it was inherently wrong but because she thought it a complete waste of time. She jumped to the first debriefing back in July, pulled up the list of nanobot inclusions, and compared it to the second visit in August. The lists were extensive, but nothing unusual stuck out. "I see nothing, Mr. Spearman. Everything seems in order. The typical nanobots for increased motor functions, healing, and immunity. They're all here. There are some variances for mission specifics, of course, such as language sets, building schematics, and personal contacts. The usual."

Spearman clenched a fist, then cursed under his breath. *Another dead end.*

"Wait a sec." Dr. Misra squinted at the screen. Leaned in close. "I'll be damned."

"What? Did you find something?"

"No. The opposite, actually."

"I don't follow."

"The problems with Cypher have nothing to do with the insertion of errant nanobots. The real problem is that he's had some left out." Dr. Misra pointed to the screen.

Spearman bent over the counter, following along.

"Two nanobots are missing. MR71, which we use to manipulate or even suppress memories. As you can imagine, it's in our best interest if the assassin doesn't always remember their missions. By manipulating memories, we can enhance an assassin's ability to kill without remorse. To face danger without fear. And to suppress any emotion. In essence, they perform more like machines than men."

"This MR71…it wasn't administered during either debriefing?"

"Correct. But that's not all. The ES44 series is missing as well. It's responsible for suppressing the soldier's moral sensibilities. We can suspend their sense of right and wrong by applying transcranial magnetic stimulation to the right temporoparietal junction. Only the mission matters."

"So what's the likely outcome of denying Cypher the MR71 and ES44 nanobots?"

The doctor stood up and stretched her back. She yawned, then looked him in the eye. "Anarchy. He would slowly lose his emotional detachment. In layman's terms…he would start caring."

"Disobey an order?"

"Naturally. At least if it goes against his better moral judgment."

Son of a bitch. "Doctor? As of now, Henry Shepherd is considered a fugitive of the law. Until we can find a permanent replacement for him, you will head up the lab here at CINS."

"What? But I'm not qualified to—"

"You will do—for now. At the moment, I have more important things to consider. It's clear that Cypher has been compromised and is no longer under control. I need to bring him down."

Dr. Misra snorted. When Spearman glared at her, she folded her arms, and the smirk on her face melted away.

"Is there a problem, Doctor?"

"Sorry. No. Well, yes—there is a problem! It's a rather big one, actually. You can't just take down an NT. They're designed to handle anything you throw at them. NTs are incredibly smart and entirely self-reliant. They don't get sick; if you wound them, they can repair themselves. They're trained to disappear—indefinitely if need be. And if you press them—force them to fight instead of flee? A trail of dead bodies will be left in their wake."

Spearman glowered at her. He knew she had a point, but he found her mousy demeanor irritating. "What do you suggest? We let him run free and kill as many people as he sees fit?"

"If he is regaining a sense of morality, that scenario seems highly unlikely."

"Are *you* willing to take that chance, Doctor?"

"Of course not. But I don't think you can run him down like a common criminal, either. It would seem to me that if you want to catch a fox, you need to think like a fox."

Spearman stopped. Considered her reasoning. After a moment, he nodded and headed to the door. "That may be true, Doctor. But I have another theory. To kill a fox, sometimes you need a wolf."

CHAPTER FOURTEEN

Miami, Florida

"Are you telling me you had sex with Richard S. Turner? The President of the United States?"

Eliana met his eyes. Paused a beat, then nodded.

That was unexpected. Savage's orders were to look for leaked intel from Senator Kelley, which made sense since he was on the Foreign Committee of Clandestine Affairs. Perhaps it made too much sense.

"Wait a minute. That's scandalous but hardly noteworthy. They wouldn't put a hit on you because you slept with POTUS. That sort of stuff has been happening for nearly as long as the office itself has been around. There has to be protocol when covering that sort of thing up."

She said, "There is. They made me up to look like a Secret Service agent. Black suit, sunglasses. They even gave me a fake gun and an earpiece. After that, it wasn't difficult to sneak me into his suite at the Biltmore."

"Where was the First Lady?"

"I don't know. Obviously, not there. There was nobody around. Not even the Secret Service. He ordered them out."

Savage took a generous gulp of his coffee, then shook his head as he worked through the details. "This doesn't add up. Did he hurt you? Get out the whips? Dress up like a woman?"

"No! Nothing like that. The President was drunk. He was—what do you call it—shit-faced. He just kept talking about himself."

"What do you mean? He was bragging?"

"He wouldn't shut up. I guess that's why it took him forever to get it up. He was too busy talking. It's like he was trying to impress me. He kept talking about how he was the most powerful man in the world."

Savage said nothing. Waited.

Eliana grabbed her mug with two hands, her eyes shifting, unfocused. She took a sip of her coffee. Made a face. "He said something strange…I didn't understand it. Something about how he could eliminate his enemies, and nobody would be any the wiser."

Savage straightened, his dark green eyes locked on to hers. "He said that?"

"Hm. He said *that* was true power." She stopped, cocking her head. "Well…he might have used the word rivals, not enemies. I'm not sure. But he's crazy. Doesn't matter."

Savage raised his eyebrows. The pieces of the puzzle were falling into place. "You're right. It doesn't. To President Turner, though, they're one and the same." Savage leaned in, his face mere inches from hers. "Listen. About a year and a half ago, there was talk about philanthropist Conall Bennett contemplating a run for the White House. He was one of President Turner's most vocal critics, particularly on climate change, and he was making waves."

"I don't understand what that has to do with—"

"According to his closest friends, Bennett was about to announce his candidacy. A week before the announcement, he was found dead at his vacation home near Vail alongside his wife and his daughter's family, who had been there for the weekend. The official autopsy concluded they died of carbon monoxide poisoning…a faulty fireplace or something."

"I remember hearing about that. It was sad. But I still don't understand how—"

"Eliana. Think. President Turner was drunk that night, and his inhibitions were lowered. He was trying to brag about how powerful he was…how he could eliminate his rivals, and nobody would ever know."

She gasped, her slender fingers reaching for her mouth.

"So here's the kicker, Eliana. Somebody already knows. *You* do. President Turner practically admitted to you he had a political rival murdered. That's why you're marked."

"But bragging about something and doing it are two very different things. Maybe you're right. Maybe the President had Connal Bennett murdered. But he never mentioned a name."

"*He* doesn't know that…not for sure. The President was drunk. He barely remembers. Might as well eliminate all doubt."

"*Maleït sigui!*" *Damn it!* "This isn't happening. Even if what you're saying is true, Savage, we have no proof."

"No. Not yet."

"Not yet? You mean never! It's not like we can just ask the President if he had a political rival murdered, and he'll come clean."

Her point was valid. But there had to be hard evidence somewhere, even in a black op like Darkwater. Plans had to be formed, orders issued, and funds allocated even for the simplest missions. Savage himself was proof of that. He got paid and paid well. But where to start? That was the rub.

For now, their safety was paramount. He could disappear. Stay off the grid. Vanish like a puff of pollen in a brisk breeze. But Eliana…that was different. He needed to get her to someplace safe, somewhere they couldn't touch her. Public opinion was her only recourse. "We need to get you to a news station. Put you in front of a national audience."

The sudden volume change of the diner's TV caught Savage's attention. His eyes shifted to the small group of people gathered around it, their mouths agape like baby birds waiting for their next feeding. The news was on.

"*…Federal agents say that Brent Savage is the primary suspect for the Miami Sniper killings that occurred over the last several weeks and is considered armed and dangerous. Eliana Bautista is suspected of killing two undercover police officers tonight during a raid on her Idyll Tower apartment in downtown Miami. Miami Police spokesperson*

Officer Paula Alvarez said the suspects were last seen near the 500 block of South Miami Avenue.

"Bautista is of Spanish descent, twenty-three years old, five foot seven inches tall and weighs a hundred and twenty-five pounds. Not much is known about Savage at this time. Should you have any information on the whereabouts of either suspect, please notify the Miami Police Department immediately."

Savage could feel Eliana's eyes on him, her mouth working to free the words that wouldn't come. But he had no time for it. His sole focus was on their survival, the moment at hand.

When Eliana's driver's license photo splashed across the TV screen, the cook and waitress must have recognized them. They whispered to each other, their expressions animated and out of place. Their lack of eye contact was telling. But when the old man at the counter turned around to see who they were talking about, it was apparent the jig was up.

Savage feigned ignorance, making as if he was listening to Eliana's ramblings. Coherence be damned.

The waitress shuffled over to their table, sheepish and unconvincing as she topped off their coffee. She returned to the counter, her plastic smile glued in place, and said, *"Li se asasen an. Rele lapolis! Prese!"*

Savage threw a glance at Eliana, his right brow arched. "Did you catch that?"

"A little. She's speaking Haitian Creole. I really don't understand it word for word, but I believe she wants them to call the police."

"And to hurry," he added.

Eliana paused, her eyes flashing like high beams.

Savage noticed her expression shift from concern to genuine curiosity. Questions were sure to follow. But he paid it no mind. His attention was on his surroundings, as it had been from the moment he had walked into the diner. While Eliana had been concerned with sticky floors and burned coffee, Savage was taking mental notes.

Everything was in the details and not always as apparent as the TV in the corner. There was a fake surveillance camera mounted on the far wall. A cordless phone by the register. There were two fire extinguishers. One over by the grill, the other on the wall nearest Savage—fourteen months since its last inspection date. And tucked away on a shelf above the cook a conventional channel scanner was belching severe thunderstorm warnings every few minutes. Most notably, there were only two ways out: the entrance at the front of the diner and a rear exit accessible through the kitchen only.

Savage stood and said, "I believe it's time for us to leave."

"What about the bill?" she asked, easing out of the booth, awkward and unsure.

"I'm sure our friends in the corner over there would be happier if we just left." The cook, waitress, and old man were eyeing them, no longer showing any pretense of ignorance. The waitress let her arm slip to her side, likely reaching for her cell phone. But Savage let his eyes burn right through her, scalding her like a hot branding iron. She stopped and wiped her sweaty palms on her threadbare apron instead.

Savage didn't hesitate. He moved toward the kitchen, the exit in the rear offering the best avenue of escape without being noticed. That all changed in an instant.

The bell rang above the front door, and two Miami patrolmen walked in, water dripping from the brims of their hats, clothes sopping from the torrential downpour. *How did they find us?* The people in the diner certainly hadn't tipped them off, and Savage had been careful to park the motorcycle behind some shrubbery and an old olive tree in the side parking lot. It would be hard to spot it from the street.

The officers gave only a perfunctory glance around, wasting precious little time zeroing in on Savage and the woman.

But Savage didn't miss a beat. He changed directions, gently herding Eliana to his side and coaxing her behind the officers and toward the front door instead. He maintained eye contact with Eliana, pretending to laugh in a brief exchange with her, but never deviating from his plan of escape. It was simple. They wouldn't question his intentions because he acted as if he belonged there and didn't have a care in the world. It almost worked.

"Sir?" The nearest patrolman turned in their direction. "Folks? I need you to hold up a second."

Savage hesitated, giving the officers the appearance of compliance. He was easing his hand toward the gun tucked in his pants, hidden beneath his shirt. But one glance at Eliana stopped him dead. Her breathing was heavy. Stilted. Her eyes were as wide as dinner plates, pleading for him to reconsider. *Damn it.* This went against his instincts, what he was trained to do. He let his hand drop to his side.

It turned out to be a wise decision. Both officers had their hands resting on their holsters and had positioned themselves on opposite sides of Eliana and himself.

"What are you folks doing here at this time of night?"

Savage looked at the patrolmen. Noted their name tags pinned above their shields. Officer Maddox and Officer Sullivan. Maddox was young. Ripped. Mid-twenties. Sullivan had salt-and-pepper hair, but with features so sharp they could cut. Close to fifty.

"I asked you folks a question."

Eliana cleared her throat. "Just getting something to eat."

"In the middle of the night? It's getting pretty late for a date."

"We hate crowds," she said.

Officer Maddox snorted. "Where you headed?"

"Home."

"You in a hurry? What's the rush?"

Savage felt his pulse quicken, his fist clenched into a ball. He knew this was pointless. They weren't being inquisitive. They had entered the diner *looking* for them. The rest was all bullshit. "Sorry," he said, "but we never liked the smell of bacon."

"Don't get smart!" said Maddox, spit launching from his lips.

The situation was deteriorating fast. But Savage continued to push them hard. He said, "Why? Is smart too much for you?"

"OK, wiseass! Let's see some hands!" Officer Sullivan pushed Eliana toward the table to handcuff her while Officer Maddox tried to pull his pistol to cover them. It never cleared the holster.

Savage reached across his body and grabbed Maddox's right arm, yanking him off balance and bringing him into close quarters. He stopped the man's momentum with a vicious elbow to his face. There was a resounding crack, a spray of blood, and the sound of bare skin screeching across the tacky floor. Officer Maddox was now writhing in agony and out of play.

By the time Savage spun around to face Officer Sullivan, the man was already screaming into his shoulder mic, calling for backup and drawing his pistol. He was out of arm's reach, a chasm between them.

Savage delivered a sidekick, the blow catching Sullivan in the wrist, knocking the gun out of his hand and sending it skittering across the dining room. The man glanced at his empty hand and shook off the sting. He wasn't as quick to anger as Maddox. He was confident. Disciplined. Decisive. Sullivan pulled out his nightstick and began lunging at Savage, using his size advantage to press him. He swung twice, first right, then left, each a miss.

Savage backpedaled until he ran out of real estate, his body pressed up against the booth behind him. Time slowed, expanses closed, and adrenaline ignited in him like a match put to gasoline.

Sullivan swung the nightstick for all he was worth, an overzealous shot meant to take Savage out for good. But Savage twisted clear, the table taking the full force of the blow. He saw his opportunity and seized the napkin dispenser on the table. It was a heavy box of brushed steel, and he used it to absorb the next blast from the nightstick. The crack from the blow sounded like a cannon shot. Again and again. *Pow! Pow! Pow!*

Savage righted himself while he braced the steel box tight against his wrist, a makeshift shield that held its own against the wooden baton. He pushed the officer back, taking one last strike with the box before he drove his elbow into Sullivan's face. His head jerked back, his eyes fluttered. His legs nearly buckled.

Savage didn't hesitate. Supporting the steel box with his left hand, he held it against Sullivan's face and struck it with his right, each blow pummeling him into submission until he crumpled to the floor.

Savage tossed the crushed napkin dispenser to the side and checked to see if Eliana was OK.

She was still crouched by the dining booth, somehow having kept out of the shitstorm that had just gone down. *Smart girl.*

Savage's eyes focused beyond her immediate vicinity. Saw danger looming just a few feet away. Eliana screamed and fell flat on the floor.

Officer Maddox had stumbled to his feet and was pulling his pistol, taking a bead on Savage's head. He could have drawn the SIG from his waistband and dispatched him with never a thought. It was in his training. But this wasn't a mark, and it certainly wasn't the Wild West. The last thing they needed was to kill a police officer. You might as well poke a hornet's nest with a stick.

Savage snatched a glass sugar dispenser from the table and hurled it at Maddox, resulting in a direct blow to his head. His gun discharged, an errant bullet blowing out the front picture window of the diner.

The staff and their lone patron scattered, running for the rear exit, the waitress's screams wailing in the distance like a passing freight train in the night.

Then there was silence. Sullivan was flat on his back, some ten feet away, groaning. Maddox was face down, crumpled on the floor, twitching.

Savage tested his shoulder. Felt no pain. It had underperformed slightly but held its own.

Eliana was nearly hysterical, grabbing her head and pacing frantically. "*Fotre!* We could have been killed! How did they find us so quickly?"

"I don't know."

"But they came right to us! Like they knew we were here."

Savage had a revelation, one more piece of the puzzle falling into place. "You're right. They did."

Eliana was still spewing a string of expletives, trying to wrap her thoughts around the events unfolding.

"Hey! Focus! We need to get out of here. They know exactly where we are. They're tracking me through my biosensor!"

Eliana snapped out of it, her eyes focusing on Savage. "Well, throw it away! Or unplug it, or whatever you do to get rid of it!"

"It's not that simple."

Savage grabbed Eliana by the elbow and pulled her behind the service counter. He opened a couple of drawers—rummaged through them haphazardly. Nothing. He spun around and quickly searched the preparation table by the grill. A takeout order was left uncompleted: hamburger wrapped in foil, fries overloaded in a paper pouch, and a large Coke, without a lid, still bubbling. Savage grabbed the burger and led Eliana to the front door.

"Let's go! They're almost here."

CHAPTER FIFTEEN

The thunderstorm had arrived and with it came a deluge of rain. It fell hard and fast, with drops so huge they looked like grapes falling from the sky. Savage made a mad dash to the Yamaha, dragging Eliana behind him, urging her to keep up. Police sirens blared in the distance, their warning distinct and eerily foreboding. They had run out of time.

Savage grabbed the first helmet off the seat and tossed it to Eliana. "Hurry," he said. He then pulled on his own and fired up the bike. The sirens were getting closer. He could see squad cars in the distance, fast approaching, their orbs of red and blue piercing through the curtain of heavy rain. Quarter mile. No less.

Savage tore the wrapper off the hamburger he'd grabbed from the diner, tossed the sandwich aside, and secured the foil to the back of his neck by wedging it between his shirt collar and helmet.

Eliana was frantic. "What are you doing?" Her voice sounded muffled beneath the shield of her helmet and the din of the downpour. But even then Savage heard her screaming. *"Està boig?"* *Are you crazy?* "They're almost here!"

And she was right. The first squad car easily had a half mile on the other responders. It charged in like a lioness in pursuit, screeching to a halt and swinging broadside. The driver wanted to throw open the door and take point while the patrolman on the passenger side would bail and provide cover from behind the squad car. Neither of them succeeded.

Savage pulled out his SIG and, with machinelike precision, fired a single shot into each of the driver's side tires. A third shot followed, blowing out the front window, forcing the police officers to duck beneath the dash of their car.

In that split second's reprieve, Savage noticed something strange on the horizon. A sheet of lightning blanketed the sky, illuminating the Bell LongRanger police chopper rapidly approaching from the northeast. The sound of rotors thumping in the distance confirmed his worst fear: an eye in the sky.

Savage fired another potshot at the police cruiser, ensuring the officers kept their heads down while he leaped onto the motorcycle. He reached out for Eliana, pulled her onto the back of the bike, and they launched like a rocket down 1st Street. The other police cars in pursuit never even tapped the brakes as they arrived just in time to pick up the chase.

Miami's roads followed a grid system. West-East routes were ordinal numbers and labeled streets, while the North-South routes were avenues. Savage knew this. Could see the city map before him like a fighter pilot's head-up display. Despite this, their chances of escaping weren't much better.

The traffic light was red at the first intersection. Savage refused to ease off the throttle. But luck played a huge part in the first card he played that night. No traffic.

They cleared NW 1st Avenue. The multi-tiered Metrorail flashed overhead, followed by a patch of herringbone brick paver on the road. The Stephen P. Clark Government Center. Courtyard. Trees. At ninety miles an hour, it was all Savage could do to focus on the cityscape streaking past him. Sirens wailed behind him.

Though he couldn't see the chopper overhead, he could feel it, sense it devouring the distance between them. *Damn it!* Why the hell wasn't the chopper grounded in the first place? The thunderstorm was raging, a veritable light show of lightning strikes. Certainly, there was protocol for such things. Why risk the lives of the pilots? Savage could think of only one reason. They were desperate enough not to care.

A barrage of spinning lights and flashing strobes appeared directly ahead, diverting Savage's attention back to the road. A wall of police cars raced toward him, preparing to cut off his only avenue of escape. It almost worked. He couldn't go forward. Couldn't turn back.

Savage hit the brakes hard, wrestled to keep the bike under control, and leaned to the right as he swerved into the park just past the government building.

The rear tire wanted to slide out from under him, but Savage kept the bike from dumping with an aptly placed foot. He made a beeline for the next street, cutting the corner and veering away from the police. But a minefield of trees littered the courtyard, each evenly spaced about ten feet apart. It took a herculean effort to maintain control of the bike. But the limited visibility and excessive speed were too much, even for Savage. He swerved left. Then swerved right. The bike's tail end didn't clear, and it smashed into a tree. Plastic cowling shattered. Eliana screamed. And just like that, Savage knew he had failed her.

The pilot felt the high winds pummel the Bell 206L LongRanger, forcing him to overcorrect to maintain a straight line. They had reports of the two suspects making a break from a diner on NW 1st Street but couldn't lock in on their target. Their forward-looking infrared camera, or FLIR, was at a distinct disadvantage in this severe weather. Typically, the camera could pick up the slightest hint of thermal radiation and then process that information into a clear picture, even during the darkest of nights. It was an invaluable tool in tracking fugitives. However, heavy rain severely limited the range of the FLIR due to the scattering of light off the water droplets. Tonight, they would have to be practically on top of them to get a distinct picture.

"Ground units, we have visual on suspects. Two perps fleeing on foot. Negative. Strike that. They're away on a motorcycle. I repeat, suspects are on a motorcycle. Heading west on NW 1st Street."

The pilot felt the floor drop from under them, the helicopter rapidly descending in altitude before he gained control.

The co-pilot was doing his best to keep his eyes glued to the imaging monitor but struggled with the turbulence. "Jesus Christ! What the hell are we doing out here? This is outside normal protocol, and you know it!"

"We have our orders," the pilot said.

"The hell with orders! Why is the FBI involved, anyway? If they want these fugitives so damn bad, let them get their asses up here and fly in this shit!"

A burst of lightning split the sky and set the night ablaze.

The pilot flinched—and then tried to hide it by making light of the situation. "What? And let them have all the fun?"

The co-pilot snorted. "Fun my ass! If the high winds don't knock us out of the sky, the lightning will."

"One suspect is the Miami Sniper. And they killed two undercover officers tonight. Assaulted two more." He offered a sidelong glance to his partner. "We have our orders," he repeated.

The pilot diverted his attention to the chatter on the emergency channel and understood that the police officers on the ground were coordinating their maneuvers to trap the fugitives.

Though the motorcycle was barely distinguishable on the monitor—a blurry streak, really—the pilot knew there were several squad cars behind them in hot pursuit, driving them directly toward the converging eastbound units.

What happened next was unexpected. The motorcycle driver stood on his brakes and somehow swerved right and circumnavigated the roadblock, disappearing beneath the canopy of trees in the park by the government building. He couldn't tell for sure. The image was jumpy. Distorted. But he swore he saw the impact.

"All units! Suspects down! I repeat, suspects down!"

The bike shook from the impact. But it remained upright. Somehow, Savage kept it headed in the right direction. A blip of the throttle sent them past some modern sculpture in the park, a giant shattered bowl, and eventually beyond the roadblock. Northbound. The bike's 1000cc engine was voracious, hungry to eat more pavement. Clearly, the damage to the Yamaha was cosmetic only. Savage wished he could say the same for his passenger. He had heard Eliana cry out. Curse from the pain. Yet she held on tight, clutching him with all her might.

More trees flanked them on both sides of the road. A smattering of cover from the eye in the sky. He took an immediate left, his left foot dragging on the ground as he pushed the bike to its limit. Water pooled on the roads. Wind-driven rain pelted his visor. Lightning exploded like flash grenades all around. Yet his focus remained razor sharp.

Local tax building, big and blocky on the right. Parking garage. Again, Savage stood on the brakes, back tire locking up. He turned right, raced through a parking lot, and then slowed as it funneled down to a narrow lane. A chain-link fence forced them to ease their way through the rear parking lot of the County Juvenile Services department. The rain fell in buckets. A lonely darkness surrounded them, punctuated with a brilliant flash of light and the crack of thunder. They had shaken their pursuit.

★　　★　　★

The radio squawked. *"Air One. We need visual. Repeat. We need visual."*

The pilot swung the helicopter around to the south, disregarding safety protocol while maintaining a low altitude. Despite their proximity to the ground, the FLIR was still ineffective. Worse, at that altitude, buildings were also affecting their line of sight. "Correction. All ground units. That's a negative on visual. Fugitive is on the run."

All ground units mobilized again.

The pilot increased his altitude to a safer level and tried to hold their position. The suspects were last seen making a line to the northwest, and his instincts were to follow them. But he had to clear the area first.

The howling winds buffeted the craft, but the pilot maintained his heading.

"Anything on the FLIR?" he asked.

"Negative," the co-pilot said. "Significant distortion. Nothing but ghosts."

"Flip on the searchlight."

"Roger. Flipping on the sun."

The effect was immediate. Sixteen million candlepower had a way of burning away the deepest of shadows. The question now was, could they remain airborne? Despite his bravado, the pilot was having significant doubts.

It was slow going. They circled the government building and began working their way outward. The new Children's Courthouse. Public library. Tax building. Each area had to be swept with the searchlight. Each demanded their attention, but the storm wouldn't allow it.

"Swinging around the juvy building," the pilot said.

The radio crackled. *"Air One. Do you have a visual?"*

"Negative, dispatch. Hold on…wait a second." The pilot nodded to his partner, pointing through the windshield. "I think we have them!"

CHAPTER SIXTEEN

Savage could hear the sirens drawing near. From which direction he couldn't tell. Their urgent shrills were stifled, choked out by the rain and swirling winds. But the helicopter—that was different. It was close. It cleared the box-shaped parking garage, its bright searchlight piercing the darkness like the searing finger of God.

Eliana leaned forward, screaming through her helmet. "They've found us!"

Savage wasted no time. He weaved his way toward the west in search of an exit. It was a dead end. The exits were blocked with massive chain-link gates and topped with barbed wire. *Of course!* It was a detention center.

Savage put his foot down, spun the bike around, and headed back in the direction they had come. The police helicopter was right on top of them, leaving Savage only one avenue of escape: a small walkway nestled between the parking garage and a couple of palm trees leading directly to the street. It was clear of fencing—just a small jump over the curb and then down a few low-level steps to make their escape.

Savage kicked the bike in the ass and headed westbound. Again, the traffic light was red. And again, Savage cleared the intersection unscathed. The searchlight was hot on their tail, but at the last second, they found cover beneath the I-95 overpass. They shot out the other side and fishtailed as they turned north at the next intersection. It was a grave mistake. They were now headed in the wrong direction down a one-way street.

Savage wasn't convinced that the police chopper had spotted them. But he wasn't about to take any chances. Seventy. Eighty. Ninety miles per hour. The rain pierced their skin like needles at that breakneck speed. Pain aside, he had his hands full just keeping the bike upright. Southbound traffic fired toward them like heat-seeking missiles. A black Cadillac streaked by on the left. Then a black Porsche Cayenne and a white BMW coupe approached in the two center lanes, staggered, with no room between them. He gave them a wide berth on the right before weaving back to center.

Another intersection ahead. NW 5th Street. The light turned red. Savage didn't hesitate. He had to create space between him and the cops. So far, he had played his cards right. He had been lucky. But luck had a way of running out, even in the most skilled of hands.

At just one hundred yards from the traffic light, an eastbound metro bus entered the intersection. Savage had but an instant to make a choice. Pass in front of the bus or behind it. He chose behind. The space was so tight he nearly clipped the back bumper. As it was, it forced him to use the sidewalk on the left. It had been the right choice. Had he gone in front of the bus, the I-95 overpass support beams promised them certain death.

That was too close. He needed to find another road—one where they didn't have to avoid oncoming traffic. Savage slowed, steady and controlled. He then made an immediate left.

Better. Not a single car in front of him. Savage let the bike loose and felt Eliana tighten her grip and bury her head against his back. He was driving on pure instinct now. Despite knowing the Miami streets, Savage couldn't know where his pursuit was, on the ground or in the sky. His senses were on edge. A roadblock could appear before him, leaving him with nowhere to turn. He needed to ditch the motorcycle, and fast. Somewhere they couldn't spot its heat signature with their thermal cameras. And Savage knew precisely where he wanted to go.

"Over there! Beneath the overpass!"

"I don't see a thing," the co-pilot said.

"I swear I saw a motorcycle dart under there."

The co-pilot continued to scan the FLIR imaging and looked for any movement that suggested a motorcycle on the run. "Negative. Nothing on the FLIR but some passing cars. Distorted, though. Jesus Christ! This is a goddamned monsoon!" He swung the searchlight around, waited for the pilot to follow suit, and lit up the west side of the overpass. Nothing.

The co-pilot craned his neck, trying to get a better look. "Can you get any lower? I'd like to get a good look under there with the FLIR."

"Not without landing on 3rd Street."

A gust of wind slammed the helicopter sideways, almost pushing it into a cluster of trees on the corner. Even the overpass was dangerously close. The pilot pulled back the stick. Climbed to a safer altitude. "This is out of control. We can barely stay in the air. There are ground units on the way. Let them put eyes on it."

A bolt of lightning lit up the sky, a strike so close there was virtually no time-lapse between the flash of light and the deafening crack of thunder that followed.

The co-pilot shielded his eyes, though the obvious delay looked silly and out of place. "That was too close!"

"I'd say! Damn near burned the paint off the fuselage."

"Sir. I don't like the idea of these bastards getting away any better than you do. Especially seeing how they've killed a couple of our men. But there will be two more if we don't land this bird…and soon!"

"I'm beginning to think you're right, son."

"All units, be advised. We have an emergency call complaining of a motorcycle heading down a one-way street in the wrong direction. They're northbound on NW 3rd Court."

The pilot turned to his partner. Made eye contact. Neither said a word.

The pilot turned the helicopter. Changed its heading to a north-northwesterly direction. It soon became clear that the suspects had been heading that way. The road north was open. There was still some lingering southbound traffic that had swung clear of the crazed crotch rocket. Maybe they were just waiting out the storm. But the pilot played his hunch.

The co-pilot pointed through the pilot's side of the windshield. "Up ahead. I think I have eyes on them. No. No. Maybe not."

"Do you have eyes on them or not?"

"Looked like a possible target heading west."

"NW 6th Street?"

"Affirmative. All units. Possible suspects westbound on NW 6th Street."

It was nearly impossible to see a thing. Eyes, FLIR, and spotlight were all at the mercy of the raging downpour. They started in a westerly direction, paused at a crossroads, and scanned the streets the best they could. There was traffic, of course, even at this late hour. But their own safety dictated they fly at a higher altitude while the FLIR continued to paint a muddy picture. Once again, the co-pilot thought he spotted motion—a streaking bullet heading north—this time with his naked eye. He was looking from the side window, where the driving rain wasn't as severe.

"Northbound, NW 6th Avenue. Looks like a motorcycle, two passengers."

"Affirmative."

"That road dead-ends there, doesn't it?"

"Yeah. Ends at Reeves Park."

"Call it in?"

"Negative. We don't have hard confirmation yet. All we're doing is stirring the pot. We have ground units scattered as it is," the pilot said. "Swing the spotlight around and—" He never completed the thought. There was a blinding flash, followed by a clap of super-heated gas. Sparks jettisoned from the control panel, followed by sudden darkness. "We're hit! Son of a bitch—we're hit!"

"Where?"

"Looks like the tail rotor. Have limited response."

"Hell! Half the instrumentation is gone. We're flying blind!"

The Bell LongRanger wanted to spin. The pilot fought for control.

"We've got to land this bird, sir. There's nothing more we can do out here."

"Affirmative. Ground. This is Air One. We've taken a lightning strike and lost some instrumentation. Partial flight control. Returning to Opa-locka."

As air control barked out instructions for an emergency landing, the pilot glanced out his side window and looked at the urban sprawl of northern Miami: Overtown, Wynwood, and Little Haiti beyond. The city lights were just glass beads on a black velvet blanket. The cop killers were out there still, on the run. He knew without a doubt they would be apprehended. But not by them, not tonight.

Savage couldn't hear the thump of the helicopter's rotors. He had a helmet on. The throaty roar of the Yamaha and the blast of rain on his face shield camouflaged its approach. But he could sense it. Feel it. He risked a glance over his left shoulder and spotted the Bell 206L LongRanger low on the horizon. It turned and made a direct line toward him. He responded without delay and took the next right. NW 6th Avenue. The street stopped a mere hundred yards later, a city park blocking its path. To his sides, there were identical low-income, two-story apartment buildings with sun-faded yellow stucco and steel bars on the screen doors. They were boxed in. *Damn it!*

Savage scoured the city map in his head and placed it neatly on the roads in front of him like a transparent overlay. The park wasn't a barrier. It was an escape. And the trees in the park provided the perfect cover.

Savage cranked his wrist back, propelling the superbike like a grenade from an RPG launcher. He navigated through the inky shadows of the park, avoiding the surrounding trees by utilizing a sidewalk that cut lengthwise across the lawn. Picnic tables, playground equipment, and basketball courts zipped by like pictures on a storyboard. NW 10th Street lay waiting for them just thirty yards away. Cop cars raced by, heading from west to east—three of them. Probably headed for their last known position. *Perfect.* Savage took advantage of the opportunity and took off in the direction they had just vacated.

He and Eliana had just cleared the park when a bolt of lightning shattered the night, its thunderclap bouncing off their backs like a physical assault. It was close. Too close. But Savage never looked back. His destination was clear.

Eighty. Ninety. One hundred miles an hour. One hundred ten. Twenty. Thirty. One hundred fifty miles an hour before Savage had to apply the brakes. By anyone's standards, it was a crazy thing to do. To Savage, it was necessary—a calculated risk. Eliana screamed the entire time, pounding on his right thigh in protest.

Savage turned down a street that ran parallel to the Seybold Canal, approached the next intersection, hit the green light, and continued west along the elevated Metrorail. His destination was a football's throw away: a short bridge on 11th Street that spanned the canal.

Moments later, he had Eliana dismount from the bike and take refuge a few feet away beneath the Metrorail. He revved the engine a couple of times and launched it into the canal. And that was that. No more heat signature from a red-hot engine. No more visual from a patrolman's spotlight. No more ride.

"I hope the owner had full coverage on his bike," she said.

Savage raised an eyebrow, took their helmets, and tossed them into the water. "His choice. His problem."

"I think it's our problem now," she said, downtrodden but doing her best to sound chipper. "I can't walk." She was clutching her knee, trying to suck it up, but was in obvious distress. "I smashed my leg back there on a tree. It's swelling up."

"Can you put any weight on it?"

She tried hobbling on it, but clearly couldn't take a step without stumbling. Tears welled in her eyes.

"You're right. We have a problem."

CHAPTER SEVENTEEN

Aurora, Colorado

The short drive back for Spearman was uneventful but productive. His conversation with Dr. Misra had gone better than expected. He had learned a lot. During their discussion, a seed had been planted and taken root in the back of his mind. By the time he got to I-225, a fully developed plan to eliminate Cypher had formed. Bold, decisive. Even risky. But for the moment, it would have to wait. The bungled hit in Miami had preoccupied his thoughts and forced him to find answers to impossible riddles. A riddle like Dr. Shepherd. His deliberate sabotage had caught Spearman off guard, certainly. But that wasn't the whole of it. Something wasn't adding up, and it was niggling at the back of his mind. Dr. Shepherd was a brilliant man. This was without question. But he was incapable of pulling off this stunt by himself. Yes, he could deconstruct Cypher's programming, but he didn't have the clearance to assign him a contract—even an insignificant contract. The hit on a call girl didn't require an NT agent to carry it out. Hell. Agent Mendoza's grandmother could have pulled that off. So who was fucking with his program? Only a couple of people had the authority to assign a hit: himself and the tactical authority coordinator, Neil Blevins. So either Dr. Shepherd had help from the TAC, or he had help from somebody with incredible computer skills. A hacker. Somebody who could rewrite the assignment.

Spearman made a mental note to visit Neil Blevins. Soon. But right now, the current state of affairs in Miami demanded his full attention. He answered the incoming call on his car's Bluetooth.

It was Rutledge from the Control Center.

"What's our status in Miami?" asked Spearman, turning up the volume through the car stereo. Control was abuzz. Noisy. Conversations cluttered with crosstalk, making it difficult for him to hear.

Rutledge gave a quick brief on the Miami situation. He was concise. Thorough. He missed nothing. In a matter of thirty seconds, Spearman had the complete picture: the police had trapped Cypher in a diner, but he managed to disarm them and flee unscathed with the prostitute. Spearman's attention sparked to life. "Say that again, comm. They found Cypher with the mark?"

"Yes, sir. They've stolen a motorcycle."

Spearman remained quiet, his gears spinning again.

"We have authorities in pursuit. The Miami PD and the FBI are tightening the circle on our target with units on the ground and in the air."

"So we have full cooperation with the locals?"

"Negative. Miami PD is throwing a fit. They're giving pushback on the FBI's authority. They're claiming this is a local matter, not federal."

Spearman snorted and clutched the steering wheel until his knuckles turned white. "I don't give a damn what the Miami PD claims. They're nothing more than a tool. And right now, they're my tool. Inform them that the fugitives are wanted on a domestic terrorist charge. That's federal enough."

Rutledge acknowledged this, scratching a quick note on the sticky before him. "There's severe weather that's moved into the area. It's played havoc with the air support."

"Have we reacquired the target yet?"

"We've been tracking them, sir, despite the weather. Apparently, the pilot took matters into his own hands. He heard that our mark killed a few of his police buddies and he's taken it quite personally. He's inbound to target."

"Excellent. Can we tap into the pursuit chopper's video feed?"

"Already on it, sir. Unfortunately, the FLIR's performance is spotty right now. Heavy rains are distorting the imaging."

Spearman swore and jerked the black BMW hard to the shoulder of the road. "Of course. Why should this be easy?" He closed his eyes and clenched his teeth as he tried to maintain his cool.

"Just a sec, sir. We've got a situation."

He waited. He could hear the background din of the Control Center. The room was abuzz, swarming with activity, each man searching the cyber-highways for a quick track on their target. Nothing was off limits: the air support's closed-circuit, patrol cruisers, traffic cameras. Even security cameras from local businesses. They just had to find it. "Talk to me, comm."

"We may have target reacquired, sir. Air One believes it has visual of a motorcycle snaking through a park, using the trees for cover. It's probably them."

"I don't need reassurances, Rutledge. I need results. Is it them or not?"

Spearman heard a sudden uproar from the Control Center, a flurry of activity. Loud voices, angry outbursts. Then silence.

"Control?"

Nothing.

"Rutledge? Status!"

"Sorry, sir. We've lost all visual from air support. It appears lightning has struck the chopper. They're out of play." Then a pause. An uncomfortable one. "We've lost them, sir."

Spearman could feel his neck prickle as his anger blazed like a firestorm in dry tinder. The situation had quickly escalated out of control. *His* control. He wouldn't tolerate it. But he needed answers, and he needed them now. And he knew just who to get them from.

Spearman hung up the phone with a quick stab of his finger to the car's touchscreen. He stabbed it again, this time placing a new call using its quick dial feature. His fingers tapped rhythmically while the phone rang. Four rings. Five. Six. An unsure voice answered the phone, still thick with sleep, not bothering with a cursory hello. "Neil Blevins."

"It's Spearman. Meet me at Benedict's. Half an hour."

"What? It's one in the morning, sir."

"It is. And you have half an hour." Spearman hung up. It was time to regain control.

CHAPTER EIGHTEEN

Denver, Colorado

Spearman had no problem securing a parking space at Benedict's, a familiar twenty-four-hour dive that had seen better days but was still popular amongst locals from all walks of life. Blacks, browns, whites. The wealthy. The poor. Blue-collar. White-collar. Sometimes at unusual hours. But not usually, and not tonight. Two cars were sitting in its pocket-sized parking lot, one of which was Blevins' white Mazda, the other a beat-up eighties-era Ford Ranger. He parked his beamer right on East Colfax.

Benedict's was some sort of historical landmark built in the early fifties; its distinct jutting eaves, large plate-glass windows, and upswept roof design were some of the last remaining examples of mid-century architecture in Denver. The food was edible. Coffee passable. Spearman couldn't have cared less. He needed seclusion.

Ignoring the parking meter, he entered the diner and immediately spotted Neil sitting in the far corner, his clothes frumpy, hair disheveled. He looked to be making quick work of a stack of blueberry pancakes.

The diner's ambiance was straight out of the seventies, its retro color palette tired and lagging, dominated by golds, browns, and burnt orange. They were left over from the last makeover, no doubt. There was a long sit-down counter with round vinyl stools, but Blevins was smart enough to procure a booth.

Spearman sat down, a poof of air escaping from the cushion as he slid across the seat to meet his man.

"Blevins."

The TAC took his elbows off the table, sat up, and then nodded in acknowledgment. "What the hell is going on, Spearman? Couldn't this wait until morning?"

"It is morning."

"You know what I mean. Daylight, then. My wife was pretty pissed, you know."

"She'll get over it. If not, there's always divorce."

"Jesus."

"Are you done?"

"It's just highly unusual is all I'm saying."

"Cut the crap, Neil. If I say jump, just do it. With or without a parachute. Got it?"

Blevins blinked, an ember of understanding beginning to flicker. There was more going on than he realized.

He swallowed. "Sure. Yeah. Sorry. I'm listening."

"We had a hit scheduled tonight. A soft target in Miami. Set for twenty-three thirty hours Romeo."

"OK."

"Sniper shot from the seventh floor of a downtown hotel. Ring a bell?"

Blevins scratched his head. "Yeah. Yeah, I remember. That's the hit on the prostitute, right? Jade something?"

Spearman waited. He said nothing.

"What about it?" Blevins asked.

"It failed."

Blevins shifted his weight; the spongy seat beneath him groaned in protest. "What do you mean *failed*?"

Spearman said nothing as their waitress greeted him, poured him some coffee, and removed the remaining menu. He wasn't hungry. Once out of earshot, Blevins started again, his whispered voice growing with intensity.

"Failed," he said again, his face contorting like he had just licked something nasty off the movie theater floor. "I don't understand. If I remember correctly, this was supposed to be a simple hit on a simple mark. Assassin snipes her from long range, packs up his gear, disappears, and leaves the mark as the prime story for the *Miami Herald*'s front page in the morning."

"It didn't go as planned."

Blevins pushed his gold brow-bar glasses up on his bulbous nose, their oversized square lenses out of place on his round, ruddy face. "The asset missed?"

"Never took a shot. Least not at the mark." Spearman paused, glancing at his steaming mug of coffee before striking a hard stare with the TAC man. "Let's talk about the asset."

"OK."

"Who would you assign for such a hit?"

"Well, as far as I know, she's not a terrorist, foreign dignitary, or political rival. Not a drug lord or mob boss. Just a prostitute, right? I'm not sure what she's marked for, but I would hardly consider her worthy of an elite asset—being a soft target and all. I'm sure I assigned standard issue."

Spearman leaned in and rested his elbows on the table. "It was an NT."

Blevins was speechless.

"Why did you assign an NT operative to the mission, Blevins?"

"What? *I* didn't!" He was straining to maintain the level of his voice.

"Well then who did? Because I certainly didn't put in a request for an NT. I left the details completely up to you."

"Hell with that! It wasn't me! That's asinine."

"Nevertheless…"

"Why would I do that?"

"That's what I'm trying to determine."

"And I'm telling you, I have no idea. I'm positive I assigned a low-level hit. There should be proof in the database. Besides, dozens of snipers could have taken that shot."

Again, Spearman said nothing. He just watched, sizing up Blevins, weighing his words, studying his eyes. There were always telltale signs of whether the subject was telling the truth: body language, voice inflection, movement of their eyes. It was a conglomerate of things—an art, really—and he was good at it. Blevins was telling the truth.

"Wait a minute," he said, his eyes flashing with surprise. "You said the asset didn't take the shot. Why not?"

"I don't know."

"But you said he was an NT. How is that possible?"

"I don't know."

"Broken?"

Spearman shrugged.

"But he can't disobey his orders."

Spearman shrugged again and exhaled through his nose. "Somebody is fucking with my operation."

"Who?"

"That's the question now, isn't it?" For Spearman, it was like solving a crime from a shit mystery novel. Who had a motive? Who had the means? And who stood to benefit the most from the crime? He had some clues, but little else. "I have a pretty good idea who fucked up my NT. But he was the gun. Not the hand that pulled the trigger."

"But why?"

"Unknown. I'll be sure to ask them when I finally get the chance. My primary concern now is who had the means to pull off the assignment change?"

"I swear, man. It wasn't me. You can check the assignment orders in the database!"

"We did. Tonight's operation had Cypher assigned to it."

"No way! I'm telling you, I didn't assign an NT!"

"Relax, Blevins. I believe you."

Blevins swallowed. Nodded. Spearman noted his posture, then observed his shoulders relax as he sat back in the booth.

"If not me and not you, Blevins, who could override the assignment? Who could alter the data on the computer?"

Blevins shook his head, his brow furrowed in thought. "I don't know. It's not possible, really, at least not from the outside. We have level-five security on all Darkwater hardware. Highest level of encrypted software. It has to be. This operation is so volatile that we must keep it safe at all costs. Can you imagine what would happen if a foreign threat breached our security and figured out we were targeting our citizens for assassinations? It would be utter pandemonium. Armageddon, even."

"Inside job then?"

"It would have to be. But I still don't see how. They'd have to be seriously tapped into our program to pull this off. I don't even see how an inside hacker could do it. Not without serious help. I suppose your first priority is finding out who—if anybody—is capable of such a feat."

Spearman shook his head. "My priority is to find out who would employ such a person…and to what end?"

Blevins sensed their conversation was coming to a close. He gulped his coffee and plopped the empty mug down on the table. "What about Cypher? Has he been recovered?"

The deputy director swirled his fingers on the table, the tiny granules of sugar there forming into indiscriminate patterns. "No. He's still off the reservation. But not for much longer."

Blevins smirked. "You have a plan to capture an NT?"

"Capture?"

The man's face turned ashen. He corrected himself. "Eliminate."

There was an uncomfortable pause. Then Spearman wiped his mouth with a napkin, tossed it on the seat, and stood up to leave. "Get some sleep, Blevins. You look like shit."

CHAPTER NINETEEN

The warm night air met Spearman as he stepped outside, its soft breeze agreeable and somehow soothing. He lit a Marlboro, taking a long drag from it as he marched to his car. His thoughts raced with the potential consequences of his decision. However, Spearman didn't achieve the position of deputy director by doubting his ability to foresee all outcomes. He knew the FBI would take jurisdiction from the local authorities, and they would put their sheer numbers to good use. They were likely already creating a two-mile perimeter around the last known position of Cypher and his accomplice. With a bit of luck, they might even find him. Dispatch a SWAT team. It didn't matter. Spearman was certain it would do no good. Just as sure as the sun would come up in the morning.

There was a better way. His way.

Spearman took a few more drags off his cigarette before flicking it to the curb. He then opened the door of his beamer and slid across the black Nappa leather of its front seat. He took his cell phone from the inner pocket of his suit jacket and entered a unique sixteen-digit security code he knew by rote. Three staccato electronic tones repeated in response. The encrypted line was now open. He entered the corresponding four-digit directory code to the asset. NT-8. Assassin. Spearman's wolf.

There was an abrupt *click-pop* on the line, followed by sterile silence.

He started to speak, then hesitated. He waited.

Then a voice broke through, distinctly male. Abrupt but unhurried. "Yes."

Spearman ran his hand briskly across his chin, his whiskers bristling beneath his fingers. "Code in."

"Mike. Three. Three. Zero. Five. Five."

Confirmed. He had his man.

Spearman looked around before glancing in the rearview mirror. Nothing but sterile streetlights cutting through a hazy swath of shadows on East Colfax's deserted streets. In the distance, the brief double chirp of a police siren interrupted the stillness of the night. "You have a new mark," he said finally. "Runner. Extremely dangerous. Federal and local authorities are on the hunt. I'm transmitting the assignment to you now." He punched the code to transmit the assignment. The mark's photo, physical description, background information, and last known position. Anything the assassin could need on the other end.

A pause. Silence.

A moment more. "Understood."

If the assassin had any concern that his assignment called for eliminating such a formidable foe as another NT, he didn't let it show. Nor should he. NT-8 was the apex predator. Perfection incarnate.

Spearman terminated the connection and returned the phone to the inner pocket of his jacket. Then he smiled.

CHAPTER TWENTY

Miami, Florida

Savage found the restroom deserted. At this time of night, at a Bag-N-Go just off NW 17th Avenue, he would have expected nothing less. He immediately searched the empty room for anything that might be useful. Nothing caught his eye, though he wished he could have said the same for his nose. The room reeked of piss and mildew.

The restroom was spacious, with a minimalist design and gray and white ceramic tile walls. A half dozen standard-sized urinals lined the wall like obedient soldiers at attention, a couple of their pint-sized cousins hanging next to them. Two stalls were tucked in the corner, and several waist-level sinks were opposite the urinals, with accompanying pink hand soap and water-stained mirrors. And for easy access, there was a pair of continuous cloth towel dispensers placed on either side of the sinks.

Eliana was out of breath, leaning up against the far wall, the crown of her head resting against the tile, its surface sporting condensation like a Coke can left out of the fridge. The failing fluorescent lights flickered overhead, casting deep shadows across her crestfallen face. She favored her right leg, as the left was slightly bent at the knee, the tips of her toes grazing the floor.

It had been about a mile walk to the convenience store, but it had been agonizingly slow. Savage carried her the entire way, though he struggled with the extra burden on his wounded shoulder. Blood was still oozing from the blackened hole. He had to do something. He couldn't continue to carry Eliana and expect his shoulder to fully heal.

Savage looked at her. Studied her. Tried to troubleshoot all angles of what needed to be done. But he knew. There was no question. He knew he needed to cut his losses and make a break for it. He needed to abandon her. Eliminate her if need be. He was in survival mode now. Nothing else mattered, and she would only slow him down.

He was staring hard at her. Studying. Then she opened her eyes, and their eyes met—a fleeting gesture. At first, he turned away, unsettled by the moment, but then he forced himself to meet her gaze again.

She smiled faintly, her deep brown eyes betraying secrets, telling tales of her fatigue and weariness. "What now?" she asked. "Are you going to leave me behind?"

Savage straightened but said nothing. He took a few steps toward one of the private stalls, never relinquishing his gaze, and ripped out a wad of toilet paper from the roll. He began stuffing the paper beneath his shirt, packing his wound.

"You should, you know. Leave me." She tested her leg again by putting a touch of weight on it. She bit her lip as it buckled. "I'm useless now, not that I would have been much help to you in the first place."

He grabbed some more toilet paper and added pressure to his makeshift dressing, then returned to the center of the room. He studied the taut lines of her face—and noticed the slight grimace she had pressed into a smile. She was right, of course. Mostly. But not completely. She wasn't useless. She was important. And she could help discover what was wrong with him. She was the missing piece to a greater puzzle. A puzzle he couldn't fathom. And now they were trying to eliminate her, attempting to cover up some politician's fly-flapping indiscretions. A mistake that the DCS intended to rectify. And Savage had been the means. But something was amiss. Something didn't feel right. He almost felt remorse for Eliana. But why?

"You're coming with me. I need you."

Eliana scoffed, then smiled. A slight crinkle of amusement played around her eyes. "I haven't heard that line in a while."

CHAPTER TWENTY-ONE

Near Santa Marta, Cuba

Davidson had barely set down the helicopter in the flats of an abandoned farm field when he noticed a shadowy figure appear from a nearby copse of palm trees. Dressed in all black with a duffel bag slung over his shoulder, he made a direct line to the helicopter. The DCS pilot knew immediately it was the package he was to deliver to Miami. It was some high-end asset known only to his superiors. Designated NT-8. *Whatever.*

"Is that him?" asked the co-pilot, leaning toward Davidson to get a better view out his window.

"Looks like it. Damn. Well, we won't have time to run a check on that turbine. It's still running a little hot."

Robbins nodded as he continued throwing switches and methodically checking gauges. "Affirmative."

The two DCS pilots were flying an experimental reconnaissance helicopter dubbed the *Velociraptor*. It was a fast compound design with stiff coaxial rotors, allowing a top speed of 273 mph and a maximum range of just over 350 miles. Developed by the U.S. military, its radical design made it the perfect bird for their mission. "At least it looks like that low-pressure system is starting to break up off the coast. Should be an easier return flight."

"What's the fun in that?" Robbins deadpanned. "Easy is overrated."

Their flight over the strait was anything but easy as they had to maintain impossibly low altitudes over dark, open waters to evade radar. One rogue wave and their flight would have ended like a bug hitting a windshield. Still, they managed to reach Cuba undetected by lifting some high-priority intel from the Coast Guard—that, of course, and their balls of steel. The mental fatigue left in its wake, however, left both pilots exhausted. "To think I could have been suffering with a margarita poolside this weekend. Fuck easy."

Davidson nodded in reply, though he wasn't listening. His attention was on the mystery man as he made his approach. The asset walked with quiet confidence, each step careful and purposeful. A leopard on the prowl. Despite the severe rotor wash and his proximity to the helicopter, the asset never lowered his head. He merely opened the door to the rear passenger compartment, stowed his bail-out bag, and climbed aboard.

Davidson swiveled in his seat to ensure the package was secure and ready to depart. "I'm Davidson, and this is Officer Robbins," he offered with a practiced smile. "We need to get airborne ASAP to make target time, so if you buckle in, we can get this bird in the air."

The asset met his gaze with piercing eyes of his own, a shade of gray so pale they looked void of color. He had a long, angular face, a light brown complexion, and black hair. He looked to be in his mid-twenties. But he had a hard look about him, a seriousness in his manner that suggested a man of greater years and vast experience.

When the man said nothing in reply, Davidson gave a wayward glance to Robbins and then turned back to the asset. "The flight over the strait was rough, and we'll be traveling at low altitude for the entirety of our return trip. Best strap yourself in…um." He paused, realizing he still didn't have the man's name. "Best to strap yourself in, sir."

The asset remained stoic. His gaze focused somewhere out the window, as if studying the northern skies. Processing. He said, "*Dudo que el cinturón de seguridad me ayude mucho en caso de chocar con una ola.*"

Davidson didn't speak Spanish. Robbins knew just enough to get by. "He says he doubts the seatbelt would help much…you know…should we crash into a wave."

Davidson sighed and returned his attention to the flight controls. *Smartass.* "A one-hour return flight, and it's already shaping up to be the longest flight of my life."

The turbines whined as they powered up for liftoff; the asset, Marcos Gullardo, settled back into the bucket leather seat, staring out the side window. He felt the inertia of the bird suddenly claw skyward. Saw the thrashing canopy of palm trees fall away while the inky black ocean became a vast expanse before him. The waters looked rough. Angry and unforgiving. And as they reached top speed, a mere fifty feet above the ocean, the white-capped waves began streaking by like star trails in a sci-fi movie. To any other observer, it would have been exhilarating.

But not Marcos. He wasn't easily impressed. He simply felt nothing. No fear. No doubts. No concerns. He was an assassin. The latest of the NTs. The omega. *The Ghost.* For him, only the thrill of the hunt mattered. And in less than an hour, he would touch down in Miami. Then the hunt would begin.

CHAPTER TWENTY-TWO

Somewhere near Denver, Colorado

There was a definite change in mood at the Control Center. The feverish buzz that consumed it just an hour ago was on the decline. Most of the operation officers had been dismissed for the night, leaving a mere skeletal crew. Along with Mendoza, only Rutledge and a smattering of cyber-warriors remained. An abrupt call from the deputy director saw to that. And as far as Micaela Mendoza was concerned, it was the perfect opportunity.

Her fingers tapped feverishly at her keyboard as she looked over previous intel to see if there was something she had missed. Some clue she should have picked up on, allowing her to foresee the pending disaster that was about to unfold that night: a failed hit. A failed hit by *her* asset. Cypher. And it just didn't make any sense. Cypher was solid. Capable. Followed orders. It wasn't the first time she had worked with him, either. She had never met him face to face—that wasn't how it worked—anonymity and all. But she had been his handler on at least two occasions prior, and there had never been a problem.

She had been trying to call him since the breakdown—at least that's what she was calling it—but to no avail. Not exactly a surprise. He would have ditched his sat phone immediately. Or left it in the hotel room. Perhaps drowned it in the pool? Regardless, there was no direct communication with Cypher anymore, and damned if she could figure out a way to fix it. Even the ability to track him through the biosensor in his nanoport had become shoddy. The signal was weak. Intermittent. Perhaps it had been damaged while making his escape. His last known location was in the Allapattah neighborhood. It was as good a place to start as any.

Mendoza exhaled sharply and brushed her bangs off her damp brow. *Did the A/C stop working in here? Ha. Not likely.* With all the electronics and high-tech hardware in the room, the place was nominally chilled to sixty-five degrees Fahrenheit. *Glacial.*

She wiped the sweat off her forehead using the back of her hand and proceeded to gather her long, dark hair into a ponytail. She continued searching. She attempted to access Cypher's personnel file from the mission database, but a formidable firewall blocked her. Her computer terminal let her know in no uncertain terms that she didn't have proper clearance to make the breach, presenting her with an annoying red banner and a razzing alarm.

She tried to gain access to the NT's R&D database. No luck. She even tried accessing the greater umbrella of Operation Darkwater, which offered a somewhat vague overview and a synopsis for those without level five clearance. But she already knew those things.

The development of super-assassins sprang forth from DARPA's desire to make the perfect soldier. They had been working on that for decades, so it wasn't exactly an enormous leap of logic to see how the same biotech could benefit the United States with their clandestine affairs. As a result, Darkwater was created. Like any black ops program, it had its dark tendrils hooked into many areas of research: biotech engineering, genetic modifications, and even cyber implants. This was where Cypher and the other NT assassins had been developed and trained. She was sure that they utilized nanotechnology. To what end, she had no idea. The only certainty was that the NTs were without equal. Deadly.

Mendoza's train of thought was interrupted by a sudden understated beeping in her headset. Incoming call. Deputy Director Spearman. *Great.* "Sir?"

Spearman didn't announce himself. He had little time for such pleasantries. "What's the status of our mark, Mendoza?"

"Ms. Bautista?"

"The whore? God no! NT-Zero." His voice had an edge to it. Impatient.

Mendoza hesitated. "Uh, yes, sir. We're still trying to get a hard fix on him. We lost him during the high-speed chase. Our best guess is that he's in the Overland neighborhood. So the federal authorities are setting up a two-mile perimeter, fanning out for a search and recovery."

"On foot?"

"We believe he ditched the motorcycle."

"Have we found it?"

"Negative, sir."

"Of course not."

She heard Spearman give a long, drawn-out sigh on the other end of the line and pictured him rubbing his tired eyes. Not a good sign of things to come.

"Shut it down, Mendoza. I'm going home to sack out for a couple of hours. You should do the same."

"Sir? But Cypher…he's still on the loose. And Ms. Bautista. Certainly—"

"She's a loose cannon. Off her hinges. Look, I appreciate your passion, Mendoza, but we don't need an NT to take out a hooker. The feds believe her to be a terrorist. Cop killer. Hell! They'll likely shoot her on sight. Perhaps they'll get lucky. Maybe they'll kill them both. Maybe not. But I'm hedging my bets. I have my own plans for the NT."

"But sir, if we can capture him before that happens, we'll have—"

"Your objections have been duly noted, Mendoza. I said leave it be."

"But there's still a chance we could capture him, bring him in for analysis. Fix him."

"Stand down, Agent!" he growled.

Mendoza clenched her jaw, her lips smashed together. She was doing her best to tamp down her rising temper.

Spearman lowered his voice, his words dripping with acid. "This isn't a search and capture. It never was. We need to find this rogue and eliminate him from being a potential threat to the public."

"Threat? But he's one of ours!"

"He *was*. Now he's fucking broken."

"But—"

"You're off, Agent Mendoza. In fact, take a few days. You obviously need the rest."

The line went dead. Mendoza sat there, blinking at the monitor. Speechless. Icy coils of fear snaked through her veins. Spearman had no intentions of bringing in Cypher. He had no interest in recovering him, fixing whatever was broken. It just didn't make sense. His value was unfathomable. They had invested countless millions into Darkwater's funding: the research and development of new biotechnology, highly specialized combat and survival training, and intel gathering, not to mention the operational costs of support and logistics. And now Spearman just wanted to toss Cypher aside like he was some outdated surplus WWI sniper rifle? *Prick!*

Mendoza ripped off her headset and threw it down onto her console. She stormed across the room to the outermost ring of the Control Center. There she found Rutledge standing at his station, talking on his headset, his words clipped, his hands animated.

"I need to talk to you," she said. Mendoza had worked with Rutledge numerous times, and though she would hardly call him a friend, she at least knew him to be competent. "Now."

Rutledge eyeballed her but said nothing as he continued to address some unknown party on the line. He was a good-looking man, dark-skinned, his hair short and well-kept. But he rarely smiled. He was all disciplined.

"Rutledge…it's important."

He once again met her gaze. He raised a finger to ask for a moment. "Do you have eyes on him? OK. Then how do you know? OK. Understood. It goes without saying, Commander, that you should proceed with extreme caution. I repeat, extreme caution. Yes. Of course. I'll see what I can do."

"What the hell was all that about?" asked Mendoza.

"Miami PD believes they have a twenty on the target. They think he entered a Bag-N-Go over in the Allapattah neighborhood."

"They have confirmation?"

"No. Eyewitness. The clerk at the counter saw a man and a woman enter the store and head to the restrooms."

"So?"

"They've been in there a while. The clerk thought they were up to no good. Gang violence or something. He said when they entered the store, the woman was limping, and the man had what appeared to be blood on his t-shirt. He didn't want to risk approaching them, so he called 911."

Mendoza froze, her mind catching up with the new information. "Oh my God, Rutledge. That's what I want to talk to you about."

Rutledge lifted his mic away from his mouth. He was shuffling through papers, making sure to keep his uncovered ear toward her voice, nodding for her to continue.

"They're not interested in recovering the asset. They want to eliminate him."

"Who?"

"Spearman!" Mendoza felt the back of her neck turn hot. "The government. The talking heads of Operation Darkwater. Hell! I don't know. Someone with a much higher pay grade than either of us, I can tell you that."

Rutledge spun toward her, his indifference suddenly melting from his face. He asked, "What makes you say that?"

"Spearman just called me. He told me to stand down. To call it a night and get some rest."

"You *do* look like shit, Mendoza. We could all use some rest about now."

"No! You don't understand. He said this is no longer a search and recovery. He said the asset was broken and needed to be taken out before he hurt someone."

Rutledge stiffened.

"Spearman said he no longer cared whether the FBI got to him first. He *wants* them to kill the asset!"

"Spearman said that?"

"Well, not exactly. He said maybe they'll get lucky…" She stopped. Tried to rein in her runaway thoughts. "He doesn't even think they'll succeed. He said he has some other plan to eliminate him—"

"Look, Mendoza. I appreciate your passion. But—"

Mendoza paused, her eyes narrowing.

Rutledge noticed her expression slip into something unreadable. "What? What is it?"

She tilted her head ever so slightly. "Say that again?"

"What?"

"What did you just say?"

"I said that I appreciate your passion."

Mendoza inhaled deeply, then let it trickle out of her nose. Those were Spearman's words verbatim. She pinched her lips together. Nodded.

"Look…if Spearman has decided he needs to eliminate the asset along with the mark, then there must be a pretty damn good reason. We're not always privy to the goings-on of the overall mission arc, Mendoza. You know that as well as I do."

She nodded once, then sighed, allowing her eyes to drift away, biding her time. She placed her hands on her hips. Grimaced. "Yeah. You're right. I just get…you know…a little overprotective at times. I've worked with Cypher before."

"Of course."

Rutledge's eyes lit up, and he quickly lowered his mic to his mouth. "Go ahead, Commander. Uh-huh. Affirmative." Rutledge hit a button on the controller on his hip, muting the mic, and leaned in close to

Mendoza. "Miami PD says they've just arrived on the scene and are setting up in a vacant lot adjacent to the Bag-N-Go. The FBI is en route, but they don't want to wait for them. They want an update on the suspect's last known position."

Mendoza nodded in earnest, her brow pinched in thought. "I might be able to help. Our ability to track Cypher through his nanoport has been spotty at best. Ever since the high-speed chase. But I might have found another way to pinpoint his twenty."

He nodded. "Make it happen." He then mashed the button to unmute himself and addressed the senior officer in charge. "Copy. FBI on approach. Stand by to receive intel from the target's controller. Opening channel."

Mendoza raced back to her station, not giving Rutledge another moment to see past her poorly veiled deceit. Her ability to reacquire Cypher's twenty was complete bullshit. But Rutledge didn't know that. Not yet. It was up to her to buy Cypher a little extra time.

CHAPTER TWENTY-THREE

Miami, Florida

Eliana winced. The deep pucker wound near Savage's shoulder continued to seep, a thin veil of bright red trickling down his chest. It looked awful. But even with her untrained eyes, she had to admit it wasn't as horrific as she expected. It looked…well…smaller. Older. Healed some. "You need to go to the hospital."

"That's not possible. Nor is it required," he said, prodding at the surrounding muscle tissue as if checking for further damage. "The bullet passed through. It will heal on its own."

Eliana snorted, thinking he was kidding, but after seeing the no-nonsense determination burning in his eyes, she realized he was serious. Dead serious. "What are you talking about? I don't see how unless you plan on waving a magic wand and wishing it away."

"Yeah. Something like that. I need to rest a bit. That's all." She started to protest, but he continued. "I could probably use something to stanch the bleeding, wrap it tight to keep it from leaving a blood trail."

"Are you sure you didn't hit your head while—"

"How's your leg?"

"What?"

"Do you think you can walk for me?"

"Well, I think I can master the drag and shuffle," she said, a slight smile tugging at the corners of her mouth. "Why?"

Savage gestured to the sales floor. "I need you to buy a few things. I'd go myself, except sporting this bullet hole will draw too much attention."

Eliana nodded, unable to find any fault in *that* reasoning. She shuffled across the tacky floor, trying to keep the pain from showing on her face. Savage met her at the door, stuffing a wad of cash into her hand. "See if you can find gauze or cotton balls. An elastic bandage. Make it two. Something for pain. Tylenol. Advil."

"Are you in pain?"

"They're for you."

Eliana felt her cheeks redden, though she couldn't say why. "Ah."

"Maybe find some cornstarch to stanch the bleeding. Flour if not."

"How about some alcohol, then? You know…to help keep that pending bacterial infection in check?"

Savage glanced away, looking toward the door. "Unnecessary. Infections won't take on me. You should get us some water and some quick snacks. Maybe almonds or something. Don't know when we'll be able to stop and eat again."

Eliana nodded, knowing it made all the sense in the world. "Anything else, boss man?"

"Yeah. I need a fresh shirt. Something in a large."

"Color?"

"Something without blood."

Eliana made her way through the cluttered aisles in search of the supplies, doing her best to keep her shuffling to a minimum. The clerk at the front counter was trying to look like he wasn't watching her, keeping himself busy by restocking the cigarette rack. But Eliana knew better than that. That much was obvious. But why? Did he suspect she was a shoplifter? Or something else? Maybe he had seen Savage's bloody t-shirt when they came in. It was sort of hard to miss.

The Bag-N-Go was empty, not surprising for that time of night. It looked like any other convenience store in the neighborhood. A mishmash of unkept shelves filled with impossibly unrelated shopping items, as if the store owner was trying to anticipate every need of the Greater Miami populace. All six million of them.

The checkout counter was near the front door, the tobacco and lotto tickets tucked away behind glass for safekeeping, while the drink coolers and restrooms were near the back.

Eliana had finished most of the shopping list for Savage, though it had become necessary to use a basket to carry all the items. She worried she would forget something. She grabbed two bottles of water from the coolers, the type with pop-up spouts—liter size—and found a small bag of almonds for Savage. Eliana looked for something else as almonds were too bland. She preferred to eat healthy, however, so candy bars were out. Chips too. In the end, she settled on a small bag of trail mix. She hadn't been able to find cornstarch or flour, though she had been up and down the aisles three times. *Now what?*

Eliana limped to the checkout and plopped down the heavy basket on the counter in front of the twenty-something sales clerk. His name tag read Sanjay. He looked to be of Indian descent and had a dark, patchy beard reminiscent of prepubescent boys and a hawkish nose. He had no chin to speak of and bluish lips that disappeared behind a scowling expression.

"Do you carry cornstarch here?"

"No. We do not."

"Flour?"

He waved dismissively at the aisles. "No. No flour. Just what you see."

Short and to the point. Not a surprise, really. He barely spoke English. But there was something about him—something not right. He seemed nervous. Beads of sweat were tracking down the sides of his face, and he kept looking off to the side, unwilling to meet her eyes. He rang up the items from the basket, his gestures short and jerky. *Nervous.*

Then it dawned on Eliana. He wasn't afraid to meet her gaze. Something outside had caught his attention.

Eliana gasped and immediately turned to look outside. She struggled to see much of anything, the store's fluorescent lights reflecting off the windows hampering her ability to see past the pallet of washer fluid next to the front door.

She snapped her attention back to the sales clerk and then found the security monitor above his head. The different camera angles were displayed within a 6x6 grid, capturing shots of the register, aisles, and the far reaches of the store. Among them were a couple of exterior shots of the parking lot. It was there she spotted movement. Not just a car passing by. But men approaching the store. Uniformed men with tactical gear and shotguns. Eliana groaned. *Not good.* She turned to flee, calling out to Savage as she did so. "We've got company!"

Savage watched her hop back to the restroom, favoring her good leg, pushing herself hard. He opened the door for her as she rushed past him, eyes wide and panting from the exertion. "There are men with guns out there!"

"Where?"

"I saw them on the security monitor up front. They're across the street. Next door. I don't know—everywhere!"

Savage nodded, still holding the door open, and leaned out to get a better look at the front of the store. Through the windows, he could make out a fleeting glimpse of parked vehicles in the neighboring lot and some men taking positions behind them. Law enforcement. FBI? SWAT? It was too soon, but they were likely on the way. Miami PD? Probably. Didn't matter. They were in trouble. He ducked back into the restroom, sweeping the area, eyes searching, his mind racing for answers.

"How did they find us?" she asked, her accent becoming more pronounced. "I mean—how could they find us so fast? It's like they knew where we were the whole time!"

Savage looked to Eliana, a sudden burst of clarity raking through his thoughts like lightning across a stormy sky.

Savage didn't reply. He scanned the restroom, his mind already racing five steps ahead to correct what was a horrendous mistake on his part. And there it was. Crumpled on the restroom floor, beneath the middle sink, lay the foil wrapper he swiped from the diner. During their escape, he had wedged the foil between his shirt and motorcycle helmet, hoping to disrupt his biosensor's signal. With the ensuing chaos of the chase, he forgot about it when they ditched the motorcycle and helmets in the canal. It may have stayed in place for a while, tucked in the collar of his t-shirt, but it fell out when he was seeing to his wounds. He reflexively reached for the back of his neck, his fingers fumbling about the nanoport. "They're tracking us through my biosensor."

"What do you mean?"

"I have a nanoport implanted at the back of my neck. It makes it easier to receive my injections of nanobots during mission planning."

Eliana's eyes flashed, her mouth agape. "Nanobots? I don't understand. Like robots?"

Savage nodded, pulling his Ontario MK III knife from its sheath, and walked to the mirrors. "Yes. Tiny. Programmable. But there's a biosensor built into the port designed to upload my vitals to Control. Heart rate, blood oxygen saturation. Enzymes. Even toxin levels. The point is, they can use that passive signal to locate my exact location by satellite."

"Like a cell phone."

"Yes."

Savage could see the color drain from her face, which looked ghostly pale under the dim fluorescent lighting. "*Oh Déu meu!* What are we going to do? If we run, they'll just find us again."

"Not if I can help it."

"Can you turn it off?"

"No. I'm going to remove it." Savage reached up, and using one hand to stretch the skin on the back of his neck, he used the other to wield the knife and make a deep incision near the base of the nanoport. A stream of bright arterial red appeared, trickling down the back of his neck. His fingers fumbled around the tiny device, searching blindly.

The mirror offered no help. But he continued to make a generous circular incision, ensuring he erred on the side of caution.

Eliana swallowed hard. "I can help you with that," she offered, though she wasn't entirely convinced that was true.

"No. We don't have time for squeamishness—no time to be delicate. You'll be slow-moving, afraid to hurt me. We don't have that luxury."

Eliana bit her lip. She knew he was right. She turned back to the door, cracked it, and peered out. "Savage—I don't think we have enough time."

"You're right. We don't."

CHAPTER TWENTY-FOUR

Corporal Scully of the Miami PD took one last drag from his cigarette and crushed it beneath his boot. The crabgrass he was standing in was long, coarse, and littered with sun-faded paper cups, chip bags, and burrito wrappers from the nearby Bag-N-Go. His pants clung to his legs, sodden with water from the summer rain, while lightning flashed around him and his team, a fresh wave of storms threatening a repeat performance in short order. *Damn! Foul weather.* His mood was faring no better.

They had just arrived on scene, set up a hasty perimeter, and were told to sit tight. No—*ordered* to sit tight! The FBI SWAT was on its way, ETA less than ten minutes, and would take charge of the scene. *Jurisdiction, my ass!* Domestic terrorists or not, it was Miami's own who were murdered by these two lunatics. Scully's backup would be there in less than five.

One of his officers hurried over to Scully, crouched low and scurrying across the ground like a wounded spider until she found refuge behind the police cruiser. It was Jennings, one of the first patrolmen to arrive. "What the hell is going on, Corporal? Why are we just sitting here cooling our heels?"

"We have orders to set the perimeter and sit tight. FBI SWAT en route."

Jennings was still gasping for breath, resting her back against the cruiser, checking her shotgun. She scoffed. "Perimeter? We have—what—five patrolmen? Not going to be much of a net."

"We have word that there's only one rear exit. I have Riley and Edwards covering the back of the building, north and south corners. It will do for now." Scully could hear the whooping and wailing of sirens on approach—knew it wouldn't be long.

"Dispatch is saying there's an employee in the store. He's the one who made the 911 call." Her voice cracked, and it had developed a tremor. "This is bad, Corporal. What if the perps take him as a hostage?"

Scully peeked over the car's hood, trying to get a better understanding of what was happening inside. He knew the employee had taken cover, trying to stay hidden. "I don't know. If he's smart, he'll make a break for it. Still no sign of the perps. It's well lit in there, and we have some decent sightlines."

Jennings adjusted the brim of her cap, lowering it on her brow. She exhaled sharply, blowing the nervous energy from her lungs. "They say he sounds panicked. Hard to understand. If we wait for the feds, sir, there's a chance this goes south quickly."

"Yeah, I know. An absolute shitstorm headed our way."

"Unit four, be advised that 'hotel' is looking to make a break for the front door."

Both officers turned down the volume on their radios in unison. The store employee was looking to make a break for it. "Unit four, copy." Scully gave a sidelong glance to Jennings, then advised his men to hold fire. He took a deep breath and steeled himself. He had to remind himself to relax his grip on the shotgun. His cell phone rang just then, destroying the fragile silence like a screeching metal band during Sunday prayer. "Jesus Christ!"

Scully snatched his phone from his pocket and hesitated when he didn't recognize the caller ID. It rang again, and despite his better judgment, he took the call anyway. "Scully…"

"Corporal Carl Scully?" asked the voice on the other end.

He paused. "Yeah. Who the hell is this?"

"Corporal, please listen carefully. My name is Agent Mary Shelley. I'm with the CIA, out of Langley. I need your help."

CHAPTER TWENTY-FIVE

Somewhere near Denver, Colorado

Mendoza scanned the satellite image of the surrounding area, canvasing the neighborhood for avenues of escape. There weren't any.

She had been monitoring the police chatter and knew things were about to get hairy fast. She needed to influence the situation from afar, but to do that, she needed to keep it shielded from outside sources. Limit the conversation to one person. She quickly worked out who was in charge but had a hard time hacking the personal phone numbers of the officers already on scene. It's not like Mendoza was any sort of hacker, but somehow she pulled it off.

Under the guise of CIA agent Shelley, she got a preliminary report after she contacted Carl Scully, the Miami PD's senior officer onsite. He communicated to her the number of team members, approximate location, and general overview of the current situation. The building had only two exits: front and back. Team members already had them covered. In short, despite the lack of team support, Cypher and the girl had very limited avenues of escape. And if the FBI SWAT arrived before they made their break, there wouldn't even be that.

Mendoza's mind was racing. She didn't know what to do. Or even if she should. But there was something that was gnawing in her gut, deep down. Something that continued to tug at her, urging her to do something. Anything.

Adjusting the mic on her headset, she called Scully on his phone again. "Status." Her inflection was flat. Nondescript. Yet it was a question, not a statement.

Scully had been reluctant to answer any of her questions when she first called, but Mendoza's ruse of being a CIA agent and her insistence that the fugitives were truly dangerous convinced him that federal involvement was inevitable. She would attempt to contact him and convince him to surrender with no need for FBI intervention or, more importantly, loss of life. That appealed to him.

The corporal responded. "We have the store employee exiting the front door now. Stand by."

"Copy."

The store employee ran out of the store, hands up, waving manically, crying for the police not to shoot. Two officers met him halfway and ushered him to safety behind one of the police cruisers.

"Clear. The hotel is in custody. I repeat. Hotel removed safely."

"Affirmative." *This isn't good*, she thought. Hotel was law enforcement's lingo for non-hostile. Now that the store employee was no longer a part of the equation, there was nothing to stop a tactical team from storming the building with full force.

Mendoza's fingers clattered noisily across the keyboard as she tapped into a nearby security camera. It was a barely adequate infrared camera mounted on the wall of an appliance repair shop across the street. It was farther down the block, but it would have to do. She could still see the front of the store. She couldn't see the entire perimeter, but she knew they had operators there to cover the rear exit. FBI's arrival was imminent. She had to buy her asset time. "Corporal. We have a no tango. I repeat. No tango."

A pause. "Please repeat."

"I say, no tango. No tango." She could hear muffled chatter in the background, as if Scully were relaying messages to his team with his hand smothering the phone. She continued. "Signal lost. Will attempt to locate."

"What do you mean the signal's lost? How?"

"Uncertain, Corporal. Signal comes and goes."

"The fuck!" he snapped. "I need to know. Is tango in the damn building or not, Agent?"

"Sorry, Corporal. I'm working on it."

There was a long silence. Apparently, there was a discussion amongst his team members. A change of plans. This was precisely what Mendoza had been hoping for: trying to throw the proverbial monkey wrench into their cognitive machine. She knew a SWAT team would have a huge tactical and numbers advantage if it came down to a full breach. Still, Savage was extraordinary. Dangerous. And if working with him in the past had taught her one thing, it was not to underestimate him. He was cagey. Slippery. He might even escape through the rear exit, though it would probably mean using lethal force. It wasn't a certainty that he would do so, but she knew she was unwilling to take that chance.

The silence between her and the corporal thickened like swamp mud on a hot summer's day. But Mendoza was oblivious. Her mind was racing, locked into the moment. She needed to gain access to Florida Power & Light's system and cut power to the Bag-N-Go. She hoped it would create a tactical advantage for Cypher, though it would be precious little. Typically, the opposite was true. Law enforcement often cut power to buildings, giving their men a tactical advantage over a target. But that was if they had the benefit of night vision technology. Something that wasn't standard issue for Miami patrolmen.

The Serpent software developed for the DCS was incredible for tunneling through security systems, lifting the heavy load for unarmed hacks like herself. But there were limitations to it. And Mendoza knew hers.

Tapping a few keys, she paged the middle ring of the Control Center, which was staffed by just a couple of remaining cyber-warriors. The response was immediate.

"Freeman."

"Freeman…it's Agent Mendoza. I have a situation here that requires expediency. I've locked down the twenty on an asset but need your help."

"Is this about the NT that went off the reservation?"

Mendoza hesitated. *Shit!* The tech sounded like a teenager. "Yes. That's correct."

"I thought we were told to stand down and let local law enforcement handle this."

Definitely young. She sounded like she should be out on a Friday night date with the high school's star quarterback instead of hacking into security networks for the government. "Affirmative. I'm working with the Miami PD and currently on a call with the corporal in charge." At least that was true enough. "But like I said, I can't do this alone. I need an expert."

"Great!" Her voice brightened, cheery even, sounding like she'd had one too many Red Bulls for the night. "How can I help?"

"I need the power cut at a Bag-N-Go in Miami." She relayed the address. "And I need this pronto."

Mendoza could hear the clickety-clack of the tech's keyboard as she whispered to herself out loud. "Florida Power & Light…"

"Yes."

"Bag-N-Go…"

"Yes."

"This is quite the firewall. Impressive."

Mendoza could feel time slipping away, feel the heat from Corporal Scully's impatience burning on the other line. "Did I mention I needed this right away? Like…before he gets away."

"Yes, ma'am. Their security is quite good. It's not like lifting a brownie recipe from your next-door neighbor's PC."

"You can't get in?"

"I didn't say that. It's just going to take a little foreplay."

She harrumphed. "Keep working on it." Mendoza tapped a button on her keyboard. "Scully. I need more time. I think the heavy storms in the area are interfering with the asset's tracking beacon. Stand by."

"I'm sorry, ma'am. That's a luxury you just don't have. I have inbound cruisers due to arrive any second and the FBI nipping at their heels. Now, if he isn't in the Bag-N-Go, I need to know that before we waste our resources on a red herring."

"I understand."

"With all due respect, ma'am, your understanding doesn't matter. We're running out of time."

Again, she switched calls. "Freeman?"

"Working on it."

"We're out of time."

"Almost there…"

"Freeman! I need the power cut now!"

"I'm in. Money shot!"

"Pardon?" Mendoza shook her head. Now that was a jarring thought. Was she even old enough to see an R-rated movie yet? She shook her head. Of course she was!

"Give me a second to navigate their software."

"We're out of time, Freeman. Make it happen!"

Mendoza couldn't wait for her response. She switched back to the phone call with Scully, hoping like hell he hadn't hung up on her yet. "Corporal. I show no tango. I repeat. No tango. Your target isn't in the building." She considered misleading Scully further and telling him that the fugitives were headed in a different direction. But she wanted to keep all avenues of escape open for Cypher in case he made a break for it. "He's not in there."

There was a pause. "Then where are they?" he asked.

"Undetermined," she said.

Another pause. "Then how do you know they're not in the building?"

Mendoza cringed, clamped her jaw tight. "Come again?"

"Excuse me, Agent Shelley, but I call bullshit. Knowing the targets aren't in the building means your equipment is working with certainty. And the only way to know *that* is if your intel shows them elsewhere. I think you're making shit up as you go along. So, I'm going to assume they're still in there."

Mendoza closed her eyes. Shook her head. *Damn it!* "Look, Corporal…what I mean is—"

"No matter, Agent Shelley," he said, cutting her off. "I'll take it from here."

The blare of sirens overwhelmed her headphones; a cacophony of screeching tires, slamming car doors, and orders being barked garbled Scully's last response. But it was clear enough.

"Backup has arrived. Your time's up." The line went dead.

CHAPTER TWENTY-SIX

Miami, Florida

Savage chanced a look out the door. Eliana was right. Their time was up. Four more patrol cars screeched to a halt at the parking lot's perimeter, with no effort to squelch their sirens or douse their lights. Too many. They would be surrounded in no time. And if SWAT arrived…well, that would be a whole different matter.

Savage glanced at Eliana, who was suddenly wide-eyed with an open hand splayed across her chest. She spoke no words, but the desperation in her eyes said it all. She looked at him for answers, for any sign of hope. He had none to offer. There was just the stark, cold reality of their predicament.

Then there was darkness. Complete and all-consuming. And in its wake, silence followed, pouring in around them like water from a broken levy. The power was out.

Savage felt Eliana clutch at his arm and then heard her gasp. It was nothing more than a soft croak escaping from her throat.

"Power is out," he said.

"The thunderstorm?" she asked.

Savage eased the door open and took another look. Outside, strobes of emergency lights flared off the dirty glass of the front window, scattered like laser lights in a nightclub. The store was awash in red and blue, lighting the interior of the store well enough for Savage to see it was deserted. Someone had tipped off the police, likely the sales clerk, and he was long gone.

Savage took stock of the police cruisers parked outside and the officers taking cover, mobilizing. He could see lights on in the houses across the street and down the block, just visible over the cases of washer fluid stacked against the front window. "No," he said finally. "It's not the storm. The buildings across the street still have their lights on. For some reason, they've cut the power to the store."

Eliana's face was pinched. "That can't be good. They're going to storm in here, aren't they? They're going to kill us."

He turned to her and put steel into his voice. "No. Not if I can help it. But something else is going on. It's too soon to cut the power. SWAT isn't here yet, either local or federal. They wouldn't chance making a breach, especially in the dark, without night vision equipment. It wouldn't be a tactical advantage for them." Savage paused, his mind racing through all the possibilities before him. A tangled web of missteps and lost opportunities yet to come. But then he saw the answer. An avenue of escape. "But it *is* a tactical advantage for us." He sighed. "However brief."

Savage stooped down and hurried out the door onto the sales floor, snatching a backpack off a rack near the snack aisle. He returned to Eliana, took the remaining goods from the shopping basket, and quickly stuffed them into the pack. He looked at Eliana, assessing, knowing damn well her leg was killing her. But there was nothing he could do about it. Not now. Then again, he could at least lighten her load. He slipped her knit bag from her shoulder and dumped its contents into the backpack as well. "Okay. Ready? You've got this. Now, keep low and follow me."

Eliana nodded grimly and followed him.

They snaked their way through the aisles, being careful not to expose themselves, but with an urgency that belied their need for stealth.

Eliana couldn't understand why Savage was making his way to the front of the store. It seemed counterintuitive to head toward the police. The thought terrified her, but not nearly as much as being left behind. Damn the swelling in her leg! Its stiffness. The throbbing pain. She was going to push through it if it killed her.

They reached the relative cover of the front counter, and then Eliana understood why Savage had risked coming to the front of the store. Behind the counter were rows of prepaid burner phones, a plethora of various brands and models to choose from.

After a quick once-over, Savage knocked several from the shelf, dropping them directly into the open backpack. He turned back to her, showing he had got what he came for, and was ready to leave when he paused. Something had caught his attention on a shelf just below the counter. The sales clerk's cell phone. He must have fled and forgot about it, she thought. Out of sight, out of mind.

Savage didn't think twice. He snatched the phone and tossed it into the backpack along with the others. Eliana began to protest and ask him why he needed to take the man's phone when he already had a bag full of burners, but the intensity of his stare silenced her. *Damn it, Eliana! Stop thinking like you're the victim.* Savage must have seen value in taking the cell phone. This was survival.

A moment later, they were already working their way back through the store, scooting past the restrooms and into a large storage room. The sign on the door warned it was for employees only.

The room was pitch dark with the emergency lights on the exit sign not working, its batteries dead and long forgotten. Savage pulled the SIG P226 from his waistband and flicked on the tactical light to get a better look around, its narrow beam stabbing at the darkness like a pointed finger. The room was an absolute wreck. Half-empty boxes were strewn about, their flaps torn open, contents spilling over. Old fixtures, gondolas, and long-since-expired sales signs were stacked like picket fencing against the far wall. In the near corner, an old Frigidaire stood sentry, its white dented surface scarred with battle wounds, its door littered with company bulletins and labor law posters hanging limply, yellowed and outdated.

The acrid smell of gasoline and musty grass lingered in the air, and Eliana spotted an old push mower parked in front of the exit door. A weed whacker was perched across its handle—a plastic gas can stacked on its engine. "Is that our way out?"

Savage didn't offer it a glance, continuing his turn around the room, using the tactical light to search high and low. "No. Not if you plan on escaping, anyway. They will have some men posted around the perimeter of the building. At least a couple on the corners with sightlines to the door."

Eliana found it hard to swallow, her tongue feeling unusually thick and unresponsive. This just wasn't happening. "Do you think you could overpower them like you did back at the diner? I mean, maybe we could make a break for it—"

Savage snapped his attention to her, his expression hard. Then it softened, understanding washing over him. "No," he said. "Make no mistake about it. This isn't like the diner. No witnesses are lingering about. And they're not here to arrest us. As far as they're concerned, we're cop killers. If we step out that door, they will shoot to kill. No witnesses, no crime."

Eliana forced another swallow but said nothing. She nodded.

Savage then swept the gun-mounted tactical light to the far corner, cast its intense light across a maintenance ladder, and followed the beam to the roof, where it ended at a push door. He had an idea.

He looked around and spotted a series of galvanized pipes in the nearest corner. He studied it for a moment, found the main water valve for the building, and turned it off. Then he brushed past Eliana, grabbed the full gas container off the mower, and started back to the sales floor.

"Stay here. I'll be right back."

CHAPTER TWENTY-SEVEN

Corporal Scully continued to take cover behind his police cruiser, staring out at the dark tomb of the Bag-N-Go. And in his mind, it *was* a tomb. One waiting for him and his men should he be foolish enough to put them in harm's way. He had a bad feeling about this. Something wasn't right. Power had been out for almost ten minutes, ostensibly for no good reason. He called it in to dispatch, and the department immediately got Florida Power & Light on the horn.

He had heard murmurs that the FBI was trying to exert their authority before their arrival, but Scully wasn't so sure. That seemed unlikely. None of this added up.

Scully was just about to give orders for the newly arrived patrolmen to form a better perimeter when Sergeant Cody finally found him. He was taking command and needed an update on the current situation.

Scully filled him in, explaining the 911 call from the clerk, his eventual escape from the building—if you could call it that—and his men's current status and position.

"Why is there no power?" he asked.

Scully shrugged. "Unknown."

The sergeant gave a cursory glance around him. "The surrounding area seems to have power. Did the perps cut the power at the electrical box?"

"We don't know. Our boys are in contact with FPL now, but they're claiming no power is going to the building at all. Like it's been turned off."

"Well, shit! Just turn the fucking thing back on! How hard can that be?"

Scully shook his head, offering a slight shoulder shrug. "They're saying they can't," he said. "They're locked out of that part of the system."

"What the fuck?"

Silence hung between them momentarily while the sergeant tried to make sense of it all. He asked, "Do we even have confirmation the perps are in there?"

Scully hesitated. He thought about his conversation with Agent Shelley and wasn't convinced she was telling the truth, at least not about the perps' whereabouts. She seemed forthright about other things, however. She claimed she was with the CIA and that they had a rogue agent on their hands who needed to be recovered at all costs. Alive, she said. But she never denied the perps' culpability in the murder of two undercover cops. And how the hell did she even find his phone number? It was all so confusing. But Scully kept that information to himself.

"We haven't seen or heard from anybody since our arrival. Now, the sales clerk claims he didn't see them leave, but it's possible they slipped out the back while he was making the call. Hell. He was hiding behind the counter."

The sergeant shook his head in disgust. "Any other employees in the store? Customers?"

"No," Scully said. "The sales clerk said the store was empty."

"Well, that's one damn thing in our favor."

Scully knew that wasn't much. They were at a standstill. They weren't in a position to breach the building. Besides, there wasn't any current risk to life to consider—except their own, of course. And that risk would soar considerably if they were stupid enough to search for the perps in an unlit store. All they could do was reinforce the perimeter with some more officers.

The sergeant started barking out orders when a caravan of black sedans and armored vehicles rolled in, announcing their arrival with a couple of quick chirps from their sirens. The FBI had arrived, and the operation was in their hands now. "Shit. That was fast."

"Got that right."

"Well, at least it's their shitshow now," said the sergeant.

Scully shrugged. But then a flicker of light caught his attention from the corner of his eye. He pivoted from his crouched position and looked back at the Bag-N-Go. He was stunned to see the front of the store ablaze, the interior entirely obscured by a ceiling-high wall of flames. It was a veritable inferno. And where were the fire sprinklers? He shook his head. In less than an hour, nothing would remain of the Bag-N-Go but a black husk.

For once, Scully couldn't agree more. He was happy that someone else was in charge.

★   ★   ★

By the time Savage had returned to the storage room, the front of the store was engulfed in a raging firestorm. Clouds of toxic black smoke began billowing through the open door. The flames were growing in intensity, spreading quickly as they searched for more fuel to satisfy their insatiable appetite. It wouldn't take long to find it.

Eliana responded by trying to shove the lawn mower out of the way and escape out the back door, but Savage stopped her, pulling her back to the ladder. "Climb!" he said.

OK. She wasn't even sure she could. Her leg was still stiff and unresponsive. But Savage heaved her up on the ladder several rungs higher and followed behind her. He used his shoulder as extra leverage to support her weight, straining with gritted teeth as he pushed through his own handicap.

"Climb, damn you! Climb!" The roar of the fire was louder now, and Savage had to yell for her to hear him.

Adrenaline shot through Eliana's veins like a fighter jet launched from an aircraft carrier. She tried to hurry, clambering up the ladder, one hand in front of the other, step by step, her mind on autopilot, oblivious to anything other than survival. It was painfully slow.

They finally reached the hatch above, and Eliana struggled to open it, yanking on the lever to unlatch it. It wouldn't budge—stuck from a lack of use. *Collons!* This had to work. She growled and tried again, forcing the lever into the open position. The door gasped as she flung the hatch up and crawled onto the roof. Savage followed, pulling himself up and over, then lay down beside her.

Eliana coughed, her lungs rebelling from the intake of noxious smoke. Her eyes were watering, tears smearing her face, but she palmed them away. Then she took in a deep, delicious breath. Above, the sky was still hiding behind a thick blanket of ominous clouds, the air hot and sticky, oppressive. But it soothed like sweet water, relief to a parched throat.

Eliana lifted her head and glanced around, trying to get her bearings. The occasional flash of heat lightning burned away the pitch of night, random and unbidden, and offered very little to see. The roof was nothing more than pea gravel over tar, its expanse unremarkable, broken up by the occasional vent pipe and an undersized A/C unit.

She took a couple more deep, cleansing breaths, then looked at Savage as he pulled himself up into a crouched position, scanning the horizon.

The roof's edge limited any direct line of sight to the dozen or so emergency vehicles parked below, but their pulsing lights bounced off the surrounding buildings, leaving no doubt they were still there. Out of the frying pan and into the fire. "What now, spy boy?"

Savage raised an eyebrow, then shook his head, scowling. "I already told you…I'm not a spy."

"You're no boy scout either." A wry smile eased across her face.

He said nothing. Eliana knew she was being snarky, but she couldn't help it. She always became flip when she was nervous. Savage didn't seem to be bothered by it, though. He just made his way over to the edge of the roof to get a better look at the parking lot below. He kept low, duck-walking until he needed to drop to a belly crawl.

Eliana went to follow, but he waved her off. She froze, suddenly unnerved. The thought of just sitting there, doing nothing, made her skin crawl. It took little imagination to know it would be only a matter of minutes before the flames reached the roof. Would the building collapse around them? Escaping the police only to be killed in a fire was of little solace to her.

The slow rumble of thunder sounded in the distance, a dichotomy to the harsh sirens of approaching firetrucks a mile or more away.

Savage surveyed the situation, paused as if taking inventory, then eased his way back from the ledge and crawled over to her. Their eyes met, but he said nothing as he continued past. He then crept his way to the western edge of the building and scanned the perimeter below. This time, Eliana didn't hold back. She joined him, careful to stay low, while dragging her swollen leg behind her. She could see a patrolman below, about thirty yards away, armed with a shotgun and standing in the shadows of the building next door. It looked to be a Cash Express store. She then glanced to her left and spotted another officer, similarly armed, monitoring the exit from the other corner of the same building.

Eliana gave a sidelong glance to Savage. She couldn't read his face. It was hard. Cut from stone. "Any bright ideas?" She glanced over her shoulder, half expecting to see a hole open up in the roof, fire bursting forth from its depths like a volcano spewing molten ash into the atmosphere. "Savage?"

His eyes flicked toward her, but he wouldn't allow himself to be distracted.

Eliana swallowed, reaching for her voice. "I don't want to die."

Again, he glanced at her, his head tilted ever so slightly in acknowledgment. He then looked right. Then left. Neither of the patrolmen had their eyes on the exit, much less on the roof. They were too busy trying to understand all the commotion created by the fire out front. Savage didn't hesitate. He pulled his 9mm SIG from his waistband, checked the clip, and stood abruptly. "*We* won't."

Quick and deliberate, he fired his first shot at the patrolman on the northwest corner, the impact of the bullet spinning the man to the right and putting him to the ground. Despite the silencer, the shot rang out like the crack of a small firecracker.

The officer posted on the opposite corner of the building must have heard the oddity because he looked around, trying to quantify the sound. Suddenly, he looked up, spotting Savage in his shooting stance, his gun pointed directly at him. Before Eliana could cry out, Savage fired again. This time, the bullet struck the man center mass and knocked him off his feet.

Eliana threw her hand to her mouth, gasping in horror. "No! No! No! What have you done?"

"Nothing that wasn't needed." He said nothing more. Offered no explanation. Savage spotted the dumpster below them and jumped down onto its lid. He landed easily and turned back, his arms reaching up for her. It was only six feet below where she stood.

She felt like retching. These weren't evil men coming to rape her and leave her for dead. They were innocents, just men doing their job. "I…I can't."

"Yes, you can. I'll catch you."

He misunderstood her. He assumed she was talking about her injured leg. But that was not what she was talking about at all. She felt like her mind was shrouded in a fog, her thoughts thick and muddled. She tried again, but the words wouldn't come.

"Eliana?"

"They were just doing their jobs," she said. "You didn't have to kill them."

Then something changed in his eyes, his expression morphing into something new, as if coming to an epiphany. He didn't answer right away, just stared at her instead. Not harshly. And not without patience. The tension eased at the corners of his eyes and softened into something like concern. "I know you don't trust me. I can't say I blame you. But everything isn't as it seems."

Eliana shook her head and then slapped the tears from her face.

"Our situation isn't that black or white," he continued. "You keep thinking those officers are innocent. But take a second and think about it. Do you honestly think they saw *you* as innocent? In their minds, we killed two undercover cops. Assaulted two others. Are you willing to bet on your life that they would have just taken you into custody? Not taken a shot at the two armed and dangerous murderers on the run?"

Eliana shuddered. Held back a sob. She felt like her heart was being torn apart.

"Eliana. I didn't kill them."

Shocked, she looked over at the first patrolman. He was still on the pavement, groaning, rolling back and forth, trying to tamp down the pain. She gasped. *What?* She snapped her attention back in the other direction. The second officer was lying prone on his back, less animated but still pounding the ground with his fist, fighting off the pain as he tried to catch his breath.

Eliana blinked, and a new well of tears spilled over and ran down her cheeks. She didn't understand it—couldn't see how those men survived. But they had. She looked back at Savage. He was still waiting below her, his arms ready to receive her. "Eliana…please. We have to go."

She nodded but said nothing. What could she say? She stepped off the roof's edge and landed easily in his arms.

CHAPTER TWENTY-EIGHT

Miami, Florida

At ten miles out from the coast of Florida, the *Velociraptor* swung into a wide arc to take a northwesterly approach to the City of Miami. Marcos could feel the inertia change and glanced out his portside window, taking in its dazzling skyline. The high-rise condominiums of Brickell were concrete behemoths with sleek modern lines and reflective glass. The vehicles on the luminescent streets below were nothing more than matchbox cars being pushed across a toy mat.

Out the starboard window, the neon lights of South Beach spilled across the landscape to the north. The Art Deco architecture, restaurants, and dance clubs of Ocean Drive dominated the upscale neighborhood. It was a virtual spotlight for the partygoer scene. Even at this late hour, the painted streets below remained a bustling hive of cars and people, all jostling for the same space.

The *Velociraptor* slowed as it reached Watson Island. It eased down on a helipad, one of several on the island's southwestern side. It was the future site of the Watson Island Heliport, but at the moment it was nothing more than a barren strip of pavement.

The pilot glanced over his shoulder, more of a polite gesture than an attempt to make actual eye contact with Marcos. The overhead speaker in the back of the cockpit crackled as he announced their arrival. "On behalf of BlackOps Air, we would like to welcome you to Miami. Local time is, uh…too damn early. The current weather is a balmy eighty-two degrees with scattered thunderstorms, though it looks like most of the heavy stuff has rolled out of the area. Uh…we thank you for flying with us tonight, and we hope you'll have a pleasant stay." The co-pilot in the adjacent seat was busy running through his system checks, reading gauges, and flipping switches overhead. He was grinning from ear to ear, apparently amused by his cohort's impersonation of a commercial airline pilot.

Marcos felt nothing, said nothing, and it choked the life right out of the cockpit.

"Too much?" asked the pilot.

Again, Marcos said nothing. It wasn't worth the effort.

Both of the pilots shifted their weight uncomfortably in their seats. They shook their heads and prepared for takeoff with scarcely a glance between them.

"Hope you don't mind me saying so, sir. But we certainly won't miss your lively conversation after your departure." He paused a beat, then cleared his throat. "That means you can get out now."

But Marcos was way ahead of him, having already opened the passenger door. He grabbed his tactical bag and hoisted it over his shoulder as he slipped out of the helicopter and walked away.

Despite a gentle offshore breeze, the night air was hot and oppressive, carrying the slight taint of fish and ocean brine. The recent rainstorms had left the tarmac soaked and littered with deep puddles, leaving Marcos to step around them as if navigating a minefield. Far to the south, lightning flashed intermittently, silent and incalculably distant on the empty horizon of the ocean.

Across the harbor, an extensive line of cruise ships was moored, most of them engaged with loading and unloading passengers, supplies, and trash. Those that weren't were doing nothing more than biding their time for departure later that morning.

By the time Marcos got his bearings, the *Velociraptor* had taken off and was heading out over the Atlantic in a northeasterly direction. In less than a minute, it was gone, the thumping of its rotors still audible for miles, long after disappearing over the horizon.

Marcos started walking down the shoulder of the road. There wasn't an arranged pickup. No ride waiting for him. Like all of his assignments, he needed to procure his own transportation by any means necessary. It wouldn't be a problem. Though the island offered little more than a few charter services and ocean-side restaurants, Marcos knew precisely where to find a car. He could see the streets of Greater Miami in his mind, could access them from the microchip implanted in the hippocampus of his brain. He could see every business, construction zone, and detour as if navigating an interactive map online. What's more, he knew *exactly* where he was heading. In the hour-long flight over the strait between Cuba and the United States, Marcos has been listening to the radio chatter of the Miami PD.

He followed along as they issued a BOLO on two fugitives suspected of murdering a couple of police officers. He didn't even have to hear their names to know the suspects were Brent Savage and Eliana Bautista. They were his marks.

Law enforcement had corralled them at an all-night diner. But their subsequent escape led the Miami PD on a high-speed chase across the city. At one point, they even lost them, though for the life of him, Marcos couldn't figure out how they managed that one. Eventually, the police caught up to Savage and the girl at a Bag-N-Go in Allapattah. And that's where the chase would end. The police would be overconfident, convinced they had them surrounded, with every avenue of escape cut off. Marcos knew better. He knew he had to hurry.

He went north along MacArthur Causeway, his head on a swivel, looking for a car that would fit his needs. There wouldn't be many choices at this time of night. But he would make do.

He soon found his answer at an ocean-side restaurant along the west shore sporting a nautical theme. The building's wood siding was stained gray and left to weather in an apparent attempt to make it look older. Along the front of the building were three oversized picture windows, accented with faux shutters and several decorative port holes. A heavy dose of maritime hardware comprising tarnished lanterns, anchors, and vintage lifesavers accented the walls. The entrance completed the schmaltzy look with a knotted wooden deck and handrails made of thick mooring ropes. And, of course, at this hour, it was closed.

But there were still a few cars parked out front. Probably a small crew of employees finishing out their shifts, cleaning, and making preparations for the next opening of business. Marcos approached the cars without adjusting his pace, walking by each one, giving each of them careful consideration. A sun-faded Nissan Sentra. A Jeep Wrangler with a heavy-duty brush bar. An older model Honda Civic—missing hubcaps. And a brand-new red Ferrari F8 Tributo, likely belonging to the owner of the restaurant.

Marcos walked between the Honda and Ferrari, looking for telltale signs of car alarms. Maybe some keys left in the ignition. The obvious was so often disregarded. But he made his choice.

Marcos closed his eyes and listened for the sound of approaching traffic and people laughing or talking, but he heard none of that—just the soft rustle of palm leaves flitting in the trees above.

Then time stopped. The metallic double click of a gun cocking echoed across the empty lot, disrupting the night's fragile silence. "Stop right there, asshole!" a man ordered.

Marcos opened his eyes and immediately focused on a short, rotund man standing a few meters away. He held a stainless steel Taurus PT92 in his right hand, and it was pointed directly at him.

Marcos feigned confusion, offering slightly raised hands as if asking not to shoot. *"Por favor, no dispares. No entiendo inglés."*

"Get the fuck away from my Ferrari!" he growled.

Marcos carefully produced a folded piece of paper in his right hand, took a tentative step forward, and offered it to the man. "No English," he said, his tongue sounding thick.

The man tilted his head, eyed him suspiciously, but reluctantly reached out to take the note from Marcos. "What the fuck is this…"

He never finished the sentence. Marcos pulled his silenced .22 pistol from behind his back and fired a solitary round into the middle of the man's forehead. The motion was a rattler strike, precise and unseen by the naked eye. The man died instantly, falling straight back as if his bones had suddenly turned to soup. Then Marcos finished the man off with a second shot, this time putting a bullet straight through his heart.

He didn't have time to linger. He spun around and headed to the other side of the car, not wanting to wait and see if the man's employees would join the party.

He opened the unlocked door, slid into the seat, and deftly hot-wired the ignition. Then, without delay, he backed out of the parking space and sped away in the Honda Civic. After all, he knew exactly where he was going.

CHAPTER TWENTY-NINE

Somewhere near Denver, Colorado

Mendoza blinked and rubbed her eyes. It was useless. She had been staring at the monitor for hours now, and her vision was becoming bleary. But the image on the monitor remained: Cypher breaking cover from the rooftop of the Bag-N-Go and shooting two police officers.

So, he *was* still capable of murder. No, that wasn't quite right. He was capable of self-preservation. That was quite different. She was unsure of his mental state. His behavior was erratic. But she didn't know if Cypher was broken. Maybe he was. Maybe he wasn't. All Mendoza knew was something wasn't right, and Deputy Director Spearman wanted the asset eliminated. No—*her* asset eliminated.

Mendoza tapped a button on the keyboard and rewound the video feed. Started it again. The first officer looked to be shot high and off-target as the force of the impact spun the man to his right before knocking him to the ground.

Wait a second. Off-target? No. Mendoza scrolled through a few menu options and then tapped a key. The video feed was piss poor. Dark. Grainy. She enhanced the image, reducing the noise, and zoomed in. There. Blood splatter, a barely perceptible spray. The shoulder of the shooting hand. Mendoza raised an eyebrow.

She continued, watching the video of Savage taking a shot at the second officer. He dropped him where he stood. He simply collapsed and fell straight onto his back. Mendoza increased the exposure on the image and, again, reduced the noise and zoomed in. There was no tell-tale sign of blood splatter—or, for that matter, a wound of any kind. Once again, the image quality wasn't the best. But she could see the shock wave of the bullet's impact transfer through the man's uniform like ripples in a pond. He was wearing a vest.

Wow. Somehow, Savage could discern in a split second which officer was wearing a Kevlar vest and which was unprotected. These were no errant shots by Savage. They hit precisely where he intended.

Mendoza's mouth was agape, her cupped hand trying to hide it in arrant disbelief. She hastily pulled it away, berating herself. She hit the continue button again, allowing the video feed to play out. The fire was raging all around them, out of control, and by this time, the black, billowy smoke and searing flames had created an opaque shroud over the rooftop. She could barely see them. But they were there. She watched Cypher jump down from the rooftop onto a dumpster, then turn and catch the girl as she did the same. After that, they headed north, fading from view as the shadows of the surrounding buildings quickly swallowed them whole.

Mendoza pulled up a street map, trying to get a bead on where Savage was heading. He had to have a plan. NTs always did. She just had to put herself in his shoes and think like a fugitive on the run. So what did he need? Well…he needed to get as far away from the gas station as possible. Shit. He needed to get out of Miami altogether. And pronto! But law enforcement would be monitoring all public transportation. That would mean no airplanes, trains, buses, or rental cars. His best bet would be to steal a car, of course, but he may not have time for that.

Then something caught her eye on the map. The Metrorail. Miami's above-ground rapid transit system. And Santa Clara Station was only about a half mile away to the northeast. Damn! What was she thinking? The Metrorail presented Savage with the same problems as any other form of public transportation: it would be monitored. *Think, Micaela. Think! What would you do if you were a fugitive?* Wait! She had to stop thinking that way. She wouldn't be just a fugitive because Savage wasn't just a fugitive. He was an NT! One of the best. And NTs weren't pigeonholed into linear thinking. The universe wasn't just a rolled-out map on a table. It was multidimensional, alive with intricate moving parts, and complex beyond imagination. It required you to look at it from different points of view. To seek solutions beyond the obvious.

Mendoza lifted the microphone from her headset and made a call. This was going to be tricky.

"Corporal Scully. It's Agent Shelley. Listen. I've got a lead for you. Corporal—shut up for two seconds and listen! They made a break for it and are headed north." He tried to say something, but Mendoza cut him off, drawing upon her tired frustration to put steel in her voice. "I understand you don't trust me. That's not my problem. That's yours. I'm telling you, the fugitives are heading north. They're making a break for Santa Clara Station. Whether you choose to heed that advice is totally up to you." Mendoza flashed a satisfied grin. She could hear him gather his breath to reply, probably to argue, but Mendoza would have none of it. She hung up on him.

She knew Scully wouldn't believe her, and there was no way in hell that he would pass along the info to his superiors. Not after her fuckup. She was a known liar. And that was exactly what she was counting on.

Mendoza made a quick backup of the night's intel on her thumb drive. Then she shut down her console, the gentle whine of its cooling fans slowing down and fading to silence. It was time to heed Spearman's suggestion and take the rest of the night off. Actually, he'd suggested taking several days off. He undoubtedly didn't want her around, digging into what was quickly becoming a sticky situation. And for once she had to agree with him. She didn't want to be around for that either.

CHAPTER THIRTY

Miami, Florida

Eliana was out of breath, her lungs on fire. She wiped the sheen of sweat from her brow with the back of her sleeve as she looped her other arm around Savage for support. Her leg tolerated her weight, but not much more. She would have never made the half mile to the metro station without Savage bearing her load. How he managed, she couldn't say. He was wounded. Shot in the shoulder—and still suffering from the rudimentary surgery he performed on the back of his neck. And yet he kept going, without faltering, without complaint.

They found themselves below the elevated platform of Santa Clara Station, resting and being careful to remain in the shadows of the giant cement pillars. There would be cameras. There always were.

Savage had just finished setting up one of the burner phones and was searching the internet for a local news station. "We need to get you on television. Try to tell somebody your story."

Eliana took a deep breath and slid down the pillar, taking a seat on the ground. The immediate relief was palpable. "Do you think it really matters? I mean, they've already spread lies about us and announced it on the evening news. The entire city is looking for us. *Maleït sigui!* All of Florida! Who would listen?" she asked, clearly excited, her accent prominent.

"Once we expose the President's dirty laundry, the wheels of politics will take over. Every investigative reporter in America will be turned loose, digging for intel, leaving no rock unturned. All the major networks will trample on each other to be the first with an exclusive. Even if nobody believes it, there'll be such a controversy left in its wake that it will be almost impossible to eliminate you."

Eliana felt the blood drain from her face. That wasn't exactly a reassuring thought. "Won't your agency—what did you call them—the DCS? Won't they be waiting for us? They must have planned for such a thing. I mean…it could be a trap."

Savage nodded, conceding the point. "Only one way to find out."

She suddenly felt queasy. She didn't like the sound of that.

Savage pulled out the clerk's cell phone from the Bag-N-Go and placed the call. "Yeah. Channel 7 News? I need to talk to somebody in charge. News desk or something. Yeah. Tell them it's Brent Savage. Well, then…I suggest you find somebody who can. Uh-huh. I will. But you have less than a minute."

"Està boig?" Are you crazy?

Savage shrugged as if to say he wasn't sure. Maybe. "Yeah. That's right. That's the one. No. I'm with Eliana Bautista right now. No. She didn't kill the police officers. I don't care what you've been told. I'm telling you, she didn't kill anybody. She's being set up. Framed."

It didn't go unnoticed by Eliana that he didn't exonerate himself from the killings. She started to argue, tried to silence him, but he waved her off. Why was he doing this? He knew damn well he hadn't murdered any cops. Those men were DCS agents. And they were going to kill her. He—he *saved* her!

He was silent for a moment, listening. "No. That's no good. It will be on her terms. I'll call you." Savage snapped the flip phone shut, then crushed it beneath the heel of his boot.

"Why didn't you explain you were innocent too?"

His brow furrowed, his head slightly cocked. "Because I'm not."

A car approached from the south, causing the conversation to be put on hold as they waited for it to pass. At this time of night, the traffic had slowed considerably, but it was far from desolate. They remained tucked away in the shadows of the elevated platform above, unseen from the road.

The car passed without incident, and Savage began rooting around the black backpack they'd boosted from the gas station. She wanted to say so much more but knew it would do no good. He had dismissed her objections without so much as a word.

He found the elastic wrap at the bottom of the bag, pleased with himself, and scooted over to where she was sitting. "Wish we had some ice. We need to get that swelling down. But this will have to do for now." He gestured for her to roll up the bottom of her capris to access her right knee.

Eliana did as he asked and gingerly exposed her tender knee. It had already turned a deep shade of purple, darkening by the minute, and had swollen like a ripe melon. She winced as he groped her knee, apparently feeling for structural integrity. He looked up and saw her mouth pressed into a thin line. "Sorry," he said. He paused and considered her knee. Then he sighed. "Pain's not my thing," he added, his touch softening.

Eliana lifted her chin, met his eyes, and, for once, didn't feel an immediate urgency to look away. His gaze was always so disarming and unflinching that it left her feeling exposed. Raw. But not this time. It somehow felt comfortable.

"You'll be all right," he said. "Nothing broken, anyhow. Banged up and bruised, no doubt, but hopefully nothing torn." Savage unfurled the elastic bandage and began wrapping Eliana's knee. He started wrapping around the leg at mid-calf and circled the leg a few times. Then he made a wrap diagonally up behind the knee and continued around the leg, above the joint. He continued wrapping the leg diagonally, making several figure eights until he ran out of bandage. He secured it with a clip.

"How's that?"

"Well, wasn't it you who said there's only one way to find out?"

He nodded in agreement. But when she tried to stand, Savage quickly took hold of her shoulders, urging her to stay put.

"There's another car coming."

This time it was a low rider, a glossy orange 64 Impala, the tireless thump of gangsta rap rattling its windows. They were slow-rolling.

Cruising. As they passed, the ear-splitting bass assaulted Eliana like cannon blasts to the chest. She gasped and eased back deeper into the shadows. They passed without incident, disappearing around a corner nearly a mile down the road.

Eliana realized she had been holding her breath and finally let it out. "That was a little too close for comfort."

Savage nodded. Then he stood up. He took her by both hands, urging her to do the same. With a grunt, she pulled herself up and then put some weight on her leg. To her surprise, it held. "It's still throbbing like hell," she said. "But at least I can put some weight on it."

Savage shook out a few extra-strength Tylenol and handed her a bottle of water.

Eliana felt parched. She sucked down the water until she drained the bottle, its plastic crackling in protest. A satisfied smile tugged at the corners of her mouth. "I needed that."

He agreed absently, his gaze fixed elsewhere, lost in his thoughts. She could almost see the gears of machinery turning in his head.

In the awkward silence, Eliana became all too aware of sirens wailing in the not-too-far distance. Half a mile. No more. She looked in that direction, expecting to see the flashing strobes of emergency vehicles, but there were none. Just a brilliant ball of orange light dominating the horizon, eerie and out of place.

Eliana turned to Savage, about to say something, but before she could do so, a police cruiser raced southbound on 12th Avenue, startling her. It screamed on by before she could hide, lights and sirens going full bore, its V-8 engine roaring in kind. As luck would have it, the officers never saw them. *Merda!* "What are we doing here, Savage? You know it won't be long before the police find us. We need to get out of here."

"Yeah, you're right." Savage crossed the road and walked down 21st Street toward the station entrance. It was gated but hardly secure.

Eliana fell into step after him, but then stopped. "Wait. You mean the Metrorail? The trains don't run this early in the morning." She rarely took the Metrorail, preferring to take the bus instead. But she had lived in Miami long enough to know they didn't run twenty-four seven. "They start at five in the morning and run until midnight."

He stopped and looked over his shoulder at her, bemused. "I know."

"You do? OK. Sorry. I figured since you weren't from around here, you may not know that."

"I do," he said, walking again, still careful to remain hidden behind an oversized live oak. He kept throwing glances at her, encouraging her to follow.

She did, though it wasn't without reservation. "Then where are we going?"

Savage stopped and pointed to the railway above. "There."

"Wait a second. Even if the trains were running—which they're not—I thought we wanted to avoid public transportation. Won't the police be monitoring all the airports, trains, and bus stations?"

"Yeah," he said, still looking up at the platform above as if accessing some unknown database. "Taxis, car rental companies, Uber. Just about everything. And like you said, not just law enforcement but the DCS too."

Eliana shook her head, still uncertain where this was going.

"You said it yourself. There's a lot of law enforcement looking for us. The Miami PD. County sheriff. Highway patrol. Hell, even the feds. But Greater Miami is a big place. It's nearly thirteen hundred square miles of urban sprawl and has over six million people living in it. That's an enormous area to canvas and a lot of people to keep track of. Maybe we can use that to our advantage."

"I don't follow."

"Well, put yourself in their shoes. You have a rather sizable police force, but it's finite. You can't realistically cover that much area and sort through that many people. It's a mathematical impossibility. So what would you do?"

"I'd try to narrow my search. Limit my focus to the areas where I'd most likely find the fugitives. Airports, I guess. Bus stations. Car rental companies?"

"Exactly. And don't forget to keep searching the city streets and highways. They're not exactly going to be looking for us by knocking on doors. This isn't Mayberry. So…they need to allocate their resources to the most likely places. Why invest those limited resources into a mode of public transportation that isn't even running?"

"But if no trains are running, how will the Metrorail help us?"

"We walk it. I figure it's five miles to Northside Station. We'll get off the rails there, near West Little River. There's someone there we need to meet. Someone who can help us."

Eliana felt the heat of her temper reach her cheeks. "Five miles? *Estàs boig?* I couldn't walk five blocks, much less five miles!"

That stopped Savage in his tracks. He turned to her and studied her face, recognizing the anger burning in her eyes. Then he slowly nodded, lowering his gaze. "Sorry. I have to stop that. I've never had to look out for anybody other than myself. My mission parameters have always been about how I will accomplish my objective. And handling pain, dealing with injury…that's just a part of my job. An obstacle to overcome."

Eliana sighed and immediately felt the tension in her shoulders ease. "It's OK. I guess I understand. But there's still one thing I don't. Don't you feel pain? You obviously can be hurt," she said, nodding at his bullet wound.

"No. I don't. At least not in the way you understand it."

She waited for him to continue, but he said nothing more. She decided not to press the issue. "You say you've only ever had to think about yourself, and you haven't had to think about others. Well…try thinking of me as a mission objective…precious cargo, if you like. A valuable source of intel."

"You *are* a valuable source of intel. But not to me. I'm no spy."

Eliana sighed in frustration. "OK. You're not a spy. But what if I was nothing more than a duffel bag full of valuable guns and ammunition? And your shoulder won't allow you to carry that extra weight for five miles."

"Hm. I'd have tossed it in the river a long time ago."

She swallowed. *Poor analogy, Eliana.* "OK. What if you needed those weapons to escape?"

"I would still toss them in the river."

"Oh."

"But I'd find another way to make my escape. There's always another way. You just have to think of it."

She smiled. *Better.*

Eliana watched Savage make his way down the sidewalk of 21st Street, using the cover of the nearby trees to keep himself hidden from prying cameras. He had asked her to stay put while he looked for something. But for what, she couldn't say. He kept looking up at the power lines.

"What are you doing?" She kept her voice low, afraid it would carry.

"We need to get up on the Metrorail, and I want to ensure they can't watch us doing it. I need to take the cameras out."

Another pair of headlights turned down the street, and she and Savage melted back into cover. It passed without incident, and Savage reappeared. He then pulled out his silenced pistol, took a firing stance, and fired a burst of four rounds into the transformer perched high on the utility pole.

Eliana flinched, clapping her hands over her ears, as there was a sudden violent explosion. A concussion of sound waves ricocheted down the block, bouncing aimlessly from building to building. In an instant, the surrounding area was doused in darkness.

She laid her hand across her chest, gasping. "OK. That's wonderful. But now what? We can sneak up on the Metrorail but a lot of good that's going to do us. Are you planning on carrying me?"

Savage stopped. He looked back at her. He had that faraway look again.

"*Estava fent broma!*" *I was kidding!*

He nodded absently, as if still considering his options. "OK," he said. He holstered his weapon and crouched behind one of the cement parking pylons. It did nothing to hide him, though it may have broken up his outline.

Eliana exhaled sharply. *He's so exasperating!* "Well, what then? You plan on flying over the rail?"

"Something like that."

Eliana could feel the slow burn of frustration crawling up her spine again. She gnashed her teeth and said nothing. They stayed hidden from view like that for what seemed an eternity. Savage crouched down amongst the pylons while she leaned against one of the larger live oaks. Several cars passed while they stayed hidden, and minutes went by. He didn't move.

Finally, another headlight turned down 21st Street—a solitary headlight. Eliana immediately recognized it as a motorcycle or some sort of dirt bike.

As it neared, Savage leaped from hiding and lunged at the man riding the motorcycle. He never stood a chance. Savage knocked him from his perch and latched onto the handlebars, promptly taking control of the motorcycle. He planted his foot, spun the bike on its axis, and gunned the engine, coming to a rest next to Eliana. "Climb on. Before he recovers."

"Uh-uh. No. Way. You expect me to climb on the back of a motorcycle again—with you?"

"Do you have a better idea?" His stare was unflinching, his jaw clenched with hardened determination. "You were the one who said if a problem seems insurmountable, you just need to keep thinking until you find another solution."

Eliana stared at him, her mind grappling with the fear of climbing on a bike again. "I never said that."

"Close enough."

Savage reached out his open hand to her, ready to help pull her aboard. Then the hint of a wry smile eased into place, his eyes bright with amusement.

"My God! You *are* crazy."

CHAPTER THIRTY-ONE

Washington, DC

President Richard S. Turner folded down the bedcovers and sat up in bed, allowing his legs to dangle over the edge. He scratched an itch on his scalp, yawned, and blearily wiped at the sleep in his eyes. *What time is it?* He reached for his readers lying on the nightstand and tried to focus on the digital clock. The electric blue display was overwhelming, too brilliant for him to look at comfortably. *Four thirty in the goddamned morning.*

He was used to running on limited sleep as his tight schedule allowed little freedom to enjoy the luxury of sleeping in. Lately, the ongoing problems in Honduras—not to mention the federal budget debacle—had cut into his leisure time even more than usual, lopping off any hopes of getting a few extra winks of shuteye. Then he was interrupted by that damn phone call in the middle of the night. By Victor, no less. It was of grave importance, he said. Couldn't wait. Well, by-god, he was going to wait. He had insisted it wait until morning, at least until he had commandeered a few more hours of sleep.

The President shuffled his way to the bathroom, where he managed to relieve himself of the previous night's bender. But at the age of seventy, his prostate tested his patience as much as his senior staff did, and it took a while. He then washed his hands, brushed his teeth, and barely had time to call the kitchen to send up some coffee before the Secret Service was knocking at the door.

"Good morning, Mr. President. Director Blackburn here to see you."

"All right, Peter. Send him in." Punctual as usual.

President Turner wiped his still-wet hands on his pajamas before extending his hand to Director Blackburn. "Victor. Good to see you, son. Come on in and take a load off your feet." The President's Texan drawl dripped from his mouth like synthetic motor oil. It was useful when he wanted his guests to feel like he was just a good ol' boy, an old friend that they could confide in. Then, just as quickly, he could turn on the charm of an articulate and formally educated graduate of Rice University.

"Good morning, Mr. President."

President Turner scoffed at the formality, clearing the morning phlegm from his throat as he found his voice. "For Christ's sake, Victor. We've known each other for what—twenty-five years now?" He knew they had, of course, but back then Victor had been nothing more than an intelligence officer at Quantico and he himself just a junior congressman from Texas. "Just call me Richard when we're alone."

"Yes, Mr. President."

"By-god you're a stubborn man, Victor."

"Yes, Mr. President."

President Turner chortled, waving a dismissive hand at the DIA director and offering him a seat in one of the nearby chairs. His furrowed brow and clenched jaw vanished from his face like a mirage fading in the desert. "They're already sending up some coffee for us. Can I call down for something to eat? Some breakfast?"

"No, thank you, sir. Too early and too many pressing needs to attend to this morning."

President Turner clasped his hands on his lap, then crossed his legs, making himself more comfortable. "I'm normally a biscuits and gravy man myself. But it's too goddamn early to be eating something that heavy in the morning. Stomach isn't even awake yet."

"Still having trouble sleeping at night?" he asked, no doubt eyeing the empty rock glass on the nightstand.

President Turner grunted. "It's this damn job, by-god. Trying to wind down after a day at the White House is like trying to land a 747 on an aircraft carrier. It can't be done. Anyway, a little nightcap helps lube the chassis after a hard day. It's these goddamned congressmen. They're vultures, picking away at me from all sides, all day, every day. I'm telling you. It's nonstop! It's like a one-armed man trying to fend off a tank division with a bow and arrow." He chuckled humorlessly, all the while eyeing the wet bar over the director's right shoulder. "You're a scotch man, Victor."

"Yes, sir. Johnny Walker Blue."

"Don't mind me saying, son, but a drink sounds good right about now."

Victor Blackburn raised an eyebrow and said nothing.

President Turner straightened, walked over to the bar, and began making himself a drink. "On the rocks?"

"No, thank you, sir. I still have a long day ahead of me. In fact, that's why I'm here. I apologize for disturbing you at such an early hour, but as I told you on the phone, we have a problem. And unfortunately it just can't wait."

President Turner scowled. *Problem? You have no idea!* He finished pouring himself a double. Then he returned to the chair across from Victor, sat down a bit stiffly, and eyed him with cool disdain.

The director, a lieutenant general in the Marine Corps, was dressed to the nines, his uniform starched and pressed with clean, straight lines, the ribbons and bars neatly arranged to military protocol. He was fit, his broad shoulders square, his posture ramrod straight. Though his short-cropped hair gleamed like sterling silver, Victor appeared much younger than the President, his complexion smoother, his eyes clearer. In truth, he looked every bit the eleven years younger than the President.

"What is it, son?"

"They botched the mission last night."

President Turner nodded, waiting for him to continue. His mind still felt tired and muddled this morning. He wasn't sure what mission Victor was referring to.

"Operation Peregrine?" Victor cleared his throat. Tried again. "Target *Jade Dove*."

The fog cleared, and President Turner nodded with recognition. He frowned. "They botched the job?"

"Yes, sir. FUBARed."

President Turner nodded as he processed this information. He found the "cutesy" mission names annoying. The falcon, the hunter. The dove, the prostitute from Miami. Just words to paint a prettier picture than the dark reality of what it truly was: murder. "Is this really necessary?"

Before Victor could answer, there was a knock at the door, and a kitchen attendant brought in a cart with an ornate silver coffee service. It was freshly brewed and smelled heavenly. The attendant was about to pour them both a cup but was dismissed instead. They deferred and left without further delay.

After he watched them close the door, Victor answered. "Is this necessary?" he repeated, parroting the President. "And just what are you specifically referring to, sir?"

Heat colored the President's face. "Come off it, Victor! Let's cut the crap. Why are we targeting some cheap call girl from Miami in the first place?"

"I don't recall her being all that *cheap*, sir."

President Turner's eyes flashed. "Watch yourself, Victor. You know damn well what I mean."

"Yes, Mr. President. I do. And if I might be so bold to say it, so do you."

"Yeah." President Turner exhaled through his nose, rubbed his forehead. "I do." He downed the rest of his drink and leaned forward, setting the empty glass on the serving tray. He remained there, resting his elbows on his knees. Despite no one else being around, he lowered his baritone voice to a whisper. "But kill her? She's a nobody."

Victor shrugged. "Isn't that why we started Operation Darkwater in the first place? To stop swimming in the mediocrity of politics and finally get things done? To finally make a difference? Mr.

President…you were a congressman, for Christ's sake! You know more than anybody that our federal laws do more to protect the criminals than put them away." He chuckled. "Look, this isn't our first rodeo. Countless other targets have come before this girl in Miami."

"That was different, Victor. We're talking mafia bosses, drug kingpins, known domestic terrorists…"

"Political rivals?"

President Turner stopped. Sat up. He wanted to reply but knew there was nothing to say to that. He swallowed and met the man's gray eyes, cold and hard like two steel rivets. "Yeah," he said finally. "That too." He sighed and leaned back in his chair. "But kill her? Why not just pay her off like all the others? If she blabs to the press…"

"This isn't about your sexual indiscretions, sir. This isn't a matter of the press finding out and us having to spin some story about Senator Kelley being unable to keep his dick in his pants. It's a matter of national security. Hell! It's a matter of us being charged with treason! And we're not talking about jail time here."

President Turner groaned and rubbed his hands roughshod across his face. "Dammit. I can barely remember that night. I was drunk."

"Understood. But the following day, when you were a bit more lucid, you claimed you may have bragged about being the most powerful man in the world. That you could knock off anybody that got in your way."

"I don't know. As I said, I had a lot to drink that night. I don't even remember the girl, much less mentioning Conall Bennett. You know, we didn't exactly do a lot of talking."

"Are you willing to bet your life on it? Because I'll tell you what, sir. I'm sure not."

President Turner's stomach roiled. He tamped down the urge to vomit. Kept the belch to himself. He knew the director was right. He had been in politics for most of his adult life. There would be no reprieve if the press ever found out. The extramarital indiscretions alone would be enough to ruin him. His legacy. He wasn't made of Teflon, like Bill Clinton had been, fending off impeachment with a silvery tongue, standing defiantly against his accusers, the First Lady "standing by his side." Hell. Elizabeth would never go for it. She'd castrate him like a Texas bovine. No. The actual issue was the assassination of Americans on U.S. soil. He couldn't pull off Ronald Reagan, either. A suspect memory and "I don't recall" just wouldn't cut it under the scrutiny of an official congressional hearing. Once the press had their hooks in the story, it would be like dripping blood in piranha-infested waters. Game over.

"So let's have it. What happened?"

"The operation called for our asset to shoot the mark from a sniper's blind less than two hundred yards away. We had planted a plausible cover story two months prior by having some criminal kingpins murdered by a sniper."

"To make it look like random killings…"

"Yes, sir. It would have been days before anyone would've discovered the call girl's body. Maybe longer, depending on how long it took the surrounding residents to smell the telltale stink of a dead body. Either way, it would be a clean getaway for our asset, with nobody the wiser. But he balked. He couldn't—or wouldn't—pull the trigger. Not only did he disregard his orders, he took out some undercover agents we had sent in to clean things up. Killed them both. What's worse, he helped the mark escape."

"Just what are you saying, Victor? We have a rogue agent on the loose?"

"It would appear so. His code name is Cypher. NT-Zero. And he's extremely dangerous."

"NT? You're talking about a super-assassin. And he disobeyed an order? I didn't even know that was possible."

Victor shook his head, his lips pale as he pressed them into two thin lines. "It shouldn't have been. I set the mission parameters myself. *I* assigned the NT. This was too important to leave it to random chance. Yet, somehow, someway, Cypher snapped. Broke. And we don't know why. This leads me to our second problem. Somebody sabotaged this mission. Wanted it to fail."

President Turner stood up, his temper quickly burning off the remaining fog of a hangover. "This just keeps getting better all the time! Do we have any idea who the hell it is?"

"Yes, sir. We believe it's Dr. Henry Shepherd. He's the lead scientist for the NT program and the man responsible for advancing this nano-technology in the first place. He was the first person we called when the mission started breaking down. The only problem is that we can't get a hold of him."

"What do you mean you can't get a hold of him? You lost him?"

"He's disappeared, and we think he's on the run. He could have re-programmed Cypher somehow, causing him to disobey orders. I don't even know if that's possible. But something tells me it is. We need to find him, Mr. President. Now."

Victor Blackburn stared out the window of his limousine, watching the first blush of dawn peeking over the Potomac and the cherry trees of the nearby park. The scene was a picture postcard. Somehow queerly serene. Tranquil even. And utterly deceitful.

There was a big problem on the horizon. The President wasn't protected from this disaster in the making. Neither was he.

They were fighting a war now—a war to keep their secrets from reaching enemy hands. And they were fighting it on two fronts. You had a rogue agent on the loose in Miami, evading authorities, capable of burning the whole thing down. And then you had Dr. Shepherd in hiding, probably the man responsible for throwing a monkey wrench into the entire goddamned machinery in the first place.

Victor figured it could be worse. If the NT and the call girl separated, they would find themselves fighting a war on three fronts. A tactical nightmare. But the more Victor thought about it, the more he realized it was an unlikely scenario. The girl wouldn't be able to make it on her own. She was only safe if the NT stayed by her side. Protected her. She would be as good as dead without him. But that's where the NT's weakness lay. She would be the albatross hanging around his neck.

CHAPTER THIRTY-TWO

Miami, Florida

Marcos eased the white Honda over to the curb, allowing the engine to idle as he canvased the surrounding area. It was less than an hour before sunrise, the sky still dark with just a hint of light on the horizon, promising another hot, blistering day for the residents of Miami.

Out of the front window, he could see the blackened heap of rubble that was once a Bag-N-Go, its metal framework warped and jagged like the rib cage of a dead animal, burned and unrecognizable.

A veritable parade of emergency vehicles surrounded the building's remains, lights flashing in reverent silence. Police cruisers, FBI armored vehicles, ambulances, and no less than three firetrucks were on scene. There was a Channel 7 News van parked across the street, a young woman doused in the bright lights of a camera forcing a cheerful smile and giving an energetic report on the Miami sniper and his ensuing escape.

The worst of the fire had been put out. Some of the fire crew were gathering up equipment and preparing for departure. However, Marcos noticed that a significant police presence remained, including the FBI and Miami PD. Around the perimeter, a few pockets of gawkers from the surrounding neighborhood were milling around, ever nosy and cluttering the scene. But they were thinning out. Irrelevant. It was time for Marcos to head out on foot.

He slipped out of his car, slung his go bag over his shoulder, and strolled on over to the emergency scene. The boundaries were marked with portable barricades and yellow police tape. Marcos eased a black ball cap on his head and slipped underneath the tape. There was no hesitation. Not the slightest hint of concern. He merely continued toward the greatest concentration of police officers. They were engaged in a heated discussion, trying to cobble together some sort of plan. Attempting to coordinate their efforts. It was a fool's errand.

Marcos took his time as he breezed by them. He was neither fast nor slow. Just another person working the scene, like he belonged there. He was a ghost, unseen and unworthy of their attention.

"Why didn't you tell us about the phone call earlier?" somebody asked. Their voice was taut. Authoritative.

"It didn't seem relevant. I received a call from her once before this all went down. She claimed she was with the CIA. But she was obviously lying. Trying to distract us. Buy time."

"Well, fuck, patrolman! It worked! Say again what she told you during the last call."

The lanky Black man wearing the gray suit and blue tie was in charge, clearly FBI. Marcos didn't make eye contact. Didn't even look their way. He just listened as he walked on by, his task at hand, his destination clear.

"She said her agent was making a break for it. That he was headed north toward Santa Clara Station."

"And this being the same woman who claimed they weren't in the building in the first place?"

The man grunted an affirmative.

"And this was Agent Shelley?" The man glanced at his shorthand scribbles on his notepad. "Claimed she was with the CIA?"

"Well, that's what she said."

"Yeah. Unlikely. Who knows who the hell she really is, but it's probably safe to assume any information she gave out was complete bullshit. We'll follow up with the CIA boys, anyway. And let's get a hold of your phone carrier and see if we can get a bead on her. In the meantime…Santa Clara is what? Northeast from here? Let's focus our attention on the west or to the south, then. But we'll cast a wide net, just in case."

"OK. But what if the perps aren't even out there? What if they perished in the fire?"

The FBI man scoffed. "Then who shot your fellow officers, Riley and Edwards? Burning buildings don't carry guns, Sergeant. No. The fugitives shot their way out. Got away—apparently with the help of some unknown caller."

"Maybe she was working with the fugitives…"

Marcos finally walked clear of the FBI debriefing and could no longer hear their words. He made sure he didn't stop. Didn't hesitate. He just kept his eyes forward and continued past the charred remains of the convenience store. He didn't need to hear anything else. The FBI man was right. No bodies had been recovered yet. And they wouldn't. Cypher probably started the fire to cover his escape.

But…the unknown caller. That was a different concern. She muddied the waters on what was an already murky situation. But one thing was clear to Marcos. The mystery woman had pulled a classic bait-and-switch with the information she doled out. She supplied a patently false narrative first so when she finally provided the truth, the police wouldn't take it seriously. Marcos, however, couldn't be so easily dissuaded. He knew his marks were headed to the Metrorail station because he knew Cypher. He was brought up through the same program. Trained by the same people. *Made* by the same people. Strong. Fast. Intelligent. Incredibly dangerous. An adversary worthy of respect. But not fear. Never fear. For Marcos was the same…only better.

CHAPTER THIRTY-THREE

Columbia, Missouri

It wasn't the piercing overhead lights that woke him. Nor was it the jarring clamor of people trying to talk over each other, though after several hours of primarily silent travel, it should have. Ultimately, it was an abrupt blow to the shoulder from somebody's heavy purse as they waddled their way down the aisle that woke Dr. Shepherd.

He reflexively clutched at his shoulder, shooting an irritated look at the rather overly large woman, pear-shaped and easily a hundred pounds overweight. Her disheveled hair was matted on one side as if she had been sleeping on it for days, her gray roots blooming through her three-month-old dye job like an explosion of fireworks. He figured his hair fared no better. Regardless, she was ignorant of her atrocities and kept on moving.

Dr. Shepherd wiped the sleep from his puffy eyes and tried to squint through the reflections on the bus's tinted windows. He couldn't get his bearings, but the driver announced their stop one last time: Columbia, Missouri. For those reaching their final destination, their luggage would be unloaded and left curbside. He was lucky he hadn't overslept.

Dr. Shepherd got up, stretched, and stifled a yawn as he exited the bus. This wouldn't be his final destination. But this was where he and the Greyhound parted ways.

The morning air was damp and heavy and held on to him like a pile of wet leaves. A stark contrast to the thinner and more arid air of the Mile High City. But it was pleasing in a warm, almost familiar way. Those distant days spent as a young child on a small farm in Illinois. Innocent and unburdened.

It was early enough in the morning that it was still dark. The bus station was a part of the Midway Truck Plaza along Interstate 70, surrounded by coarse grass and drawn-out clusters of hardwood trees as far as the eye could see. The far horizon was dappled with thin ribbons of rain clouds, the skies above favoring the gray of predawn. At least there were no police.

Dr. Shepherd located his duffel bag amidst the clutter of luggage on the curb, stretched and cracked his back, then made his way across the parking lot toward the highway. He had never been to Columbia before, but had memorized his route months before. He knew the roads. Knew his final destination.

He crossed Highway 40, then walked a short distance before veering left onto West Cunningham Drive, an insignificant side road that shadowed Interstate 70 for a short distance. He wouldn't be traveling that far.

All the arrangements had been made and meticulously planned down to the finest detail. Each step had to be executed without deviation. The impending result would otherwise be nothing short of failure. Capture. Perhaps even death.

Dr. Shepherd gave that some thought. Would they kill him? Of course they would! With nary a thought. And as he looked down at his feet plodding along with deliberate certainty, he knew that was true. He had always understood it was a possibility. Even likely. But he had to try. He couldn't let his lifework—and all the medical advancements he developed within the nanosciences—be perverted into something sinister. That was never his intent. He wanted to help people.

He was only a junior at the University of Illinois when his mother passed away from colon cancer. It had been a grueling, hard-fought battle she had never relinquished. But in the end, the cancer won. It always did.

He had always been close to her. After his father died ten years prior, she became his world. A lone beacon of light in a suddenly large and pathless world. She was everything a mother could be. Loving.

Nurturing. A strict but guiding hand. Then she was simply gone, and he was left all alone. Lost. And it was during that dark, tumultuous time in his life he decided he needed to find his way. Nobody was going to do it for him. He needed to pull himself up by his bootstraps. So that's just what he did.

He had always been smart. Brilliant even. But he had also been listless without direction. In the end, his mother's death became his motivation. Drove him to become better than he was, greater than the sum of all his parts.

He finished his BS in chemistry, graduating summa cum laude, and then received his master's and doctorate degrees from Stanford University. There was a two-year postdoc at MIT, where he realized he had an affinity for the nanotech sciences. He worked at various labs and universities for the next ten years, including a four-year stint as an associate professor at UCLA, before moving on to Harvard as a full professor.

He was always learning, continually building upon previous fields of study. And he excelled at them all. Nanoscience and nanotechnology. Materials physics. Biology. Neuroscience. He made advancements in them all.

But he could never have foreseen that he would one day be working for the Department of Defense. They sold him on the dream of making a difference, like a starving salesman pushes cars on a holiday weekend. *Imagine the possibility of soldiers being able to heal themselves from battlefield wounds! Think about all the poor soldiers coming back from war, suffering from PTSD! Might the targeting of specific memories help heal their traumatized minds?* They'd claim, *The sky is the limit!* And he bought it. And for a time, he even believed it. But no longer.

Dr. Shepherd drew back to the here and now as a car approached, then passed him, allowing for a generous distance between them. He couldn't imagine this being a busy road, especially this early in the morning. It certainly caught his attention. But after a quick jaunt down the road, it turned left onto Schotte Lane and disappeared from view.

He let out a sigh of relief. It was just somebody out on a morning milk run.

He continued his walk, occasionally allowing his attention to drift from the scrub grass along the side of the road to the distant fields beyond the interstate. A low-lying mist hovered over the tilled earth, a soft throw blanket still and without form. It would burn off quickly once the sun came up, but Dr. Shepherd had no intention of being around by then.

He continued to make his way down the two-lane. Now and then, the toe of his walking shoe would catch, causing small rocks to skitter across the pavement. Crickets chirped. He all but ignored the constant rumble of traffic on the interstate.

He was close now. Yes. And there it was. Holcom Industries. A local aluminum fabricator set back off the road a short hop, its parking lot set on a low-rising hill. Though the company didn't maintain a third shift, it was a big enough place that some cars were always parked on the property, either out front or on the west side of the building. Dr. Shepherd was pleased that the first shift had already begun their day. His plans continued to fall into place.

He had arranged for his cousin Becky from Mansfield, Ohio, to rent a car locally and drive it to Columbia, Missouri. She was to leave the car in a prearranged location in the parking lot of Holcom Industries. Her husband Gary would follow in their car, and after making the drop, they would leave together and go back home. It was a huge favor to ask as he had never been particularly close to Becky—or, if he was truly being honest, that whole side of the family. But there had been no grumbling from either of them as he promised to compensate them well. You couldn't always count on family. But money? It never failed.

He proceeded to the west side of the building, where most of the shift workers parked, and then counted out four parking spaces. Found a silver Ford Focus. Kentucky plates. If this was the correct car, the door would be unlocked, and the key would be hidden under the passenger-side floor mat. He eased the door open, half expecting a car alarm to go off, but it opened without a hitch. The key and its spare were right where they should have been. *Perfect!*

Dr. Shepherd gave the sedan a once-over. Checked the glove box. User's guide. Rental agreement. He snaked around his seat to inspect the back of the car. Nothing unusual. Except for a small red and white Igloo resting on the floor, wedged between the front and back seats. To his delight, it was stocked with some easy travel food: sandwiches, chips, bottled water—even a few apples.

Dr. Shepherd twisted the top off a cold bottle of water and took a deep, greedy drink, draining it in one go.

He fastened his seat belt, adjusted his mirrors, and sat deep in the seat, making himself comfortable. He still had a long drive ahead of him. Morgantown, West Virginia. He needed to avoid all toll roads. Truck stops. Rest areas. Anywhere there might be video surveillance. *With any luck, I'll be there by tonight.*

God willing, he wanted to say. Or perhaps, *if fate allows*. He believed in neither.

CHAPTER THIRTY-FOUR

Denver, Colorado

Steam rose from his mug of coffee, its slinky trail dissipating into the crisp morning air. Typical weather for Denver in the early fall. Mild sunny days followed by clear, crisp nights. It wasn't unusual for this time of year to have a temperature swing of forty degrees in a single day.

On the balcony of his downtown condo, Theo Spearman looked out over the city streets below, watching people clad in their pressed Armani suits and armed with over-the-shoulder briefcases make their morning runs for lattes and bagels. Prepped for battle, they were, and the slog that followed on their daily commute. The early signs of the morning traffic were just beginning to stir from slumber, the soft halos of streetlights fading as the sun tickled the landscape with its first rays of early morning.

He yawned. How pathetic, he thought. A literal rat race. All those working-class people scurrying amongst the corridors of life, looking to make a few bucks and improve their station in life. Looking to be rewarded with the prize cheese at the end of the maze. But the joke was on them. There was no cheese. No prize. Only a new maze.

As foolish as that seemed to Spearman, pointless and mind-numbing, he figured it was more humane to live that way—to not know—than to face the cold and much darker reality that their lives didn't matter. They each were but one cog of the wheel in a world of eight billion.

His thoughts drifted, flipping through the previous night's memories like pages in a picture book. He thought of Cypher. Clenched his jaw. This morning's update said he had eluded capture, and his current location was unknown. Spearman took a cleansing breath and let it trickle out of the corners of his mouth. He willed himself to relax. There was nothing else to be done. He had known all along that the police would fail. That's why he had hedged his bets. The Ghost would track down and eliminate Cypher, come hell or high water.

Spearman straightened and went back inside. It was past time he got to work. He needed to head to Control despite having had only four hours of sleep.

As he closed the door behind him, Spearman heard his phone ring. He paused, looked around, and remembered placing it on the kitchen counter. It was Director Blackburn. He knew this before he even read the caller ID. He answered it without formality.

"Spearman."

"Theo. Let's have it. What news do you have for me?"

Spearman looked down at his free hand. Watched it clench and unclench as if marveling at the simple physiology of the human body. It looked simple. Basic physics at work. But it was ingenious, wonderfully complex.

"Cypher has slipped past the perimeter of local law enforcement. His and the girl's whereabouts remain unknown at this time."

"That isn't what I wanted to hear, Theo. Please tell me you have a plan."

"It's all under control."

"Control? You think this is under control, Theo? Because I can't fathom how."

Spearman shook his head and pinched the bridge of his nose with his thumb and forefinger. "I've activated another asset from the program. He's not only capable of tracking down Cypher but can take him out when he does."

"And Ms. Bautista," Blackburn reminded him.

"That goes without saying."

"I'm beginning to wonder."

Silence hissed between them.

Then Blackburn added, "So you've activated an asset from the Centurian Project?"

The director was referring to the eventual successor to the current program, Project Dragonfly. While the NT series of super-assassins was built off the previous program's advancements in genetic modification, the new Centurian assassins, the CY series, were being developed to utilize direct cyber implants and bionic modifications.

"No, sir," said Spearman. "The Centurian Project hasn't launched yet. We're still a year or two away. I've called up NT-8, code name the Ghost. He has some CY modifications, however. He's the latest and most advanced of the NTs, sir. Consider him the final run-up, if you will."

"So your solution to eliminate a broken NT—a very dangerous one at that—is to unleash another one onto the general population? So instead of one problem, we now have two!"

"With all due respect, sir, there won't be two for long. Cypher is a zero. A prototype. Even though they've tried to keep him upgraded, he's still no match for the Ghost. An eighth-generation NT—the omega in the Dragonfly Project. He's the apex predator."

Spearman could hear the man sigh on the other end, his voice cutting like a knife's edge. "And what if *he's* broken, too? What if Dr. Shepherd has sabotaged the entire program? Did you ever think of that? We should be shutting this down! Not opening Pandora's Box!"

Spearman opened his mouth, wanting to argue, but the words wouldn't come. No. He hadn't thought of that. It's true, Dr. Shepherd was very resourceful. Highly intelligent. But to sabotage the entire program made little sense to him. To what end? If Dr. Shepherd was taking some sort of moral high ground and wanted to shut down Darkwater, he wouldn't do so by setting a nest of super-assassins upon the American people. He would want to help them. Shield them from such unlawful atrocities.

Spearman finally said, "No. The good doctor wouldn't reprogram—if that is even possible—the entire nest of assassins in the program and put innocent people at risk."

Blackburn scoffed. "Isn't that what he's done?"

"No. I don't believe so. He might try to expose the program. Put it in the public eye so it gets shut down. But he can accomplish that through a conscientious objector."

"Excuse me?"

"Cypher. He was programmed to be the ultimate weapon." Spearman paused and considered how much he should tell Blackburn about his discoveries at the institute. He kept it generic. "If he regains a conscience—develops a moral compass—he would stop being a weapon and become a mouthpiece instead."

Once again, there was silence on the other end of the line, as if the director had blown a fuse trying to wrap his simple mind around the idea. Spearman almost snorted out loud but had the good mind to stifle it. The smug bastard. He was speechless. But not for long.

"Well then, Theo. Then it's like I said. You still have—at *minimum*—two very serious problems on your hands. And they are likely going in two different directions."

"How do you figure? The doctor isn't dangerous. He isn't going to kill anybody. He's a scientist, for Christ's sake!"

"Yes, he's a scientist," Blackburn said patiently, as if talking to a small child. "The architect of the NT program. And may I remind you, Theo—he has a mouth, too. We don't know where he's at or where he's going. For all we know, he has a vendetta against the United States. He could expose the entire program. Burn the whole damn thing down to the ground, Theo. And take us with it."

Spearman gnashed his teeth. The man's insipid tone was infuriating. It was a wonder that he could hold his temper in check at all. And usually he did. But not this time.

"What the fuck are you talking about, *General*?" he snapped, purposely forgoing the rightful title of director like an insolent teenager. "You're talking treason here!"

"I am."

"Well, I don't believe it. If he wanted to talk to the media, he would have done so before this whole thing blew up as a twenty-four-hour news run on CNN. He's on the run because he's afraid. Afraid for his life. And he wants to be as far away as possible when this whole damn thing blows up!"

"And it will. So this ends now. Take him out, Theo."

"Wait. You're talking about killing the lead scientist in the Dragonfly program. If you take him out, you will kill any opportunity for him to fix all of this mess—especially if your doomsday scenario with all the NTs going rogue comes to fruition."

There was a brief pause on the other end, as if the director was weighing his next words carefully. And when he finally spoke, his voice was a sizzling crackle of raw energy, a fiery bolt of lightning. "This discussion is over!" he growled. "And this is *not* open for debate. I've made my decision, and you will follow the chain of command! Is that understood, *Deputy*?"

Spearman clutched the empty coffee mug on the counter, squeezing it so tight his knuckles turned white. "Yes, sir."

"Fine. I'm going to activate all DCS stations around the country. We will have an active presence in all media outlets, across all the major cities. New York, Chicago, LA…wherever. In addition, we will have our best hackers tunnel into their networks, keeping a tab on all incoming calls and emails. We have to keep a lid on this. In the meantime—"

"We don't have the resources—"

"In the meantime, Deputy, we will activate other agents in the Midwest and on the East Coast to track down Dr. Shepherd and take him out. By *any* means necessary. Understood?"

Spearman voiced agreement, but his tone revealed his disdain. It didn't matter. Beneath the pompous Director of the DIA title, the man was still a three-star general. He was used to giving orders and having the men beneath him follow those orders. Agreeing with them was irrelevant.

And Theo Spearman didn't. He said, however, "Understood."

After he ended the call, Spearman stood at the kitchen counter, seething, the muscles in his arms twitching, his hands trembling. He counted backward from ten, trying to put a lasso around his raging emotions. *Ten, nine, eight, seven…*

It usually worked. *Six, five, four…*

This time it didn't. *Three, two, one…*

Spearman screamed. A blast of primordial anger, white-hot and unbound, exploded from his mouth. With the heavy coffee mug already in hand, he threw it with all his might at the kitchen wall, obliterating it into a cloud of black ceramic dust.

Fucking idiot!

CHAPTER THIRTY-FIVE

Miami, Florida

Eliana was bone tired. The motorcycle ride on the Metrorail tracks didn't help matters. Yes, Savage insisted he could avoid the third rail and keep them from getting electrocuted—and who was she to doubt him—but that did little to ease her fear of flying off the platform and plunging to their deaths twenty-five feet below. Even so, she could barely keep her eyes open. She found herself drifting off to sleep, only to be jarred awake by an unexpected bump. A rev of the engine. The shift of body weight. But somehow she kept her arms cinched around Savage's waist.

It took them less than ten minutes to reach Northside Station. It was just another ten through some rundown industrial complexes before they reached their final destination in Westview. Eliana figured it was far enough north to be considered part of Opa-locka.

Sleep was all she could think of as they stood at the entrance of a cookie-cutter house in a cookie-cutter neighborhood, waiting for somebody to answer the door. A door, mind you, sporting iron bars.

Eliana tried to be patient as they waited. She started looking around, attempting to appear relaxed but not doing a very good job of it. Not a friendly neighborhood, she decided. All the houses were the same. They were nothing more than small stucco ranches on slab foundations, looking more like pastel-colored tissue boxes than homes. Unkept lawns, overrun by crabgrass and thinned out with large patches of sandy dirt, were the best of the lots.

Iron cages barricaded the windows and doors, apparently standard issue, while the unchecked crime rate in the area locked people inside as much as the bars kept the undesirables out. Few of the homes had garages, some without paved driveways. And most everyone kept their cars off the street and parked in their yards instead, comforted nominally by the rows of chain-link fences.

Eliana watched Savage knock on the door again. Still no answer, so he tried the doorbell. The sound was cheery and inviting but muffled, as if buried deep in a distant catacomb. She saw him look up and followed his eyes to a small security camera on the cracked stucco near the roof. He looked back at the doorbell and she saw an oversized button with a bright blue light. Definitely not standard issue.

Savage leaned in close, his nose practically touching the button. Then he straightened and offered the video doorbell an upturned middle finger. He held it there, making sure there was no ambiguity about his message. She caught Savage's amused expression and then heard a noise from inside. Footsteps. Quiet at first. Getting closer. The door creaked open, maybe a foot. Just enough for a man to peek out.

"Qué coño quieres?" What the fuck do you want?

"I need a new pair of shoes," Savage replied. That drew a raised eyebrow from Eliana.

"Luego, joder, vete a Walmart!" Then fucking go to Walmart!

"No. I need a cobbler."

The man sounded Cuban. He was of slight build and weather-worn, with skin like tanned leather. He had a curly mop of oily hair and a toothpick dangling from his lips, which he now twitched nervously from the corner of his mouth. "Both of you?" he asked, slipping into perfect English as easily as if he had flipped on a switch.

Savage nodded.

The man stepped back and opened the storm door for them to enter.

Eliana joined Savage inside and was immediately met with an arctic blast of cold air. The place had air-conditioning. That was a pleasant surprise. But then again, so was the whole interior. Despite the home's ramshackle exterior, the interior looked recently remodeled and—she dared say—had been done so tastefully. The floors throughout the house had glazed ceramic tiles in sandy pink, resembling marble. The smooth plaster walls were buttery white and understated. She judged the furniture as pedestrian but functional and was likely picked straight out of an IKEA catalog. But the rooms were of decent size and the kitchen had been recently updated with new stainless steel appliances.

The man gestured for them to follow, so they made their way to the back of the house. She counted two bedrooms—no, three. The last bedroom was just past the kitchen and down a small hallway, serving as the man's workshop.

Cluttered tables filled the workspace, littered with surveillance monitors, printers, laminators, and photography equipment. In the center of the room was a robust electric standing desk with a new iMac.

Eliana leaned in toward Savage and whispered, "Who the hell is this guy?"

"He's a cobbler—a professional forger. And for a fee, he'll provide us with passports, driver's licenses, birth certificates. Whatever we need."

"Yes," the man said, forsaking any illusions that he hadn't overheard their conversation. "Your *amigo* is right. I hook up my clients with all the legal docs they need. I got you covered on more than just those documents he mentioned—green cards, work visas, fake signatures, you name it. The works. Though I prefer to think of myself as a legal document designer."

Eliana smirked. "Legal? Don't you mean *illegal*?"

"Ha! I like you," he said, a toothy grin splitting his face. "It's only illegal if you get caught. And if you do, it won't be because of my documents."

"And why is that?"

"Because they are the real McCoy. Right down to the ink and paper they're printed on."

Eliana wanted to probe further but felt completely out of her element. She politely nodded instead.

"So how do you two *turistas* know of my little operation? You with the NSA? CIA?"

Savage said, "Something like that. You were on my list of viable contacts in the area. If things should…well, not go as planned."

"And these things…they have not gone as planned?"

Savage glanced at Eliana. Shrugged. "No. Not as planned."

"I see. And are these things that didn't go as planned…are they illegal?"

Eliana felt her stomach flip. Why was he even asking that? Should they come clean? She didn't know. She was relying on Savage, hoping he knew what to say. "Yeah," he said. "They're illegal." Then he added, "And I'd wager they're illegal even if we don't get caught."

This seemed to amuse the little Cuban man. His smile widened. "I like you, *gringo*. You're the real McCoy, too." He then looked at Eliana, took the toothpick out of his mouth, and pointed it at her. "How about you, *chica*? You in trouble, too?"

Eliana felt her nerves fraying, ready to snap. She exhaled slowly. "Would I be here if I wasn't?" She looked at Savage. He was calm. Collected. And a smooth glance from him told her he was in complete control.

Savage said, "We both need new identities. Complete with passports, driver's licenses, birth certificates, and social security cards."

The cobbler nodded. "*Bueno*. We'll need to take a couple of pictures then. *No hay problema*. My going rate for fake identities, complete with supporting documents, is usually three thousand."

"For both?" asked Eliana, already thinking of the limited supply of cash they had safely tucked away.

"Each," he said flatly. "Which is usually my going rate for *mis amigos*. Yes? But only for *mis amigos* who have minor problems. But perhaps your problems aren't so minor. No? And you're not *mis amigos*. I don't know you." He paused, looking up at the popcorn ceiling, his brow lines deepening. "I've done some side jobs for the government. Very hush-hush. I usually charge them extra when they need to keep their hands clean. An extra thousand. Because—well—because I don't like them. And they can afford it." He seemed amused by this. Laughed at a joke only he understood. "But you two *turistas*…you're involved in something big and *very* illegal. I'd say you're in deep shit. But at least you have one thing going for you. Neither of you are government employees." He worked the toothpick to the other side of his mouth. He twitched it up and down as he considered them. "At least not anymore."

The cobbler walked over to the work desk behind him. Grabbed a folded newspaper from a stack of documents. He tossed it onto the counter in front of them. It was the morning edition of the *Miami Herald*. The headline read *Miami Sniper Duo at Large*, followed by the smaller subtitle *Escape After High-Speed Chase*. The accompanying article included pictures of them both.

Eliana gasped, clasping her hand over her mouth. Her heart started racing, pounding so hard she felt like it would burst through her chest. Her first response was to run. To get the hell out of there. But she froze like her feet were encased in a block of ice. "That's not true!" she snapped, her voice strained and wavering with emotion.

The Cuban man had turned to walk away, but he stopped and turned his attention back to her. He said nothing at first. He just raised his eyebrows. Surprised? Amused? She wasn't sure.

Eliana scooted closer to Savage. Her arm brushed against him, and without thought, she entwined her arm through his and took his hand. It was so warm. It surprised her.

The cobbler smiled. Amused, then. "No, Eliana. I figured it wasn't true. Not completely, anyway." He rocked a level hand back and forth in a see-saw motion. "Should we expect anything so noble from our local police? The government? Sadly, it's the way of the world." He tsked.

"You know my name?"

"Sure…or at least what the paper says it is. And you must be the one they're calling Brent Savage," he said, turning to face him. "The deadly sniper. Murderer." He waved his hand in disgust. "*Pura mierda!*" *Pure bullshit!* "CIA is more like it. And as I figure it, you must have pissed them off. But honestly? *Me importa un carajo!" I don't give a fuck!* "It's none of my business. Besides, my work requires me to maintain a certain level of confidentiality for my clients. It's the nature of the beast. But what *is* my concern, *mis amigos*, is the payment for said services. Five thousand. And yes," he said, eyeing Eliana. "That's for each of you."

Eliana let out a sigh and squeezed Savage's hand. Then she blushed. *What the hell am I doing?* She totally forgot she was holding his hand. She started to pull away but then felt him squeeze back. Her body tingled with electricity. *Shit!*

There was a brief pause, just a heartbeat, then Savage said, "Three thousand."

"You insult me, *amigo*. This isn't a simple green card we're talking about. We're talking about a full workup. Five thousand."

"No. Three. It's the same amount of work for you whether I'm an illegal alien or the Miami Sniper."

"But much more risky. Dangerous. I insist on five."

Savage worked the muscles in his jaw, trying to keep control. The man had no idea just how dangerous it was. "Fine. You're putting your neck on the line. And you feel more money is justified. But I say you still owe us a discount. We're your *amigos*. You said it yourself. So we'll give you four a piece."

The man frowned, then smiled sheepishly. *"Amigos?* I just wanted to make you feel welcome. Feel at home. I'm sorry. I lied. It's still five. And not one dollar less."

Savage exhaled sharply. Grimaced. He was growing tired of this game. "And I said we will only pay you four. That's three thousand for your friends and family discount, plus a thousand dollar kicker for the risks involved."

"I already told you, *gringo*. You and *la chica* aren't *mis amigos…*"

"Yeah, yeah. I heard you the first time. We're not your friends. And I really don't care." Then he lowered his voice, and it went cold. "But understand this—she's *my* friend."

Eliana blinked, his words somehow sounding strange to her ears. Foreign.

The cobbler rubbed his scruffy chin and thought about it for a moment. Well…that was eight thousand dollars—a good chunk of change. Certainly more than a simple green card or birth certificate could fetch. "OK. You drive a hard bargain. But you've got it, *amigos*. Four thousand each."

"Agreed. We will pay you half now and the rest tonight when we pick them up. They must meet our approval, naturally."

"Tonight?" He laughed. "No good! I won't be able to finish all that by tonight."

"Of course you can."

"No! I—I don't—that's not enough time! I have other customers, you know."

"For eight thousand dollars, I'm sure you can clear your busy schedule."

The man wanted to argue, but Savage cut him off. "Tonight. You will have it done by tonight."

"Yeah, well…that's going to cost you extra."

"Fine." Savage reached behind his back and pulled the SIG out of his waistband. He didn't have to point the gun at him to show him he meant business. He did it anyway.

Eliana gasped and placed a staying hand on his arm. Shook him to get his attention. "Jesus! What are you doing, Savage?"

"Renegotiating."

The room fell silent. Not a word was spoken. The two men just stood there, looking at each other. Savage, deadly serious. The cobbler, in utter shock. Beads of sweat immediately sprouted from his forehead.

"We need those documents, Eliana, and your money won't last long. Not if you're going to stay ahead of the police, the government. Since our friend, the cobbler here, wants to keep changing the rules, I thought I'd oblige."

There was a long, agonizing pause. A writhing, twisting serpent in the room, threatening to strike.

Eliana didn't know what to do or what to say. She let her arm slide down his arm and gently placed her hand on the gun. Moved it away. She looked into his eyes. They held each other's gaze for what seemed like an eternity. Unspoken words passed between them. Understanding. He nodded. Lowered the gun.

But in that one moment of hapless insanity, she had unwittingly broken the tension in the room. The cobbler let out a roar of laughter, slapping at the table with loud bravado. "Ha! I knew I liked you, *amigo*!" he said, wagging a finger at Savage. "You are quite the haggler. And have some mighty big *cojones*! No?" He then looked at Eliana and grinned. "You too, *chica*. I think maybe some small *cojones*. But yes. Definitely c*ojones*."

Eliana sighed and closed her eyes. She began kneading her temples. "*Oh Déu meu!* I need some sleep."

CHAPTER THIRTY-SIX

Eliana and Savage had their pictures taken. After sorting out the details about their payment and when to expect the documents to be finished, they left the cobbler's house and made their way down Highway 9 to a hole-in-the-wall motel called Echo Bay. The sun-faded marquee, sporting a jumping dolphin in neon lights, boasted of air-conditioned rooms and free cable TV. Cheap rates and by the hour. Eliana doubted, however, that outside of the neon logo on the marquee, they would see any dolphins during their stay. Nor a bayside view. They were seven miles from the nearest beach.

The room was dark and smelled of wet carpet, the air conditioner rattling its discontent from beneath the dirty window. There were two full-size beds, a table between them, and an old RCA television. It wasn't as clean as Eliana had hoped; the cockroaches could attest to that. It didn't matter, as the motel suited their needs. They accepted cash, and no ID was required.

"I'm going to take a hot shower," she said, "if that's all right?" She could feel the filth sticking to her, and a hot shower sounded heavenly.

The bathroom was small, just a simple sink and toilet, and the grout on the floor tile was stained with mildew. But the shower worked, and the water stream was strong. She buried herself under the surge, allowing it to wash the grime away and, along with it, the stress.

The attempt on her life weighed heavily on her mind. She had almost died at the hands of an intruder, then was almost gunned down again by yet another. But Savage showed up. Saved her. *Yeah. And then he told you he was supposed to kill you.* Eliana shook her head. *But he didn't.* He saved her life. More than once. He had been protecting her. *Why?*

After ten minutes of deep therapeutic bliss, she finally shut off the squeaky faucet to the shower. She towel-dried her hair, then took another towel from the rack and wrapped herself in it. She had forgotten that she didn't have a change of clothes, and the outfit she had been wearing reeked of burned plastic and smoke. The towel barely covered her modesty—if there was such a thing anymore. But what choice did she have? Then she remembered the night before, in her condo. Listening to her earbuds after her shower and… *Oh Déu meu! He was watching me!* Eliana suddenly felt like she was going to vomit. And she had no idea why. Considering what she had been doing to make ends meet for the last couple of years, that seemed trivial in comparison. *Shit! And the sponge bath at the kitchen sink, too!*

She left the bathroom, still toweling her hair dry, only to find the room almost entirely dark. Savage had pulled the curtains closed, and though it was broad daylight outside, the black, heavy curtains darkened the room as if it were midnight. Eliana left the bathroom door open, allowing its light to spill into the room.

Savage lay on the bed, his uninjured arm tucked up beneath his head, seemingly in deep thought.

"Your turn," she said, fidgeting with the bottom of her towel, trying to keep it from riding up her thighs. "I'm sorry. I had to use two towels to dry off and…you know…have something to wear."

Savage sat up, his eyes flashing in surprise. Or was that something else? Eliana felt her cheeks grow hot. *Get a grip on yourself. He's just another guy.* "There's still one more towel on the rack."

He nodded and said that was fine. He then reached down to the floor, picked up a plastic bag, and tossed it to her. "I went down to the lobby and got us a couple of robes. A couple of toothbrushes and some toothpaste. Had to pay for the robes though…" He shrugged.

She smiled. "Thank you. That was very thoughtful."

Again, he shrugged. Then he excused himself and went to take a shower.

Eliana finished drying off and slipped into her robe. She brushed her teeth at the vanity sink, then combed her fingers through her damp hair, trying to keep it from getting too tangled. But it was a losing battle, and she gave up.

She plopped down onto the corner of her bed and began surfing the TV channels, looking for something—*anything*—to watch. She needed a distraction, something besides the news, so she settled for an old black-and-white movie on the local Spanish station. But she was barely paying attention as her mind kept drifting back to Savage.

The shower cut off a few minutes later. He must have been drying off as a couple more minutes passed without another sound. Then she heard him brushing his teeth. Finally, he reappeared wearing a towel of his own. *Shit!* No robe.

"Oh, hey. There's nothing on," she said, sounding bored, trying not to look at him. She did anyway. His hair was still wet and spiky, like it had been the first time she had seen him. He was a little taller than average height and lean, the muscles in his arms and chest sinewy like steel cord. His stomach was well-defined. But it was his shoulder that caught her attention. The bullet wound. It had stopped bleeding, and the dark purple bruise had faded to a sickly yellowish brown. The skin was slightly puckered and flushed red where he had likely been tending to it. But it scarcely looked like an entrance wound anymore.

"Amazing," she whispered. She stood up and walked over to take a better look. She leaned in close and placed her hand gently on his chest as she observed. "I've never seen anything like it."

"Yeah. I suppose not," he said, sitting on the edge of the bed. "There's not too many of us left who can do this." He unzipped the backpack on the floor and began rummaging through it, looking for the medical tape and gauze. When he found it, he angled his back toward the giant mirror on the wall to get a better look at the exit wound. It looked like an X marked the spot where the skin had started to knit itself back together, but it was no worse for wear than the front side.

Eliana realized that the wound from his impromptu surgery on his neck had vanished, too. Just a minor scratch now, as if he had somehow scraped it on cement. "Is all this because of those little robots you told me about?"

"Nanobots. And yes. Some."

"Nanobots," she repeated quietly.

"They're microscopic machines designed to run through my bloodstream, making my body more efficient. They provide me with extra oxygen and adrenaline when needed, and are capable of destroying invading bacteria—even viruses."

"Viruses, huh? So you never catch a cold?"

Savage chuckled. "No. At least I haven't for a really long time."

Eliana watched him struggle to reach his arm behind his back and dress his wound. She sat down beside him and laid a hand on his. "Let me help." She took the alcohol and cotton balls from him and carefully began cleaning the wound.

He jumped at her touch.

"Sorry. Did that hurt?"

"No," he said, amusement playing in his eyes. "Just cold."

"Oh, good. So, these…nanobots. They help you heal?"

He nodded, then hesitated, unsure how much he wanted to share with her. When he looked over his shoulder and looked into her eyes, she smiled at him, encouraging him to continue.

"Yeah. Some. But mostly because of my genetic modifications. Rapid cell regeneration. It was developed by DARPA, with designs to create a super soldier."

She was methodical as she worked, careful with how much pressure she applied to the gauze when taping it down. "But you're no soldier."

"No."

Eliana smiled. "And we've already established you're no spy."

"Right. I'm no spy."

Eliana finished the dressing on his back, then slid down onto the floor, kneeling between his knees. She looked up at him and saw his face tighten as she leaned in close, her face mere inches from his stomach. She reached around him to grab the tape and gauze again. He smelled good—clean, like soap. But there was something more. Something uniquely him. *Oh, God. I'm losing it.*

She then tended to his chest, placing a clean dressing over the entrance wound. It didn't need much attention. It looked much better than it did just a few short hours ago. But she figured it couldn't hurt. "Well, if you're not a soldier, and you're not a spy, just what does that make you?"

"An assassin," he said, his voice dropping to a whisper. "A murderer."

That gave Eliana pause. She looked up into his eyes, searching for answers, and what she found surprised her. There was pain. Confusion.

Eliana looked away, the feelings too raw, too uncomfortable for her to digest. She gathered her thoughts for a moment, then nodded and looked back into his eyes. "Maybe. Maybe you have done some bad things. I don't know. I'm certainly not in a position to judge anybody. But I've also seen how you've risked your life to protect me. Maybe…maybe you're not an assassin…not anymore."

Savage just shook his head, his thoughts seemingly far away.

Eliana hesitated. She wanted to ask him something but was afraid of how he would take it, and she fumbled over the words. "I need to ask you something, Savage. I really need to know. But I'm not sure how to ask, so I'll just sort of let it fly."

"Yeah, sure. Go ahead."

"Why didn't you kill me?" Her voice quivered, and she struggled to keep a pool of tears from falling. "I mean…you were given orders to shoot. But you didn't. Why?"

Savage sat for a moment, trying to sort through his thoughts and remember the events that had unfolded the night before. "I…I don't know. It's hard to remember. But it somehow seemed wrong—out of place. Look, I won't sugarcoat this. I've killed a lot of people. Evil people. Murderers, rapists, and pedophiles. There's been drug lords and mafia hitmen. People so evil that they left little doubt why they deserved to die. But then there was you. And yeah, Control tried painting you like you were some treasonous terrorist. But I had been watching you around the clock for almost two weeks. Studied you. It felt like I knew you."

"And did you?"

"I knew you weren't evil—that you didn't do anything worth dying for. But I don't know if it was all that clear to me at the time. I had never disregarded an order before. And up until that night, I never felt the slightest inkling of doubt. That's when I knew I was broken."

Eliana took his hand in hers, squeezed it. "And do you still think that way? That you're broken?"

Savage inhaled deeply and looked away. Outside their room, the maids were starting their morning routines, calling back and forth in loud voices while their cleaning carts rattled noisily down the sidewalk.

Savage turned back to her. He was clearly uncomfortable. "Yes," he said finally.

"Oh. I see."

"No…no, you don't. I'm not broken because I wouldn't take the shot. I'm broken because I once thought I should have. Eliana…*that* is evil."

Tears spilled down her cheeks, and she quickly swiped them away with the back of her hand. She sniffed. "Listen to me, Savage. I don't believe you're a bad person, and you certainly aren't evil. They've trained you to kill. They've turned you into a weapon. But you don't have to be. Do you hear me? You can be whatever you choose to be. OK?"

"I don't think that's possible anymore. Did you see how I pulled my gun on the cobbler? Threatened him?"

Eliana nodded. "Yes, of course," she said, biting her lower lip.

"Well…it wasn't for show. I wasn't bluffing. I could feel my finger twitching on the trigger as every fiber of my being urged me to shoot him. And for what? He didn't do anything. Not anything worth dying for, anyway."

"But you didn't."

"I wanted to."

"But you didn't!"

Silence fell between them. Their eyes danced with each other. "Look, Savage. I don't know what they did to you. I don't know if it can even be fixed. But I've seen what you're capable of. And I know you have a good heart."

With a smile on her lips, Eliana's hand found its way to his face, cradling it gently. She caressed it with her thumb. And for a long, enchanting moment, she lost herself in his gaze. She leaned in and felt the warmth of his breath as she softly kissed the corner of his mouth. "You're a good person, Savage. Don't you ever forget it. Because I won't."

With that, Eliana stood up, offered him a playful smile, and said goodnight.

CHAPTER THIRTY-SEVEN

The morning sun was still low in the sky, obscured by a veil of distant rain clouds, yet the temperature was already on the rise. It was going to be another sweltering day. For the Ghost, it felt like any other day back home in Baracoa. Hot and muggy, with no prospect of relief. And all completely irrelevant. Only the elimination of his targets mattered.

He approached Santa Clara Station from the west, having snaked his way through the streets of Allapattah until he reached NW 21st Street. There was no way for him to know the route Cypher and Bautista would have taken to the Metrorail station. There were just too many streets, too many possibilities. In truth, he was uncertain if that had even been their destination. But Marcos knew that's exactly where he would have headed if it had been him on the run. And that was all the certainty he needed.

Down the street, a Florida Power & Light service truck was parked beneath a utility pole, its yellow lights flashing, a worker high in its lift bucket working on the transformer. A Miami-Dade police cruiser was parked on the other side of the road. It, too, had its lights flashing. That caught his attention but did little to dissuade him from investigating further. Marcos adjusted his go bag to the other shoulder, freeing up his right hand should he need to pull out his concealed pistol. He approached with caution.

He reached the service truck and was standing beneath the lift bucket before the utility worker even noticed. The man offered no hello. He just cursed under his breath about the "damn punks" and how it was going to take hours to replace the transformer.

Marcos had noticed the electricity was out for the entire city block but gave no more thought of it, figuring at some point it must have suffered a direct lightning strike during the storm. But upon closer inspection, he saw that it had been shot. Multiple times. It had to be Cypher.

Marcos looked around, searching the surrounding sidewalk and curb for any clues. He immediately found the spent bullet casings. Four of them. 9mm. *Common caliber.* Still, he knew it was Cypher who had shot up the transformer. He could feel it. But to what end? An electrified rail powered the trains. And those rails had their own substations to keep the Metrorail running in case of a power outage. What couldn't continue operating, however, were the stations. Even with emergency backup power, it was limited, and the station would have to be shut down for safety reasons.

Without a doubt, the disruption of services at Santa Clara would cause widespread inconvenience this morning for commuters along the entire line and probably result in some financial loss for the city. But if Cypher intended to make a clean getaway—and there was little doubt that he did—he'd made it impossible to use the Metrorail.

The Ghost took a mental note of his surroundings. He was struggling to connect the dots on why Cypher destroyed the transformer in the first place, not to mention determining where he and the girl had escaped to. Marcos was at a loss.

Across the street, about twenty-five meters away, the Miami-Dade police officer was talking to a young—and rather animated—Caucasian male. The officer was questioning him, taking notes, and didn't appear in the least interested in what he had to say. Routine.

At the station entrance, a security guard for Miami-Dade Transit was turning away a group of angry commuters. Before the morning was out, there would be plenty more.

Marcos had an idea. He looked into the cab of the utility truck and found a tool belt on the front seat and a clip-on ID badge hanging from the visor. He swiped them both and put them on. The city worker in the bucket above never noticed.

Marcos crossed the street and headed to the Metrorail entrance. A live oak sat on a small rise just off to the right of the officer and young man, so he slipped by on the other side of it, giving them ample room. He made a quick adjustment to the listening device in his ear and continued by, eavesdropping on their conversation as he did so.

The young man had been riding down the street sometime early that morning when he was accosted by some unknown assailant. He was knocked off the motorcycle and must have hit his head on the pavement and blacked out. When he awoke, the bike was gone. He was questioned about the reason behind his early morning joy ride but failed to provide a satisfactory explanation.

"What the fuck took you so long to get here?" the man demanded, throwing profanity around like candy during a Memorial Day parade.

"We've been a little occupied responding to other emergencies in the area."

That nearly stopped Marcos in his tracks. *Emergency.* Emergency, as in a police standoff. A three-alarm fire. And fugitives on the run. The kid wasn't the target of some random bike-jacking. Marcos quickly regained his composure. He kept walking toward the entrance, his gait relaxed and unhurried.

Now, it was all making sense. Cypher had made a clean getaway all right. He blew up the transformer to knock the power out, thus disrupting rail services at the station. It had the added merit of knocking out the security cameras as well. Stealing the motorcycle was the whiskey chaser for this drink. He avoided the city streets and the ensuing manhunt by avoiding them altogether. It was nothing more than a magician's trick. A sleight of hand. Genius.

Cypher and Bautista had made their escape via the Metrorail after all. It just wasn't by train. In some ways, this benefited Marcos. They were either heading north or to the south. But which one? If they traveled south, they would be going back the way they had come, deeper into Miami and straight into the trap set by law enforcement. Opting for the northbound line would put them on a trajectory to not just one but two airports. Marcos didn't think this was likely, however, as Cypher was too intelligent to risk the heightened security of an airport. No. He calculated they would steal a car and then head north. That offered a plethora of escape routes, all leading away from Florida and ultimately to destinations unknown.

Marcos pushed his way through a group of commuters that were still milling around the front entrance to the station, bitching, only to be met by the MTA security guard. He was a ruddy-faced, heavyset man, and the early morning heat had left him drenched with sweat. He ordered Marcos to turn back around, but when he tapped the ID card clipped to his shirt, the man nodded with relief and waved him by.

Marcos headed to the stairs that took commuters to the station's mezzanine level and immediately noticed the condition of the handicapped security gate. The swing barrier bars had been torn off their hinges and now lay strewn on the ground, twisted like some discarded lemon peel. That was unfortunate. It wasn't going to be some simple repair job. It would need to be replaced entirely. Which meant maintenance workers would be dispatched soon.

Marcos looked around, searching high and low for security cameras. He spotted two immediately. One covered the security gate, or rather what remained of it, while the other overlooked the exterior steps and walkway. Both had been destroyed by gunshots.

Marcos needed to work fast. When maintenance discovered the shot-up cameras, the police would also be dispatched—and not just some random traffic cop. It would be the FBI. ATF. The works.

Here in the recesses of the station, the daylight outside barely made a difference, and the stairwell was deep in shadow. The power outage made it darker still. Yet Marcos had little trouble seeing as the smart contacts in his eyes allowed him visibility even in low-light conditions. But he wanted to reach the mezzanine level, hoping it would provide additional clues in determining the direction the fugitives went.

He took two steps before he heard a man's voice call out from below him.

"Stop right there! Put your hands up and keep them where I can see them!"

Marcos hesitated, slight and imperceptible. But again he didn't stop. He continued to climb the stairs as if he hadn't a care in the world. As always, an idea quickly formed in Marco's mind. It wasn't a thought-out plan. It was reactionary. Ingrained in his very matrix. The darkness was an advantage for the Ghost. The man below him couldn't see him clearly. Certainly not well enough.

Then a flashlight clicked on, and Marcos suddenly found himself bathed in a beam of light. At that, he allowed himself to react, putting on a show of surprise and turning around with his left hand shielding his eyes. His smart contact lenses immediately adjusted to the bright glare. It was the security guard.

"Put your hands up where I can see them. No—keep your hands away from the gun! Raise your hands! Do it now!"

So that was it. He must have seen my gun. Again, Marcos feigned confusion and squinted against the bright light, though he saw him as plain as day. He raised his hand to his mouth and showed him the hand sign for deaf and mute. The security guard didn't understand American Sign Language. Even if he knew the basics, it was far too complex of a message for him to piece together with his pea-sized brain. But it had achieved what Marcos had wanted it to do. He planted the seed that he was unable to communicate normally.

The security guard ordered him to put his hands behind his head and lie down, yelling even louder now, as if that would help, and oblivious to the fact that he was standing on stairs. Just how did he expect Marcos to lie down?

Marcos took slow steps down toward the man, once again offering him the sign for deaf and mute.

The security guard hesitated, not entirely sure how to proceed.

Marcos offered the man a folded note.

He reached out for it, tentatively at first, fully aware that Marcos couldn't communicate, nor understand, his instructions to comply.

As he was handed the paper, the security guard unfurled it and began to read. It must have confused him when he discovered there were no words written on it. If only for a second…

CHAPTER THIRTY-EIGHT

Golden, Colorado

It felt good to be home. It took Micaela Mendoza almost an hour to get there. She was so tired that she walked straight to her room and fell asleep on top of her bed, never bothering to change out of her clothes. For eight hours, she was dead to the world. It wasn't until the sun began its slow descent to the western horizon that the daylight reached her bedroom window, waking her. It was three o'clock. Apparently, at some point, her brother Andres arrived unannounced and let himself in. That was typical. He then helped himself to the food in the refrigerator. She found *that* annoying. But the familiar smell of fresh coffee brewing teased her awake and eventually brought her shuffling into the kitchen.

"If that coffee is fresh, just pour it into my eyes." Her voice was phlegmy, still thick with sleep.

Her brother stood at the stove, grilling something in the iron skillet. He glanced over his shoulder. Smiled. "Rough night?"

"You have no idea."

Andres chuckled, walked over to Micaela, plastic flipper in hand, and gave her a quick peck on the cheek. "Good to see you, sis." He walked back to the stove to tend the skillet. "I'm making myself some dinner. You're welcome to have some."

Micaela stepped closer and peered around his shoulder. Smiled. "Grilled cheese?"

"Hm. Soul food."

"You have the soul of a four-year-old, big brother." She patted him on the back. "You'd think you might have learned to make something besides grilled cheese by now."

"I can order pizza, too."

Micaela had to laugh at that. A genuine, deep-in-the-gut belly laugh. How long had it even been since she'd felt like doing that? "Well, I guess I figured you might be able to hire a personal chef with you being a big-time litigator and all. You know? Or at least be able to afford to eat out at one of those fancy restaurants in Denver once in a while instead of mooching off me."

Andres took a bite of his sandwich, then nodded his head, savoring the experience. "And what? Miss all this?" He took another bite. "You sure you don't want any, sis? It's the bomb. So good it'll stick to your ribs."

Micaela cringed. Rolled her eyes. "Having food stick to my ribs isn't what I had in mind. Coffee. I need coffee." She padded across the kitchen's wooden floor, its old boards creaking beneath her feet as she made her way to the coffee pot and poured herself a giant mug of joe. Black. No sugar. She slurped at it greedily and smiled in satisfaction. "My compliments to the chef. This is class A shit."

Andres smiled warmly at her, then nodded knowingly. He walked over to Micaela and wrapped her in his arms, his embrace warm and reassuring. "How you doing, sis? For real now. You look tired." For a moment, neither said anything. Then he grinned and said, "Well, actually, you look like shit."

"Thanks a lot," she said, laughing. "Love you too."

"Aw, come on. I'm only teasing." He slipped away from her and reached for a ceramic mug neatly stacked in the white kitchen cabinet above the sink. He poured himself some coffee, then drowned it with cream and sugar.

"Jesus, Andres."

"What? I'm not an army grunt like you. I have a refined sense of taste." He tugged at her elbow, pulling her along after him. "Come sit outside with me on the back deck. It's a beautiful day."

Micaela joined him outside and sat in one of the gliding wooden deck chairs. She closed her eyes and took a deep breath, soaking in the late afternoon sun. The aspen trees were getting an early jump on fall, golden and dancing in the warm breeze, just an artist's brushstrokes amongst a sea of evergreens. Up above, white puffy clouds drifted without purpose across a vast and carefree sky.

"God, I needed this." Micaela took a deep, cleansing breath, savoring the sweet and familiar tang of sunbaked pine. She settled into the peaceful silence as though it was a comfortable throw blanket and looked at her brother. He was smiling, but the emotion didn't carry over to his eyes. She ignored it and broke the silence before he could. "You got off early today?"

"Yeah. It's a holiday weekend. There were no appointments after lunch, so I took a half-day. You?"

Micaela snorted. "God, no. Just the opposite. I worked all night."

"Wow! That blows. And they allow that?" He always referred to her workplace as "they" since he knew so little about her job. All he knew was that it involved working for the government, and she didn't discuss it.

"They were the ones who sent me home. Forced me to go, actually. Told me to take a few days off." Micaela took a long draw of coffee from her mug. Shrugged.

"Maybe that's not such a bad thing. Maybe take a couple of days off to clear your mind. Relax a little. Maybe do some kayaking on the Poudre."

"Yeah. I miss that. I've been putting in so much time at work lately."

Andres leaned back in his glider, stretching his long legs out in front of him. He was lanky, and at six foot three, he was nearly a foot taller than Micaela. Where he got those long legs was beyond her, as neither their mother nor father were tall.

"What's going on at work that's got you so bummed?"

"I'm not bummed. I'm just tired."

Andres scrunched his face, giving her a *come on* look that she understood all too well.

Micaela sighed. Nodded. "Yeah, well…I'm not so sure I know who I'm working for anymore."

"The United States government?"

Micaela shot him a look. "What I mean is that I'm not so sure if I'm on the right team."

Andres said nothing to that. He waited. Allowed her the space to gather her thoughts.

"I used to think I knew it all. Had it all figured out. There was order in this world. Everything had its purpose. Everything had its place."

"But?"

"Things aren't so black and white for me anymore."

Andres raised an eyebrow, then leaned forward and rested his elbows on his knees. "Hey, look, sis. I'm aware we don't discuss too much about where you work. There's always been an unspoken boundary between us, a mutual agreement not to discuss it. I always respected that. I always figured with your intelligence background in the army, you were involved in some of that CIA, hush-hush, spy bullshit."

Now it was Micaela's turn to raise an eyebrow.

He grinned, raising his hands in mock surrender. "Clandestine operations," he corrected. "Anyway, as I see it, the world of government intelligence, by necessity, has to be kept secret. I get it. They're dealing with some seriously dangerous assholes out there, extremists who love nothing more than to hate us. Or as the lawyer in me would say, acting with extreme prejudice and deliberate malice. Right? Doesn't the government bear the responsibility of protecting us at all costs? Stop thinking that the world is your personal footlocker, sis. You're not in the army anymore. Not everything is measured, neatly folded and stacked, and put in its proper place. By its very nature, this is a very messy world. It's not black and white. It's gray."

"I used to think that way," she said, her voice subdued and barely audible over the breeze washing through the trees. "That the government needed to walk that fine line of gray. To protect us all. To protect its self-interests." She paused, choosing her words carefully. "I'm realizing that our government—the people I work for—operate in a world far darker than I ever imagined. Far greater than I can accept."

Andres sat up in his chair. "I never heard you talk this way before. You've always been country first. Your underwear is red, white, and blue, for crying out loud! What the hell is going on, Micaela?"

She looked at him, studied the tight lines forming at the corners of his mouth, the worry pinched on his brow. She wanted to tell him. He was her brother, for God's sake! But how much should she tell him?

"The hell with it. You're right. I work for the government. But not for the CIA. I'm part of a black ops program that works independently from direct oversight. I'm a liaison for agents in the field. Very specialized agents who operate out of the most extreme and dangerous places. Doing the dirty work, as you might say, in those darkest corners of the world."

"You're a handler for spies?"

Micaela tilted her head, diverting her eyes. "Handler would be accurate." She looked back at her brother and met his eyes head-on. "Spies?" She shrugged. "OK. As good of a word as any."

Andres stiffened, an uneasiness washing across his face. "Uh. Maybe you shouldn't be telling me this."

Micaela plowed ahead, ignoring the offhand remark. "This spy's job is to…stop…bad people. Terrible people. The worst."

"I get it. Evil people."

"Yes! Exactly! Evil people. And this organization I work for tries to *stop* these people."

"OK," Andres said. "I see where you're going with this, and I get it. They're *stopping* evil people. But it sounds like they're stopping these bad guys for the greater good of others."

Micaela shook her head, nearly choking on her words. "No. I don't think so. At least not anymore."

He waited.

"There's this…this *spy* that I've worked with before. A few times now. He's one of the best. He's never failed to complete a mission…"

"Stopping these bad guys."

"Yeah. Anyway, on the last mission, he balked at his orders. He didn't carry out his orders to stop…this target."

"OK, let's cut the crap—no more dancing around the subject. Let's call it like it is. This *spy* is an assassin, and he kills people to stop them from committing heinous crimes. I said it. Not you. I'm your lawyer, so let's just consider this attorney-client privilege."

Micaela nodded. "Yeah. All right, fine. They usually reserve these assassinations for the heads of drug cartels, mafia bosses, and terrorists. People that are hard to get to through legal means—at least not without putting our people at significant risk."

"Reasonable. So who did this assassin refuse to kill?"

"A call girl."

"Excuse me?"

"A high-end call girl."

"A suspected terrorist?"

"No."

"A foreign spy?"

"No."

"Murderer? Traitor?"

"No."

"Tax evasion? Failed to pay off her parking tickets? Crossed the street without looking? Help me out here, sis. What warrants killing a call girl?"

"Nothing! I think she might have turned a trick with a well-known government official—some senator or something who wants to keep it a secret. But I'm not sure. You just hear certain rumors whispered around the water cooler."

"That's a bit of overkill, don't you think?" Andres winced as soon as the words left his mouth. "You know what I mean."

"Yeah, I know. And I agree. It doesn't make sense to me either. But here's the thing—that's not all. After he disobeyed orders, he eliminated—"

"Killed."

"Killed the backup team sent in to finish the job."

"He killed the…killers? Yeah…that sounds weird. The other team?"

Micaela nodded. "And now he's on the run with the woman. He's helping her escape. He's *protecting* her!"

"Whoa." Andres put up his hands, his mind reeling. "This is some crazy shit."

"And now the organization is trying to eliminate them both. They're trying to kill their own asset, Andres." She threw her hands up in the air. "Why is that? Never mind that he's one of us. Never mind that the government has invested millions into the training and development of these assassins. They invested time. And time isn't something they can get more of just by buying it."

Andres steepled his hands around his nose, thinking. Then he said, "They have something to hide."

"Something's not right, Andres."

"No shit."

"No. I mean, something isn't adding up. This assassin was trained—created—by our government to kill and follow orders without fail. And yet he didn't. So, I ask again, why?"

"What do they say?"

"They say he's broken." Micaela rolled her eyes. "Well, hello! No shit, Sherlock! But saying he's broken is like saying someone died of heart failure because their heart stopped beating. They want to kill him, Andres. They want to murder him, and we're all supposed to be on the same team!"

Andres nodded and looked at her thoughtfully, his eyes widening with understanding. "You feel responsible."

She fought back tears of rage, her face burning with frustration. "I *am* responsible. He was my responsibility."

"Ah."

Micaela took another sip of her coffee, clutching the mug with both hands as if she were cold. "I tried helping him, you know. I created a diversion for him and the woman to escape by sending the police on a wild goose chase. I figured I could stall them. Send them in the wrong direction. As far as I know, they got away."

"You don't know their current whereabouts? Where they're heading?"

She shook her head. "Not anymore. The deputy director didn't want me nosing around. That's why he sent me home for a few days to get some rest. It was like a parent giving their damn kid a dollar to go play somewhere else."

Andres tipped his mug back and downed the rest of his coffee. "Well, one thing is for damn sure. Your employer won't stop until they eliminate them both." He stood up and stretched. "Want some more coffee?"

When she didn't answer, he said, "I don't know about you, but I think I'm ready for a beer. Want one?"

She shook her head, but she wasn't really listening. She had that faraway look on her face—the one she wore for the world to see when she felt lost and helpless.

Andres walked back into the house, and when he returned, he had a couple of Dos Equis in his hand, leaving one on the table for his sister. He plopped back down across from her, leaning forward, his elbows resting on his knees. "So what are you going to do?"

Micaela looked up, startled, as if suddenly aware that he was still there. "I really don't know. I want to warn him. But I have no way of reaching him. He lost his sat phone. He's no longer trackable through his biosensor. And he's certainly not going to reach out to me. How the fuck do I help him?"

Andres grinned. Sat back up. "Oh my God."

"What?"

"You like him."

"Who? The asset?"

"No. The Pope. Yes, the asset...this...this guy on the run."

"No. It's not like that. It's not like that at all," she said, but her cheeks were bright with color.

"OK. A friend, then?"

Micaela sighed. "No. Not really. I don't know him that well. All of our communication has been through encoded emails or by sat phone. And I only know what he looks like because of his picture in a dossier file."

Andres got up and went over to Micaela, putting a reassuring hand on her shoulder. "Then what is it? Why are you putting everything on the line for this guy? You don't even know him. And you just said he's broken."

Micaela nodded, her eyes far away. "I know I did. It's just that…I don't think so. My gut is telling me this guy isn't broken. He's not a damn machine."

"OK. He's not a machine. And he's not broken. Then what does that make him, besides a fugitive of the law?"

Micaela thought in silence, trying to get her mind wrapped around her feelings. Then she said, "It makes him human. Certainly more so than me. Probably more than most." She turned to her brother, looking him dead in the eyes. "You asked me why I was putting everything on the line for this guy. But I'm not risking anything. Not really. He is! He's risking his career, prison—his life! To protect someone he believes is innocent."

Her brother grinned. Took a long pull from his beer bottle.

"What are you grinning about, you overgrown boy scout?"

"You. You're still that little twelve-year-old girl back home on the ranch, hand-feeding a calf too small to suckle. Too stubborn to quit, even when Dad said it was a waste of time. You probably averaged three hours of sleep a night for a month!"

A smile swept across Micaela's face, warmed by the memory—a memory separated by eighteen years and over two hundred and fifty miles. "Yeah. But he pulled through."

Andres shrugged. "For a little while, anyway. I'm sure hamburger was his endgame."

She scrunched her mouth closed and shot him a glare.

"Let's face it, sis. You've got a thing for wanting to save the underdog."

Micaela raised her eyebrows. "Believe me. This guy is no underdog."

"Sure he is. It's him against the world."

"Yeah." She peered intently into her mug, the dark and impenetrable coffee swirling around like the thoughts in her head. He was right. Mostly. "Them," she corrected. "It's them against the world. There's the woman, too."

Micaela's phone rang. She eyed it on the circular wood table between them and thought about ignoring it altogether. She sighed. Then she leaned forward and retrieved it before it stopped ringing. "Agent Mendoza."

It was Skye Freeman, the overly exuberant cyber-warrior from last night. *How did she get my number?* That was a stupid question. "What is it, Freeman?"

"Just checking to see if they assigned you to tonight's operation?" Her voice sounded tinny and far away. "We were killing it last night."

"There's an operation tonight?"

"Well, yeah. Didn't they tell you?"

"No. They pushed me out for a few days."

"Oh. Sorry. I didn't know. I thought Blevins would assign you to be the liaison. Especially since they pulled you off the manhunt for Cypher."

Micaela's heart dropped. "Jesus! They're still looking for him?"

"I don't think so. They've pulled everybody off it and assigned another assassin to hunt him down."

"An assassin? One of ours?"

"Yeah. Another NT. At least I think so."

"Shit! Look, Freeman. I need to track down Cypher before the other assassin does. But I can't do it on my own. I need access to some information only you could get."

"You mean real spy shit? Like legit?"

Micaela laughed. "Yeah. Real spy shit. Can you help me?"

"Fuck me! I'm on duty tonight, remember?"

"Then call off sick. Make some shit up or something. They've banned me from work, so I need you to come to my place in Golden. Can you do that for me?"

"Bet! All this cloak-and-dagger shit is dope!"

Young. Definitely young. "Good. I'll send directions to your phone."

Micaela stabbed the end call button and stood up. "I've got work to do, Andres."

"OK. What are you planning on doing?"

"What I do best. Try to save the underdog."

CHAPTER THIRTY-NINE

It was a moonless night, but Cypher's eyes adjusted to the dark long before he reached the shoreline. There was a warm, southerly breeze pushing in off the ocean, the rustling of the palm fronds above mere whispers in his ears.

He left the cover of thick jungle behind, made his way across the narrow strip of beach, and approached the docks with extreme caution. The lonesome clanging of a buoy bell in the distance warned of danger, its sound both mournful and foreboding. Strings of lights illuminated the pier, but burned-out bulbs provided deep pockets of shadows along its many berths.

Cypher kept a low profile as he slipped amongst the yachts and pleasure boats of the Bahía Perdida Marina, keeping in their shadows, moving down the dock from pillar to pillar.

He checked his watch. It was a quarter after three, and most of the boats were moored for the night, lights off, and their well-to-do owners fast asleep in their luxurious cabins below.

At the end of the pier, the fifty-meter luxury yacht, Negro Mako, sat idle, its sleek modern hull painted a glossy black, rendering its silhouette nearly invisible against the pitch of night. Despite the late hour, Cypher knew there would be a small security detail patrolling the upper decks, well-trained and highly motivated by the generous income of their patron, Berto Ramón Maduro.

He methodically worked his way closer to the yacht, painstakingly slow, burning precious time he didn't have. Hushed voices spoke without form in the dark, their colloquial Spanish rapid and almost indiscernible to Savage's rudimentary understanding of the language.

The faint sound of club music thumped somewhere deep within the bowels of the yacht. This was not unexpected.

He needed to slip down into the water and make his way to the starboard side of the ship, where his approach would go unnoticed.

The sheltered waters of the bay were warm like a tepid bath, waveless and inky black. Its surface, smooth and reflective, was like a looking glass.

It would be a fifty-meter swim beneath the water to the portside of the boat. Cypher cycled through several relaxed breaths to prepare his lungs for the final breath and then dove beneath the water. He had no light to see by, no sense of direction in the murky water. Just a diver's watch he used to keep his bearings. He glided through the water, maintaining excellent form to reduce drag and increase efficiency. With no oxygen tank and no fins, there would be minimal bubbles breaking the surface of the water to alert his approach. The black pitch of night would ensure the rest. Cypher checked his watch, noted the distance traveled, and allowed himself to float to the surface.

As his head broke the plane of the water, a bright beacon of light stabbed through the darkness, spotlighting Cypher as if he were an inmate breaking out of prison.

"Tú en el agua! Identifícate!" You! In the water! Identify yourself!

Damn! Cypher only had a moment to react. He was capable of holding his breath for over two hours. If he could just make a quick dive beneath the surface...

There was a muzzle flash, the sharp crack of a rifle shot...then nothing but darkness.

Savage gasped and sat up in bed with a start. Around him, there was nothing but darkness. Ravenous and all-consuming. It took him a moment to get his bearings, then he realized he was still in the motel room in Miami, the curtains drawn to keep out the sun. On the far wall, the air conditioner hummed and clanked defiantly, blasting its cold arctic air into the small room. It was freezing.

"Savage?" It was Eliana from the bed next to him.

He blinked, his mind still in a fog, trying to sort through—what? A dream? No. A memory. He wasn't really sure. "Yeah?"

"Are you OK?" The sound of her voice seemed tentative, nervous. "You sounded like you were having a bad dream."

Great. You woke her. "Yeah. I guess I was. I think I was remembering something. Something that happened to me a long time ago."

Silence.

She must have thought him some sort of nutcase. More silence. *Did she fall back asleep?*

"Are you scared?" she asked.

"No. Not really. It startled me. But that's not the same thing as being scared. It was reactionary. A fight-or-flight mechanism."

Silence fell upon them again. Then she finally said, "I'm scared, Savage. I'm so scared."

Savage lay back down, put his hands behind his head, and stared at the ceiling. A ceiling he couldn't see. He wasn't very good at this sort of thing. He was so used to working alone that he never knew what to say to someone. It was usually the wrong thing, so he learned to say nothing. But somehow she was different. She awakened something in him. And he ignored the warnings. "Why?"

"They're going to kill us, aren't they?" she asked, a slight quiver in her voice.

Savage thought he heard a sniffle. "They're going to try," he said. "But I'm going to give them one hell of a fight."

She said nothing at first. Then she whispered, "I know."

The air-conditioning cycled off, and the room fell morbidly silent again. It was an uncomfortable feeling, but she continued. "Let's say we somehow get away. What then?"

"We go into hiding."

"And if they find us again?"

"We kick and claw, we fight, and if we're lucky, we run again."

"But they're never going to stop, are they?"

Savage hesitated, thought about sugar-coating it, but decided against it. He owed her that much. "No. Not until they succeed."

Eliana began to cry.

Wow. Great job, asshole. That's why you keep your big mouth shut. He sighed. "I'm sorry. I'm not very good with this sort of thing. You know…talking to people. Girls…uh…women." Savage closed his eyes, rubbed away the tension in his temple.

Eliana's cries slowly turned into quiet sobs and, after a while, into just a few sniffles.

"Savage?"

"Yeah?"

"I don't want to be alone."

"You're not alone. I'm here."

"I mean…is it all right if I come over there and lie with you?"

"Um…I don't know if that's such a good idea…"

Eliana hadn't waited for his answer. Before he finished talking, she was already climbing into his bed. She slipped under the solitary sheet he was using to cover himself. As he had no clean clothes, he was completely naked.

She snuggled up against him, her arms tucked tight against her body. "It's so cold in here. I'm freezing."

"I could turn off the air-conditioning…"

"No. Don't get up. Just…just hold me."

Savage felt his heart skip a beat, and then it was off to the races. He hesitated, then removed his hands from behind his head and tentatively placed his arms around her. Eliana repositioned herself and turned into him, draping her leg over his and sliding her hand across his bare chest. She had been wearing her robe, but as she climbed into bed, it had fallen open, and they were now skin to skin. She purred. "Hmm. Much better."

Savage closed his eyes, trying to think of something else—anything else—but the warmth of her body pressing against his. *My God! She certainly doesn't feel like she's freezing.* Her body was on fire. And his body responded in kind. *Oh, shit.*

Savage felt her lift her head, and when he opened his eyes to look at her, she was staring back, a smile playing across her lips.

She laid her head back down, her shoulder-length hair spilling across his chest in soft curls, her fingers tracing delicate circles across his bare skin. Her hair smelled heavenly, sweet like honeysuckle, and her soft skin smelled clean, like soap—and of something else. Something indefinable, he thought. A scent that was both sweet and musky, and distinctly her.

"Savage?"

"Hm?"

"I want to ask you something. And I *really* don't want to offend you. So I'm not sure how to go about doing it."

"I find it best just to ask."

Eliana laid her hand flat across his chest, began caressing it. "You told me the government trained you to be an assassin. To take a life dispassionately. And to suppress your emotions. But I don't know if that's a deeply ingrained discipline or the nanobots. So…could you…" She stopped and took a breath to steady herself. "Are you able to feel? I mean…emotions and things?"

Savage blinked, caught completely off guard by the question, though he tried his damnedest not to let it show. "Yeah," he mumbled, feeling strangely hurt by the question. "I feel emotions…sometimes. Sometimes I feel angry. Sometimes I'm sad. And there are times I even feel happy. Why?"

"And how did I make you feel last night?"

Savage didn't follow, so he said nothing.

"You told me you've had me under surveillance for almost two weeks. Monitoring me."

"That's right."

"Last night, right before all this madness began, I had just finished taking a shower. I remember towel-drying my hair and then lying down in bed."

Oh, no. Savage closed his eyes, shook his head. He was in deep shit.

"You remember?"

"Yes."

Eliana turned her head toward Savage, resting her chin on the back of her hand. "Did you watch me?"

Savage looked into her eyes and held her gaze. He should have felt uncomfortable, expecting to find burning accusation and resentment staring back. But he found neither. "Yes."

She smiled, her perfect white teeth peeking beneath parted lips. If it had been a test of honesty, he passed. A test of virtue? Not so much. Then again, how much virtue could one expect from someone who killed people for a living?

"I see. Well, you have me at a distinct disadvantage, then." She lowered her eyes playfully, then looked back again. "You've seen me…most intimately. And I haven't seen you at all." Eliana rolled onto her stomach and scooted forward until her face hovered over his. She was staring deep into his eyes, her hair falling softly against his face, the tips of her breasts brushing lightly against his chest. She was so close he could feel her breath whisper across his lips. "I want you."

"Um. I'm not sure we have a lot of time. It's almost four o'clock, and we still need to eat before returning to the cobbler. Well, that, and we probably need to use some cash and buy new clothes…"

Eliana cupped her hand against his face, gently guiding his mouth toward her, and ever so softly pressed her lips against his.

Savage was stunned. He felt an electric shock fire from his head straight down to his toes. But he didn't know what to do. He tried to say no, that this wasn't a good idea, but the words wouldn't come. She kissed him again, allowed her lips to brush against his, teasing, nibbling at his lower lip. She tasted wonderful. Still, he didn't kiss back, though God knows he wanted to. *I need to stop this before it gets out of hand.*

When he didn't respond to her kisses, Eliana pulled back, opening her eyes. "Don't you want me?" she asked, her voice still soft and breathy.

"No. Well, I mean, yes! I do! But I think it's a terrible idea." *OK. I need to shut up now.*

"Oh. So you don't like me? Is that it? Or is it you just don't find me attractive?"

"Are you kidding? You're one of the most beautiful women I've ever seen."

"One of?" She raised an eyebrow, glaring at him with mock indignation.

Savage sighed. "I told you I'm not very good at this."

"I see. So it's just *who* I am that bothers you. Because of what I do for a living." Tears were welling in her eyes.

"No. Not at all, Eliana. Look at me. Look at who *I* am. Who am I to judge you?"

Eliana swallowed, tears spilling down her face.

"We're not all that different, you and I," he continued. "We've been dealt a bad hand in life, and all we're trying to do is make it to the next day by any means necessary. I can't admonish you for that. I admire you. You're tough. You're smart. Brave..." He let his words trail off. "You're a survivor, Eliana. We're both survivors."

She smiled. She understood him. Nodded in agreement. Then she leaned in and began kissing him again. And again he tried to protest in as many words, though he couldn't help himself, and was surprised to discover he was kissing her back. Another moment passed, and again he tried separating from her, to reject her advances. "We need to stop. We shouldn't be doing this. It's too distracting, and I need to be able to think straight."

Eliana laughed at that, a huge smile lighting up her face. "I like you, Savage. I really do. But you think too much. Sometimes you just need to stop thinking and allow yourself to *feel*."

She kissed him, more urgently now, her mouth greedy for more, her tongue testing, exploring. The sensations Savage felt were sensory overload, and he opened his mouth to hers. He was just as hungry, just as needy. His stomach was bursting with butterflies, terrified he would somehow mess it up. Afraid he would say the wrong thing. *Do* the wrong thing. Afraid it would end.

Eliana pulled her leg over and slid on top of Savage. She caressed his face, both hands guiding him to her mouth, ensuring he wouldn't draw away as she covered him with ravenous kisses. He slid his arms around her, his hands lightly stroking her back, feeling the tautness of her body, the smoothness of her skin. His hands continued to explore her back. Slowly. Gently. Lovingly. Until his hands came to rest on her hips. When the heat of their bodies finally merged, she groaned and slid her hands down to his chest and sat up.

He watched her succumb to the pleasure until he, too, was overwhelmed by the maddening sensation, and he closed his eyes. She began moving, slowly at first, rhythmic. Without thought. But he wasn't an idle spectator anymore. He sat up, his hands firmly gripping her waist, and his mouth found hers once again.

He opened his eyes, and he could see her in the dark. Her arms wrapped around his neck as she leaned back, her eyes still closed, her mouth open, moaning with approval. He couldn't remember the last time he had been with a woman, but he was certain he never felt anything like this.

"Déu meu…Savage!" Eliana's face was a mask of exquisite anguish, and she arched her back, allowing gravity to pull her down onto the bed. Savage had no choice but to follow, and he found himself on top of her. She wrapped her legs firmly around him and held him fast, urging him to continue.

Outside, in the late afternoon sun, the world continued without them. The rush of traffic passed. Sirens wailed, then faded into the distance. Out in the parking lot, a hooker and her john yelled at each other, cursing and carrying on. These things they didn't hear.

Inside their little motel room, Savage and Eliana found solace in each other's arms. They held each other's gaze, refusing to close their eyes, and finally offered their souls up to each other as only lovers could. They gasped, out of breath…moaned in ecstasy…and whispered sweet passions to each other, their voices quivering in surrender. These were the only sounds they heard.

There was no more fear. No danger. No need to run. There was only the two of them. And they made love. They made love until the sun slipped beneath the horizon and surrendered to the night.

CHAPTER FORTY

They lay in each other's arms, blissfully spent and not wanting for anything. Save another hour of sleep. That was a luxury they didn't have.

But Eliana didn't want to move. She continued to lie in Savage's arms, her head snuggled beneath his chin, purring with contentment. She didn't want it to end. Eliana wanted to hide away from the world. She wished she could spend more time just enjoying Savage's company. She thought of going out to breakfast at a cute little diner—Savage ordering bacon and eggs, her a platter of fruit—and sipping their coffees without care. Or better yet, she could cook him something at her place, hotcakes with maple syrup, and serve him in bed. Of course, after that, they would make love again, hot, passionate, and exquisitely slow. At *least* until noon.

Her thoughts continued to wander. She thought of them spending the day at the beach. Or maybe just shopping for clothes together. It would all seem rather mundane to most people. But not to Eliana. Right now, it seemed so perfect, so heavenly, that it made her want to cry.

She knew it was nothing more than a dream. Outside the motel room, reality awaited them both. But it made her want to hold on to Savage—and that fantasy—even more. To cradle that dream in her arms, next to her heart, for just a little while longer.

In the end, they had to leave it all behind. Savage found a thrift store just a few blocks down the road and, armed with Eliana's wardrobe sizes, bought a couple of clean outfits for them—some denim jeans and basic t-shirts along with a darling teal-blue sundress for her. On the way back, he stopped by Z-Bo's Beach Shack across the street and bought them a couple of bags of food to go. Not exactly health food: a couple of cheeseburgers, some fries, and a large Coke. Eliana didn't care. She was famished and devoured it all.

They took another quick shower and changed into their new clothes before leaving their little sanctuary behind.

Eliana wanted to wear her new dress but knew it wouldn't be practical, so she settled for the faded jeans and gray V-neck tee. The swelling had gone down on her knee, and it wasn't nearly as stiff, but Savage insisted she wear the elastic bandage, and he re-wrapped it for her. Then Savage changed into his clothes, abandoning his usual dark attire in favor of a simple white t-shirt and blue jeans. It was all about blending in now, but wow. He looked *amazing*.

"Where are we going?" she asked as they headed out the door. "Back to the cobbler?"

"No. Not yet. I need to check on our little friends at the news station and see if we can talk to somebody. We need to expose Operation Darkwater to the American people. Blow it wide open. Right now, it's the best way I know how to protect you."

The ride to WSVN was a little over eight miles, but Savage kept off the main roads as much as possible, so it took them twenty-five minutes to get there. When they arrived, he didn't go directly to the television station. He parked behind a building across the street called Grove by the Bay, a four-story commercial leasing complex that offered the perfect vantage point. It housed a diverse array of businesses ranging from daycares and ministries to cafes and medical offices. While the building wasn't readily accessible, it was a simple matter for someone with Savage's skill set. He just disabled a couple of cameras and picked a few locks. They made it to the top floor without incident.

They bypassed the push-bar security door and exited onto an open expanse of bare concrete roofing. There were no other structures to offer them cover. No decorative walls. No protective railings to keep them from falling. Just a small pile of discarded lumber that maintenance had been using to repair the stairwell walls.

There was a handful of commercial-grade AC units scattered about. The largest was only fifteen feet away from Savage and Eliana. That would give them a hide to work from and break up their profile to wandering eyes.

Savage crouched behind the bulky AC unit, and Eliana followed his lead. They focused their attention to the north, toward the Sunbeam Television building, home to WSVN and Channel 7 News.

He pulled out his compact monocular from his pants pocket and scanned the Sunbeam property for any signs of federal presence. It was an Invizera ND 6-12x25 monocular, capable of twelve times magnification and a field of view up to 210 feet at a thousand yards—even in low-light conditions. Savage calculated 150 yards.

He scanned from left to right, looking at the various trees and landscaping on the ground, and worked his way up two floors to the roofline. He found nothing. Nothing seemed out of place. No people loitering about. He turned to Eliana. "Are you ready for this?"

"Yeah. But do you think it will do any good?"

"No. Not really. There's no way that the feds would allow a major broadcast company to report the truth about us. But we should at least try."

"OK."

He handed her one of the burner phones, then the monocular. "Remember, it's important to stick to the plan."

"I know."

"It will take me a few minutes to get into place. Just stay put. Keep that phone with you. I need you to be my eyes in the sky for me."

"OK." Her voice sounded light, but Savage could tell she was nervous by the tautness of her face.

"After I make the phone call to the news desk, I'll call you back. We'll both keep watch. What we do next will all depend on how the news station responds. OK. Ready?"

She pursed her lips, then blew a loose strand of hair out of her eyes. "Ready."

★   ★   ★

Savage made his way down the stairs and crossed the street to an abandoned parking lot next to the television station. An unkept row of trees with undergrowth along its length created a natural blind for him to set up surveillance.

He watched the occasional car come and go, people employed by the station changing shifts. A Channel 7 News van returning from a remote broadcast. A couple of coworkers chatting over a cigarette break out by the entrance doors under the walkway canopy. Satisfied there were no police around, he retrieved his burner phone and made the call.

"News desk," the anonymous voice said.

Savage hesitated. It wasn't the same person he talked to last time. "I need to talk to your boss."

"Speaking."

Again, Savage paused, processing. "And you are?"

"This is Ken Levasseur. How can I help you?"

"*You* can't. I need to talk to the person in charge, not some lackey go-between. I need to speak to the woman I spoke to last night. Carol Henderson."

"Wait a minute. Let's back up. Who am I speaking to?"

"Brent Savage. I've talked to Carol before, and she's expecting my call."

"Did you say Brent Savage?"

Savage said nothing.

"Hello?"

"I'm still here. And I'm still waiting. And you still aren't Carol Henderson."

"Well, I'm sorry—Mr. Savage, is it? She's not here right now. Carol is taking some paid time off, and I'm filling in for her."

"That's a damn shame because I'm out of here, along with the biggest news story to hit Miami in the last ten years. So long…"

"Wait! Wait! *Wait!* Maybe I can help you."

Savage glanced at the phone and checked how much time remained before he hung up. "Fine. Let's see if you can. But first, let's cut the crap. You know who I am, Ken. All of fucking Florida does. Everybody is looking for me and Ms. Bautista. Every last patrolman, troopie, special agent, and traffic maid. But it's all bullshit. I'm not the Miami Sniper, and Ms. Bautista isn't a cop killer. All of that's been hung around our necks to slander us. To keep people from believing the truth, even when they hear it."

"Well, to be honest, Mr. Savage, I'm finding it difficult to believe you. What exactly *is* the truth?"

"That this is all an elaborate coverup. The U.S. government is running a black ops program that's targeting American citizens."

Silence.

"Do you have proof?" he asked.

"Yes."

"Then I need you to come on in. Let's get the real story. We might still be able to get it out on the ten o'clock."

"No. Can't trust you. We do it my way. Meet me at PortMiami, Terminal C. One hour. Come alone." Savage ended the call. Looked at the time. Satisfied, he took the SIM card out of the phone, removed the battery, and smashed it under the heel of his shoe. Then he took out another burner phone and made his call to Eliana.

"I still don't see a thing," she said, feeling pensive. But another minute passed, and she was giving in to hope. Maybe the feds hadn't been monitoring the television station after all.

"Keep checking," Savage said. "And keep an eye on the roof. They might send a team up there as a precautionary."

She placed the phone down and put him on speaker. "No...nothing. Just a bunch of junk. Air-conditioning units and things."

He said nothing. Just dead air.

"Savage?"

"Copy…take a look at the front entrance. The tall, bald man headed toward the parking lot. He seems to be in a hurry."

Eliana swung the monocular around to the front of the building, zoomed out a little, and then spotted the man Savage was talking about. He wasn't running, but almost. He practically skipped over the grassy median and went to the white Channel 7 News van. "Is that Levasseur?" Eliana felt her heart pounding. "Maybe he wants to break the big story after all."

"Maybe. But I don't think so. We'll let it play out. Copy?"

"OK…um, copy. You don't think it's him? You told him to come alone, right?"

"Yeah. But that isn't Levasseur. It's not even a reporter. Probably FBI."

Eliana didn't understand.

"Did you see what he was wearing? What would a beat reporter be doing wearing a black suit and tie? He's not a news anchor. And why take the news van at all? He has his own car. There's no need for all that equipment. There's no cameraman. Just him, remember?"

She zoomed in with the monocular and watched the van back out of its parking space and race away. The driver headed for the exit, made a sharp turn onto the causeway, his tires squealing, and then disappeared down the road.

Seconds later, more men came pouring out of the front of the building. At least half a dozen. All of them ran for their cars.

Eliana's heart sank. "Damn it." It felt like a rug had been pulled out from under her. All her hopes of freedom hinged on a single moment. And just like a house of cards, that moment caused all their plans to come tumbling down.

"It's all right," Savage replied, suddenly sounding far away. "It wasn't unexpected. At least we know."

"What *do* we know?"

"What we've always known. That we're going to have to find proof. Concrete evidence that the government is trying to kill you. All because the President fucked up—told you too much about a black ops program being used to terminate U.S. citizens."

"But he didn't. Not really."

"They don't know that. They're hedging their bets. Anyway, I'm living proof that it exists. But we need more. A lot more."

"What do you have in mind?"

"I need to think. But not here. Not now. What we need to do is get the hell out of Miami. Tonight."

Eliana watched all the men in suits hop into their cars, as the other man did before them, and speed away. Then they stopped at the causeway, yielding to the armored FBI SWAT truck advancing from the west, their lights ablaze. *We've sure stirred the hornet's nest now.*

Then she saw them: two men running across the parking lot, heading directly toward the Grove by the Bay building. Directly toward *her.* "Savage?"

"On my way."

"Um, Savage? There are a couple of men wearing suits heading toward this building. They're running this way. I think they're armed."

"OK. Don't move! Stay put! I'm on my way."

"Savage?"

There was no answer.

"Savage? Come in!"

Silence.

Eliana ducked behind the AC unit. It was running now, its exhaust fan buzzing in her ears. It was far too loud to think clearly. But she didn't know what else to do. "Savage!"

She turned off the hands-free speaker on the phone and placed it to her ear. "Savage?"

Nothing.

She crept forward, away from the fan noise, so she wouldn't have to raise her voice. She tried again. "Where are you?" Her heart was beating like a jackrabbit's.

When there was no answer, Eliana walked toward the front of the building, keeping low, trying to spot Savage. When she couldn't, she peered over the roof's edge for a better view. She then saw the two men in suits dashing across the sidewalk and heading to the main entrance of the building. They were coming for her!

"Oh, cagar!" Oh, shit! Eliana ran back to the stairwell door. She needed to get out of there before they figured out where she was hiding! She would have nowhere to run if they made it to the roof.

She pulled open the door to the stairwell and leaned partway in to see if she could spot the two men. Nothing. She took a few steps forward and peered down over the railing. She could see straight down to the ground floor, but still nothing. Then she heard it. Voices. Men's voices. They were bantering back and forth, insulting each other like a couple of college roommates. Then she heard the slam of a heavy steel door and the unmistakable sound of footsteps banging up the stairs.

Eliana gasped and ran the only way she could—back out the door and onto the roof. She started for the AC unit, wanting to hide, but quickly decided against it. That would be the first place they'd look.

She whirled around, saw the stairwell enclosure, and realized it was the only place for her to hide. It was a sizable L-shaped structure, with the farthest side being a four-story drop to her death. The exit to the roof, however, was on the west side. Perhaps she could hide behind the north wall, wait for them to pass by, and then make a mad dash to the door.

She tried to think of what Savage would do in such a predicament, with no weapons at his disposal. She choked back a laugh. What the hell was she thinking? Savage didn't need a weapon. He was the weapon!

The footsteps were louder now. They had made it to the top floor. They would come through that door any second now. Eliana looked down and spied the discarded pile of lumber she had seen earlier. She leaned down just far enough to grab a two-by-four and ducked back behind the wall. Then nothing.

She strained to hear, her breath coming in quick, shallow gasps. There were no more footsteps. No shouting. What the hell were they doing?

Then the door crashed open, startling Eliana so badly she nearly screamed and dropped the board. But as the man stepped out into the open, she lunged forward and swung the two-by-four with all her might. And she just missed Savage by mere inches. His incredible reflexes were all that saved him from having his head taken off.

"Oh my God! Savage! I'm sorry! Are you all right?"

Savage straightened and looked at Eliana. He nodded with appreciation and raised his eyebrows as if surprised. "Yeah. I'm fine. The question is, are you?"

Eliana threw herself onto him, wrapping her arms around his neck and pulling him tight against her. "Thank God you're all right! I was so worried. When I didn't hear from you right away, I thought something had happened to you. And there were some men—Savage! There are some men with guns coming up the stairs—"

"No. It's OK. They're not. Not anymore, anyway."

"Oh."

Savage remained silent, prompting Eliana to lean back from her crushing embrace to get a better look at his face. "Did you—"

"Kill them? No."

She offered him a little smile, keeping her arms around his neck as she looked up into his beautiful green eyes. Savage was a master of hiding his emotions. His face was all latex and putty. Malleable—able to take on any shape he chose for the world to see. Right now, he was smiling, but the expression never reached his eyes. And that, she knew, was where she could find the real Savage. There, she saw confusion. Frustration. And…anger? "Hey…what's wrong?"

He cast his eyes away, the tension in his jaw tightening. He shook his head, his brow pinched as he tried to find the words. "It's just that I—I thought you were in danger. The thought of them hurting you made me want to—"

"Hurt them?"

"I *did* hurt them. But I wanted to do far worse." He balled his hands into fists and looked back at the door. His knuckles were scraped and bloodied.

Eliana gave him a moment, allowed him the room to navigate his thoughts. She then gently cupped his chin and pulled his attention back to her. She smiled and caressed his cheek with her thumb. "I know you did."

"They would have killed you, Eliana. I promise you, they have orders to shoot on sight. And I can't—won't—allow them to hurt you."

CHAPTER FORTY-ONE

Somewhere near Denver, Colorado

This had been a piss-poor day. It was a cluster fuck and a complete waste of time. And time was something Spearman had precious little of. After he drove to the Control Center earlier that day, he got the teams pulled together and began working the problem: to locate Dr. Shepherd immediately and eliminate him at all costs. That had been his orders. Straight from the top. And complete bullshit.

He knew they still needed to find Dr. Shepherd. He had caused this nightmare in the first place. Sabotage. Pure and simple. Worse, he possessed the knowledge to expose the entire program—blow the whole damn thing up! But Spearman also knew that he could make things right again. He was the leading authority on nanotechnology in the country—hell, the world! And certainly the driving force behind all the recent advancements. As far as Spearman was concerned, to kill Dr. Shepherd was to kill the Dragonfly Project. That would be asinine. The good doctor could be brought back into the fold. He was certain of it. What they needed to do was stop Cypher, and Dr. Shepherd was the key.

They had lost track of the doctor outside the airport in Kansas City. They had spent the entire morning canvassing through the records of every bus station, taxi service, and rental company in the city to no avail. So they spent countless work hours scouring closed-circuit security cameras—not just the transportation hubs but across the entire city. Traffic cameras. Weather stations. Local mom-and-pop shops. Every camera from the airport to the state line, and still nothing.

But as good as the FRS was, Spearman knew it was far from perfect. Multiple things could cause software failure. Poor picture quality.

Obstructed views. Hell, even latex prosthetics could throw it off if Dr. Shepherd had the mind to use them.

Then, they finally received a break. They had got a hit on the FRS on a travel plaza's security camera just outside Columbia, Missouri.

Spearman stabbed out his cigarette and ran up two flights of stairs to the Control Center. He burst through the glass doors and leaped down onto each landing until he reached the center ring. "Talk to me, Blanton. What do you have for me?"

"The FRS just captured a positive ID on Dr. Shepherd. Probability sitting at ninety-seven percent. We have him unloading from a Greyhound at Midway Travel Plaza just outside Columbia, Missouri." Blanton nodded to the senior cyber-warrior assigned to the station, and the agent brought up the fuzzy black-and-white image onto the main screen. It offered about as much clarity as the 1969 TV broadcast of the Apollo 11 moon landing. That's to say, you couldn't see anything at all.

"And just as pretty as you please," said Spearman, smiling. It was the first thing that had gone right all day. "Clean up that image and see if you can stabilize some of that camera shake." The computer tech did as instructed and, with the aid of some specialized software, sharpened the image right up. "Roll it."

The recording advanced, showing Dr. Shepherd exiting the bus behind a large, heavyset woman. He almost disappeared behind the behemoth. Spearman made a face and rolled his eyes. "Well, at least we know why the FRS had such a hard time picking this up before now. Couldn't see him. When was this video captured?"

"Six twenty-five hundred hours, Juliet time."

Over fifteen hours ago! "Listen up! We are at least fifteen hours behind our target, which means he could be anywhere from LA to New York City and everything in between. Hell! By now, he could be sipping margaritas at a beach in Bora Bora. I need you to work the problem. Find every dipshit aunt, uncle, cousin, neighbor, or side-pussy Dr. Shepherd has ever known. And get yourself some coffee because it's going to be a long fucking night."

In an instant, the din in the control room jumped thirty decibels, the room bursting into a bustling hive of activity.

Spearman watched the doctor struggle to find his duffel bag amongst the pile of luggage left curbside by the bus company. He found it soon enough and began walking away from the station.

Spearman rested his hands on his hips, his eyes narrowing. *Just where the hell are you going, Doctor?* "Somebody get me an exact twenty on our target. Put it up on the MVS."

A few key taps later, the main video screen came alive with the security camera footage already rolling. Dr. Shepherd sidestepped a couple of cars entering the travel plaza and continued making a direct line to the main road.

"That's U.S. 40," somebody called out.

Dr. Shepherd looked both ways and did a half-trot across the road until he reached safety on the other side. It wasn't quite sunrise yet. The image was dark. Grainy. "Is there any way to clean this shit up? Can't see a damn thing!"

"No, sir. That's the best we got."

"That's West Cunningham Drive," a voice added.

"From there, we have five side roads," another interrupted. "All of them dead ends, with no other access. The longest of them is less than a mile."

Spearman watched the MVS until the washed-out gray of predawn swallowed the doctor into its grainy abyss. "What do we have back there?"

There was some more keyboard tapping, some banter back and forth, and then someone in research spoke up. "A whole lot of nothing. A smattering of houses, a few businesses—and a high probability of cow patties."

Spearman frowned. "What businesses are back there?"

"Missouri Pork Producers Association. Holcom Industries. And a small engine repair shop. Looks to be run out of their home."

"We can presume he isn't going to the small engine repair shop. The Pork Producers sounds like a small outfit, a little office. What the hell is this Holcom Industries?"

"It looks like a local aluminum fabricator. Employs around fifty people."

"All right, folks. That's what we're looking for. Get me into their security feed. I want to see everything in the last twenty-four hours. Inside the plant. Parking lot. An angle of the road, if we got it."

"We got nothing, sir," said a junior agent who looked stick thin but spoke in a surprising baritone. "No security cameras. No eyes inside or out."

Spearman leaned forward, resting his hands on the console in front of him. He exhaled through his nose, long and audible. "Fucking backwoods hillbillies. Whatever." He looked over to mission-com and made eye contact with Rutledge. "Get me somebody in charge on the horn. I want to know if anyone noticed anything unusual in the last couple of days. Strangers loitering about. People asking strange questions. Anybody walking by on foot, lugging a duffel bag on their shoulder." He tossed his hands in the air. "That ought to fucking stand out. There's nothing back there!"

"On it." Rutledge made the call.

CHAPTER FORTY-TWO

Miami, Florida

Marcos took a sip of his Cuban coffee, oblivious to its taste or effects. He didn't enjoy it. He drank it out of habit. Like muscle memory. A tic. Besides, he'd become impervious to caffeine—like all stimulants— when he joined the program two years ago. His tostada remained untouched.

The cyber cafe was dead. Not a soul around, save for the barista and the lifeless TV hanging from the gallows in the corner. Nobody wanted to be wired at this time of night unless you were a student cramming for a test. And they weren't interested in the free Wi-Fi. The students at Miami-Dade College had different ideas on how to spend Labor Day weekend. Marcos tapped away feverishly on his laptop, his hands striking the keys so fast it looked as if he didn't know how to type at all and was faking it. Typing two hundred and fifty words a minute required more than fast hands. It required a brain fast enough to process all that it was seeing and put it to use.

He had tracked Cypher on foot for a while, but the physical trail had gone cold. He needed a fresh approach. For most of the afternoon, he had spent his time scouring the web for clues that could lead him to the rogue agent. In less than an hour, he had tapped into the security feed of Miami-Dade Transit. In half that time, he found the video evidence he had been looking for: Cypher and Bautista on a dual sport motorcycle, riding the elevated platform of the Metrorail. Though they had knocked out the cameras at Santa Clara Station, the other security cameras down the line were still operational and captured them passing through various stations along the way. The last camera to capture them passing through was at Dr. Martin Luther King Jr. Station. There was nothing after that. A quick Google search and Marcos discovered another power outage reported by the MDT at Northside Station. He didn't need to go there to understand what had happened.

He had a starting point. Their last known position. He spent hours more systematically tapping into security cameras surrounding the station. There were sporadic hits, fleeting glimpses of them passing by on poor-resolution cameras. A Marathon gas station. A McDonalds. Even a kids' shoe store. But the truth was, there weren't enough of them to piece together even a best guess at their destination. And he was falling behind.

He had to ask himself why he was even trailing them. That was too linear. Ineffective. It just wasn't good enough to know where they had been. He needed to know where they were going. Get ahead of them.

He began with accessing old intel from previous missions. Not just what had been programmed into his cerebral cortex but also old CIA, FBI, ATF, and DCS databases.

There was a plethora of information still available to black-op agents who needed to contact the seedier side of Miami. Confidential informants, dealers, pimps, and loan sharks. Money launderers. Mafia hitmen and their cleaners.

Of course, many contacts and locations found in those files could also benefit his marks. These would be doctors, weapon suppliers, and even safe houses. Marcos found no evidence of Cypher having ever arranged for a safe house in Miami, although there were still a few around, maintained by various government entities. Cypher might have been looking for a doctor to patch him up. But he was just as capable of healing battle-grade wounds as Marcos, and he found this highly unlikely. He considered the possibility of the woman sustaining a severe injury. But again, he didn't think so. However, one thing in the database caught Marcos's attention. A cobbler. A forger of official documents. There were two listed in the Greater Miami area. An old Bosnian artist living in Brickell. The other, a slick Cuban pawn shop owner living near Opa-locka. That was where he was headed. Marcos knew this with absolute certainty. Cypher and Bautista would need to get new identities if they were to go into hiding. And they would need a passport should they try to leave the country.

The coffeehouse owner busied himself with wiping down empty tables and sweeping up floors that hadn't been walked on for hours. He kept working his way closer to Marcos. When he noticed the empty mug on his table, he tucked his damp rag into his apron pocket and quickly returned with an order pad. He offered Marcos a practiced smile. "May I get you another espresso, sir?"

It would have only been his second cup of the day. After spending hours at the cafe, occupying the old man's table and using his free Wi-Fi, Marcos had only ordered ten dollars' worth of food and drinks. When Marcos refused to order another, the old man's face soured, and he left to retrieve his check, grumbling as he walked to the service counter.

Marcos felt something akin to anger flash across his face, igniting his blood like an incendiary bomb. His posture remained unchanged, his expression cemented in stone. The owner popped his head into the kitchen and barked something unintelligible to one of the workers in the back. Moments later, a young girl returned to his table with his order ticket. She was deeply tanned and had long, straight hair reaching down the length of her back, with wide deep-set eyes that were as dark as the espresso in his mug. Her name tag read Anita, and he figured she was no more than sixteen. "Here is your bill, sir. Are you sure there isn't anything else we can get you tonight?" Her eyes shifted subtly to the untouched tostada. "Maybe something else to eat, more to your liking?" Marcos's eyes narrowed.

The owner was probably a relative of the girl. An uncle, perhaps. A distant cousin? Not a father—not hers, anyway. It was apparent that he had intended for the young woman to flirt with him, to pique his interest enough to stay. Spend a little more money. And perhaps that would have worked with some freshmen attending the nearby college. But

Marcos wasn't susceptible to such cheap manipulation. A teenager or not, if he had wanted her, he simply would have taken her. And for a moment, he considered this. But in the end, he decided against it. Not because of moral reservations. Nor for a lack of interest. Lust was primal, an innate animal instinct, and did not require an emotional response. He simply had more important things to attend to, and he was running out of time.

The girl must have seen something in his ghostlike eyes, cold and lifeless. The blood drained from her face, and she hurried away, leaving the check on the table for him to pay.

But Marcos had no intentions of doing so. He pushed his chair back from the table, its legs scraping on the wood floor like a squealing pig. Silence followed, and the check remained on the table.

The owner stood behind the counter, next to the girl, and he stiffened as Marcos approached, fighting an overwhelming urge to run. He opened his mouth to speak, but wisely said nothing.

Marcos drew in close, and the girl's eyes widened with fear. She turned to leave, but he grabbed her by the arm, forcing her to stay. His eyes never left the owner's. "You are lucky, *viejo*, that I am only leaving you with debt." His Cuban accent lay heavy on his clumsy attempts at English. He gestured to the teenage girl, then slowly returned his attention to the old man. "There are things far worse I could have taken from you than your time and money. Lucky for you, I have more important things to attend to. *Dulces sueños, viejo.*" *Sweet dreams, old man.*

CHAPTER FORTY-THREE

Somewhere near Denver, Colorado

"Let's hear it, Rutledge. What do you have for me?"

"OK. I got a hold of the plant manager. His name is Blake Caldwell."

"Good. Patch him in."

Spearman switched on his headset, adjusted the mic's position, and leaned on the console. "Mr. Caldwell. My name is Theo Spearman. Thank you for taking time out of your busy schedule today to help us out. Any information you'd care to share with us would be greatly appreciated and considered a great help to your country."

"Sure. Your man said you guys are with the FBI?"

"Clandestine Services," he corrected, knowing all too well that without context, it was just useless jargon.

"Not sure I can help you, but I'll do my best."

"Fine. Thank you. I've been told you don't have any security cameras on the premises. But I know that sometimes companies secretly have one or two around the facility to monitor their staff's behavior. Do you have any cameras that others may not be aware of?"

"Well…none that *I'm* aware of!" He chuckled at that, his sophomoric sense of humor lost on Spearman. When he didn't laugh, the man added, "No, sir. We have no cameras on the premises."

Fucking hillbilly. "Don't you guys ever worry about theft, Mr. Caldwell?"

"In an aluminum fabricating plant?"

Spearman glanced at his watch. "I figured it was a long shot. So, have any of your workers seen anybody strange hanging around?

Maybe someone stopped in and asked some questions of you or your staff?"

"No, sir. But one of our workers has a wife who wanted to get out early to the grocery store this morning before it got too busy—being Labor Day weekend and all. Anyway, she noticed a man walking down the road with a duffel bag over his shoulder. It stood out to her at the time because he seemed as determined as a Missouri mule to find his way to the end of a no-outlet road. I heard some men joking about it in the break room earlier today."

Spearman pointed to Blanton and nodded.

"Thank you. That's very helpful. Anything else odd or out of place?"

"Well, sort of…not sure if it's relevant, though."

"OK. Shoot."

"Well, we don't have a third shift here, but we start pretty early. Being the plant manager, I get here about an hour before anybody else. When I arrived, a car with Kentucky plates was sitting in our parking lot. The windows had been collecting dew, so it looked like it had been there all night."

"So you've never seen that car there before?"

"No, sir. And I asked around. Nobody here at Holcom has recently bought a new car, so I don't have a clue where it came from. But here's the funny thing. I had a small custom order ready for delivery to one of my repeat customers. It needed to be there early and was on the other side of town. I probably left about seven o'clock. But that car with the Kentucky plates was gone. Just an empty parking space."

Spearman pointed at Blanton again and began snapping his fingers, trying to get his attention. He gestured to the outer ring of the control room, letting him know he needed the cyber team to get a jump on this. He flipped a switch, turning off the microphone to the headset. "I need eyes on that video feed from the truck stop this morning."

Blanton asked him, "What are we looking for?"

Spearman turned the mic back on. "Can you tell me, Mr. Caldwell, what make of car it was? Model. Year. Even a color would be helpful."

"You bet. It was a silver Ford Focus."

"Four doors?"

"Yeah. And it looked brand new. Probably this year's model."

"Anything else you can think of?"

"No. I guess that's about it. But if I think of anything else, I'll call you."

"OK. You do that. Thank you so much, Mr. Caldwell. You've been an incredible help. Bye now." *Fucking simpleton.*

Spearman tapped a button on the console computer, and the video feed from this morning pulled up on the MVS. "All right, people. I need to locate a new Ford Focus sedan, silver with Kentucky plates. It will exit West Cunningham Drive sometime between six and seven a.m. And for those directionally impaired, that will be right toward the camera, folks."

They fast-forwarded through the video until just before the forty-minute mark. They stopped the image when a silver Ford Focus appeared at the intersection across the street—turning left toward the interstate. The sun had crested the horizon by then, and the lighting was much better. Still, they failed to get a positive ID on the driver. What they came away with was a better read on the license plate.

"Let's find out who this car belongs to—now, people! Tomorrow does me no good."

The rapid fire of fingers tapping keyboards filled the room. People cross-chatting. Computer drives whirling. A cacophony of agents diligently working. This was how it was supposed to be.

"I have it," an agent said. "The car is registered to Avis Rentals, purchased in December last year."

"I need more, Agent."

"Yes, sir. Working on it…"

He jumped through a few more windows on their work portal and had what he was looking for in less than a minute. "Last rented yesterday in Indianapolis at sixteen-oh-two. The East 82nd St location.

Rented by Gary Fischer from Mansfield, Ohio. As of this morning, it has not been returned to any of their nationwide locations."

Spearman just nodded, offered no ridiculous platitudes or sentiments. It was their job. "Send it to my console, Agent."

The agent complied and continued with his work.

"OK, people. Listen up. Our target has outside help. We need to find everything there is to know about Gary Fischer. I'm transmitting an image of the rental agreement to each of your stations. You have a birthdate, address, phone number, and signature. I need to know everything you can find on this guy. Is he married? How about kids? Where does he work? And most importantly, I need to know his connection to Dr. Shepherd. This is the break we've been waiting for. I need answers! Let's cast that net, folks."

Spearman flipped off his mic, then turned to Blanton with a stone-cold expression on his face. "Put out a BOLO on the Ford Focus. And while we're at it, let's have someone pay Mr. Fischer a visit."

CHAPTER FORTY-FOUR

Morgantown, West Virginia

The sound of the Jake Brake growled like two pit bulls fighting, jarring Dr. Shepherd out of his deep, toe-warming slumber. His eyes opened and narrowed into two thin slits, unable to focus on the dimly lit interior of his rental car. He felt a trickle of saliva oozing from the corner of his mouth, and he wiped it away with the back of his hand. He fully opened his eyes, hoping to see through the cloudless fog of sleep, and struggled to remember where he was.

A sharp rap on the driver's side window startled the doctor, causing him to jolt upright and sending his heart racing. A piercing bright light shined into his car. "Hey, buddy. Are you all right?"

Dr. Shepherd shielded his eyes with his left hand like a sun visor, wincing at the intrusion. *I'm dead! They found me.*

"Oh, good. You're still kicking. You had me worried there. Thought you were dead or something," the man slurred, his voice sounding muffled and far away. The man switched off the torch on his cell phone and tapped on the car window again. He gestured for the doctor to roll down the window.

The fog in his mind cleared, and Dr. Shepherd complied. He was immediately greeted by the snap of the chilly night air. And the stink. The man's breath reeked of whiskey, and his cheeks burned with the aftereffects of a Saturday night out on the town. It wasn't the police. *Thank God!*

Now he remembered. He had driven for twelve consecutive hours, except for that quick pit stop he made just outside of Dayton. He stopped at a burger joint long enough to relieve himself, grab a coffee and an order to go, and was on his way again. By the time he reached Morgantown, the doctor had been up for forty-six hours straight, and he could no longer keep his eyes open. A hotel room was out of the question. And he knew enough to avoid any rest stops or any other place that might have cameras. He found an isolated gravel lot behind a local bar and laundromat off University Avenue and immediately fell asleep. He glanced at his watch. *That was what? Two hours ago?* He sighed.

"You OK to drive, bud?"

"I haven't been drinking," he said. His tongue felt thick, and his lack of sleep left him feeling punch-drunk, like he had been in a boxing match. "I'm just tired," he croaked.

The man grinned and gave him a sharp nod. "OK. Well, just an FYI, you don't want to hang around here in your car. This area is patrolled pretty heavily by the campus police. There's a motel just down the road, about two blocks down. Local college kids use it all the time, if you know what I mean. I'm sure they charge by the hour."

"Thanks. I think I'll do that."

"Sure. Goodnight. And be careful now."

There was a moment of silence between them. Then it was broken by the slow and steady roll of tires over gravel, the rocks beneath crackling and popping as they gave way. It was the police.

Oh, shit!

The cruiser came to a stop, and the patrolman rolled down the window. "Are you two in need of assistance?"

Of course, what he really meant was, *what are you two up to?* Up to no good, no doubt.

Dr. Shepherd's heart sank. He had spent meticulous, unimaginable hours planning his escape. Going over every detail. Every little step of the way. Only to have it derailed by a nosy drunk and a sleep-induced lapse in judgment on his part. Why did he choose a bar parking lot—of all places—to crash? It must have looked like he was trying to solicit drugs from a dealer. Even if this neighborly busybody had no drugs on him, which was questionable, he was clearly drunk. Naturally, the police officer would then question Dr. Shepherd, ask him to step out of the car—ask to see his driver's license. After that, nothing else would really matter. It would all be over.

Dr. Shepherd heard the officer shift the cruiser into park, preparing to call it in and step out of his car. But out of the blue, a pickup truck full of college kids blasted on by, music blaring, girls screaming, hootin' and hollerin' down University Avenue.

The smugness on his face shattered like glass and fell away. He had lost interest in Dr. Shepherd and the stranger. He gave them both a withering glare, the kind dads give their misbehaving children, and said, "Stay put. There's another patrolman on the way."

Of course, there wasn't. Not really. And even if there was, Dr. Shepherd wasn't about to find out. When the police cruiser took off in pursuit of the rowdy college kids, Dr. Shepherd put the car in drive and tore out of the parking lot, a rooster tail of gravel spraying in his wake.

With adrenaline now pumping through his veins like rocket fuel, Dr. Shepherd would have no more problems staying awake for the three-hour drive to Baltimore.

CHAPTER FORTY-FIVE

Miami, Florida

They took it slow down the stairwell. Savage knew Eliana's knee was still stiff and considered taking the elevator, but decided against it. He didn't want to walk into an ambush. So they took their time instead.

The swelling in her knee had decreased significantly since yesterday. It obviously didn't bother her so much that it had kept her from performing acrobatics in bed earlier. Not that he was complaining. He figured it must have been the adrenaline.

They passed the unconscious bodies of the two FBI men on the third-floor landing, their faces noticeably swollen and bloodied. One was face down, their right arm bent at an unnatural angle. The other? It would be a long time before he walked again—at least without the aid of crutches.

Eliana hesitated, but didn't stare for too long. "What about them? Won't they call this in?"

"You mean when they wake up? Inevitably. But we don't have the time for me to lock them up in a closet somewhere. We need to get going while we still can."

Eliana said nothing at first. She just took his hand and allowed him to coax her along. When they reached the ground floor, she finally said, "By yourself?"

"What do you mean?"

"How would you take two full-grown men down several flights of stairs and put them into a closet?"

Savage chuckled a little, pushed on through the doors to the back parking lot, and walked with Eliana to the motorcycle. "Well, I could have just asked them nicely to go in the closet, but I'm sure they would have been reluctant."

Eliana returned the smile, her eyes crinkling with amusement. She played along. "Oh? And what would you do then?"

He raised his eyebrows, shrugging. "I've already done it."

CHAPTER FORTY-SIX

The ride to the cobbler's house was uneventful. The FBI and local law enforcement were converging on PortMiami, deploying enough firepower that it wouldn't have shocked Savage to find they emptied the city streets of all police presence. They would be severely pissed off when they found out they had been duped. But it would be at least an hour before they figured that out. In the meantime, there was nothing in their way of a clean getaway.

The cobbler was expecting them and, as agreed upon, had all their documents finished and ready for them to review.

Savage looked them over and reluctantly admitted they were of excellent quality. As good as anything Control had ever set him up with. Eliana's were equally good. *Mitch and Karyn Fields.*

"Just two *turistas,*" the cobbler said, beaming. "Enjoying their vacation in sunny Miami."

"Before I pay you the rest of the cash, what assurances can you give us you've kept no record of our fake personas or any of the other forged documents?"

"Oh. I am very careful, Mr. CIA man. Nobody has access to my information. I assure you, your business transaction with me is secure and will remain private."

That amused Savage. He still thought he was with the CIA. But what was more amusing was that he still thought his assurances would be good enough for Savage. "Sorry. That won't do."

Savage pulled out the Glock 17 he lifted from the FBI agent earlier and pointed it at the Macintosh computers the cobbler used for photoshopping. He fired three rounds into each of them, sparks and smoke bubbling up in the aftermath.

"*Santa Madre de Dios!*" *Holy Mother of God!* "Why in the hell did you do that?" The cobbler reached back for a pistol he had stashed away in the waistband of his pants. He'd learned fast from their earlier encounter. However, it wasn't unexpected. Savage already had his Glock trained on the man, leaving him with no choice but to stop and raise his hands in compliance.

"The forged names are simple enough for you to remember. There's nothing I can do about that. But I need to ensure there's no evidence left behind that's traceable back to us." Savage gestured for the cobbler to turn around. He did as he was told. The man let out an audible cry, choked off deep in his throat, terrified he was about to be assassinated. But Savage only tucked the gun back into his pants and told him to turn back around. "Here's the cash we agreed upon." He tossed it down on the counter in front of them. "Good thing you charged us the extra fees. Now you can afford to replace your computers."

The cobbler groaned. Savage just shook his head. He knew the original price agreed upon wasn't that important to the cobbler. The real value was the data he kept on all his clientele. Criminals, law enforcement—and the government—would all pay handsomely to obtain it. In all reality, the cobbler just lost out on hundreds of thousands of dollars on future money ventures.

"It was nice doing business with you."

"I wish I could say the same, *amigo*."

CHAPTER FORTY-SEVEN

Their problems were many. They needed to get out of Miami, and time was of the essence. The longer they were on the run, the more time Control had to lock them in, to trap them. And the deeper their bullshit story would become entrenched in the public's mind.

Savage had a destination in mind, but to get there fast, they would need to fly. That was the second problem. They couldn't just march into Miami International and expect to buy tickets. There would be cameras everywhere, heightened security, and an unimaginable number of undercover federal agents walking the concourses. Maybe even handing out flyers for people to keep an eye out for them. But a civil airport. An airport like Opa-locka? That was a different story. They needed to charter a private plane, and Opa-locka gave them a better chance of avoiding scrutiny. And circumventing security. Probably. They would address that problem when they got there.

Another problem was they would have to find a pilot to fly them out of there. Someone who wasn't above a bribe or, at the very least, being paid an overly exorbitant fee. Again, that would be something they would have to address later.

It was only a short distance to the airport from the cobbler's house. Even with the extra precaution of taking back roads when possible, it was only a fifteen-minute ride. That should leave them enough time to do what they had to do.

Then the motorcycle died. Right there on Superior Street. Just one more problem heaped onto the pile.

Savage tried to start it, but it wouldn't turn over. He checked the tank. The fuel was low, but there was enough to keep it running. He gave the engine a quick once-over, but nothing was immediately apparent. Vapor lock? Fuel filter? Maybe a blocked fuel line? It didn't matter. It wouldn't start anytime soon.

"Can you fix it?" Eliana asked.

"No. We don't have the tools or the time."

"What are we going to do, then? Walk?"

"Yeah. But I figure the airport is two to three miles from here. About a forty-five minute walk." He glanced at her leg. "Maybe. But that'll take too long. I don't see we have a choice. We're going to have to steal another vehicle."

"But won't that take time, too?"

"Not if I find the right one."

Eliana gave a quick nod, resigning herself to the inevitable. "OK." So, they walked, looking for a car to steal.

It was another steamy night, the kind where the moisture in the air oozed across your skin and weighed you down like a wet mohair suit.

The neighborhood looked rough. Dangerous. And a definite step down from the cobbler's. It was equally clear they shouldn't be there after dark. Not even to pass through.

There was no one around, the streets abandoned for the night. Residents barricaded themselves and their possessions behind their chain-link fences, giving themselves a modicum of security. Those without figured they had nothing worth stealing, though their yards remained littered with a veritable treasure trove of trash: kids' sunbaked toys, folding chairs, wheelbarrows, and flat tires. There was even a yard with a broken commode.

The ratcheting buzz of the cicadas in the trees was overpowering, nerve-racking, like a dentist drill. The streetlights were few and far between, and most of the houses were unlit, though occasionally the soft flickering light of a TV could be seen through the window curtains. All else was dark.

They walked only for a short distance—maybe half a block—when Savage spotted an older Hyundai Accent parked along the side of the road. It was a faded blue, and like the neighborhood, it was in rough shape. The body was rusting out, and some sort of collision had left the front panel and bumper crumpled. If it would start, it would do.

Savage peered into the driver-side window to see if the car had keys in the ignition. It didn't. Nor did it matter. The door was unlocked, and a USB phone charger was plugged into the dash.

"Is this what you were looking for?" Eliana asked. "It doesn't look like much."

"No, it doesn't. But I'm not interested in what it looks like. I just need it to get us to where we need to go."

She looked skeptical.

Savage smiled and reached for his multi-tool. "This model of car is lacking an immobilizer. I just need to tear off the plastic panel around the steering column and pop off the ignition cylinder." He leaned into the car and pulled out the phone charger. "I can turn the engine over with this. We'll be out of here in a couple of minutes."

No sooner had he said the words than a car turned the corner down the road and started toward them. Its LED headlights bounced up and down, a lowrider doing its dance, as the cannon speaker in the trunk thumped its driving bass, warning everyone of their pending arrival. *Gangbangers.*

Eliana's first response was to run, but Savage grabbed her hand and forced her down behind the front of the Hyundai, away from the approaching car's field of view. He met her eyes and put a finger to his lips.

As it drew nearer, they skirted their way down the length of the Accent, always keeping the car between them and the approaching threat. And as they reached the trunk, the pimped-out car slow-rolled on by, as if suddenly on alert. A shark smelling blood in the water. It was a gold 1982 Olds Cutlass with black pinstripes, custom wheels, white-walled tires, and a hydraulic suspension. But it was no longer bouncing. They were on the hunt, the engine just idling, rumbling, as the Olds continued to roll down the street.

Savage and Eliana had made it around to the back of the car. Silent. Watching it drive farther away.

The car stopped, its taillights painting the road red. Then the backup lights lit up, and the car slammed in reverse. The tires squealed, rubber burning, as great clouds of billowing white smoke obscured their view.

Their cover was blown. The gangbangers knew they were there.

Savage's heart rate ramped up like a top fuel dragster, going from zero to a hundred. Adrenaline poured into his bloodstream. His muscles tensed, his fists clenched. Fight or flight. Those were his choices. There would have been no question if this occurred during his time with Operation Darkwater. He would have killed them all with no second thoughts. No remorse. But now…things were different. Different in ways he couldn't fathom.

But Savage knew they couldn't run away, either. Eliana would never be able to keep up, never match his speed or endurance. And he could never leave her behind. It was a no-win situation.

Savage took Eliana by the hand and pulled her along, urging her to hurry. They ran toward the nearest yard, a house with no gate to keep the riffraff out.

Four Black men jumped out of the car, ran into the yard, and quickly closed the gap between them. They were whooping and hollering, badgering them. Hurling insults like foreplay. "Hey, lil' *mamacita*! What's the hurry?"

"What da fuck, bitch? Your spic ass too good for us? You in the wrong hood, bitch."

"She's a fuckin' spic," one of them repeated. He was just a kid. Looked to be about thirteen.

"Yo! What you doin' with this white cracker, then?" another asked, wearing sunglasses as if it were high noon.

The gang moved in on them, pressing their position, shoving Savage in the chest. Lunging for Eliana. Their movements were fluid. Ever changing. But always pressing, always aggressive. Savage kept Eliana moving backward toward the house, keeping his arm extended toward her, forcing her to retreat, keeping her on the move.

The gang continued to badger, cackling like a pack of hyenas nipping and harassing a solitary lion. "What da fuck, bitch. Your man a limp dick?" said the man with a gold-plated mouth grill.

"Nah. He ain't got no dick," said Sunglasses.

Eliana reached the porch. Her eyes were wide with terror. She turned and pounded on the barricaded storm door. "Help! Please help us!"

There was no response. No lights turned on in the house. No door opened. There was only silence.

"Open the door!" she screamed, her voice becoming shrill.

"Maybe she needs a real man," said the one with tattoos covering his face. He was older. Had clearly done some time. The leader.

Grill Mouth laughed. "Yo! Fo sho! How about you, BG? You a player?" He was talking to the kid. Baby G.

"Hell, yeah!" the kid said, lowering his voice to make himself sound older. Tougher. But his wide eyes told a different story. He looked scared.

Savage felt the tension in the air change. This was it, he thought. The moment had come. He looked around, his mind racing. Scouring his surroundings. Using his mind's eye to see the battlefield. Noting avenues of escape and looking for objects he could use as improvised weapons.

The yard was littered with a motley collection of kids' toys and had an odd assortment of gardening supplies, fertilizer, and bug sprays. The owners had even tilled the yard as if it were perfectly normal to plant a garden in front of their house. But it didn't matter. There were enough items for Savage to work with.

Switchblades appeared as if out of thin air. Snicked open. At least one of them, maybe two, had a gun. Sunglasses was one of them. He pulled out his Hi-Point .45 ACP and shot it at Savage.

Savage moved so fast it was disorienting. Surreal. In one fluid motion, he sidestepped Sunglasses, grabbed the gun barrel with his left hand, and pushed it away. The gun fired a second time before Savage used his free hand to bend the man's wrist in on itself. It snapped like a twig. And the man fell away, screaming in agony. Savage held on to the gun, ejected the clip. Then tossed it away.

He spun toward the large man with the gold grill. But it was too late. Grill buffaloed him with a brutal right punch, knocking him to the ground. The man was a big, no-neck, muscle-bound behemoth who hit so hard that Savage nearly blacked out from the blow. And Grill wasn't about to wait around for him to get up. He was going to stomp him in the head, but Savage caught his foot at the last second and gave it a sickening twist. The man's ankle spun around like spaghetti on a fork, and he collapsed beneath his own weight. He landed on one knee, his face contorted in a silent scream.

Savage performed a kip-up, springing gracefully to his feet like a cat, then kicked the man in the face, breaking his jaw and knocking him out. Grill was down and wouldn't be getting up anytime soon.

"Motherfuckin' cracker! I gonna kill you, white boy!" screamed Sunglasses, finally staggering to his feet, his shooting hand hanging limply at his side. In the other, he held a sawed-off semi-auto shotgun. Savage had no idea where it had come from, but he wasn't about to take the man or the gun too lightly. Even with Sunglasses being forced to shoot off-handed, he still held a formidable weapon. Savage ripped the gun from his hands, elbowed him in the face, and swung the shotgun hard into his temple. Sunglasses collapsed as if a breaker switch had been thrown. Two down.

Again, he ejected the shells from the gun and tossed it over the fence. He turned his attention back to the others, but before he could turn around, Savage heard Eliana scream, "Look out!"

Savage ducked and twisted his body, pivoting as if on a swivel. Years of training as an assassin had honed his skills, created muscle memory. His reflexes were now instinctive. The knife struck him any-way. Its blade stuck through his forearm. It would have been buried in his back if he hadn't reacted so quickly.

It was the tattooed man. He was reaching for another weapon and found it. Then charged. It was another knife.

Savage saw a kid's plastic wiffle bat at his feet, flipped it up into his hand with a nifty kick move, and received Tattoo's charge head-on. He caught the knife in the bat's barrel, then yanked it away, ripping the knife right out of his assailant's hand. The man blinked, not understanding what had happened. But before he could react, Savage slammed the butt of the bat into Tattoo's throat. The bat wasn't heavy. But it applied sufficient force into such a small surface area that it crushed his larynx. The man's eyes fluttered. Then he dropped like a stone, falling flat on his face. He gurgled. His legs twitched. Three down..

Savage glanced down at his arm and saw the switchblade sticking in it. There was no pain. Just a minor inconvenience. He grabbed the hilt of the knife and pulled it out. A pool of blood spilled down his arm. But there was no major artery damage.

Eliana must have seen the wound. She screamed and ran to him. She made it halfway before he held up his other hand. Yelled for her to stay back. "I'm fine!"

Only Baby Gangster remained. Who, up to this point, had been too scared to enter the fray. Smart. Until now. Whether it was a sense of loyalty to his gang family or not wanting to be labeled as a chicken, BG pulled a Smith & Wesson M&P pistol and raised it to shoot. He fired, blinking in anticipation of the recoil. He missed.

Savage reached down into the pile of garden supplies and grabbed a canister of wasp and hornet spray. *Accurate up to twenty feet.* It would do. Savage took two steps forward and sprayed BG directly in the eyes. He collapsed to the ground, clawing at his face and howling like a scalded child. The last one was down.

Savage walked over, grabbed a folding chair, and placed it down over the thrashing kid's throat, effectively pinning him to the ground. He rested one foot on the seat to make his point: he was in control. "A piece of advice, kid. Get the hell away from here, as far as you can. And don't come back. You don't need this. Trust me. You'll live longer."

Savage dropped his leg off the chair, reached down, and picked up the kid's pistol.

Then he heard someone scream, "Drop it! Drop it, muthafucker, or I'll fuckin' cut this greaser from ear to ear."

Savage froze.

Fifteen feet away, another gangbanger had Eliana in a lock hold. He held an eleven-inch switchblade to her throat.

Where the hell did he come from? Savage had been wrong. There weren't four gangbangers. There were five.

He dropped the gun.

CHAPTER FORTY-EIGHT

Eliana watched in horror as the gangbangers surrounded Savage. Attacked him. Tried to kill him! But he was so fast, so elusive—they couldn't get a hold of him. And one by one, he disposed of them. Swiftly and efficiently. Brutally.

She continued to pound on the iron bars of the door until her knuckles bled. Screamed until her throat burned. It was useless.

She had to help Savage. She couldn't fight. Didn't know how. And she was probably more of a hindrance than a help. But Eliana couldn't just stand by and watch them attack Savage.

Then she noticed the man with the tattooed face making a run at Savage, knife in hand. He was going to stab him in the back! Ice-cold terror washed over her. She screamed, "Look out!"

Savage spun around just in time, barely avoiding the stab in the back. Instead, his left forearm took the brunt of the blow. It didn't slow him down. She watched in amazement as he took a kid's toy and put the man down in seconds.

That's when she saw he was wounded. A switchblade was sticking out of his forearm, with only the knife's hilt still visible. She completely lost her mind. Screamed. And ran into harm's way.

She only managed a handful of steps before something hard struck her in the head. Dazed her. The world swam around her, her eyes going in and out of focus. Her legs wilted like a dying flower, and darkness pressed in around her. She felt herself passing out. But she never hit the ground. She then realized that one of the gangbangers had her in a headlock, keeping her up. Holding her hostage. His right arm was so tight around her throat that she couldn't speak, couldn't breathe.

He wasn't a big man. Not much taller than her. His arms were thin. Wiry. And surprisingly strong. He had long dreadlocks, thick like strands of rope, and reeked of sour body odor.

She watched Savage put the teenage boy down through blurred eyes. Watched him take his time. Heard him talking to him. But she couldn't warn him, scream for him to watch out. She was entirely at the mercy of her attacker.

When Savage turned to her and saw that she was being held hostage, it broke her heart. He had fought so bravely, with a confidence that only absolute certainty could provide. There was never a doubt in his mind about the outcome. Until his gaze met hers. His focused, determined eyes fell flat, doused by the inevitability of defeat. When the man told him to drop the gun, he did as he was told.

The gangbanger shifted his stance, lowered his arm from her throat, and dropped it to her chest. For a second, she thought she might be able to break free. But then she felt it. The cold steel of the switchblade on her throat.

"Now step back, mothafucka! Leave it. I said leave the gun!"

Savage backed away slowly so as not to startle him, his arms raised chest high. He moved back ten feet.

"Yeah, you smart. Now get down. Put that mothafuckin' grill down in the mud, cracker! Now!"

Savage didn't move. He kept his arms out to his sides, palms up, showing him he wasn't a threat. Had no weapons.

Eliana's heart was racing so fast, she was sure the man could feel it pounding in her chest. She was terrified not just for her own life but for Savage's.

She tried to stomp on the man's foot and strike him in the balls. But his sideways stance protected him, kept her from reaching him. It proved to be nothing more than an annoyance to him—a stick poking a bear.

"Naw. Naw. None of that, bitch. I'll fuckin' cut you, fo sho." The man pressed the knife up against her throat, a thin trickle of red beading up along its long, sharp blade.

Savage took a step forward, but then stopped. His fear was overriding his instincts.

They were in a standoff. And both men knew it. Despite his bravado, the gangbanger wasn't stupid. He knew Eliana was his only protection against this crazy white man in front of him who had taken out four of his friends in a matter of seconds. He stood no chance one-on-one in close combat.

Savage must have known it, too. He refused to lie down.

"Don't think I won't do it!" he warned, his voice growing hot with frustration. "Yeah. Yeah. That's right. Maybe I'll just cut up her fuckin' pretty little face. Cut it up real good." He held the knife up in front of her face, flicking it around as if showing Savage how he would do it.

Eliana choked back a cry, heard it strangle in her throat. She closed her eyes.

The man leaned in close, his lips pressing against her temple. His breath was revolting. It smelled strangely of licorice. Anisette. And something far worse. Foul. He whispered, "Be a shame to cut up a fine-lookin' greaser like you."

She felt the knife press against her cheek, knew he meant to cut her. She swallowed hard and screwed up enough courage to open her eyes.

In that instant, everything about Savage had changed. Gone was his passive demeanor, his non-threatening expression. It was replaced with something far more serious. Far more sinister.

Savage stood rigid, a steel spring coiled tight, ready to unload. His muscles were taut and twitched with a nervous sort of energy. His brow was weighed down by an angry scowl, his jaw tight. But it was his eyes…his eyes were on fire. They burned with an intensity she had never seen before. A raging inferno gaining momentum, about to explode.

If the man wasn't already shitting his pants, she thought, he soon would be. Eliana moved—a sudden, violent act. With the man's lips still pressed against her temple, she reared back and head-butted him across the nose. He jerked back and howled, unconsciously releasing his hold on her to clutch his broken nose. Then she dropped low and grabbed the handheld garden trowel off the ground. She stabbed him deep in the thigh; all of her pent-up rage and fear released in a single devastating blow. He screamed a tirade of curses, blood spewing from his mouth. "I'll mothafuckin' kill you, bitch! You're dead!"

Eliana tried to scurry away, but he lunged and grabbed her by the hair, yanking her back. He was in a blind rage now, blood pouring from his nose, dripping off his chin. He swung the knife down on her.

CHAPTER FORTY-NINE

The move startled him. He hadn't seen it coming—none of it. But Savage's reaction was instantaneous. Before the man started his downward swing of the knife, he had already pulled his SIG from his waistband and fired two shots into Dreadlocks' forehead. The man was dead before he hit the ground.

But Savage wasn't finished. He stepped straight over to the twitching body, stood over it, and fired several more rounds into the man's chest. The clip emptied, but Savage kept pulling the trigger. *Click. Click. Click.*

"Savage!" Eliana screamed. "He's dead!"

Click. Click.

"Stop. Savage, honey! You can stop. It's OK! *I'm* OK! You can stop." Eliana stood and wrapped her arms around him, pulling him close. "We're OK."

Savage stopped pulling the trigger. He let his arm drop. Released his hold on the gun. Then he screamed—a roar of primal rage. And Eliana held on.

They stood for several minutes, just holding each other. Offering no words.

Savage regained his breath, and his heart slowed. As he calmed, he became conscious of his surroundings again. And he sat down.

Eliana joined him, leaned her head against his shoulder, and sighed.

Savage finally spoke. "We can't stay here," he said. "We need to leave before the police arrive." He listened for sirens in the distance, but there was nothing—just the constant buzzing of the cicadas.

"I don't think they've been called," Eliana said. She looked down at her right hand, the knuckles bloodied from pounding on the barricaded door. "The people around here are terrified of the gangs." She let out a small laugh. "We probably did them a favor."

Savage nodded but said nothing. He rested his elbows on his knees and continued staring at his dirty, scuffed boots. His thoughts were elsewhere.

Eliana sat up and took hold of his bloodied arm. She winced. "Are you OK? It looks like you're bleeding pretty bad."

"Yeah. I'll be fine."

She stood back up, walked across the small yard to the sidewalk, and returned a moment later with their backpack. She sat down beside him and applied a pressure bandage to his wound. "This may need stitches."

Savage looked at her. Shook his head.

She smiled weakly. "Probably not, huh?"

"No."

"Hey," she whispered. "Are you OK?" She still had a hold of his arm. "Not this," she amended, referring to his bandaged arm. "But this." She placed her hand over his heart.

When Savage didn't reply, she gently cupped his cheek and turned his attention toward her.

He looked into her eyes. "No. I shot that kid. And now…now he's dead."

"You had no choice, Savage."

"Yeah. I know. Maybe that's the problem."

"What is?"

"That I had no choice. That I'm nothing more than the monster they created."

Eliana's eyes grew wide. "You're not a monster, Savage! My God! You saved my life!" She kissed him and wrapped her arms around his neck, hugging him tight. "For the umpteenth time, you saved my life!" She paused, took a deep and stilted breath to calm her nerves. "He's dead. And I'm not. I think you, of all people, would find that agreeable."

Savage had to laugh at that. She was throwing his own words back at him. The words he spoke to her when they first met.

"Yeah. I do."

CHAPTER FIFTY

Golden, Colorado

It was well after dark before Skye Freeman arrived, and dinner had long since passed. But she had brought a pizza as if they were having some sort of teenage slumber party.

She handed Micaela the box. "You ever had Colossal Pizza before? Colorado style? It's the bomb!"

"No, I can't say I have."

"Oh my God! It's sooo good! It has a shit ton of toppings on it. And a huge braided crust. And you dip that in honey."

"Honey? Really? And here I thought pineapple was weird."

"Legit."

"Oh! And I brought some Dew to wash it down with. Where would you like it?"

Micaela pasted on a smile. "Here. I'll take it." She took the sixpack of Mountain Dew from her, ripped two free of the plastic rings, and put the rest in the fridge for later. She handed Skye hers. "Any problem finding the place?"

"Nah. I just used my phone. But wow! It gets frickin' dark out here, doesn't it?"

"Yeah. But I like it. It's quiet. Gives me the space to think. Anyway…you ready to get to work?"

"Bet!"

Micaela took the pizza box, along with her bottle of pop, and led Skye down the hallway and into the second bedroom, where she had an office set up with all her computer stuff. Pretty standard fare. It was immediately apparent that the room wasn't on display for visitors. She had papers scattered about in cubbyholes, and there was a nest of computer components and tangled wires in a cardboard box. In the corner stood a folding table with a giant half-finished puzzle on it.

Micaela grabbed a folding chair and moved it over to the work desk. Then tidied up by moving a few of the days-old dirty dishes out of the way. "Sorry about that. Haven't had a lot of time to clean the house."

If Freeman seemed put off by the clutter, she didn't show it. Micaela had a feeling that her own home office was no better. Maybe worse.

"No worries," she said, settling into the bigger, comfier office chair. "So what do we have?"

Micaela remained standing and leaned in, resting her forearms on the desk. "I have an asset in the field who's on the run, and he needs my help. He's damaged his sat phone or lost it. Either way, I've lost communication with him. And I need to get it back. I need to find him ASAP."

"You're talking about the NT that Control is trying to find. Cypher?"

"Yeah. NT-Zero. They're trying to kill him, Freeman."

"One of ours? Like, what the fuck? What did he do?"

"They ordered him to terminate some call girl in Miami. He questioned his orders. Then balked by refusing to pull the trigger. Now they have *him* marked for termination."

Freeman shook her head and quirked her mouth to one side. "They have another NT hunting him down."

"Yeah…look. I know he's broken. I get it. But they're trying to kill him. He either stumbled on something the government wants to keep secret, or they're afraid he will find it."

"And they're willing to kill him over it."

Micaela sighed. Nodded.

"Well, maybe there's something about this call girl we don't know. Maybe she *is* dangerous."

"Yeah, but is she dangerous to the security of this country or just to some asshole who wants to keep a secret?"

Freeman shrugged.

"Have you ever heard of them putting a hit on a mark that wasn't over-the-top evil? Or, at the very least, dangerous to the security of this nation? Known terrorists. Traitors. Human traffickers? Look, I love our country. So do you. But where do we draw the line? Cypher isn't evil. He refused to follow orders. That's all. God forbid if *we* ever make a mistake. Question our orders. Hell, how about thinking for ourselves?"

"Like we're doing now?"

Micaela arched an eyebrow. "Yeah," she said, nodding gravely. "Just like now."

Freeman thought for a moment. The room fell silent, save for the soft murmurs from the TV in the other room. She smiled, bright and cheery. "Let's hit it! What do you need from me?"

"I need access to information that only you would be privy to. Not exactly cloak and dagger shit—no back door hacking or anything like that. You already have access to most of these areas."

"Oh." Freeman seemed disappointed. She started typing. She logged in to her work portal remotely while Micaela talked.

"Won't they be able to see that you logged on after you called off sick tonight? Track you?"

"Nah."

Micaela raised her eyebrows. Waited for her to explain.

Freeman smiled. "Cloak and dagger shit. You know…a little back door hacking."

"OK. Great. You mentioned earlier on the phone that they pulled the entire team from locating Cypher and assigned them to another target. Who's this other target?"

"Good question." Freeman started typing, her fingers working the keyboard like a jazz pianist. She looked through the assignment logs issued earlier in the day and quickly found what she was looking for. "Dr. Henry Shepherd."

Micaela straightened, thought for a moment, and then leaned back down to get a better look at the monitor. "Hmm. I remember them talking about this guy last night. What's so damn important about him that they called off the manhunt for Cypher?"

Again, Freeman typed, jumping through multiple portals and menus, looking for any info on Dr. Shepherd. At first, it was slow going. Little tidbits of background info. Birthdate. Education. Work history. Each new revelation led her to another doorway. Another puzzle that needed to be solved. By the time she had reached the end, she was deep within the bowels of Darkwater and its origins. "Fuck me! This guy Shepherd is a genius. He's responsible for developing the nanotechnology used in the Dragonfly program—stage two in their efforts to develop the perfect super-assassin. He not only handled the design and fabrication of these nanobots, but also how they could transfer information directly into the brain's cerebral cortex."

"That's way over my head."

"Legit. But sounds dank."

"So, outside of the fact Dr. Shepherd developed this technology, what use does he have to Theo Spearman on the night of the failed hit? The little Napoleon had everybody running around, scrambling to track him down. I think they eventually found him in Kansas City using FRS. He was wearing some sort of disguise or something. Anyway, they lost him. And according to what you told me, they're still looking for him. So, I ask again. Why?"

"Well, you said it yourself. The asset is broken. If your car breaks down, don't you call a mechanic?"

Micaela pursed her lips. Put her hands on her hips. "Yeah. But no. Too simple. What is it you said about these nanobots? They're capable of transferring information directly to the brain? I naturally assumed it meant they could extrapolate information from Cypher after a mission. But the transferring of information could also mean putting it in as well. Right?"

Freeman shrugged, looking lost. She reached over and opened the pizza box and quickly seized a large slice, taking her first bite. With her mouth full, she mumbled, "I dunno."

Micaela leaned in closer to get a better look at the information on the computer screen, her heart-shaped face aglow in its soft light. "What sort of duties was Dr. Shepherd assigned?"

"Besides lead scientist? Not much. I'm sure he had his hands full being a mad scientist and shit."

"No. I mean, like, mission specific?"

Freeman began typing. Cursed. Tried again. After several minutes, she stopped. "They have the mission specifics locked down tighter than a wet knot in a torrential downpour. It would take me days to hack my way in. Weeks even. Maybe never. The only documentation I can find on his assigned duties is just boring everyday things."

"What do you mean everyday sort of things? Like taking out the trash?"

Freeman laughed. "I don't know. Maybe. A lot of analytical stuff. Number crunching. But there are a lot of references to him performing routine exams on assets both before and after missions, too. Nothing very sexy."

"Debriefing?"

"Yep."

"Mission planning?"

Freeman shook her head and scrolled back up through the text on the computer screen. "It mentions he programmed relevant information prior to missions. You know, target locations, building schematics, foreign languages… Spy shit."

"So he was responsible for introducing the mission-specific nano-bots— Oh! Jesus! I know why they want Dr. Shepherd! He's the one responsible for Cypher being broken. This mission was supposed to fail all along. He sabotaged his programming!"

CHAPTER FIFTY-ONE

Freeman took another massive bite of the pizza and continued talking through a mouthful of half-chewed food. "So you're saying Dr. Shepherd purposely made it so Cypher would fail?"

"It's the only thing that makes sense. His manipulation of the programming allowed Cypher to think autonomously."

"You're saying they're programmed to follow orders, no matter what?"

"I don't know what I'm saying. Maybe. Maybe this whole thing is crazy. But I think the nanobots somehow reprogram the way they think. Lowers their inhibitions. Like when you get drunk. It makes you more open to suggestion."

"Fuck me! This is sick shit." Freeman downed the last swig of her pop, wiped her mouth with the back of her hand, then did her best to hold back a belch. "Why would the doctor want to destroy his own creation?"

"I don't believe he does. Do you think he developed this nanotechnology so the United States government could create super-assassins? Come on! The military has been stealing scientific advancements to further their agendas for centuries. I'm guessing he no longer wanted to be a part of that." Micaela took a long, shaky breath. Rubbed her tired eyes. "So, the question is, where is the doctor now?"

Freeman delved deeper into the mission logs, searching not only for clues on Dr. Shepherd's whereabouts but also for how close Control was to locating him. It took her a while to read through all the updates, but when she reached the end, she turned to Micaela and shook her head. "Not good, sis. They tracked him to a truck stop in Columbia,

Missouri. But he slipped away again. It seems he had some outside help. Someone left a rental car for him in some local parking lot, and he literally drove away."

"Do they know where he's headed?"

"Not yet. Just that he was heading east." Freeman scrolled down to the last couple of log entries. "Looks like the help came from a distant cousin—or at least one that he's not very close to. Unfortunately, they're going to send someone to 'convince' them to spill their shit."

"This is way above our pay grade, Freeman. Way above our abilities. We need some help."

"Who do you suggest?"

"Cypher. He needs answers. And Dr. Shepherd might be the only one who has them."

"Won't do him much good if they kill the doctor first."

"Exactly. So we're right back to where we started. We need to find Cypher. And fast."

"Sounds like my sort of fun." Freeman bent down and reached into her purse. When she sat back up, she had an opened bag of red Twizzlers in her hand and a rope of braided candy dangling from her mouth. "But I'm going to need some more Dew to keep my energy up."

Micaela looked at her incredulously. "You've got to be kidding me! If you had any more energy right now, you would glow in the dark."

CHAPTER FIFTY-TWO

"I just don't understand how you think you'll find Cypher. He could be anywhere by now. He could be halfway around the world."

Micaela finished the last slice of the pizza, feeling famished. She shook her head, still chewing, before speaking. "I don't believe so. But who knows where he's headed?"

Freeman's eyes sparkled, and her big-cheeked smile lit up her face. "So…what do you think?"

"Like I said, I don't know. Definitely somewhere other than Miami."

"No. I mean, what do you think of Colorado-style pizza? It's fire, right?"

"What? Oh. Yeah, it was good."

Freeman eyed the paper plate. "But you didn't eat the crust. And you didn't even open your cup of honey. That's the best part!"

Micaela blanched at the thought. Rolled her eyes. "OK. Can we get back on subject here? Cypher. Remember?"

Freeman nodded, crestfallen, and pursed her lips. "Sure. But I don't understand why you think he's still in Miami. I told you about his phone call to the news station and the FBI's subsequent shutdown of PortMiami. I might add that he could have made that call from any-where in the country—and from a burner phone. They weren't able to track it. So, poof! He's gone."

"I think that was just a diversion. It was a misdirection, giving him room to make his escape."

"OK. Even if that's true, even if he's in Miami, you still have no direct line of communication with him. It's not like you can just jump on a plane and fly to Miami. Even if he's there, where would you even begin to look?"

"I don't know."

Freeman sighed and tried to solve the problem like she was scouring lines of code for a syntax error. She eyed the untouched crust on Micaela's paper plate, pulled it on over, and polished it off with some honey. Then she said, "What about his biosensor? I read the doctors use a sensor-equipped port to inject nanobots and track the assassin's vitals."

"Yeah. That's true. I was using it to track Cypher for a while. But it stopped working. Probably wised up and got rid of it."

Freeman made a face. "Do you think?"

"He's pretty resourceful."

"Jesus! He's the fucking GOAT. That was our best bet for tracking him down."

"Goddamn it! I don't know, Freeman. Maybe we're approaching this wrong. We need to think like a super-assassin. If you were in Cypher's shoes, where the hell would you be headed?"

"I'd be getting the hell out of Dodge!"

"OK. Jumping out of the frying pan and into the fire accomplishes nothing. He has to have a plan. A destination in mind."

"Somewhere he can find help."

"Yes! Good." Micaela started pacing, her hands resting on her hips. "OK. Let's try this. Pull up anything you can find in the NSA's database for a list of friendly assets in the Greater Miami area."

Freeman laughed, pouring on the sarcasm. "Sure! No problem. It's as easy as pulling up some cheat codes for the latest *Call of Duty*."

"Shit. Is it hard?"

"It ain't easy."

"Fine. It's not easy. But can you do it?"

"Yeah. Yeah. Keep your shirt on, sis. I can do it. It's just going to take some time."

"Then I feel obligated to tell you that's something we *still* don't have."

"Oh, good. Nothing like a little pressure to get the juices flowing."

"Freeman!"

"OK! Got it. Sheesh." She frowned and did a tap dance on the keyboard with her fingers. A spreadsheet of friendly contacts popped up on the screen. "Now who's the GOAT?"

Micaela returned to the desk and studied the information in front of her. There were dozens of names on the list. Addresses. Contact numbers. "Shit. That's a lot more hits than I expected."

"You realize it will take us forever to go through this and track these people down."

"I know," said Micaela. "And that's assuming those people are still alive and kicking."

"Now what?"

"I want a visual of their locations. Can you pull up those addresses and overlay them on a map of Miami?"

"Watch me." Freeman looked up at Micaela, a big smile stretching across her face. "You know what? This shit is getting good."

It took a little longer than Micaela expected. Or was the pressure cooker of time just making it feel that way? Another eight or nine minutes passed, and Freeman finally had it. A couple more keystrokes and the on-screen map popped up, now littered with a series of blue dots, each representing a potential friendly asset. She counted over thirty-seven of them. "Big yikes!"

Micaela rubbed her hand across her face, massaging the tension from her brow. "Yeah. Big yikes. Hell! There are potential targets everywhere! From Brickell to Hollywood. I even got a loner out in the Everglades. How the hell are we supposed to know which is his most likely destination? This is impossible!"

"Facts."

Micaela turned away from the screen. She started pacing again. Playing with her hair as she worked the problem. She stopped at the folding table in the corner and stared at the jigsaw puzzle she hadn't worked on in months. The picture on the box was a nonsensical cluttered 3D mess of space debris orbiting the Earth. Which, of course, made it incredibly difficult. Micaela reached back and pulled her hair up into a ponytail. Thinking. Yes, difficult. But not impossible. It just seemed that way. She just had to keep working the puzzle, one piece at a time, until she had the complete picture.

Micaela gasped and practically ran back to the computer desk. She grabbed the folding chair and plopped down next to Freeman. "I got it."

Freeman raised her eyebrows, the hint of a smirk forming in the corners of her mouth. "OK."

"I need you to access the Global Tracking Net for all our assets in Operation Darkwater."

"You mean by using their biosensors?"

"Yeah. They should all have them. Across all projects."

Freeman started typing, hopping through menu options to look for the program. "I thought you said Cypher somehow removed his."

"He did. But I'm not looking for Cypher. I'm looking for the next best thing. The assassin that's hunting him. Can you get it?"

"Bet!"

Another map pulled up on the screen. This one was of the entire world, and it was littered with numerous flashing red dots. Forty-two of them, to be exact.

"That's a shit ton."

"OK. We can disregard anything that's not in the United States. Eliminate those."

Freeman did. Now there were only five that remained.

Micaela felt her heart pumping a little faster, the butterflies in her stomach taking flight. "Good. That's it. It's safe to assume we can eliminate the targets in Los Angeles, Portland, Dallas, and Boston. But there is one in Florida. We need to target that biosensor. Let's overlay its current GPS coordinates on our map of Miami and see where that leads us."

Again, Freeman complied. A few moments later, there was a solitary red flashing dot surrounded by an otherwise sea of blue. "Bingo. Zoom in on our target. See which blue dot is the closest. Maybe we can extrapolate from that where he's headed."

"Um. That biosensor we're tracking isn't just close to one of the assets. It's on top of one!"

Micaela stood up. "Which one?"

"It's a document forger in North Miami. He calls himself the cobbler. But his real name is Carlos Romero."

"Oh my God! That's it! That's where Cypher is heading—if he's not there already!"

"Well, he's about to have company."

No! No! No! Cypher was a rabbit caught in a snare, and the wolf was about to pounce. She needed to warn him. "Pull up that phone number and call the cobbler now!"

CHAPTER FIFTY-THREE

Miami, Florida

Carlos gave up. He was tired and had enough headaches for one night. His computers were shot. Literally. He thought he might be able to recover the information on the hard drives, but damn if that son of a bitch CIA agent didn't shoot them both dead center. How in the hell did he shoot them inside the computer casing, anyway? He couldn't even see them, much less aim for them. But somehow he hit them both—the iMac *and* the MacBook Air.

Well. No matter. The *bastardo* had no idea that Carlos backed up all his information through a cloud service. Carlos cackled as he walked across the cold ceramic floor and into his kitchen. He grabbed a beer from the fridge, twisted off the top, and took a long pull of the Palma Cristal.

Damn, that hit the spot! He took another swig. Tried to relax. After all, he made a lot of cash tonight, and there was little doubt he could recover all of his clients' information. And that, of course, was where he could make the big bucks.

Carlos was about to take another swig of beer when there was a knock at the front door. He stopped. Lowered the bottle. Who the hell was that at this time of night? He returned to his workshop to check the security camera feed before remembering the computers weren't working. *Estúpido!*

Now the doorbell rang. It must be that crazy CIA man again! *"Bueno, al diablo con él!" Well, the hell with him!* He could stay out there on the stoop all night for all Carlos cared!

The doorbell rang again.

Carlos peeked out of his workshop and looked down the short hallway and into the living room. He could barely make out the front door from his vantage point. Not that it mattered.

There was pounding on the door. Loud and reverberating against the metal frame. Then nothing.

The clock ticked in the living room. The refrigerator hummed. Then there was a shotgun blast, followed by another.

Carlos nearly shit himself. He turned to retrieve his gun from the workbench, but the intruder kicked the door open before he could. Carlos yelped, frozen in place like a deer in headlights.

The man marched straight to him, his short shotgun raised, fixed on Carlos. "You there! Keep your hands where I can see them." He spoke in Cuban Spanish. Carlos raised both hands, still awkwardly standing in the workshop's doorway.

The man's black hair was shorn into a buzz cut and he had a scruffy two-day-old beard. Thick, bushy eyebrows stitched over his pale, lifeless eyes. One stare said it all. Cold.

"Where are the man and woman who were here earlier?" The intruder stepped closer, gesturing with the shotgun for him to step back into the workshop.

Carlos complied, his raised hands never wavering from the surrender position. "I don't know what you mean, friend," he replied smoothly, maintaining his native Spanish as a courtesy. It was easier for him, anyway. "There is nobody here but me."

The man struck him across the face with the short barrel of his gun, cutting his cheek. He never saw it coming, and it stunned him.

"I don't like to play games, Mr. Romero..."

Carlos dabbed at the sting on his cheek, his fingers now wet with blood. *He knows my real name.* Carlos tried to swallow, but his mouth felt dry, his tongue thick and clumsy. "Of course not—um. I didn't catch your name."

The man didn't reply. His stare never wavered. He opened his shoulder bag and removed a Baretta 71 pistol. After training it on Carlos, he stashed his shotgun back into the bag. "I never like to ask twice…"

"Yes! Of course! I remember now. There was a couple here. Earlier tonight. They broke down somewhere or something like that. I told them to get lost."

"You and I both know that isn't true." He casually reached into his bag and pulled out a suppressor. He began screwing it onto the barrel of his gun.

"OK! OK, friend. You're right—no more games. I had a couple stop by here earlier today. Brent Savage and Eliana Bautista. They wanted new identification papers and were willing to pay handsomely for them. So, of course, I said yes."

"I'm disappointed with you, Mr. Romero. You tell me what I already know." The stranger lifted the gun and shot Carlos's left knee. He collapsed, clutching at his leg as he thrashed around in agony. It was the most excruciating pain he had ever experienced, and he screamed. Shrill and mindless.

"Why!" he cried. "Oh my God! Why?"

"I told you no games. I already know who they are. Now tell me the fake names you created for them."

"I…I don't remember!" he said through clenched teeth, long strands of drool running down his chin. "Wait! Wait!"

The man didn't. Again, he pulled the trigger, this time completely blowing off the ring finger of Carlos's right hand. Carlos was going into shock. The horror of seeing his finger shot off, the sheer agony of it, made him want to pass out. "No! Please no! I really don't remember, but it's saved on the computer. I swear it! But that fucking CIA man shot them up. Ruined the hard drives. I can't access them!"

The man with ghost eyes seemed amused by this as the hint of a smile slithered across his face and found purchase on his mouth. "You think this Brent Savage is CIA?" He didn't elaborate any further. "Come now, Mr. Romero. You're a smart businessman. You would never leave such valuable information left to fate and unprotected on a mechanical device such as a hard drive. Prone to failure such as they are."

Carlos was crying now, sobbing. Not just from the terrific pain but from realizing what fate awaited him.

"I need to know their new identities. So, one last time, Mr. Romero. I need the name of the cloud service you used to save their info, along with your username and password."

Carlos told him. Then he began crying even harder. He never even heard the phone ringing. Just the cough of a silenced pistol. Double tap. Then nothing.

CHAPTER FIFTY-FOUR

Miami, Florida

It took them less than five minutes to drive to where they ditched the Olds Cutlass on Jann Avenue. They had barely spoken a word, a heavy silence falling between them—too tired, too shocked for casual conversation.

Savage kept working the fight repeatedly in his head but couldn't see how he could have played it any other way. He had no choice but to kill the young man. Deep inside, he knew this. But he couldn't help but feel like he had let Eliana down somehow. She, on the other hand, had surprised the hell out of him. Impressed him with her quick thinking. She had saved her own life as much as anything Savage had done.

He told her as much when they made their way over to the security fence at the airport. "You were great back there. You kept your cool. Did what you needed to do."

She smiled, more forced than natural. Squeezed his hand tighter. "Maybe. But knowing it doesn't make it feel any better."

Savage nodded thoughtfully and squeezed her hand back. "It never does."

They reached the fence line and Savage crouched down beside it. The fence was a typical six-foot chain-link, fortified with barbwire along the top as a deterrent. They wouldn't be climbing the fence, so that didn't matter. They would go straight through it. Savage fished the multi-tool from his pouch and began cutting the chain-link fence. He cut out an opening large enough for them to crawl through, not quite completing a full circle. Savage went first and held the flap open for

Eliana. After clearing the fence, they made their way toward the hangars and service buildings.

It was surprisingly easy, just a half mile across open grass and paved concrete with few deterrents in between to slow them down. Better yet, there was little in the way of security cameras, at least none Savage could detect. Still, they approached the hangar with caution. They waited. Observed. Made sure there weren't any extra security measures in place. And at this time of evening, there wasn't much in the way of comings and goings in the nearby facilities.

One of the bay doors was open, the overhead lights turned on. But not all of them.

They made their way along the perimeter of the building and peeked inside. In the far corner of the hangar, below the lights, was a solitary man working on a twin-turboprop King Air 260. He was alone, so they entered.

He appeared to be in his late fifties, sun-worn, with crow's feet etched deep around his eyes like cracks in a dried riverbed. His unkempt beard was gray like his hair. And he wore wrinkled beach clothes, consisting of an unbuttoned Hawaiian shirt, khaki cargo shorts, and flip-flops. He wore a tattered orange ball cap on his head, the words *McGrew's Getaways* stitched across the top in blue thread.

He had the cowling open on the port engine, checking the oil level on the dipstick. When he heard their footfalls, he turned to watch them approach. "Can I help you?"

Savage cleared his throat and put some cheeriness into his greeting. "Uh, yes. Good evening. We sure hope you can. My name is Mitch Fields, and this is my wife, Karyn."

The gray-haired beach bum climbed down the small ladder he was standing on and wiped his greasy hands on a rag he had tucked into his pants. He extended his arm to shake hands with Savage. "Nice to meet you. I'm Terry McGrew. Owner and operator." He offered his hand to Eliana and shook hers as well. "What can I do you for?" His blue eyes sparkled like bright coastal waters.

"Well, we're looking to charter a plane. We're in a bit of a hurry, you see. And we need to get to Chicago right away."

McGrew tilted his head slightly, his eyes shifting from Savage's backpack to Eliana's knit bag. No luggage. There was a sheen of perspiration on their faces, their clothes dirty and soaked with sweat. "Huh. Well. I'm sorry. I can't help you, folks. You see, I just mainly charter out regionally here in the south, mostly for traveling businessmen looking to get away on some overnight fishing trips. In fact, I just got back from Biloxi, Mississippi, tonight. A couple of old-timers wanted to do some fishing out in Back Bay." If that was supposed to mean something to Savage, it went over his head. He played along.

"Wow! Cool! I'd love to get away for a weekend, do some fishing." He looked at Eliana, giving her a play-along smile. "But unfortunately that will have to wait. We need to get to Chicago by tomorrow morning. We're supposed to be in our best friend's wedding tomorrow. But we had one hell of a day today. The worst! We had some car trouble and, well, to make a long story short, we missed our commercial flight."

"And we just can't miss the wedding," Eliana added. "As my husband said, we're part of the wedding party. Can't you please help us out?"

He exchanged glances between the two. Sighed. "Sorry, guys. Would love to, but as I said, I just got back home. I'm frickin' beat. Just wanted to tidy up a few preventative maintenance things on my baby before calling it a night."

"She's beautiful," Savage agreed, caressing the front edge of the wing. "Well. I'm sorry to have bothered you. Do you know anybody who might be willing to charter a plane tonight?"

"At this time of night? Not a chance." He gave them a nod and turned to walk away. "Good luck, folks."

"We're willing to pay you handsomely."

McGrew stopped at that. He turned back around, eyed them both from head to toe. "Oh, yeah? Neither one of you looks like well-to-do yuppies. Unless you've just won the lottery. I normally charge twenty-five hundred dollars per hour of flight time. Chicago? That's about a four-hour flight. You have ten thousand dollars you can part with?"

Savage and Eliana exchanged glances. She gave him an almost imperceptible nod. He slipped off the backpack from his shoulder, unzipped it, and pulled out a stack of one-hundred-dollar bills. "Yes. We do. As I said, we must get there as soon as possible. We need to leave tonight."

McGrew scratched absently at the tufts of gray hair on his chest. "Look. You guys seem like friendly folks. But I'm tired. Just tired enough to have lost my sense of humor for the night, so you can stop pulling my leg. Even if I thought you were serious, it would be quite a while before we could depart. I have to refuel. Run over my checklist. Heck. Filing a flight plan will take us a good hour."

"How much to forgo the flight plan?" Savage pulled out a half stack of one-hundreds.

McGrew adjusted the brim of his hat. Frowned. "All right. What the hell is going on here? Just what kind of trouble are you guys really in?" He looked at Savage's bulging backpack again. "You two running drugs?"

"No. We aren't running drugs, and we aren't criminals."

"Then what?" he asked.

"You wouldn't believe us if we told you. But this bundle of cash here is worth fifteen thousand dollars to help convince you."

McGrew took off his hat. Rubbed his hand through his wet head of hair. He looked at Eliana and saw pleading in her eyes. Then he looked at Savage. Saw nothing. Just a serious stare, void of all emotion. "You folks didn't murder somebody, did you?"

"No," Savage said. He paused long enough to consider his words. "Not murder. Self-defense. They were going to hurt Karyn. They left me no choice."

McGrew closed his eyes and sighed. "I must be crazy for even considering this. Hope I won't regret it. Give me enough time to fuel this bird and run over my checklist. And we'll get out of here ASAP."

Savage handed him the cash and then unfolded the other half stack of one-hundreds. "There's five thousand more if you push through that checklist a little faster."

McGrew laughed to himself and shook his head. "Suddenly, I don't feel so tired anymore."

★　　　★　　　★

The Ghost heard the twin-turbo engines roar and come to life. Then he saw it. A white and blue Beechcraft King Air 260. Taking off to the east. A blinding flare of landing lights on the far side of the runway. It was them. Cypher and the woman. He knew it. Could feel it.

He said nothing. Did nothing. He just watched as the plane raced toward him. Watched it ease off the ground and fly directly over his head, a wash of dirty air buffeting him in its wake. Then, the plane pulled up its landing gear and banked sharply to the left, climbing skyward like a bat out of hell.

The sound of the twin engines faded as the plane became nothing more than a distant speck, a red beacon of light twinkling on the northern horizon. Then it was gone.

He had missed them by mere minutes. But no matter. He saw the tail numbers. Put them to memory. And Marcos knew it was only a matter of time before he found them.

CHAPTER FIFTY-FIVE

Mansfield, Ohio

Becky had just finished her shower. She had soaked under the scalding hot water for what seemed like an eternity. The showerhead was set to power-massage, kneading away every ache and pain from her shoulders and lower back. A necessity after that ten-hour drive home. If there was any hot water left, her husband Gary would have to make the shower a quick one.

She left the bathroom to him while she headed to the bedroom to slip on her robe and begin her nightly ritual.

She toweled off her hair, brushed her teeth, and was cleaning the water from her ears when she heard a knock at the door. *Who the hell could that be at this time of night?*

She wrapped her hair with the towel as she made her way down the stairs. "I got it," she called out to her husband, though he likely didn't hear her with his head under the showerhead and the radio blaring AC/DC. "And turn that shit down!"

She walked over to the door to look through the peephole when there was another knock. She jumped. It was louder this time. Urgent.

She opened the door about six inches and looked at the two men standing on the front stoop. Tall. Athletic. They were both dressed in black suits and wore matching ties. They had the same short crew cut, square jaws, and broad shoulders. Practically twins. The only noticeable difference was the hair color, with the one on the left having blond hair and the one on the right having brown. "Yes?"

"Good evening, ma'am. Sorry to disturb you at this time of night. But we're looking for a Becky Fischer."

Becky's brow pinched. She opened the door a little further to get a better look at them both. "I'm Becky Fischer."

"Pleasure to meet you, ma'am. I'm Agent Scarpelli, and this gentleman is Agent Ingersoll." He paused. His eyes drifted toward the towel wrapped around her head. "Once again, I'm sorry to bother you at this late hour, but we need to ask you and your husband a few questions. Is he home?"

Becky shook her head, clearing the cobwebs of exhaustion from her mind. "What? Wait a minute. Who are you guys?"

"Ma'am…we're with the Bureau," he stated, flashing a gold and blue shield he had unclipped from his belt. "We're looking for Dr. Henry Shepherd. We've been informed you may have been in recent contact with him."

Becky swallowed. "I'm sorry. What did you say this was about?"

Ingersoll chimed in. "We're hoping you could tell us where we might find him." He reached into his suit jacket and pulled out a recent 4x6 photograph of the man.

They knew! Becky unconsciously clapped her hand over her pounding heart. "I…I'm not sure. You see…uh…I…my husband and I…"

"Do you mind if we come in and ask you and your husband a few questions, ma'am? We hate to intrude, but this is too important to wait." Scarpelli walked forward without waiting for her reply, closing the distance between them and crowding into her personal space. She reflexively stepped back, and the two agents entered the house.

Ingersoll closed the door behind him. Stopped. Locked the dead bolt. "This really shouldn't take too long."

CHAPTER FIFTY-SIX

Savage was dreaming again. Wasn't he? But it seemed too vivid for a dream. It was too lucid, lacking the nonsensical surrealism of a dream. A memory, then.

It started the same way. He was emerging from a jungle on a dark, moonless night. Somewhere in—what—a foreign country? Yes. A remote part of Mexico. He crossed a beach alongside a private marina, looking for a luxury yacht. No. Not just any luxury yacht. Berto Ramón Maduro's yacht. Negro Mako.

Again, he found himself walking down the pier, dipping in and out of the shadows created by poorly lit strings of incandescent lights.

He found the Negro Mako moored at the end of the dock. He dove into the dark murky waters, swam beneath it, and then surfaced on the far side.

As he emerged, he waited for the garbled warning from one of Maduro's men, followed by a muzzle flash. This time, it never came.

Savage looked around, gained his bearings. Pitch dark. Eerily still. Only the mournful clang of a buoy bell in the distance broke the fragile silence.

The security detail was still patrolling the decks but hadn't noticed him. Not yet. Savage swam as quietly as a whisper to the aft of the ship, to the open swim platform. There were no soldiers around. Nobody sharing a nightcap on the platform, stargazing. He climbed his way out of the water and onto the platform. Quickly, Savage removed his SIG from the watertight carrying case and tossed it aside.

Savage pressed on, making his way into the bowels of the ship. Control had prepped him with all the ship's schematics. He knew every room, every corridor as if he had lived on the ship his entire life.

He made his way to the engine room, climbing down a ladder and walking down a short corridor. At the end of the hall was a steel door. He put his ear to the door and could hear the steady hum of machinery on the other side. He tried the handle and was surprised to find it unlocked. That was odd. He slowly opened the door and eased his way into the room. Again, nobody was around.

Savage squatted beside the main battery bank and began placing C4 plastic explosives. He slid around the engine room, keeping the charges small, concerning himself with accuracy and precision rather than blunt destruction. He attached the timing device and then completed the connections. In just a few minutes, the entire ship would be doused in a veil of darkness. He needed to move.

Savage exited the engine room. Made his way down the corridor and to the nearest stairwell. The music had stopped. No more club beats bouncing off the walls of the ship. Party over? Or were they searching for him already? He heard the occasional footsteps but no voices. No whispered orders being issued. No guns being locked and loaded.

He made his way forward, through the midship, and up to the upper deck, toward the master suite. That's where he would find Maduro sleeping, isolated from the noise of the engine room and the chaotic atmosphere of the club and entertainment centers of the ship. His best soldiers would be on security detail just outside his room. As he reached the top of the stairs, Savage stopped, used a small tactical mirror to check around the corner, looking for the number of soldiers he would have to deal with. But the corridor was empty. Nobody was posted outside Maduro's suite. Savage took a deep breath. Tried to understand what trap they had lying in wait. This wasn't adding up.

He gave it a ten count before slicing the pie around the corner and approaching the door at the end of the hall. There were narrow strips of white LED lights along the baseboards on both sides of the corridor.

Primarily decorative, they only offered a nominal amount of light to navigate the halls at night.

He reached the door. Then nothing. It was slightly ajar, and he could hear the soft, rhythmic sounds of deep slumber from inside. But there were no voices. No lights. Not even a TV inadvertently left on. Savage checked his watch—three thirty-one. Planting the C4 explosives took longer than expected, and he was now running behind schedule.

Savage eased the door open, raised his silenced SIG, and took aim at the figure curled up in a fetal position on the massive elevated bed. No. It was two figures. Maduro and his wife for the night.

Suddenly, a brilliant light flooded the corridor behind Savage. He spun around, prepared to fire. But the two-thousand-lumen tactical light ensured he was disoriented. Blinded.

"Asesino! Asesino!" a man screamed. He never heard the crack of the gunshot.

★　　　★　　　★

The plane bumped along a small pocket of air turbulence until it jostled Savage awake. He sat there a moment, blinking and getting his bearings. The plane then made a steady bank toward the west, its inertia causing Eliana to stir. She inhaled deeply through her nose and opened her eyes. When she saw Savage staring at her, she smiled, her sleepy face sparking to life in the dimly lit interior of the cabin. "Did you sleep?" she asked, her voice squeaky and thick with sleep.

She sat across from him, her executive-style seating facing him directly. Savage nodded. "I dozed for a while. It was more than I expected, really. I don't require much."

"Yeah. But it sure feels good," she said simply.

Savage looked out the window, watching the smattering of city lights pass below, glittering like starlight on a dark, moonless night. "I had another dream."

Eliana straightened up in her chair, tilted her head. "Was it bad?" She swept the strands of loose hair behind her ear.

"Well…I'm not sure. I mean…it seems to be a memory of some mission I had done a while back. Not really sure how long ago. It didn't seem to be out of the ordinary, though—at least not relative to any of the other missions they ever gave me. It seems my assignment was to assassinate the head of a powerful drug cartel off the coast of Mexico: Berto Ramón Maduro. A very dangerous man. Sadistic. And I believe it turned out all right. I'm here, after all. But it's the second time I've had this dream. That seems a little more than coincidental."

"Yeah. I agree."

"I can't put my finger on it, but something doesn't feel right. I can't seem to shake this deep sense of dread, like there's a locked door in front of me. It's dark and dangerous. And the dream is warning me not to open it."

"Jesus, Savage. I don't know. Maybe it *is* just a dream. We all have them. But a suppressed memory? How could you ever know? It must be awful." There was just the hint of her accent peeking through as she spoke. She reached out and touched his hand. "I'm sorry," she said, and meant it. "Maybe you should try talking about it. Bring it out into the open. It might help you make sense of things."

But Savage said no more on the subject. And Eliana let it drop, allowing him the space to sort it out. The cabin fell quiet again, except for the steady hum of the twin-turbine engines and the occasional radio chatter from McGrew in the cockpit.

Eliana looked out the window, her thoughts seemingly far away. It was quiet for the longest time. Then she began to hum—a sweet, delicate melody. Savage just listened. Watched her. After a while, the humming turned to singing. Slowly, at first. Softly. Just a random word or two. Then they came more frequently. Started to flow. He felt himself sink into his seat and relax as the words formed on her lips and whispered around him like a warm summer breeze. Unknown and unseen. But always welcome. He had never heard the song before. A song that spoke of lost dreams. Of loneliness. And hope for better days. The dream of finding love. It seemed too perfect to be improvised. But Savage knew it was. She had a gift.

"That was beautiful," he said, his voice just above a whisper. "You have a lovely voice."

"Thank you." She smiled warmly, genuinely pleased that he enjoyed it. But she looked tired, distracted. She was still looking out the window, shaking her head in disbelief. "*Déu meu,*" she said finally. "How the hell did we ever get to be where we are now? What happened to us?"

Savage smiled to himself, rubbed the tension from his forehead as he looked back out the window. "That's a good question. And I wish I knew the answer."

Eliana was staring at Savage again, a slow smile forming. "*Jo també.*" *Me too.* She shifted in her seat and tucked her legs up beneath her.

"You should have been a recording artist. You would have made millions."

She laughed at that. "That was always the plan. It's why I came to the United States in the first place. To follow my dream. Become a big star and sell millions of records to all my adoring fans." She said it lightly, as if she were joking. He could tell she wasn't.

"You have the talent for it."

She blushed and tried to hide her smile. She couldn't help it.

"So you weren't born here."

"No. I was born in Spain. A city in Catalonia called Girona. But I didn't live there for very long. My parents gave me up for adoption when I was very young. I don't remember them. But I moved around a lot from one foster family to another for years. It was really hard on me. Some of the families were OK. They tried, anyway. Others, not so much. The last family I fostered with…wasn't good. The man was abusive. *Un puta imbècil.*" *A fucking asshole.* "So, one day, I'd had enough. I was only fourteen when I took to the streets. Learned to make it on my own. "

"And survived."

"Yes," she said, nodding. "Then one of the foster sisters I had growing up moved to the United States. Miami. Her name was Angela. She was great. She wanted to be an actress. And she invited me to stay with her. So I scrimped and saved for a couple of years until I was able to join her. We had such big plans. We were going to move to California and become these big stars. Stupid, huh?"

"Not at all." He leaned in, resting his arms on his knees. "So what happened?"

Eliana hesitated. "She died of a drug overdose. A couple of years ago. She was the closest thing I ever had to family."

"I'm sorry. I truly am." He knew what it was like to be alone. To have nobody to confide in. To depend on. "So you never left for California…"

"No. When I lost Angela, I lost everything. I had no money. I had no place to go."

Savage stood up and took the seat next to her. He released the seat from a locked position, allowing it to slide over, and swiveled close to her. Eliana did the same, and they were now sitting together. He put his arms around her and embraced her.

She nestled her head beneath his chin, her deep sigh of relief brushing across his neck. She sniffed and then wiped away a tear. "What about you?"

"What about me?"

"I mean…I know practically nothing about your past. Like who you were before I met you."

"Hm. Not much to say, really."

Eliana smiled. Tsked. "Of course there is. Where were you born, Savage? I mean…what was your childhood like? If you ever had one. Somehow, I can't see you ever being a child."

He looked away, suddenly uncomfortable. "Honestly, I don't remember that much about my childhood. I know it was short-lived, having to grow up on the streets of Pittsburgh. I know it doesn't sound

as sexy as toughing it out on the streets of New York or Chicago. But believe me, it was pretty rough."

"Damn, Savage. Didn't your parents care about you running around like that?"

"As I said, I remember little about that time in my life. My parents weren't drunks. They weren't drug users. Or abusive." Savage shrugged. "They were just too self-absorbed in their own lives to notice."

"Not even their son?"

"I was a burden. We had little money. My dad was a steelworker. My mom worked the third shift in a textile factory. They were never home. And I guess it just made it easier to pretend I never existed at all."

"That's terrible! What about friends? Other family members? Maybe an aunt or uncle? Even a neighbor?"

"No. I was always a loner. At least until I was old enough to join the Marines."

"The Marines," she said thoughtfully. "And they became your family."

Savage shook his head. "No. But it got me off the streets. Provided me with a unique set of skills. And, in all likelihood, it probably saved my life."

McGrew suddenly interrupted them. "We'll be landing soon," he said, looking over his shoulder and through the open cockpit. "You'll want to get your seats back in place and buckle up."

The plane banked hard to the right, then straightened out, finally bringing the dazzling Chicago skyline into view outside the portside window.

Eliana sat up in her chair, craning her neck to get her first glimpse of a U.S. city outside the State of Florida. Her face brightened like a child experiencing the circus for the first time.

"Wow."

CHAPTER FIFTY-SEVEN

Chicago, Illinois

Eric Newberg allowed the Lexus LS to park itself. Why not? Parking on the streets of Chicago was always at a premium, and Hudson Street in the Lincoln Park neighborhood was no different. It was a tight fit, but the car slipped into the spot without a hitch.

He normally would have parked in the garage at the rear of the building, but Helen was coming home with the kids and an armful of groceries, and she would need the space.

Newberg was careful to look before opening his door on the crowded street, then he grabbed his briefcase and headed for the front stoop of his three-story Victorian stone home. It was a 4,200-square-foot beauty on a street dominated by brick row houses and nineteenth-century brownstones. But it was the greenery he fell in love with. The streets were adorned with mature oak and elm trees, colored with flowering shrubs and ornamental gardens. And what a beautiful Sunday morning it was. Bright blue skies and not a cloud to be found.

He adjusted his suit, brushed at the wrinkles in the crease of his pant legs, and headed inside his home.

The delicate aroma of apples and cinnamon greeted him warmly. Helen must have changed the plug-in air fresheners again. According to her, the Labor Day weekend marked the unofficial start of fall. Oh, well. He didn't mind.

He quickly perused the mail left on the foyer table from the day before, saw nothing of interest, and headed up the carpeted stairs.

The living room was dimly lit, the drapes still drawn from last night. The smell of French toast and bacon lingered in the kitchen from breakfast that morning. Newberg thought it best to open up some windows, let in some fresh air and sunshine before he started the day with the family.

He slipped off his suit jacket, loosened his tie, and started for the windows across the living room.

He stopped when the table lamp next to the wingback chair turned on. His heart skipped a beat. A man was sitting in the chair, one leg crossed over the other, his arms at rest beside him. "Hello, Newberg. It's been a while."

CHAPTER FIFTY-EIGHT

"I see you've done well for yourself." Savage waved his hand toward Newberg's black Emporio Armani suit with the red power tie.

Newberg swallowed. "Hi, Savage."

"Nowadays, I go by Mitch Fields. But I'll bet it wouldn't have taken you very long to figure that out. Just a couple hours of digging on the dark web, right?"

"Sure. OK."

"Are you just as entrepreneurial as ever? Still in the same racket?"

Newberg looked down at his pressed shirt and dress slacks, suddenly self-conscious. He rubbed at an imaginary piece of lint on the shirt pocket, repositioned the gold-coated business pen. "Um…no. I'm working for a financing firm now." When Savage said nothing, he added, "Strausberg and Wickett."

"So you don't dabble in cyber *engineering* anymore?"

"No. You told me to never—no. I don't do that anymore."

Savage remained silent. The tension grew.

"I mean…I still do some business on the computer. I'm a financial consultant. You know…"

"Oh, I know."

The room was suddenly feeling stuffy. Hot. Newberg slipped his tie knot down further, unbuttoning the collar on his shirt.

"Newberg. There's somebody I'd like you to meet." Savage extended his arm out and a woman slipped in from around the corner of the dining room. "This is a friend of mine, Eliana Bautista. Once again, I know it would only be a matter of time before you discovered her alias. But just humor me and call her Karyn."

Eliana stood next to Savage.

"Hi...Karyn."

"Eric Newberg's real name is—*was*—Newman Powell. He was one of the greatest computer hackers in the world at one time. Renowned in certain underground circles for his ability to get past the Pentagon's cyber security and steal some of their greatest and most well-guarded secrets. The type that would fetch a handsome sum from foreign governments. Or the kind that they would outright eliminate you for."

"That was a long time ago." Newberg looked over his shoulder, back toward the stairs. "I'm married now. I have two beautiful little kids."

Savage continued as if Newberg hadn't spoken at all. "Anyway, it turns out that there was a government willing to eliminate him for his indiscretions. Ours. So they sent me to kill him. He was one of my first assignments. Operation Darkwater was in its infancy then. They were just beginning Project Hydra and genetic modifications—with Project Dragonfly not even on the radar yet."

Sweat was trickling down Newberg's face. His neck was flushed and blotchy from a rise in his blood pressure.

"You should have seen him. He was a pimple-faced seventeen-year-old high school dropout whose biggest worries at the time were how to beat *Call of Duty* and how to get laid."

"Honestly, I think I played *Fallout 4* a lot back then."

"Pathetic, really. He was just a kid. Brilliant, yes. But still just a boy. Unchallenged. Without direction."

Eliana nodded, understanding. "So you didn't kill him."

Savage folded his arms and shook his head. "I made a deal with him. I spared his life. Set up a new identity for him. I reappropriated some confiscated drug money from a large-scale drug bust. Then I set him up with a little trust fund. Gave him a fighting chance to make something of himself."

"From the looks of it, I'd say he succeeded," said Eliana.

Savage was noncommittal. Shrugged. "I convinced the DCS that I eliminated my mark. As far as they were concerned, problem solved. Isn't that right, Newbie?"

Newberg said nothing. Didn't move a muscle, not even to wipe the stinging sweat away from his eyes. He didn't dare.

"He had to agree on two conditions for me to spare his life. Do you remember what they were?"

"Yeah. Sure, Savage. That I would quit being a hacker. Stop breaking into security systems."

"Or?"

"You would come back and finish the job." He closed his eyes. He tried to swallow but couldn't find enough saliva to do it.

"And what was the second condition?"

"That I would owe you a favor someday."

Savage smiled. "Correct. Now, despite your claims that you have met the first condition—that you've stopped hacking your way past security systems—I find that highly suspect…"

Newberg protested, but Savage cut him off.

"But I'm willing to forgive such transgressions because I need to call in that favor from you. Now."

"But I—" Newberg stopped. Blinked as if he were accessing a server somewhere deep in the recesses of his mind. "Wait. What?"

"I need your help, Newberg."

Just then, there was the sound of the back door opening downstairs. "Honey. We're home! I bought the groceries."

Newberg's eyes widened, his attention split between Savage and the sound of his wife and kids chattering downstairs.

Savage cleared his throat. "Newbie." He didn't respond. "*Newberg!*"

That caught his attention, and he turned back to Savage.

"I'm not here to hurt you." He gestured toward the stairs. "I'm not here to hurt your family. I'm not like that. Not anymore. But I need your help. *We* need your help."

He could hear his wife's footsteps coming up the stairs. He stared at Savage, his brain working in overdrive, trying to make sense of it all.

"They're trying to kill her," he said, placing his hand on Eliana's arm. "They assigned *me* to kill her. Just because she slept with the wrong guy—someone high up in the government. And they're afraid he told her something that could incriminate him and their whole damn black ops programs. I refused to do it. And now I'm trying to save her life."

"Honey? Are you home?" The voice coming from the stairs sounded bright and cheery.

Something about what Savage said resonated with Newberg. Clicked into place. And the taut expression on his face eased.

"I won't force you to help us, Newbie. Not even sure that you'd be able to, although I suspect you might be the only one who can. But listen. If you don't want to get involved, I'll understand. We'll just walk away. No harm, no foul. And you'll never see or hear from us again."

At that moment, his wife reached the top of the stairs, groceries in hand and looking out of breath. "Eric…didn't you hear me calling? Darling? Oh! I'm sorry. I didn't know you had company."

"Oh, yes. Uh. Sorry." Newberg walked over to his wife and gave her a quick kiss. "I didn't hear you come in. I was just talking with my friends." He turned to them both, his arm extended as if he were pointing out a brand new knife set for the kitchen. "This here is an old friend of mine, Mitch Fields. Mitch, this is my wife, Helen."

Savage stood up and nodded politely. "Nice to meet you."

"And this is…" Newberg hesitated, burning through his memories, looking for the right name.

Eliana saved him the trouble and stepped forward, offering her hand. "Hi, Helen, I'm Karyn. It's very nice to meet you."

"Yes. Karyn is Mitch's sister, and they're visiting from…"

"New York," Savage said helpfully. Though he could have slapped him upside the head for saying Eliana was his sister. *Who travels with their sister? Anywhere?*

"New York City?"

"Rochester. We develop software security for small businesses and are in town for a symposium. Thought we'd drop by and just say hi to Eric while we're here. It's been so long."

"Well, great! Nice to meet you both. If you'll excuse me, I have some groceries to put away and some hungry kids to feed."

"Oh, let me help you with that," said Eliana, taking one of the bags from her hands. "These must be heavy."

"Oh. Thank you!"

Eliana took one more from her and followed Helen into the kitchen. She looked over her shoulder and winked at Savage as she disappeared around the corner, the two women kicking up a comfortable conversation as if they had known each other for years.

Newberg turned back to Savage, his chest still heaving as he tried to calm himself. "You're not here to kill me? My family?"

Savage shook his head.

"Blackmail me?"

"People can change, Newberg. You, of all people, should know that."

Newberg thought for a moment, then nodded slowly, as if coming to some sort of understanding. He walked past Savage, giving him a wide berth like a snarling dog, and opened the sliding glass doors to the balcony. There was a pleasant breeze blowing, the curtains billowing in a rhythmic dance with its partner. Birds chirped and fluttered about the trees. Kids laughed and squealed in delight as they rode their bikes up and down the street.

"I suppose they can change," he said. "But not entirely. We are bound by who we are. Deep down inside, at our very core—we are who we are."

"I'm betting on it."

There was a quiet moment as the two men stared at each other, interrupted only by Newberg's two young kids when they came thundering up the stairs, the boy whooping and hollering and the little girl screaming. Neither one noticed Savage or their father in the living room. They ran down the hallway toward the playroom in pursuit of whatever toys they favored.

Newberg rubbed the tension from his forehead. "Sure. OK. I'll help you. I suppose I owe you that much. If you hadn't spared my life all those years ago—gave me a second chance—I would have none of this."

"I was hoping you'd see it that way."

"So. What do you need me to do?"

CHAPTER FIFTY-NINE

Arlington, Virginia

President Richard Turner approached the ball and took his time lining up the shot. He visualized the chip shot, could see it arc over the sand traps and land on the far side of the pin. The angle of the green should have allowed it to roll back toward the hole. He overshot the green by a good fifteen feet. He damn near threw his pitching wedge. Instead, he slammed it to the ground.

The President usually enjoyed these golf outings to the Army Navy Country Club. It was an excellent way for him to relax. To just get away for a while. But this was turning out to be a miserable day. First, he had received word that the rogue assassin had escaped Miami and was now in parts unknown. Then he woke up to the talking heads of the major news networks blathering on about another two murders being investigated in Miami. This was after they found a restaurant owner murdered out on Watson Island. The newest victims were an on-duty security guard for the MTA and a computer repair man in Opa-locka. Or at least that was what the papers were calling him. The President could feel his blood pressure soar. The bodies were piling up, drawing even more attention to the very thing they were trying to cover up.

The President had begun his walk across the green to find his ball on the far side when a Secret Service agent hurried over to him and handed him his secure iPhone. "DIA Director Victor Blackburn on the phone for you, Mr. President."

"By-god, it's about time!" The President snatched the phone out of the agent's hand. "What the hell is going on, Victor? For Christ's sake! All the news is talking about this morning is the murders happening down in Miami! Not one damn word about my new economic package proposal. Not one! Page three in the *Washington Post*, Victor. Page three!"

"I understand, Mr. President. Things have gotten out of hand with the Ghost hunting down Cypher. Apparently, the idea of stealth has gone to the wayside in his pursuit of his prey."

There it was again. All those damn ridiculous code names. "Are you kidding me? He's leaving dead people in his wake like a trail of breadcrumbs! And we both know where that trail will eventually lead, Victor! Don't we? I won't have that! Do you hear me? Somebody is going to take the fall! And by-god, it's not going to be me!"

"Yes, sir. I understand. But these things can be a delicate matter. There are a lot of moving parts in play that aren't immediately obvious. There is a plan—"

"Delicate? You call three murders in the last twenty-four hours *delicate*? Because I sure the fuck don't! I want you to clean this up, Victor. I want it cleaned up now. And I don't care how you do it. But you can be damn sure I'm holding you directly responsible. If you want to be the director of the NSA someday, then fix it! Fix it, or by-god, I will!"

"Understood, Mr. President."

The line went dead.

CHAPTER SIXTY

Somewhere near Denver, Colorado

Spearman lit a cigarette and tossed the Bic lighter onto the table. He took a long drag of smoke and held it for a moment before exhaling it through his nose. Yesterday was another long day. Too long. Today would be no better. In the intelligence business, there were no such things as weekends off. Or holidays. The bad guys certainly didn't get a break. He couldn't either. It was a twenty-four-hour job, three hundred and sixty-five days a year. And with that sort of dedication, it usually paid off, at least as far as the world of espionage would allow. After all, there were no winners. Just survivors.

Right now, things were a mess. He hadn't been able to reach NT-8 since last night, though he knew Cypher had slipped the net and was now in places unknown. But the Ghost would see to it. Find him again. And the good doctor? That was something else entirely—an enigma.

Spearman took refuge in the conference room, using its computer system and overhead display to study a digital evidence board he had plotted out. He took another long drag off his cigarette and again held the smoke before letting it trickle out. He studied the screen. It currently had the best guess of Dr. Shepherd's escape route down Interstate 70 from Denver to Columbus. A straight line to the east coast. They should have picked him up on the tollbooth cameras at Breezewood, Pennsylvania, if he had remained on Interstate 70. But there were no hits.

Dr. Shepherd's whereabouts had remained uncertain until last night, when they caught a lucky break. There was a campus policeman out of Morgantown, West Virginia, who had spotted a man fitting Dr. Shepherd's description in a parking lot outside a local bar. He reported there were two men engaged in suspicious activity, with possible intent to either buy or sell drugs. He would have been arrested had the officer not left in pursuit of some drunk kids on a Saturday night joyride. Worse, Spearman's cyber-warriors would have missed it entirely if they hadn't stumbled across a crucial part of the officer's report. The man in the car was driving a silver Ford Focus. Kentucky plates. Fortunately, the images were captured on the police cruiser's dash cam. Given the dimly lit interior of the car, the FRS computed a probability of sixty-three percent that it was Dr. Shepherd. The Kentucky plates—clearly visible—made it one hundred percent certain.

Unfortunately, that did little to shed any light on the doctor's whereabouts. The other threads of information—background details like family members, old friends, places of residence, work history, and education—all appeared to be irrelevant. None of it made any sense. None of it tied together. He had traveled east for nearly 1,400 miles before taking a sudden detour to the south. That could mean something. Or nothing. Logically, if he continued east, that would lead Dr. Shepherd straight into Washington, DC. But to what end? Committing suicide seemed fantastical and over-the-top for a man who had otherwise maintained a level head.

Spearman stared at one of the sidebar photos of the doctor from his days at Harvard. A faculty portrait. Neatly parted hair, oversized gold wire glasses, and a neatly trimmed beard. Younger. *Fucking asshole! You're no good to me dead!*

The phone rang. It was incessantly loud, and it broke his train of thought. But mostly it was just annoying. He'd forgotten he had forwarded all his calls. He stabbed the button on the phone. Put it on speaker. "Yeah. Spearman."

"What the hell is going on out there, Theo? This is an unmitigated disaster!" It was Victor Blackburn. "You'll excuse me if I continue to stand at attention while we talk."

"Sir?"

"Well, I just got off the phone with the President, and after the ass-chewing he just gave me, I find it impossible to sit down! It seems he isn't very impressed with the operation you're running. Very subtle, Theo."

"I don't know what you mean…"

"Don't play coy, Theo. It isn't becoming. We have three dead people in Miami. The assassin you set loose to hunt down Cypher couldn't have left a bigger swath of destruction if he were an F5 tornado!"

Theo wanted to correct him. Remind him that there were actually four people dead now—if you included the gangbanger Cypher shot all to hell. But he kept that to himself.

"What's almost as bad is we have the architect of the Dragonfly Project actively searching for a way to destroy our operation—and us along with it—heading straight for DC."

"We don't know that, sir."

The director harrumphed. "No. It appears *you* don't know that. It seems everybody else does."

Spearman stood up, flipped off the wall, and screamed silent obscenities to the phone on the table. His face was a purple turnip. "Sir. If you just let me explain."

"The time for talking is over."

There was a long pause on the other end of the line. Then, the slow release of a sigh. "I'm sorry, Theo. You've left me no choice. I'm going to have to pull you off this project. As of now, you're relieved of your duties to hunt down Dr. Shepherd. We'll take it from here. In the meantime, I need you to recall NT-8 immediately. Start cleaning this up. Make things right. I'll figure something out to tell the President."

The line went dead.

Spearman slammed his fist on the table. Roared. "Unmitigated? You're an unmitigated pompous ass!"

Spearman leaned his full weight down on the table as if he were pushing it out the door, and he closed his eyes. All his hopes of one day becoming the director of the NSA just flew out the proverbial window.

There was no chance of it now. Even replacing Blackburn one day was out of reach. In an instant, his dreams had been blown away.

Seconds passed into minutes. Spearman just stood there, listening to the ventilation air exchange kick on. The A/C hum. The table creaked as it supported his weight. He took the last drag off his cigarette before stabbing it out on the lid of his Coke.

There was a sharp rap on the door. It opened before Theo could answer. It was Blanton. "Sorry to bother you, sir. But I got an update on the interrogations of Gary and Becky Fischer."

Theo straightened and turned to Blanton. "Yeah. Come on in. What do you have?"

Blanton stepped in, opening the door wider to accommodate his extra girth. "Not a hell of a lot, sir. Both of them blabbed. Once the necessary pressure was applied, the agents couldn't get them to shut up. The problem was that neither of them said anything worthwhile. They carried on about how they didn't keep in touch with Dr. Shepherd. And then, out of the blue, he mailed them a letter. He offered them money to rent the car and drive it to Missouri to a prearranged destination. They knew nothing more than that."

"Maybe they're withholding. Playing stupid."

"Not a chance. Not with what they were just put through. They were throwing out anything they could think of just to stop the pain—especially Becky. She blathered on about how, as a kid, her family traveled to Yellowstone for vacation and spent the night at the Shepherds' farm. After that, she rarely saw him. Not even at family reunions. She received the occasional Christmas card in the mail. She even received an invitation once to a wedding she didn't attend. Outside of seeing the occasional article about Shepherd and his scientific discoveries, she heard nothing of him. All pretty mundane..."

"Wait a minute. Repeat that. What was it you said about a wedding invitation?"

"Oh, nothing. She was going on about how they didn't keep in touch. They exchanged pleasantries with the occasional Christmas card. She then mentioned that she received a wedding invitation from Dr. Shepherd when she was still in college. But that was over thirty years ago. She didn't attend, of course."

"Blanton. Dr. Shepherd was never married."

"He wasn't?"

"No. Never. Did they get a name?"

Blanton put up his finger, made a quick call on his cell phone. "Yeah. Blanton. I need the name of the bride on Dr. Shepherd's wedding invitation. Yeah. That's right. Uh-huh. Uh-huh. I know it's from thirty years ago. Just get me the info. Yeah. Yeah. That's what I need. Thanks."

Blanton hung up the phone and turned to Spearman. "Josephine Minich."

"Son of a bitch. Is she still alive?"

Blanton shrugged. "Sort of. If you want to call it living. She's suffering from Huntington's disease, and she's confined to long-term care at a research facility."

"Research facility? Not assisted living?"

Blanton shook his head. "No. They said Johns Hopkins."

"Son of a bitch! That's it! Get me the local branch office in Baltimore. I want a full specials team onsite and within the hour. In the meantime, get me Josephine Minich's room number. She's about to have company."

Blanton turned to leave, then stopped when Spearman called out to him. "Belay that order. I forgot. I've been removed from the case. Instead, get Victor Blackburn on the horn and pass along the information you just told me. It's *his* responsibility now."

"Are you serious, sir?"

"Dead."

"What if we can't get a hold of him?"

Spearman picked up his pack of smokes from the table, placed another one in his mouth, and lit it. "Then just keep trying." He exhaled sharply, and the cigarette smoke billowed out of his mouth like a mushroom cloud. "I'm sure you'll eventually get through."

Spearman grabbed his jacket off the back of the chair and hurried from the room. "In the meantime, if you need anything—bother somebody else. I have things to do. Places to go."

CHAPTER SIXTY-ONE

Denver, Colorado

Spearman parked his car and walked the short distance across the street to Prairie Meadows Park. He found a spot to sit beneath a pedestrian bridge in the outer circle of the park and took a moment to have a bite to eat.

He was still fuming at being dismissed from his duties, but in truth, it had stunned him, and he was still trying to process it all. Spearman took a bite of the Cuban sandwich he bought from a nearby strip mall and savored the burst of flavor. It was delicious, which surprised him. The irony of it being a Cuban sandwich when his entire career unraveled in Miami wasn't lost on him.

There were kids playing flag football in an open grassy area, shouting, laughing, and having fun. Unabashed and loud in a way that only children could be. The park was circular, bowl-shaped, and boxed in on all sides by rows of new homes. Central Park neighborhood. Modern suburbia. Well-thought-out. Planned to the nines. With designs for future expansion.

The community was developed on the site of the former Stapleton Airport, which was decommissioned in 1995 when the newer and much larger Denver International Airport was built east of Denver. It was repackaged as a pedestrian-centric development. And, after years of expansion, Central Park was now the largest residential neighborhood in the City of Denver, home to over 30,000 residents. It boasted fifty parks, eleven schools, a recreation center, seven swimming pools, and several shopping areas and business districts. In short, it became repurposed, just like Spearman.

And Spearman had every intention of doing that very thing. The only caveat was, from now on, he would do this without the support of the DIA. Sure…they would try to keep tabs on him. Try to prevent him from doing what he was about to do: go rogue. But he would deal with that later. Success was all that mattered.

He was sure they put a tracking device on his car. Not easily discoverable, of course. He knew they were tracking him using satellites and military drones. And no doubt his phone was tapped as well, with them listening in on his every word. That was if he still had it. He had thrown it out the window into a grassy field somewhere along Peña Boulevard.

Spearman unclipped his new sat phone from his belt buckle, punched in the proper codes, and made a phone call. An appropriate response to digital tones beeped on the other end, ensuring an encrypted conversation. Spearman said, "Code in."

A pause. Then, "Mike three three zero five five."

Confirmed. It was the Ghost. "What is your twenty?"

"North Hudson Avenue. Chicago, Illinois. Five houses south of target's current location."

I'll be a son of a bitch! A smile crept across Spearman's face. "Impressive. And just how did you acquire his location so fast?"

"Tracked him through the tail number of the plane he escaped in. They landed at DuPage County Airport. Targets took a Lyft to current location and paid for the ride with a forged credit card under their assumed names: Mitch and Karyn Fields. It wasn't difficult.

"Wait a second…did you make contact with the Lyft driver?"

"Negative. Was able to extract information through digital means."

"And the pilot of the plane?"

"Was unable to locate. Do you need him eliminated as well?"

"No! Hell no! You've done enough killing already. The bodies you left behind are stacking up. Now we're getting blowback from it."

"I still have two more marks before completing the mission."

"Negative! I repeat! Negative. Do not engage the targets. Do not engage Cypher. We can't afford to have him escape again."

There was silence again. Long. Patient.

"He can't escape if he's dead."

"Negative. I repeat. Do not engage Cypher. That's an order! I have a much better idea…and it involves the whore."

Micaela Mendoza watched the Ghost hang up his sat phone. Look around. Then turn and walk away toward the south.

She was sitting on a stoop half a dozen houses north of him, blending in with her surroundings as if she didn't have a care in the world. Just a neighbor enjoying a little sunshine on a warm fall day. When the Ghost turned and walked away, Micaela leaned back, ensuring the brick pillar on the stairs broke up her outline.

He had eyes on the stone Victorian house across the street, just two doors down. If she hadn't missed her guess, Cypher was inside that house. So near. Yet so far.

She needed to contact him. Needed to reach him without drawing attention to herself. The Ghost could already have made her out, hidden from view. Watching. She couldn't just walk up to the front door and knock. She would have to be discreet.

Then Micaela thought of something else she hadn't considered. Approaching Cypher was going to be dangerous. He couldn't know she was here to help him. Couldn't possibly know that she wasn't part of some covert operation by Darkwater to get to him. How could he trust her? He didn't *know* her.

Like a solitary lioness approaching an unfamiliar pride, she would submit herself to him. Expose herself to the real possibility of death. Only then would he trust her.

It was time to risk everything.

CHAPTER SIXTY-TWO

Baltimore, Maryland

Dr. Henry Shepherd walked from the Orleans Parking Garage to the rear entrance of Sheikh Zayed Critical Care Tower at Johns Hopkins Hospital. When he arrived, Dr. Anthony Hammit was waiting for him by the door. "Henry! So good to see you."

Dr. Shepherd shook his hand, grinning, and then clapped him on the back. "Tony! It's been too long. Thank you so much for this."

"Anything for you, Henry," he said. "You know that."

Dr. Shepherd had met Tony at Stanford University when they were both studying for their master's degrees. It was the beginning of a life-long friendship between the two men. One that didn't require immediacy. Or constant contact. Sometimes years would pass without ever exchanging a single phone call. Yet their friendship remained steadfast, as if they had spoken every day for the last twenty years.

Tony was taller than Dr. Shepherd, with a neatly trimmed beard and a fuller head of hair. And though he was just a year older than Dr. Shepherd, his silver mane made him look years older.

"You look tired, my friend."

Dr. Shepherd raised his eyebrows, feigning surprise. "You have no idea."

They walked down the corridor and up a flight of stairs in comfortable silence. Upon stepping off the elevator, they passed the nurses' station and turned right at the first cross-section. Room 2103 was at the end of the hallway.

Dr. Shepherd turned to his old friend. "How's she doing? Any changes?"

Tony pressed his lips together. Shook his head. "I'm afraid none for the better. The disease is progressing rather aggressively now. I'm not sure she'll be able to recognize you or even communicate for that matter." Tony placed a steady hand on Dr. Shepherd's shoulder. Squeezed it. "If you've come to say your goodbyes…well…you probably couldn't have come at a better time."

Dr. Shepherd looked down. Swallowed. He tried clearing his throat. "Thanks again, Tony. Really. For everything."

"Sure thing. Maybe we can go get a beer later. No offense, but you look like you could use one."

"Maybe next time. Unfortunately, I can't stick around. I have to run."

Tony looked back as he was walking away, his face betraying his confusion. "Sure. OK. Next time."

After parting ways, Dr. Shepherd stood outside the open door for a moment longer, gathering his breath. Steeling his courage. Then he walked into the private room.

The room was standard fare. Nothing unusual. Just as cold as it was sterile. An adjustable bed. Side table. A couple of armchairs for visiting guests. And a TV up on the wall. *Judge Judy* with the sound muted. But the curtains were open, and the bright afternoon sun cast its warmth across the room, its rays of light splaying across Josephine like she was the only flower in an English garden. To Dr. Henry Shepherd, her beauty had always transcended such trite comparisons.

He approached with care, not wishing to startle her. Careful not to disrupt her routine. He quietly scooted a chair alongside the bed. Sat down next to her and crossed his legs.

Josephine was looking toward the window, her mouth hanging open, her tongue pushing on the bottom lip. Her frazzled hair was tainted with gray and matted flat on one side, with an out-of-control tuft sticking up on the crown of her head. She didn't move.

Dr. Shepherd felt his chest tighten. It had been twenty-three years since he had last seen her. A lifetime ago. So much had changed since then.

Once upon a time, they had been engaged to be married. She was his forever love. His soulmate. They had met in college in Illinois and had started out as nothing more than steadfast friends, really. At least at first. They were study partners. Spent countless hours in the library together, cramming for chemistry finals. Then they began studying at his place. Sometimes hers. By the end of the fall semester, they were spending the weekends together. Going to the movies. Grabbing a bite to eat. By spring break, they had moved in together. It was true love. And for the next three years, they were inseparable.

They planned their wedding for the first summer after they graduated. He would get his master's degree right there in Champaign while they began their new life together. But then something happened. Something that wasn't a part of their original plans. Dr. Shepherd was accepted into graduate school at Stanford University. It was a prestigious school with an incredible biomedical engineering program. It was a subject that had always captivated him and a fantastic opportunity he just couldn't pass up. So he took it without ever discussing it with her. He had just assumed Josephine would come with him and that she would understand. But she couldn't. Wouldn't. And it was like a dagger to the heart. A grievous injury that their relationship would never recover from. Oh, they tried the long-distance relationship thing for a while. But it didn't work out. Did it ever? Josephine couldn't forgive him for leaving. Dr. Shepherd wouldn't forgive her for not following. Looking back now, after all these years, he realized just how petty it had all been. Just how selfish. Ultimately, he became all-consumed by his need to fix the world. To keep people from suffering like his mother had.

And here Josephine lay. Now. Suffering. It wasn't cancer that was eating her alive. It was something else. Something genetic. Something that was devouring her mind, leaving nothing behind but the shell of the person she once was. For Dr. Shepherd, it was just another failure in a lifelong string of them. It was a bitter pill to swallow, knowing you couldn't change the world. And he would have given anything just to change her little corner of it, even for a little while.

"Josie? It's me. Henry."

She didn't move.

"I wanted to see you just once more before I go. You see, I have to go away for a while. And…and I won't be back."

Drool trickled from the corner of her open mouth, down onto her chin. Dr. Shepherd leaned over to the tray table, pulled a couple of tissues from the box, and dabbed it away. He leaned in closer, looking into the cool gray of her eyes. The years hadn't been kind to her, the disease unyielding. "I should have never left you, Josie—never left for California. But I was young. Full of pride. Full of grandiose aspirations. Believing I could single-handedly change the world. But I couldn't. And you know what the funny part is? In trying to do so, I left behind the only world that ever mattered to me. The world that had you in it."

Her eyes shifted toward him in a moment of clarity. "It's about time you got here."

Dr. Shepherd sat up, taken aback by the sound of her voice. "Josie?"

"You're late! I've been waiting for my medicine for nearly an hour."

Dr. Shepherd felt his heart drop and explode like an egg hitting pavement from ten stories up.

"And my bedpan needs emptying." Her words were imprecise and slurred together like her tongue was too big for her mouth.

Dr. Shepherd sighed and looked to the table where a paper cup sat crumpled and empty. She had already taken her pill. He stood up and checked her chart. She wasn't due for another three hours. He flipped through the pages. Studied the notes. Then shook his head.

"Of course," he said, his voice warm, reassured. He sat down next to her again. "How's that? You should feel better any moment now."

"I feel better now."

Dr. Shepherd nodded. He hadn't done a thing, of course. But she wouldn't have been able to remember even if he had. Her brain lacked that cognitive function.

"I was wrong. I was wrong about so many things. Too stubborn. Too self-centered to admit it. And what do I have left to show for it? How could I ever make it up to you?"

Dr. Shepherd stood up and walked over to the window, his hands neatly tucked into his pants pockets. It was a breezy day. The trees outside danced in the wind. The cloudless skies were clear and as blue as Mediterranean waters. He sighed. Wiped a tear away from beneath his glasses.

He turned and sat down next to her again. "Oh, Josie. I've done terrible things. Horrible, unforgivable things. Things that can't be undone."

He took her hand, caressed it lightly with his thumb. He looked into her eyes, trying to make a connection with her. But she was far away. Unreachable. "Josie? Sweetheart?" Nothing.

Dr. Shepherd lowered his head and wept, sobbing into the crook of his arm. For days, the anxiety of his escape had wreaked havoc on his nerves. The anticipation of seeing Josie again after all these years. The fear of capture. Not getting to see her one last time. All his pent-up emotions weighed heavily on him to the point of suffocation. And now that he had arrived, it had all come pouring out—a surge of poisoned emotions spilling over the intellectual walls he used to protect himself. "I'm sorry. So sorry."

He felt a gentle squeeze of his hand. It startled him, and he jerked his head up. Josephine was looking at him. Her face was haggard and disheveled. But her eyes—her eyes were focused on him. Not just seeing him. But knowing him. Alive and in the moment. "Henry. Where have you been?"

"I…I've been away for a while. You know…working. But I wanted to see you. I've come so far. Been through so much."

There was genuine happiness playing in the corners of her eyes—a sliver of a smile peeking beneath her pale, chapped lips. "You did it. You finally did it," she said.

Dr. Shepherd shook his head slowly, his brow pinched in confusion. "I don't understand. I finally did what?"

"You came back to me. After all this time. You finally came back to me. I always knew you would. We were meant to be, Henry Shepherd."

Dr. Shepherd nodded. He hadn't the words. He just stared into her eyes. Present in the moment. Cherishing it for all it was worth. A moment that would never come again.

Josephine's mouth parted again, and her head sagged onto its side, the light dimming from her eyes.

"Josie? Josie!"

She didn't answer right away. But hearing her name called, she turned toward the voice, saw a man sitting next to her. "It's about time you got here. I needed to take my medicine over an hour ago."

"Yeah," he said, trying to hide the crack in his voice. "I have it right here."

He reached down and picked up his bag off the floor. He unzipped it, rummaged through its contents, then removed a cylindrical metal tube. He inserted a hypodermic needle into its sealed top, filling the syringe with a translucent amber-colored liquid. Then he leaned over and gave her the injection of medicine. "This should help you feel better. Soon."

He sat up, exhaling a long, tired breath. His thoughts clouded. Muddled.

He thought back to when he first embarked on his career in medicine. His genuine desire to help people. To eliminate suffering. To find cures for terminal diseases. First, it had been his mother. Then, years later, when he heard news of Josephine's condition, he knew he had to help her as well. So, naturally, when the opportunity to do research for the United States government presented itself, he jumped at the chance. It afforded him the resources to do actual research, with unparalleled financial backing. He could finally make a difference. Hell, his technological advancements in nanotechnology and the neurosciences alone offered hope. *Real* hope.

But now he had run out of time. There were no cures. No long-term solutions. It was over now. The injection of nanobots he gave Josephine was his last gift to her. It offered her some reprieve from the ravaging effects of the disease and would improve her quality of life, even if for a short while.

Dr. Shepherd stood up. Looked into Josephine's eyes one last time. He leaned down and kissed her tenderly on the forehead. His lips felt feverish as they brushed against her clammy forehead. "Forgive me for not staying by your side. I'll always love you."

He picked up his bag and pushed the chair back to where he found it. He took one last forlorn look out the window. Then he turned and walked away. He didn't look back.

Thirty minutes later, the specials team arrived, storming the room with military precision. Team members barked out orders, armed and ready. They swept all four corners of the room, protecting each other's backs.

Nothing. Just an old woman lying comatose in her bed, ramrod straight and half mummified from whatever disease she was suffering from.

But the whole second floor was in an uproar now. Nurses were screaming while doctors ran toward the commotion. Calls for security screeched over the intercom. It was pure pandemonium.

The team leader was wearing a mic and headset. He stopped. Flipped a switch. "Yeah. Reaves here. Yeah. It's done. No, sir. There's nobody here. Just some half-dead old lady. No. I don't see how." The team leader stopped as the old woman shifted her weight and looked at him earnestly. "Wait a minute, sir. I think she's trying to say something."

The old woman opened her mouth, a wheezy breath trying to form words. So the team leader walked closer to her, encouraging her to speak up with the twirl of an impatient hand.

She said, "Where have you been? You're late. I've been waiting for my medicine for over an hour now."

The team leader squinted and then wrinkled his nose as if he caught a whiff of something dreadful. "I wouldn't worry about it, sir," he said, adjusting the mic closer to his mouth. "She wouldn't be worth our time."

There was a pause as he listened. "Yes, sir. Understood. Where? Copy that. We'll coordinate with the other team. On our way."

CHAPTER SIXTY-THREE

Chicago, Illinois

Newberg used his sleeve to wipe the sweat from his brow, then growled through gritted teeth.

Savage raised an eyebrow. Unfolded his arms. "What is it?"

"This is infuriating. I can't get past their firewall. It's incredibly complex. Way beyond anything I've ever encountered before. Certainly more than I encountered seven years ago."

Savage stepped a little closer to get a better look at the monitor. It was nothing he recognized. Just a bunch of numbers. Sequences of ones and zeros. Newberg was writing his own code. He placed his hand on the back of the office chair, leaned in. Newberg noticeably shifted away, as if Savage was plutonium and emitting toxic radiation. "Relax, Newberg. I've already told you. I'm not here to hurt you. I'm here because I need your help."

Newberg nodded and took a breath. A bead of sweat dangled off the end of his nose. "Sure. OK. But what happens to me—my family—when you don't need my help anymore?"

"Then we'll be even. And I'll be forever grateful."

Newberg looked at him, his mouth open as if he wanted to ask something. But then he closed it.

Savage wasn't sure what the problem was. "And you'll never have to see me again?" he asked, unsure of what he was supposed to say to allay his fears.

"Yeah? And what if I fail? What if I can't break into the Pentagon's database? What if I can't find the information you're looking for?"

Savage blinked. Raised an eyebrow. "I don't know. I wasn't thinking about failure, Newberg. It's not a part of my DNA. I guess we'd just have to keep running until we found another way. But I do know that I won't hurt you. Not you. Not your family. You have my word on that."

"Sure. OK."

"I believe you can do this, Newberg. If there's anybody that can do this, it's you. Trust me on this."

He nodded.

"So what's the trouble? Didn't you say you left a back door to their system? Leaving you a way back in?"

"Yeah. But I can't get to it."

"What do you mean? It's gone?"

"Yeah. Probably. I mean…it was very subtle. Undetectable. But they must have found it. And they've added additional security over the years. A crazy amount. It's like peeling away a layer of an onion only to find another one. And another one after that. Each layer creates its own set of problems. Each one slows me down. This could take months. Years even! Not hours."

Savage said nothing. Just stood there. Thinking.

Newberg added, "I can't just bust down the door trying to get to the next one. I have to be careful. Precise. Remove the layers as if using a scalpel. If I screw up, they'll know it. They'll be able to locate us. And they'll be on my doorstep before I can kiss my ass goodbye."

Again, Savage said nothing. He folded his arms. Looked around the room.

Newberg's office looked business professional, befitting his financial advisor moniker. The room was adorned with chic and contemporary furnishings, predominantly in black and gray hues, complemented by pops of burgundy in the curtains and large cushions on the loveseat and armchairs. Black-and-white photographs of Chicago were presented like a fine art exhibit, with meticulous framing and matting, perfectly level and evenly spaced. A careful balance of living plants and modern art knickknacks were included to elevate the ambiance. Savage suspected Helen had a hand in the decorating. It certainly wasn't Newberg.

It bore no resemblance to his computer room from seven years ago. A teenager's room. Floors strewn with filthy garments and discarded fast-food packaging. Walls plastered with provocative pin-up girls and marketing posters of the newest video games.

But one thing remained the same. At the center of the office was a high-tech computer system. This one had three side-by-side monitors and a CPU with enough RAM to handle almost anything the hacker could throw at it.

Savage turned back to Newberg. Nodded. "I know I'm asking a lot. This is a monumental task to complete in such a short time frame." He patted him on the shoulder and gave it a reassuring squeeze. "Just do the best you can."

Savage left him to his work and headed down the hall to the living room. As he took in the rest of the house's layout, he realized the entire place was impeccably decorated—befitting the 4.5 million dollar price tag of such an upscale house in the Lincoln Park neighborhood.

In the center of the room, the two children sat on the oversized sectional couch eating fruit snacks and watching a cartoon on the big-screen television. The boy, Lucas, was about four years old. The girl, Mia, was still a toddler, around two.

Savage walked past the kitchen, caught Eliana's eye, and they exchanged smiles. She was talking to Helen, and he left them to their girl talk. She seemed happy. Occupied, for once, with something other than running for her life.

He approached the kids and asked if it was OK if he could sit down and watch the movie with them. Lucas nodded, stuffing a purple fruit snack into his mouth, while Mia just pointed to the screen and babbled something that sounded like *ribbit*. Maybe *robot*? Yes. She had said robot.

On the television, an animated movie showed a giant Godzilla-sized robot attacking an army of humans. Soldiers firing their weapons.

Tanks rolling in, attacking from the ground. Fighter jets shooting their missiles from the air. Battleships attacking from the sea. All converging on the enormous evil robot. Savage thought it seemed a bit much for little kids, but he was hardly the person to be dispensing parental advice.

The robot looked like a three-headed Hydra. "He looks kind of scary," he said, making light of the heavy action. He wondered if they would have nightmares.

Lucas shook his head. Pointed at the TV screen. "No. He's the good guy."

Savage scrunched up his face. "Really?" He looked at Mia and asked the little girl, "What do you think? He seems scary to me."

Mia turned to him, looking at the strange man sitting beside her. Unsure of who he was, but unabashed about talking to him. "Uh-uh." She shook her head, her huge blue eyes like liquid pools sparkling in the sunlight. "What's your name?"

Savage spun around at the sound of a man screaming in alarm, "Asesino! Asesino!" The soldier had a gun pointed at his head, his face contorted in an angry growl of defiance, ready to pull the trigger. Savage blinked at the click of the gun. Then the soldier was gone. He simply wasn't there. In his place stood a little girl, the soft glow of a nightlight providing the only ambient light. She was about five, waist high, her bangs hanging across her face. She was wearing her red Christmas pajamas, with a pink stuffed dragon tucked neatly under one arm, and wiping the sleep out of her eyes. "Are you Santa?"

Savage's heart plummeted like a dropped anchor in the ocean. That was unexpected. But he was quick on his feet. Changed tactics. He shook his head and whispered, "No. Just one of his many helpers."

The girl stared at him under the influence of a sleep-induced lethargy. "What's your name?"

Savage stiffened and saw little Mia looking up at him. Innocent. Expectant. Savage shook his head, trying to dispel whatever cobwebs remained. *What the hell was that?* "Um. My name is Mitch."

The little girl smiled and put her finger in her mouth. Shook her head.

"What? Don't you like my name?"

She shook her head again.

"Why not?"

She shrugged.

Savage let it drop and turned to watch the TV. The evil robot had been about to blow up a battleship at sea when a little boy came running up, screaming for him to stop. The boy was telling him he didn't have to kill. He didn't have to be the bad guy. He could be whatever he chose. Only then did he shapeshift back into a friendlier, more relatable robot, resembling more of a giant Tin Man than a scary sci-fi monster. Obviously, the kids had seen this movie before. Perhaps dozens of times.

Lucas turned to Savage, grinning. "Told you."

Savage sat quietly for a moment, lost in his thoughts. Then he nodded. "Yeah. You did."

He looked over his shoulder, back toward the kitchen. Saw Eliana chopping some vegetables, chatting with Helen. She looked up and saw him staring at her. She smiled.

Eliana watched Savage talking to the children from the kitchen. They were sitting on the couch, watching a cartoon and chatting as if it were the most natural thing in the world. In her experience, men were uncomfortable around children. They talked at them, not to them. Savage was doing more than either of those things. He was interacting with them. Engaged in the moment. Well, except for one, when he seemed to drift off, lost in his thoughts. But it was brief.

He then looked over his shoulder, caught her staring at him, and smiled. *Busted.* She couldn't help herself and smiled in return.

She returned to slicing up the cucumbers for the salad. Helen was next to her at the counter, chopping up a couple of heads of romaine lettuce. "I don't know how you do it. How do you manage to juggle a full-time job, be a mother, and still have time to run a household? You're amazing!"

Helen laughed. "It can be a handful. That's for sure. I get up pretty early. Get a two-mile run in before work. Shower. Cook breakfast for Eric and the kids. Then it's off to the daycare before heading to the office."

"What do you do?"

"I'm a marketing manager at Hilliard and Bowers Global."

Eliana nodded in approval.

"Anyway…after a nine-hour day, it's time to come home and fix dinner. Clean up. Spend some quality time with the kids. Give them their baths and tuck them into bed. Maybe read them a story. If I'm lucky and not completely exhausted, I try to find some alone time with Eric. Just us, without the kids around."

"Wow! I can't imagine. Do you have a golden lasso and an invisible plane to go with those superpowers?"

Helen laughed again, louder this time. "No. I wish. But Eric helps a lot. He has a heavy workload, too. Yet he always finds time for me and the kids." She took advantage of the open layout of the kitchen to look in on her children as they watched TV.

"They're wonderful," Eliana said.

"Yes, they are."

Eliana finished with the cucumbers and switched to dicing up some tomatoes. She peeked into the living room, looked at Savage. She was quick about it, trying to look casual. And her face warmed at the sight.

Helen glanced at Eliana, then put the chopped salad into a storage container for later. "So…how long have you known?"

Eliana looked at her, a moment of puzzlement passing across her face. She tilted her head slightly. "How long have I known what?"

"That you're in love with him."

Oh, Crist! Obvious much, Eliana? She closed her eyes, shook her head as if she hadn't heard her right. "In love with who?"

Helen rolled her eyes, then gestured toward the living room. "With Mitch, of course."

"Wait. I'm sorry. You misunderstand. Mitch is my brother…"

"Oh, please, honey. I'm not blind. And I know my husband. He's a sweetheart. But he's a lousy liar. Besides…it's written all over your face."

Eliana cast her eyes down, oddly embarrassed, feeling like her emotions were on display for the entire world to see. Butterflies swirled in her stomach and a smile brushed across her lips. She looked at Helen and nodded. Her face was all aglow. "Actually…we've only known each other for a few days."

Helen's smirk turned to a toothy grin. "Honey. That's the way it works sometimes. One minute they're as irritating as a rock in your shoe—the next, you can't stop thinking about spending every waking moment with them."

Eliana nodded, her smile widening. "Yeah. It's a lot like that."

Helen stooped down and sorted through the canned goods in the cabinet below. She found the tomato paste and set the cans on the counter. "Well, good for you. Consider yourself a fortunate girl, then."

Eliana gave out a little laugh, sounding breathy. Shy. "Why do you say that?"

"Because it's hard enough to find love in this world. To have someone love you back? That's special."

Eliana shook her head, her face falling flat. "Oh, no. I don't think so. Um…Mitch…could never love someone…" She stopped, tried to find the words. Then she said, "Do you really think so?"

Helen nodded and gave her a half-hearted shrug. "Of course. He might not know it yet, but he's crazy about you. It's written all over his face. The way he looks at you. The way he talks to you. That's not exactly brotherly love."

"Yeah. About that…I'm sorry about misleading you."

Helen dug out the can opener, then opened the tomato paste and a couple of cans of sauce. "Look. I don't know what trouble you two are in. It's none of my business. But I know Eric is trying to help you, and that's good enough for me."

"Look. Um…maybe we shouldn't have come here. It's just that…"

"Stop right there. I don't need to know. Whatever trouble you two are in—it doesn't matter. You aren't bad people. I know that much."

"No. You're right. We're not. Mitch needs Eric's help. He feels he's the only one who…" She let her words trail off, unsure whether to proceed. "I'm sorry. I've said too much already."

Helen sighed. Thought a moment. Then she leaned against the counter, moving close enough that only Eliana could hear her whisper. "I'm not naïve, Karyn. I know my husband had a past. And I have a pretty good idea of what that was. I also know he had a life-changing event at some point—when he was younger. I think Mitch had something to do with that. Not sure how or why. I just know that I'm grateful. Because it doesn't matter what he was like back then. I know who he is now. A loving husband. A wonderful father. And that's good enough for me."

Eliana said nothing at first. She just took it all in. Considered her words. Then she smiled at Helen and hugged her. "Thank you."

Helen patted her back. "Of course." Then she made a big show of grabbing a couple of wine glasses from the hanging stemware holder. "So, do you two have plans for tonight?"

Eliana had no idea, and it showed on her face. "Oh, I don't think we have any plans. I think they have a lot of work to do still…"

"Oh, please. Don't get me started. Men are full of excuses. They'll eventually have to come up for air at some point, you know."

"Well…"

"Do you have any dinner plans? Pfft. Doesn't matter. Why don't you stay here and have dinner with us? We're having lasagna. Eric's favorite. My mother's recipe. Been in the family for years."

"Oh, that's very sweet of you, but…"

"Great. It's settled. And no excuses. There's plenty. I always make too much. Do you two have a place to stay? A reservation at a hotel?"

"Well, we just got into town. I'm not sure we have reservations anywhere…"

"Good. Why don't you guys stay the night? We have a spare room upstairs."

"Um, that's very sweet of you to offer. But we don't want to intrude…"

Helen was staring at her, her eyes practically boring a hole through her.

"…any more than we already have?" Eliana offered a sheepish grin. "Sure. That sounds great. Thank you."

Helen wiped her hands on a towel she had draped across her shoulder, then looked at Eliana, questions forming in her eyes like bubbles in an open bottle of champagne. "Looks like you could use a long, hot bath." Before Eliana could answer, she added, "Do you have anything to change into? I didn't see any luggage. Maybe something a little…softer? Pretty?"

She shook her head. Then suddenly remembered she did. "I do! I have a nice summer dress that Savage…*Mitch* bought me."

Helen tilted her head as if surprised. She smiled. "Really? Interesting. Anyway, did you bring any toiletries with you? Any makeup?"

"Uh. A little. I have a toothbrush. And a little makeup kit. You know…for touchups. I didn't have a lot of time."

"Oh, Karyn…honey. There's always time. Believe me. Come upstairs with me, and we'll see what I have."

CHAPTER SIXTY-FIVE

"Fuck this!" Eric slapped his coffee mug off his desk, sending it and its contents flying across the room.

Savage shook his head. Glanced at his watch. Six o'clock. Dinner would be ready soon. "Jesus, Newberg. Calm down. What's the problem?"

"You're screwed! I'm screwed. We're all fucking screwed! I can't bypass their security. Not in the damn time you need it. I've tried every goddamned program I can think of—Metasploit, Kali Linux, Nmap, Acunetix WVS—hell! Why am I telling you? Let's just say I've used the very best of the best hacking tools. I've even tried one of my own that I wrote. I'm sure I can do it. But it's just going to take a very long time."

"We don't have that luxury."

"Don't you think I know that? Hell, Savage! You're acting like this is done by brute force—like kicking in a door. But it's not. It takes finesse. Studying the firewall's weaknesses. Looking for exploits. Attempting to inject SQL codes."

"OK, I get it." Savage rubbed his hand across his face, feeling just as frustrated. "But getting pissed off about it isn't helping us. You've been at this for six hours straight. You need a break, Newberg. Get your head right again."

"No! We don't have the time for that!" he snapped, an errant droplet of spittle shooting out of his mouth.

Savage sighed. "We don't have time for you *not* to be thinking straight, either."

Newberg refrained from speaking. The muscles in his jaw bulged with tension.

"Why are you so upset? I don't know how many times I have to tell you—I won't hurt you no matter what happens. You're safe."

"Well, *you're* not!" His face reddened.

"What? What are you talking about?"

"Jesus! You don't get it, do you? You spared my life, Savage! I owe you for everything! Do you understand me? *Everything.* And now your life hangs in the balance. And Karyn's, too, or whatever her real name is! I have to make this right!"

Savage closed his eyes and bowed his head. "OK. I get it. You feel you owe me. But the best thing you can do for me right now is to try to relax. Get some food in your stomach. Spend a little time with your family. Maybe it'll clear your head, and you'll find a new angle to attack this thing. So what do you say? I'm sure dinner's just about ready. Come on."

★   ★   ★

There was a gentle rap at the door, followed by Helen popping her head in. "Decent?"

"Yeah." Eliana smiled and stood up from the chair in front of the vanity mirror. She ran her hands down the sides of her dress, smoothing out the fabric. "What do you think?"

"You look gorgeous."

Eliana smiled, small dimples forming at the corners of her mouth. "Really? I hope so."

Helen pulled a couple of tissues from the box on the vanity table and handed it to her so she could blot her lips.

Eliana blew her bangs up out of her face. "God. I'm nervous."

"That's understandable. There's only one chance to make a first impression."

"Oh, we're way past that. If I haven't impressed him yet with what he's seen, then covering it up with a dress isn't going to help."

Helen raised an eyebrow. Covered up a laugh. "Wow. OK then."

Eliana's eyes brightened. A hint of color shaded her cheeks. "What?"

"Nothing. No judgment here! Let's just focus on accentuating your natural beauty, then. We'll let the dress highlight your more demure qualities."

Eliana burst out laughing, then tried to stifle it by covering her mouth with her hand. "Oh? Demure. And what good will that do?"

Helen shrugged. Tossed her hands up. "I don't know. Maybe remind him how stunning you look when your dress comes off?"

Eliana laughed again, looking away with her mouth open in mock disbelief.

Helen took a hold of her arms. Looked her in the eyes. "OK, honey. You got this. Dinner's on the table. Come on down when you're ready."

★   ★   ★

Savage poured a glass of milk for Lucas, handed Mia her trainer cup, and then took his seat. Newberg sat across the table from him, his chin resting in his hands, with a dead look in his eyes. His thoughts were somewhere else. The worry lines on his forehead looked compressed, as if burdened by the weight of desperation.

Savage had genuine concerns as well. They'd bought some time by getting out of Miami. Their whereabouts were unknown to the DCS. But the time gained was finite. He knew they would never stop the hunt. Never quit until he and Eliana were dead. But the difference between him and Newberg—amongst many things—was that Savage didn't allow worry to cloud his judgment or slow him down. He thrived in a pressure cooker.

Helen set the bubbling dish of lasagna in the center of the table. Tossed the big bowl of salad. Then she took her seat at the end of the table, between the children and her husband.

Savage wondered what was delaying Eliana. "Where's Karyn? Did anybody let her know it's time for supper?"

Helen began making the plates for the children. "Yeah. She should be down any minute."

As if on cue, Eliana came down the stairs, careful with her steps, and then walked to the dining room. She stopped in front of them. Smiled. "It fits!"

Savage blinked, taken aback by her entrance.

"Well…what do you think? It's the dress you bought me down in Miami." She twirled, showing it off.

It was a teal-blue surplice dress with ditsy print and a waist tie to gather the ruffled hi-low hem. The deep V-neck and leg slit accentuated her sleek, feminine figure perfectly.

"Do you like it?"

"Wow. Yeah."

Eliana smiled. Tucked a loose strand of hair behind her ear. "Really?" She was practically glowing.

"You look stunning."

"Thank you." She tucked the skirt beneath her legs and sat at the table beside Savage. "I mean…thank you for the dress. I love it."

Little Mia applauded like it was somebody's birthday, and Lucas simply said, "Cool dude," while shoving a chicken nugget in his mouth. Helen and Eliana exchanged knowing glances, which didn't go unnoticed by Savage.

The rest of the meal continued without fanfare, without fuss. They chatted amongst themselves. Talking about everyday things. The mundane. Weather. Shopping. Places to go on vacation. But Helen didn't ask questions about his and Eliana's unannounced arrival at their home and their subsequent need for Eric's help. Perhaps she already knew. Oh, maybe not the details. But understood enough. "Any luck?" she asked her husband.

Newberg was laser-focused on the saltshaker, oblivious to the sound of his wife's voice, until she nudged him with her elbow and asked again.

"No. Not yet."

Mia squealed as Lucas began tapping her head with a half-eaten French fry.

"All right!" said Helen. "That's enough. If you two are done eating, it's time for your bath. No. I said that's enough. I didn't ask you if you wanted to. I said it's time for your baths. After that, it's off to bed."

★　　★　　★

Savage jumped at the sound of the little girl's groggy voice. "Are you Santa?"

"No, just one of his many helpers." He was walking toward her when the image suddenly shapeshifted. She was no longer a little girl standing in her red footy pajamas and clutching a stuffed toy dragon. Savage was suddenly back on the Negro Mako, and one of Berto Ramón Maduro's elite personal guards was holding a machete, ready to charge him. Before he could react, his memories changed focus, shifted to something else entirely. They were more like snapshots from a camera rather than watching a movie. Each picture a freeze frame. Each punctuated with a blinding flash of light. Jungle. Palm trees. Starry skies on a moonless night. White sandy beach. Poorly lit docks. A black yacht. The engine room. Sabotage. Finding Marcos asleep in his bed. A man standing in a hallway, gun in hand.

No, it wasn't a man with a gun. It wasn't a man with a machete. It was the little girl again; the scene queued in Savage's mind, repeated itself.

"Are you Santa?"

"No. Just one of his many helpers."

The dark-haired little girl rubbed the sleep from her eyes and yawned.

Savage walked over to her with an easy step, his arms outstretched in an invitation to pick her up. She offered him no resistance and allowed him to carry her down the hall.

He whispered, "Which room is yours? This one? Yeah? It's a very nice room."

Pink the Playful Dragon decor dominated the room from the wallpaper and lampshades to the comforter, bedsheets, and even the waste basket. White Christmas lights hung in the window, casting a soft glow.

He tucked her neatly back into bed and covered her and her stuffed dragon with the sheets and heavy comforter.

"Better? Yeah? OK. Good. Now close your eyes and go to sleep right away. You don't want to be awake when Santa arrives, do you? Of course not. He might fly past your house because you were still awake."

The girl rubbed her eyes again. Shook her head. She looked troubled. Confused.

"Are you OK?"

⋆   ⋆   ⋆

"Mitch! Snap out of it. Are you OK?"

Savage startled. A flash of light and the sound of the kids squealing snapped him back into the room. The dining room…in Eric Newberg's house in Chicago.

Eliana was standing over him, her hands clutching his shoulder, leaning in close, studying his face. "Mitch? What was that? Are you OK?"

The nanobots coursing through his blood began filtering the adrenaline from his system. His oxygen leveled out. His heart steadied. "I don't know *what* the hell that was."

"Were you dreaming again?" she whispered, her face so close to his that her hair brushed his cheek.

"No. This wasn't a dream. I was completely awake." He hesitated. Thinking. "And this wasn't the first time this has happened. It happened earlier, when I was watching TV with the kids… I think it's getting worse."

Eliana was looking into his eyes, a look of concern etched on her face. She nodded. Cupped her hand along the side of his jaw. "OK. We'll talk later."

Suddenly, there was a loud knock at the front door, and the room fell silent.

CHAPTER SIXTY-SIX

"Are you guys expecting somebody?" Savage looked at Eric. Then his eyes shifted to Helen.

"No! Not at all." Eric's eyes bulged with alarm.

Helen got up from the table, sensing the tension in the room skyrocket. "Eric. What's going on? What's the matter?"

Savage stood up and held his hand out, urging everybody to sit tight. He then silenced them with his finger. The mammoth clock adorning the living room wall marked off the passing of seconds lost, each tick a warning.

Eliana took his arm in hers and looked at the stairs leading down to the foyer entrance. "It's them, isn't it? My God, Savage. They found us already!"

Helen jumped to her feet. "Would somebody tell me what the hell is going on?"

Savage looked her in the eyes. "Helen? Those baths you were about to give the children? Now would be a good time to do that."

Helen lifted Mia from her highchair and planted her across her hip. She herded Lucas close to her side. "You guys are scaring me!"

Newberg said, "Helen. Do what…do what Mitch says. I'll explain later. Now go on upstairs with the kids."

"But why—"

"Now!"

Helen took both children in her arms and ran up the stairs.

There was another knock at the front door. Faster. Urgent.

Savage turned to Eliana. "That goes for you, too. You better go upstairs as well. Get your gun. Join Helen and the kids. Lock the door."

There was fear in her eyes, but Eliana stood her ground. "No way. I'm not leaving you."

"Eliana…"

"I said no! I'm not leaving you." She stood in front of him, forcing him to look at her.

He clenched his jaw out of frustration, then shook his head. He turned away. "Newberg. I need you to answer the door."

"Me?"

"It's your home. If they're not sure we're here and they're just checking the joint out, it isn't going to do us any good if I answer the door."

"Sure. OK. It's my home. But what the hell happens to me if they have a gun? And fucking shoot me?"

"It won't come to that. I'll be by your side, just out of sight."

Floorboards creaked upstairs. Then a door slammed, followed by the metallic click of a lock being engaged.

"Maybe it's the FBI. Maybe they've discovered my probes into the Pentagon's firewall."

"Newberg?"

"What?"

"Answer the damn door."

"No, wait!" Eliana took off and ran up the stairs to the third floor. "I'll be right back."

But they didn't wait. They couldn't.

Eric Newberg swallowed. Nodded reluctantly. He headed down the stairs to open the door. Savage trailed closely behind, then hid off to the side.

Newberg took a deep breath. Glanced at Savage, then opened the door.

A woman was standing on the stoop, long dark hair pulled into a ponytail, a ball cap pulled down low on her face. "Grubhub," she announced, sounding cheery. "I have an order for two pies from Giordano's. One sausage, the other pepperoni."

Newberg just stood there, mouth hanging open. He said nothing.

"That will be $76.77, please."

Newberg caught his breath. Shook his head. "We didn't order any pizza."

The woman leaned in slightly, pretending to read the receipt to him as if there were a problem. "I'm not entirely sure who you are, sir. My sources tell me you're Eric Newberg. My name is Micaela Mendoza, and I'm looking for Cypher."

"Who?"

She repeated it. Enunciating each syllable as if she were talking to a slow child. She was of Hispanic descent but clearly had been born and raised in the States as she had no accent.

There was the sound of a gun cocking, and the woman claiming to be Mendoza closed her eyes and mouthed a prayer. "I've come to warn him. The DCS has tracked him down. They know he's here. I'm just trying to help."

"We'll see. Step on inside," said a disembodied voice from somewhere off to the side. "But keep your hands where I can see them."

★   ★   ★

Newberg stepped back from the door, allowing her the room to enter. He was the fidgety type, bustling with nervous energy, shifting his weight from one side to the other as if he'd had too much sugar on his Frosted Flakes.

Micaela Mendoza stepped inside and handed the pizzas to Newberg. For some strange reason, he thanked her for them, then closed the door behind her.

The man known as Cypher came out from hiding, his pistol pointed at her head. A split second later, a woman ran up with dark shoulder-length hair and a gun of her own clamped firmly in her right hand.

Micaela felt like she was about to be the target in a turkey shoot. She took a deep, steadying breath. She held her arms out from her sides to show compliance, but her hands shook uncontrollably. "Cypher, I admit I'm about to pee my pants here. But I am very pleased to meet you…at last. You're a tough man to track down. We've worked together before, you know. But I've never met you in person."

He said nothing, but studied her intently.

Micaela turned her attention to Eliana and was relieved to see her alive and well. *"Debes ser Eliana Bautista. También es un placer conocerte finalmente." You must be Eliana Bautista. It's a pleasure to finally meet you as well.*

The beautiful woman looked at Savage for guidance but kept her gun trained on Micaela.

"I know you have no reason to trust me. But I've come a very long way—put my ass on the line—to warn you. Control has sent an assassin after you both. He's an NT. But he's been upgraded with some first-generation Cyborg tech."

"The Ghost," Savage added quietly.

"Yeah. That's right. He's tracked you from Miami. And he's been casing this place out all afternoon. Planning his next move. He doesn't know I'm here. Control doesn't know I'm here."

"Who are you?" Eliana demanded.

"I'm Micaela. Micaela Mendoza. I work in the same black ops program as Cypher."

"Why do you keep calling him Cypher?"

"It's my code name," he said. "Mendoza was my handler. A liaison for Control. Provides important information in real time by communicating directly with the asset in the field."

Eliana stiffened. She pulled the hammer back on her .357 and braced her arm to fire.

"Please don't! I swear I'm here to help. I think what the DCS is doing is wrong. When they turned on their asset because he failed a mission…" Mendoza closed her eyes. Swallowed. Then looked at Eliana. "I don't know what they're accusing you of—or what they think you did. I don't know why Cypher balked at his orders. But my gut is telling me this is all wrong. It *feels* wrong. Look—I've been trying to help you guys for the last couple of days. They've suspended me from duty. Hell! I'll probably be lucky if they don't fire me."

"Or kill you," Savage added.

"Oh, shit. Yeah. Or that."

"How can we trust her?" asked Eliana. "This could just be some elaborate plan to trick you, Savage. Get close enough to kill you."

Micaela was laboring for breath now. Scared out of her mind. "I know what this sounds like. I get it. I wouldn't trust me either."

"She's telling the truth," he said, reaching out and placing a hand over Eliana's. He pushed the gun down toward the ground.

"How do you know?"

"By listening to the pitch of her voice, its inflection. Watching her eyes. Her body posture. Oh, a lot of different things. But I'd say there's a ninety-seven percent probability that she's telling the truth. What's that you said about trying to help us in Miami?"

"Like I said, I don't want to be a part of what they're doing—not anymore! What they're doing is wrong. When the police tracked you down to the Bag-N-Go in Allapattah, I tried to delay them. Buy you time. I wanted to give you a fighting chance to get away. SWAT was on their way. If I hadn't cut the power to the building…"

"We'd be dead."

She paused, nodded. "I'd tried to call you. But your phone was either turned off or dead. So I tried tracking you through your biosensor in the nanoport. But I lost that signal, too."

"I removed it."

Micaela cringed, her stomach flipping like a flapjack. "I even tried sending them on a wild goose chase in the wrong direction. But somehow the Ghost managed to find you. Track you."

"And then you followed him…"

"Right. You're pretty smart."

"Apparently, so are you. And you say he's out there right now?"

"I'm sure of it. But there's more. Control has sent a specials team to kill Henry Shepherd. He's on the run. I think he's responsible for sabotaging the operation. He's been running for as long as you have. Maybe longer."

"The doctor?"

"Yeah." Micaela watched Cypher. He was thinking, and she could practically see the wheels turning in his mind as he sorted through all the scenarios and calculated their probable outcomes.

"OK. Here's what I need you to do. If the Ghost is truly watching this place, he watched you come inside. You can't stay here—at least not without tipping your hand. You need to go back out the way you came in. I assume you have a car rental?"

Mendoza nodded.

"Head back to your car. Find a place to park on another block. Then walk back to the alley behind this house and we'll let you in from the garage entrance. Then we'll get started."

"Started?"

"Making plans of our own."

CHAPTER SIXTY-SEVEN

After Savage let Mendoza back into the house from the backside alley, he immediately began preparations to fortify the place. It was a daunting task as they had three stories to protect and two entrances to barricade, not to mention a dozen or more windows. They had only four adults and four guns to defend themselves. Mendoza was ex-military and could handle a gun. Eliana knew the basics, but he would never expose her to a real firefight. Eric and Helen? The only guns they ever saw were on TV. Their only chance was to hole up in a single room. Stay close. And only have one door to defend. That was Newberg's office.

"I think the doctor sabotaged the mission," said Mendoza. "It probably has something to do with the nanobots. It appears they're used to make the assassins compliant. To remain impartial so they won't question their orders. But Dr. Shepherd did something to you. Allowed you to think for yourself. I don't know for sure. Honestly, I don't think Control knows either."

"That's bullshit. I've always had control of my thoughts. I've always known what I was doing. And the marks they sent me to eliminate were vile, abhorrent people. Sadistic bastards like Berto Ramón Maduro."

Eliana was standing next to Savage, her arm tucked into his. She looked up at him, her eyes searching his. She was worried. Scared. But she didn't say a word. She just squeezed his hand—a promise to him.

Newberg stared in silence, too. He opened his mouth to speak. Shut it again. He tossed his hands into the air as if to say what the hell. "Are you sure about that? What about me?"

"No way. I wasn't even a part of the NT program back then. It didn't even exist yet. And I didn't kill you. I spared your life."

"Exactly. You didn't kill me then. Because you *chose* not to. You said I was just a kid."

Savage pinched his brow.

"And how many missions have you balked at since that time seven years ago?"

"None!"

"Right. None. At least up until the night you balked at your orders to kill Eliana."

"The same night Dr. Shepherd disappeared," added Mendoza. "Let's face it, Cypher. He did something to you. Something to set you free. And he's been running for his life ever since."

The room fell eerily quiet, the only noise the whisper of the ceiling fan circulating the stagnant air above. Mendoza stepped forward and folded her arms in front of her chest. "We need to help him, Savage. They aren't interested in capturing him. They mean to kill him before he can escape the country."

"Do you know where he's headed?"

"End destination? Unknown. But the best guess is he's going to fly out of Baltimore. He said his goodbyes to someone he used to be really close to, a fiancée from long ago. He's leaving."

Savage stood silent for a moment. Thinking. Calculating the risks. "I can't."

"What do you mean you can't?" Her eyes narrowed. "He needs you."

"And so does everybody else in this household!" he snapped. He was angry. Not at Mendoza. But at the injustice of it all. "In case you have forgotten…there's an NT assassin out there looking for an opportunity to kill me. To kill Eliana. And he won't care who he goes through or who he kills to get to us!"

Mendoza looked away, shook her head. She knew he was right. And she was just as frustrated.

Savage suddenly realized that Helen was nowhere to be found. "Newberg. Where the hell are Helen and the kids?"

"They're downstairs. Helen's grabbing a few things and taking the kids to her mother's house in Des Plaines."

"What? Are you crazy? It's not safe for them to leave! What don't you understand about this?"

"I tried to tell her. But she wouldn't listen. She's scared…"

"I don't give a damn! Find Helen and stop her. Bring her and the kids back to this room, even if you have to drag her. Now! I don't care if she gets mad. Blame it on me!"

Newberg dashed out of the room.

"He's scared, too," Eliana said. "We all are."

"I know. I know." He drew her in close. "I'm sorry. I'm trying to do the best I can. There are too many moving parts. I can't protect everybody."

Savage looked at Mendoza and shrugged helplessly. "I can't save the doctor. I can't be in two places at once."

"Yeah. I know," she said, sounding tired. Beaten down. "I just was hoping we could save him."

"We can't. But *you* can."

"What?"

He took a step toward her. "You can save him, Mendoza. Take a red-eye flight tonight. Charter a private jet if you have to. You need to get to Baltimore and warn the doctor before they get to him. You need to convince him to come with you."

"I can't help him… I'm not a field agent. I'm just a handler."

"You have to try. Find him. Play your hunches. You're obviously good at that. You found us."

"That was different."

"It isn't. We need him. I need him. He might be the only person alive who can help me find the answers about my past—what they did to me. But it's more than that. I owe him. I'm asking you to find him, grab him, then run like hell. We'll keep in touch by sat phone. I'll give you instructions once you have him."

She looked scared. Her skin gleamed with perspiration. And she was swallowing a lot. But there was no doubt in her eyes. They were focused. Resolute. "And what about you? What are you going to do?"

"We need to find evidence of Operation Darkwater. Find tangible proof that the United States government is using assassins to target American citizens. That they're using them not only to circumvent laws and eliminate difficult criminal elements, but also to target political opponents."

That caught Mendoza's attention. She unfolded her arms. Straightened. "What do you mean?"

"President Turner had a political rival murdered. Remember the accidental death of Conall Bennett and his family about a year and a half ago? They found them dead in their vacation home in Colorado. The autopsy revealed they died from carbon monoxide poisoning. A faulty fireplace or something."

"And you think the President had something to do with that?"

Savage stared at her. He didn't have to say a word. His eyes said it all.

"Jesus. How do you know this?"

Savage pulled Eliana even closer, offering her some solace in his arms. "Earlier this summer, at the Republican Convention in Miami, he had arranged for a private escort service. And he was drunk…and he started running on at the mouth. Bragging about how powerful he was."

Mendoza's jaw dropped, her face collapsing like a sagging tent. She looked at Eliana, and all at once, the puzzle pieces fell into place. "Oh, God. I'm so sorry, Eliana." She closed her eyes and shook her head in disbelief. "I can't imagine what you've been going through."

"*Gràcies.*"

Just then, Newberg returned with Helen and the kids in tow. Both kids were asleep. Lucas in his father's arms. Mia in her mother's. Helen didn't say a word. She didn't have to. She was pissed. You could see it burning in her eyes.

Savage carried on, unconcerned. He nodded to Mendoza. "How far is your rental?"

"Not far. I parked it one block over. Why?"

"You're going to go get it. He'll know Eric and Helen's cars. He's been casing the place out all day. But he won't recognize yours. You literally can drive away and will be just another nobody going about their business. Get to the airport—catch a flight to Baltimore tonight. They won't be looking for you. At least you'll stand a chance."

Helen interrupted. "I'm not staying here! *We're* not staying here!" She stomped over to where Savage was standing and slapped him hard across the face. "Damn you! Damn you for putting our family in danger! How dare you!"

Savage blinked, moved his jaw back and forth to work out the sting. He didn't say a word. He deserved it. But Eliana pushed her way in between them. "Stop this, Helen! It's not helping. Savage doesn't want to hurt anybody. He only—"

"Savage? Is that his name? Or is that his reputation? Whatever! Is your name even Karyn?"

"No. My name is Eliana."

Helen went to slap Eliana, too, but she grabbed her hand and held it firm. Her eyes narrowed to thin, glassy ribbons. "You're right. We shouldn't have come. We needed Eric's help. But I see now we were wrong."

Helen looked like she was about to spit nails. She was rearing for a fight. But Mia started crying, and she backed away, bouncing her in her arms, trying to calm her with a soothing voice.

Savage looked at Newberg. "Go on. Get on out of here. Take your family and get as far away from here as possible."

Newberg didn't expect that. He stuttered as his mouth tried to play catch-up with his mind. "Me? I'm not going anywhere."

"Sure you are. Agent Mendoza? Get your car. Return to the rear entrance of the house. Remember, we have no idea where he's at, so be quick about it. Stop only long enough to pick up the Newbergs. Then get the hell out of here. Drop them off at Helen's mother's house and take the first flight you can get to Baltimore."

Mendoza nodded.

Helen let her shoulders drop. "Oh, thank God. Come on, Eric. We're going to Mom's."

"No. I'm not going."

"What do you mean you're not going?"

"I can't. I have to stay and try to help them."

"You don't have to help anybody, Eric. This is serious. Someone out there is trying to kill them. Now stop fooling around and let's go." Her voice wavered, her emotions laying heavy in her throat. Then it cracked. "Eric?"

Newberg walked over to his wife, put his arms around her, then kissed her on the forehead. "Go. Take the kids. I'll join you at your mother's as soon as I can."

She couldn't believe it. Her mouth dropped. "You can't be serious, Eric? You owe him nothing!"

"No! You're wrong! I owe Savage everything!" He held her by the shoulders, securing her attention. "Do you understand? If he hadn't spared my life seven years ago, I'd have nothing! There would be no you! No kids! No house, no cars. No fucking bank account!"

Savage sighed, tossed his hands up in the air. *I give up.* "It doesn't matter, Newberg. We're getting nowhere breaking into the Pentagon's database. Even if we could somehow, it would be like looking for a needle in a haystack trying to find what we need. It's like you said…we're screwed."

Mendoza walked over to where Eliana was standing. She looked at Savage and then at Newberg. "What's the problem?"

Newberg was trying to chew a cuticle off his thumb. He shrugged casually. "I can't get past the firewall. Well—I can—but it will take quite a bit of finesse. More time. Something we don't have."

Savage added, "He left a backdoor into their security system seven years ago. But the system has changed. It's not there anymore. On top of that, they've added additional layers of security. Improved it."

"What if you could bypass their newest security? Get on the inside to access their database?"

He shrugged. "I'd be able to write some code. Tunnel my way in. But that would require somebody from the inside giving us access to their operating system. Clicking on a link in an email. Signing on from an unprotected network. There are a bunch of different ways. But none of them likely."

Mendoza smiled and took her phone out to make a call. "Yeah? I think I know somebody who can help you with that."

CHAPTER SIXTY-EIGHT

The only ambient light in the room was from the soft glow of Newberg's computer monitor. Mendoza had taken Helen and the kids to safety hours ago. Eliana lay sleeping on the loveseat, curled up and wrapped like a cocoon in a fleece blanket.

Savage sat on the floor, his back against the wall, studying her slackened face. It was peaceful. Relieved from all her care, all her worries. A reprieve from all the insanity. He listened to her breathe softly through parted lips.

He had thought of joining her, holding her in his arms. But it was fleeting. He would stay awake all night, keeping watch. Protecting them both from the attack that was sure to come. It was the Devil's hour. And he was near.

Newberg sat at the desk, his fingers tapping away on the keyboard in a hypnotic rhythm, performing magic. He was in now. Thanks to the help of Skye Freeman, he bypassed the firewall and began tunneling his way through the labyrinth of endless files and databases. Her work shift had ended a couple of hours ago, but by then she had done her part. She had provided Newberg with passwords and accompanying access codes. Guided him through the various programs and how to use them. She didn't have access to the top-secret data he was looking for— mainly anything leading to evidence of Operation Darkwater. Domain. Planning. Funding. Training and assets. Presumably, those assets would include information about Cypher. But also anything constitutionally illegal that could tie the President of the United States to Darkwater. Thus far, he had found nothing useful. But Newberg made a copy of anything that seemed even remotely relevant and sent it to an encrypted cloud—a near-infinite bounty of storage that he had procured illegally.

Savage was impressed. Both Skye and Newberg were savants when it came to cyber security. Both geniuses in their own right. Yet both socially awkward. But Newberg—good ol' oddball Newberg—he was the best of the best. Once he gained entry, he uploaded the code he had written. It allowed him to manipulate the numbers, keeping the Pentagon from accurately determining the amount of data being uploaded. It also allowed him to search for specific keywords in the database and file systems.

Now and again, Newberg would make a noise, breaking the fragile silence. A grunt. An indiscriminate "hmm." Sometimes, he would curse. Then he would start typing again.

Savage stood up. Stretched. Then walked across the office and edged his way to the room's lone window. Despite the mini blinds being closed, he made sure not to walk in front of them. He took a peek from the edge of the window frame, careful not to cast shadows from the light of the monitor. He scanned the streets below. Cars were lined on both sides of the street as far as his eyes could see. It was too early for foot traffic. Too early for people to be heading off to work. A solitary cat slinked down the sidewalk, stopping now and then to look around as if checking to see if he was being followed.

Savage swept his eyes over the houses across the street, scanning them for any signs of life. Any movement. Any shadows. There was nothing. Not yet.

Newberg broke the silence when he said, "Son of a bitch!"

That got Savage's attention. He immediately joined Newberg at the desk, looking over his shoulder. "What is it?"

"This is some slick shit here. I've been reading all this information about the various programs under the umbrella of Darkwater. All the technological advancements they made for their assassin program. Genetic manipulation. Nanobot technology. Even cybernetic implants.

They're literally working on creating a bionic man. Wasn't that a show from the seventies?"

"Probably."

"Anyway, each program built itself off the developments from the previous one. The starting point was the Hydra Project. Genetic manipulation. It created assassins with better tissue generation. They healed faster, had improved muscle strength, and better cardiovascular stamina. And with their cognitive enhancements, they could go days without sleep, without degradation of their ability to think. They were even immune to pain without inhibiting their ability to react in the name of self-preservation. Incredible."

"Why are you talking in the past tense? *I* came out of the Hydra Project."

"Ok. Sure…sorry."

Savage heard Eliana stir, then yawn. He smiled as she climbed out from under the covers and walked over to join them. She slid her arms around him and laid her head against his shoulder. "Sounds like you guys found something."

Newberg guffawed. "You got that right, sister. This shit is over-the-top crazy. After Hydra, they began Project Dragonfly. They introduced nanotechnology to their super-assassins. That's where they manipulate matter on a microscopic scale to create new materials and engineer devices that work in nanoscale dimensions. Sort of like little microscopic robots."

Savage smiled at the oversimplification—if not outright inaccuracy—but it was close enough. He nodded. "Yeah. Nano-tech. I was the prototype."

"Oh. Right. You, of all people, should know. I keep forgetting. Anyway…these nanobots of yours can increase oxygen flow to body tissue, allowing you to run for miles without tiring. Hold your breath for a couple of hours. Remove toxins and other contaminants from your bloodstream. I bet that would come in handy during a party." He smiled.

Savage shook his head.

"Sure. OK. So they found a way to augment intelligence and improve problem-solving." Newberg leaned back in his chair and folded
his arms across his chest. "The nanobots can transfer information directly to your cerebral cortex, giving you instant knowledge on a subject
you previously knew nothing about."

Eliana yawned again, nestled her head beneath Savage's chin. "Like
downloading a program on a computer?"

"More like saving a file on a hard drive. But yeah…you get the
idea."

Savage rolled his eyes. This was nothing new to him. He didn't need
to hear it. He was living proof of it. More importantly, he didn't care
for Eliana hearing it. What sort of monster would she think he was?
Some kind of freak show. "Not to be rude, Newberg, but I need you to
move along. There's nothing here that helps us. Anything about Operation Darkwater?"

"Oh, shit tons! I've found all kinds of references to specific black-
op missions, including the elimination of targets through lethal force.
But tying them to a particular organization or ranking official has yet to
yield any results."

"Nothing on the President?"

"Well…that's very interesting in itself. It seems someone has gone
to great lengths to cover up his…indiscretions…in Miami. There's no
video evidence, of course. Not in the room, anyway," he added, if a bit
sheepishly. "Just the Secret Service escorting the President to his room
after the acceptance speech at the convention. But they've gone to great
lengths to pin this call to an escort service on someone named Senator
Kelley. I guess he's a dirty old fart."

Eliana gnashed her teeth. "The President's no saint either."

A dark shadow passed over Savage's eyes. "It doesn't matter to the
American public whether the President slept with an escort. They could
never prove it in a court of law. Besides, U.S. presidents have been promiscuous since the office came into existence. Dirty laundry? Sure. But
hardly felony material. They couldn't even impeach him for that."

Eliana kept her eyes down, but she squeezed Savage tighter, practically pulling him through her.

"We need something more substantial."

"Well, trying to have Eliana murdered is pretty substantial," said Newberg. "Then trying to cover it up by making it look like the random work of a serial killer qualifies as pretty illegal."

"Wait a second. Say that again. What do you mean *cover it up*?"

"Well, you should know. *You* were the assassin. You killed the Russian mob boss, Aleksei Petrenko, first. Shot him while he was eating dinner at a downtown restaurant with his family. Followed a month later by the murder of Armando Cortez, drug king extraordinaire, shot at long range while swimming in his penthouse pool. The third murder was supposed to be Eliana, of course, a deliberate attempt to make it look like the killer considered the sex trade in Miami just as dirty as the other criminal factions. You were supposed to be some crazed vigilante on the loose, if you will. There might have even been a fourth hit planned. But you kind of messed that part up, I think."

"I didn't do those hits."

Newberg tilted his head and gave a half-hearted shrug. "Well...all the evidence to the contrary says you did. It wasn't just a cover story. You actually *were* the Miami Sniper. You did much of the preliminary planning yourself."

Savage felt his chest tighten. "No. That's impossible. Don't you think I'd remember doing all that? I was in Miami for only a couple of weeks. Before that, I spent several months in Nevada. Hell...I remember all the places I traveled to. California. Brazil. Italy. And I think before that I was in Mexico."

Eliana slipped her arms from his waist and gently placed her hands on his chest, staring up at him. She knew he was struggling, trying to put the pieces together.

Newberg was oblivious, of course. He wasn't good at picking up on nonverbal cues—one of his shortfalls with social interactions. "Well, that's because those memories you have are false memories planted by

Darkwater. You see, that's the real genius behind these nanobots. Darkwater found it useful to prevent the super-assassins from remembering every mission. Some were acceptable. But not all of them. The nanobots could ensure that the darkest and most top-secret missions would remain just that—secret, with no chance of light ever being shined on the details. They weren't just erasing memories. They were creating brand-new ones. Crazy, huh? But that's just the half of it. To ensure that the assassins didn't question their orders in the first place, they had to manipulate their judgment center. And they succeeded. By applying even a weak magnetic stimulation to that part of the brain, it disrupted electrical currents to those cells, keeping them from firing. In effect, it turned off the assassin's moral compass. It made them numb to the horrors of murdering somebody."

Savage's head was spinning. He didn't like this. Didn't want to believe it. Was he just a monster, after all?

He felt his blood pressure drop. His breathing ramp up. And suddenly he felt lightheaded.

★   ★   ★

It was a moonless night, but Cypher's eyes adjusted to the dark long before he reached the edge of the tree line. It was bitter cold, with a westerly breeze pushing ahead of the low-pressure system moving in. The rustling of the pine boughs above was a mere whisper in his ears.

He left the cover of the pine trees behind, made his way across an open frozen field, and approached the house with extreme caution. The lonesome yelps of coyotes in the distance warned of danger, their sound both mournful and foreboding. There was a long wooden footbridge ahead, spanning a winding, frozen creek and festively draped with clear Christmas lights. The homeowners had illuminated the walkway with landscape lights, but burned-out bulbs provided deep pockets of shadow for him to make use of.

Cypher kept a low profile as he slipped amongst the ornamental shrubs and outdoor furniture of their yard. He kept within the moon shadow cast by the roofline, making his way down the side of the house.

His footprints were light and well-placed but still visible. Fortunately, the forecast called for heavy snowfall throughout the night. By morning, there would be a foot of fresh snow on the ground.

He checked his watch. It was a quarter after three, and no sign of life was stirring in the house. Lights were off, and the well-to-do owners were fast asleep, snug in their warm beds for the night.

At the end of the house, there was a row of basement windows. Three of them. The preliminary scouting of the property two days prior revealed that the last window had its latch unfastened. Here, he would make his entry. Cypher knew there was a security system. He had obtained the make and model, and his memories had been preloaded with the operations manual. If he were unable to disarm the security system, not only would he wake the entire household, but it would transmit an alarm to the local police. Despite their distance from the remote luxury home, they could reach the premises within thirteen minutes. With the icy roads, maybe twenty. Plenty of time for him to do the deed and escape. But none of that mattered. Body count alone didn't measure this mission's success. It was the plausibility of accidental death. No trace of his presence could remain.

He methodically worked his way closer to the basement window, painstakingly slow, burning precious time he didn't have. In the deep of the woods, the shrouded voices of nightfall spoke without form: trees creaked and groaned in the wind, pinecones fell, and animals unknown skittered away in search of shelter from the approaching storm. And just at the upper cusp of his hearing, he detected the faint sound of Christmas carols chiming somewhere deep within the hollows of the home. Despite the late hour, this wasn't unexpected. It was Christmas Eve.

He needed to slip through the window and down into the basement, make his way to the far side of the room, and find the security panel by the stairway.

The basement's stagnant air was chilly and smelled of must. The bare cement floor was icy and unyielding, like permafrost on the tundra.

It was a short walk to the keypad, though he had to navigate the basement's clutter: stored lawn furniture, archery sets, boxes of books, old golf clubs, and racks of outdated clothes that, despite the owner's good intentions, never seemed to make their way to charity. Cypher placed each step with care. Deliberate. He had no light to see by, no sense of direction in the basement's pitch darkness—just a Rangeman watch he used to keep his bearings. Above him, he heard the telltale sound of the family's eight-year-old Doberman's claws clicking against the ceramic tile as it patrolled the kitchen for unknown tidbits.

He reached the keypad, but instead of flipping open the cover and punching in a corresponding security code, he placed a small rectangular card against its surface and held it there for three full seconds. Its red LED lights blinked in tandem and then turned green. The security system was now neutralized. More importantly, there would be no record of it being disarmed.

Savage made his way up the stairs, slow, careful not to make the steps creak. Despite his best efforts, a low growl sounded from the other side of the door. Savage paused, listened. The dog was sniffing at the bottom of the door, a deep rumble sounding in its chest. He didn't have much time before the dog would start barking. He reached into his belt pouch and fished out what he was looking for: a chunk of raw steak. "Hey, Daisy, girl. Is that you?" His voice sounded warm and friendly, like they were old pals meeting again. He took a breath and opened the door. The dog scooted back, not sure how to proceed. But when she saw the cube of meat in his gloved hand, she sat in submission. "Good girl, Daisy," he whispered, tossing it to her like a ball. She snapped it out of the air, gulping it down without chewing.

Easy as that. Daisy wasn't a trained guard dog. She was the family pet. And, by the looks of it, was frequently hand-fed scraps from the table.

Daisy licked her lips and raised a paw, begging for more. Savage reached into his pouch again and tossed her another one. She greedily gulped it down. Happy. Her bobbed tail rang like a bell. She then lay on her side and yawned. One minute and forty seconds later, the spiked meat had the Doberman fast asleep. "Goodnight, Daisy."

Savage pressed on, making his way past the formal dining room and out into the grand room with exposed beams and vaulted ceilings. It was there he discovered where the Christmas carols were coming from. The TV was left on, with its home theater system streaming the holiday channel and its nonstop coverage of Christmas music.

He walked upstairs to the second level. Control had prepped him with the house's floor plan. He knew every room, every corridor, as if he had lived in the house his entire life. There were four bedrooms, including the master, and two full baths.

He made his way down the hallway to the nearest room. Then the music stopped. Bing Crosby's baritone voice no longer reverberated through the walls. Did the station lose signal? Or did somebody turn it off? There was silence. There were no footsteps. No voices. The TV was likely set to sleep mode.

He made his way toward the master suite, where he would find Conall Bennett sleeping.

There was a solitary nightlight plugged in halfway down the hall. Its cover was porcelain, with an intricately detailed nativity scene etched onto its surface. Primarily decorative, it only offered a nominal amount of light to navigate the halls at night.

He reached the door. It was slightly ajar, and he could hear the soft, rhythmic sounds of deep slumber from inside. But there were no voices. No lights. Not even a TV inadvertently left on. Savage checked his watch—three thirty-one. He was running behind schedule.

Savage used a small tactical mirror to check around the corner and into the room. There were two figures curled up next to each other, spooning: Conall and his wife, Jennifer.

He entered the room and padded carefully over to the freestanding gas fireplace in the farthest corner of the room. It was lit, turned on low, its tired flames licking at the fake logs, while its dim light sent shadows dancing across all four walls. Savage crouched down behind the fireplace, reached into his utility pocket, and pulled out a painter's five-in-one tool, its edge caulked with a thin layer of silicone sealant. In just a matter of a few seconds, he wedged its blade between the seams of the flue pipe and made a separation between the two joints. It would do. And nobody would be any the wiser. After all, somebody could have bumped it with the vacuum. Tripped over it. Knocked a potted plant onto it while reaching high on the shelf for a book. It didn't matter. It just had to seem plausible.

Savage pocketed his makeshift tool, turned the flame to high, and slipped back out of the room. He left the door open and looked in the room one last time. Sound asleep.

Then he jumped as a soft voice interrupted the perfect stillness of the moment. "Are you Santa?" He spun around and instinctively reached for his gun. But his SIG wasn't there. The mission parameters required him to leave it behind.

He didn't need it. It was only a little girl. She was standing about ten feet away. The soft glow of the nightlight draped across her cheeks like a silken shroud. She was about six years old, waist high, with bangs hanging down across her face. Conall's granddaughter. Hailey. She was wearing her red Christmas pajamas, with a pink stuffed dragon tucked neatly under one arm and wiping sleep out of her eyes with the other. Conall's daughter and her husband must have flown in from California for Christmas and were sleeping in one of the other bedrooms.

Savage's heart dropped like a woodman's axe. This was unexpected. But he was quick on his feet. Changed tactics. He shook his head and whispered, "No. Just one of his many helpers."

The girl stared at him under the influence of a sleep-induced lethargy. "What's your name?"

He didn't answer. Instead, he walked over to her with an easy step, his arms outstretched in an invitation to pick her up. She offered him no resistance and allowed him to carry her down the hall.

He whispered, "Which room is yours? This one? Yeah? It's a very nice room."

Pink the Playful Dragon decor dominated the room from the wallpaper and lampshades to the comforter, bedsheets, and even the waste basket. Christmas lights hung in the window, adding a homey warmth to the ambiance. Quite the guest room for some child that lived in another state altogether.

He tucked her neatly back into bed and covered her and her stuffed dragon with the sheets and heavy comforter.

"Better? Yeah? OK. Good. Now close your eyes and go to sleep right away. You don't want to be awake when Santa arrives, do you? Of course not. He might fly past your house because you were still awake."

The girl rubbed her eyes again. Shook her head and yawned.

"OK, then. Go to sleep and dream of all the presents you'll receive when you wake up in the morning."

Savage kissed her on the forehead, playing his part to its fullest, and walked out of the room. For her and the rest of the family, morning would never come.

CHAPTER SIXTY-NINE

Savage lay on the floor, looking up at the ceiling. Eliana and Newberg were hovering over him, talking to him, trying to snap him out of it. Then he remembered.

"Fuck! No! No!" Savage pounded at his eyes with clenched fists. A startling, undistinguishable groan escaped from his throat. It sounded inhuman. His face morphed into a grimace. Anguished. And then he was racked with violent sobs.

"Savage! Honey! Please talk to me. What's happening?"

"Oh, God! No! Not the little girl, too!"

Eliana exchanged glances with Newberg, then leaned close to Savage, taking him into her arms. She held him tight and let him cry it out. She didn't say a word. And didn't let go.

Eliana wasn't sure how long his sobbing lasted. It was probably for just a couple of minutes. But it seemed longer. The sound of his anguish, guttural sounds of despair, would last a lifetime for her.

Finally, Savage relaxed. His breathing slowed, and he lowered his hands from his face. Eliana kissed him and wiped away the tears from his cheeks. "You scared the hell out of me," she said, trying to smile. It was a thinly veiled attempt to keep it light.

He kept his eyes locked on the ceiling fan above him.

"You remembered something else, didn't you?"

He swallowed. Nodded slowly. "I remember."

"What?"

"Everything." He waited. Tried to get control of his runaway emotions. But it was impossible. "I'm responsible. I'm the one who murdered Conall Bennett. I killed his entire family. The little girl…"

Eliana pinched her lips together, trying to keep them from trembling. Tears clung to her eyes like morning dew on a flower, refusing to fall. "Oh, God, Savage. I'm sorry. So sorry."

When Savage didn't reply, she tried sitting him up, then looked to Newberg to help her get him to his feet.

He stood there for a minute, took a deep breath, then nudged them away. "I'm fine."

"You don't look like you're fine, Savage."

"I fucking killed them. For nothing. Why? They weren't evil. They were just an everyday American family who decided they wanted to do something good in this world. To help facilitate change. To make a difference." He stopped and turned back around to look at Eliana. "The only mistake Conall Bennett was guilty of was deciding to run for president against Richard Turner."

"Maybe this was all just a dream, Savage. Memories are a tricky thing, you know?"

He shook his head, turned away from her. He couldn't look at her. "It was real. I was there. Fuck! I was there."

She took a step closer to him, taking hold of his arm, and urged him to turn back around and face her. "It's not your fault."

He jerked his arm away. Spun around with burning venom in his eyes. "Then whose fault is it, Eliana? Because I sure as hell don't remember you being there. Nobody else was there. *I* was the one who broke into their house. Sabotaged their fireplace. Because of me, they all died that night."

Eliana charged right back at him. She refused to let him push her away. "That's not true, Savage, and you know it! Darkwater performed experiments on you. They programmed you to obey orders. They altered your memories. Look! You weren't even aware of what you did until tonight! Damn it, Savage! They *made* you!" Her eyes were on fire, her jaw locked in determination.

"Yeah. I know. They made me. And do you realize how close they came to making me kill you?"

The color drained from Eliana's face. Her jaw tightened. "It doesn't matter."

"It does."

"No. It doesn't."

"Damn it! It matters to me! If Dr. Shepherd hadn't done something to me—something that broke me—I would have killed you, Eliana! I would have killed you as sure as the sun is going to come up in the morning. And I would have never fucking known you. Or cared for you. Or fell in—damn it! Fuck me!" He roared. Picked up a paperweight off Newberg's desk and threw it across the room. It punched through the wall like a cannonball, landing with a thud somewhere in an adjacent room.

Newberg practically jumped out of his socks. Took a step back. But Eliana stood steadfast, placing her hand against his shoulder.

Savage stood in silence, his fist clenching and unclenching as he fought with his inner demons. "Do you know what the worst of it is? Huh? Do you?"

She shook her head, her brow knitted with worry. "No. Tell me."

"Remembering."

Eliana cocked her head, clearly puzzled.

"I wish I never knew who I was. Or knew the things that I did." He scoffed in disgust. "Did you know there was a little girl in the house that night? Conall's granddaughter. She wasn't supposed to be there. She must have flown in with her folks for Christmas. Anyway, I must have woken her up somehow. She asked me if I was Santa. What a fucking joke. Santa. I tucked her back into bed. Kissed her goodnight." He slowly shook his head, not wanting to believe it. "I actually kissed her goodnight. Lied to her. Because in a couple of hours, she would be dead. Dead by my hands as surely as if I had pulled a trigger."

Eliana said nothing. Another tear spilled down her cheek, and she swiped it away with the back of her hand, leaving a wet smear behind.

"What kind of monster would do such a thing?" he asked. "How evil would you have to be to murder without remorse? To be so cold."

Eliana shook her head again. "I don't know. How could I?"

Savage looked over his shoulder, surprised to hear her say such a thing. She was staring at him. Not with judgment, but with genuine concern.

She said, "And neither could you because you don't even know that man. You're *not* that man."

"Oh, yeah? Then who am I, if not a monster?"

"I don't know who you were then. But I know who you are now. You're Brent Savage. The man who didn't kill me that night in Miami. The man who—despite his brainwashing—*chose* not to kill me. And you're the very same man who's done nothing but protect me ever since. You saved my life, Savage. Over and over again. But most of all, you've given me a reason to live again."

Savage closed his eyes and turned away from Eliana. He couldn't get away from his self-loathing. "No matter what I do from now on…no matter how many good deeds I do for the rest of my life…I'll still be a murderer. A monster."

"Stop saying that! You're not! And you never were!"

"Oh, yeah? Really? How could you possibly know who I am?"

"Because I could never love a man like that." Eliana inhaled deeply, her nostrils flaring. She was breathing hard, doing her best to maintain control.

"Wait. What did you say?"

"I've fallen in love with you, Savage. I…I know that sounds crazy. We've only known each other for a short while—but I can't help it. It's true."

"No!" He jerked away. "I—no! I don't want you to love me! Do you hear me?"

Eliana folded her arms in front of her chest. She was trembling. More tears spilled over. "Look at me."

Savage cursed under his breath. Ran his fingers roughly through his hair. He sighed, then turned around.

"Look at me," she repeated. "Look me in the eye, Savage, and tell me you don't feel the same about me. Go ahead. I'll believe you. Because I'll believe anything you tell me. You've never lied to me. You've always been honest. Brutally so. Even when it wasn't convenient."

Savage opened his mouth, knew what he wanted to say. But couldn't. It was a no-win situation. "When this is all over, you need to get the hell away from me, as far as you can, Eliana. You need to run away and never look back. I'm not worth it."

"You don't have the right to tell me what or *who* I find worth loving!"

Savage shook his head in disgust, waved her away. His face was burning red hot. He was angry beyond words. With her. With himself. With the whole damn situation. He stared in silence at the window. Thinking. Then he said. "This has got to stop. We can't keep running. Hiding. This ends now!"

Savage ran out of the room, ordering them both to stay put. He made a mad dash down the hallway, leaped down the stairs, and crashed out the front door with an explosive release of energy. Still angry. Out of control.

He leaped off the front stoop, cleared the stairs, and landed easily on the sidewalk below, all before the first gunshots were fired. *Crack. Crack.* He dove behind a car. *Crack.* And just like that, the fight was on.

CHAPTER SEVENTY

The first two shots ricocheted. The first off the cement handrail of the stoop. The second off the stone facade of the house. Shards of stone rained down on Savage. The third took out the side mirror of the black Ford Escape Savage was hiding behind. The light crack of gunfire echoed down the street. Faded. Then nothing.

Savage pulled his SIG from his holster and screwed on the suppressor. He duck-walked toward the front of the SUV, popped up, and fired a burst of three shots toward the place where he had seen the muzzle flash: a narrow gap between two houses just up the street and on the other side. The man ducked behind the wall just in time; the bullet missed by mere inches and shattered the corner brick right where he once stood. It had to be the Ghost. And he was true to his name.

Savage stood up, his gun extended. He began walking straight for the opening. When the head appeared again, he fired two more shots in quick succession. *Pfwap. Pfwap.* Again, he missed. But this time, when the brick and mortar shattered, he heard a high-pitched yelp in response.

He started running straight for the corner of the building. He was in the open now. Vulnerable. Yet he didn't hesitate. He ran even harder. Faster. He leaped onto the hood of a Mustang, crushing it, then jumped his way clear of the yard's decorative iron stake fencing. He approached the corner blindly, only slowing down to slice the pie around it.

Nothing. Nothing but a narrow walkway no wider than he was. He pushed on, narrowing his shoulder so he could slip down the walkway with his gun extended. He had to be careful. If the Ghost took advantage of the funnel trap, he'd be pinned in with nowhere to maneuver. But he wasn't there. He was on the run.

Thirty yards down the brick path, the walls opened to a small yard. Trees and thick shrubbery clogged any obvious path to the alley on the other side. It was overgrown and unkept. Savage stopped. Waited. He couldn't see a thing in the pitch darkness. The Ghost could be anywhere in the tangle of brush and briers. He could have a gun pointed at his head right now.

Savage bent his knees, trying to lower his profile, when he heard a person suddenly crashing through the brush, running away, heading for the alley on the other side.

He jumped up and raced after the sound, his left arm in front of his face for protection, his right arm still clutching the gun down at his side. It was slow going, but he made it to the end of the lot, bruised and beaten. A five-foot wooden fence stood in his way, but he jumped over it like a gymnast hurdling a pommel horse. He landed in the open alley between Hudson and Sedgwick. He spun in a circle, his head on a swivel, his gun drawn, looking for a target. Then he saw the Ghost. He was running away, full out.

Savage ran after him, certain he could catch him. He pumped his arms and dug in hard. But he fell behind. Couldn't gain ground. This was troubling. Savage was fast. Olympic fast. Genetic modification of his leg muscles had made him that way. His improved lung capacity and the nanobots' ability to keep lactic acid from building up in muscle tissue also meant he could run long distances without tiring. But the Ghost was faster. He just about disappeared when Savage saw him stop, veer to the right, and jump over a fence.

Ten seconds later, Savage reached where he had last seen the Ghost. No. It wasn't a fence. He had jumped up onto the roof of a garage. Maybe eight feet high. Savage followed, jumping high enough to catch the roof but still needing to hook his leg over to pull himself up. He cleared the roof in another fifteen feet, and once again he was in another yard with more trees. A sidewalk led to Sedgwick Street.

He raised his gun, spun, and hit all points of the compass. He spotted the Ghost running away from him, still to the north. And pulling away fast!

Again, Savage chased after him, putting all he had into the run. Concentrating on technique. Making himself as aerodynamic as possible. Pushing hard. But the Ghost had out-distanced him with no real effort. And soon the darkness swallowed him whole.

Savage continued to run in the same direction, flailing blindly into the dark. He was less than fifty yards from the corner of Sedgwick and Webster when he spotted a side alley off to his right. He stopped. Looked around. Saw nothing. The Ghost had disappeared. But Savage had an eerie feeling, his sixth sense kicking in, and he removed himself from the middle of the street. He made his way over to the side alley, taking cover by the brick house on the corner. He looked down the side alley and saw it leading to the east before turning back toward the south, thirty yards in or so. Another blind curve. A perfect place for an ambush. But Savage was fueled by anger now. He had to put an end to this for Eliana's sake. Even if it meant him dying, he had to try.

Savage eased his way down the street, keeping his back against the stone wall of the house. He kept an eye out for the Ghost. High and low. Nothing was out of the realm of possibility. There were a couple of hidden corners just down the wall of the building. Two garage doors cut into the building at an angle. Either could have been a perfect ambush point.

Savage switched sides of the road, increasing his field of view to the bay doors. There was no one there. The next thing that caught his attention was a community of garbage cans lined up single file along the curve and disappearing around the corner. Another place for the Ghost to lie in wait.

Savage stopped. Waited. He searched for any signs of disturbance. Any movement. But there wasn't any. He waited some more. Waited until his skin crawled. He walked toward the garbage cans and stopped. He took a few steps past them. Just enough to look toward the south.

Nothing. Savage sighed. This was taking too long. And he had strayed too far from Newberg's house. From Eliana.

Suddenly, a phone rang, and Savage's heart leaped to life as though it had been jolted with an electric cattle prod. He looked around. He didn't see a phone, but he could hear it. He took a few steps back. Turned around and walked his way back to the first garbage can. The ringtone grew louder. Hesitantly, he lifted the lid. There, sitting on top of an overstuffed black garbage bag, was a cell phone. He picked it up. The caller ID said unknown. But Savage knew.

"Yeah?"

He heard breathing on the other end of the line. Steady. Not labored at all. "Finally. A real challenge," the voice said, thick with a Cuban accent. "You surprised me back at the house. I didn't expect you to come charging out the front door like some crazed shoot-'em-up John Wayne cowboy. You almost got me."

"Shame I missed."

A pause. Then he said, "You wounded me. I took shrapnel in my left eye."

"Now I feel real bad. So close, yet so far."

"You're a funny man, Cypher. But you won't find this so funny. I've taken the girl."

Savage felt a rush of adrenaline blast through his body, and he started running back toward the house. *He doubled back on me!*

"No need to hurry. It's too late. I've already taken her. And if you ever want to see her alive again, you'll do exactly as I say."

"Fuck you!" Savage kept running.

"Tsk. Tsk. I'd be careful what you say to me, Cypher. You've hurt me. You took something from me. So now I'm going to take something from you. Hurt you even more."

Savage gritted his teeth. Spat. "What the hell do you want?"

"Hmm. Plenty. But I'll tell you what…I'll give it some thought. I'll call you back later. Give you specific instructions. Oh! And Cypher? If

I were you, I'd make sure I'd keep that phone close by. I'll only call once."

"You son of a bitch. I'll fucking cut your heart out."

The line went dead.

Savage didn't stop running. The Ghost had played him. Suckered him in. And now Eliana's life was in danger. Newberg's too! The Cuban assassin never even mentioned him, so Savage feared the worst.

When he arrived at the house, he noticed the front door was open and hanging awkwardly from its hinges. Savage continued without slowing down, jumping over the front stoop, onto the landing, and into the house. He raced up the stairs to the second floor and ran down the hall toward Newberg's office, his gun leading the way.

The door had been kicked in, and a faint tinge of gunpowder was in the air. The computer at the desk had been destroyed. Smashed to pieces.

At first, he thought the room was empty and that the Ghost had taken Newberg, too. Then he saw his body crumpled in the corner. The worst of his fears were playing out in his mind.

"Newberg!" Savage ran to the prone body lying face down on the carpet, resting in a pool of fresh blood. He checked the carotid artery for a pulse. He found it immediately. Strong and steady. He was alive!

Savage set the gun down on the floor and carefully rolled Newberg over. There was a gash on the top of his forehead that was bleeding profusely. An egg-sized lump had already started to form. Savage retrieved a clean towel from the linen closet and applied steady pressure to the gash. It wasn't deep. Just an open crease where the bullet skipped off his forehead. But like all wounds to the head, it bled easily and was difficult to stanch the flow. But he would be all right.

Newberg groaned. His eyes fluttered. Then opened. "Fuck me. Am I dead?"

"No. Looks like a bullet skipped off that hard head of yours. Must have come in at a shallow angle."

"Oh, God. Yeah. OK." He swallowed dryly. "The assassin came for us."

There was a pause. "Yeah. I know. What do you remember?"

"I'm not sure. I remember he busted into the house. Came straight for us, as if he knew exactly where we were. He just kicked in the door. Raised his gun and shot me." His brow creased as the pain in his head thumped. He probably had a concussion. Then he remembered something. "Eliana had her gun with her. I think she fired it at him."

Savage looked behind him. Saw a giant divot and a corresponding hole in the plaster where the bullet struck. There was no blood. He re-folded the towel and placed it back on Newberg's forehead. "Sounds about right. Her shot must have taken him by surprise. Distracted him. Caused him to make an errant shot. And you…you must have flinched just at the right moment because the bullet just skimmed off you. You're one lucky son of a bitch, Newberg."

"I don't feel lucky."

"Oh? Your brain must be muddled. I spared your life seven years ago. And now the Ghost missed you. You have managed to survive two separate attempts on your life from an NT assassin."

Newberg chuckled. Then he smiled, though he kept his eyes closed. "You mean I'm not dead?"

"Sorry to disappoint."

"And here I thought you were the angel of death."

Savage sighed. "Perhaps I am, Newbie."

Newberg opened his eyes, suddenly remembering something. "Wait. Where's Eliana? Is she…is she OK?"

"For now. The Ghost took her. I don't know where they are or where they're heading. He's using her to get to me. To ensure I comply."

"Jesus, Savage. It's all my fault."

"No. It's mine. I let you guys down. I should have never left the house."

"What are you going to do? He'll kill her, Savage!"

"Yeah. He will. Eventually. But not right away. He's going to find out what she knows first. Then use her to lure me in. Kill us both."

"Oh, shit! What are you going to do?" he asked again.

"Whatever he tells me to."

Newberg's eyes widened, some clarity of thought peeking through. "But if you do that, you'll both die."

Savage nodded slowly. Looked up at the window. The first rays of dawn were peeking through the mini blinds. "Yeah. Probably. But there's a slim chance that I can save her while trying. I'll take out as many of them as I can. Especially the Ghost."

Newberg took a deep breath and sat up. "Is there anything I can do to help?"

Savage looked at what was left of Newberg's computer. Nothing but parts and pieces scattered about the desk. On the floor. "He destroyed your computer. Probably took your storage drive. I'm not sure you can."

Newberg coughed, clearing the frog from his throat. "I have a laptop. A good one. And he can keep the SSD. I saved all the data I collected in the cloud, and I never save passwords. Good luck to them."

Savage smiled. "Then let's get to work."

CHAPTER SEVENTY-ONE

Baltimore, Maryland

Micaela didn't know where she was going, but she knew she had to get there fast. Time was of the essence.

She said, "Look, Skye…I need to know what flight and which gate." She was out of breath. Baltimore Washington International Airport wasn't particularly large, but her flight had arrived in Concourse D, and she had to double-time it back to the main terminal. She didn't even know if Dr. Shepherd would fly out of Baltimore, much less where he was headed. It had all been one big hunch in the first place. But moments after she reached the main entrance, Skye informed her Dr. Shepherd had bought a ticket to Reykjavik, Iceland. That was international flights and on the other side of the airport.

Now she had to hurry. She had to reach him before the federal agents arrived. After all, if she knew he had bought a ticket, they did as well.

Skye's voice chirped into her earpiece. "The ticket is for Flight 102, Play Airlines. Departs in less than an hour." Micaela heard her fingers tap across a keyboard. "It looks like gate E8. But that's irrelevant. Unless you plan on buying a ticket to Reykjavik, you won't get past security anyway. You need to catch him before he gets past the checkpoint."

"Shit!" Micaela was speed-walking as fast as she could. She started to jog.

The terminal was packed with travelers, though she shouldn't have been surprised. Labor Day weekend was one of the busiest travel days of the year. Now she found herself pushing through the crowds, struggling to find the path of least resistance. She practically knocked an old lady down as she ran into her. She managed to catch her—barely—but had little time for apologies.

More people crossed her path, all in a hurry, and none were considerate of those around them. "This is a madhouse!"

"Facts. And it's about to get even crazier, Mick. I've got radio chatter from Control confirming the arrival of the FBI. They're onsite and heading to the security checkpoint for international flights."

"Damn!" Micaela ran.

"You know…you might just have to take the L here."

"What?"

Skye giggled into the earpiece. "OK, millennial. Take the L…you know…quit?"

"Not a chance."

"You're cray cray, girl. How did you even guess that he was flying out of Baltimore in the first place? There's like three major airports in the metro area. Five if you count the ones that are within driving distance."

Micaela let out an *oomph* as she took an over-the-shoulder bag to the gut, but she kept moving. "Because the doctor is through running. He accomplished what he set out to do, which was to reach Baltimore and say goodbye to the woman he loves. Now that he has, it doesn't matter to him anymore. No more games. No more tricks. If he escapes, he'll consider himself lucky. If he doesn't, so be it. Either way, he's done caring."

"But Iceland? WTF? Who the hell wants to live on an ice cube in the middle of the Atlantic?"

"How the hell should I know? Maybe he likes reindeer. My guess is it's a layover to his final destination. Maybe Switzerland? They have a hell of a healthcare system over there. And if I'm not mistaken, Switzerland has ignored extradition orders from the U.S. before."

"Wow. That's thin."

"Look, can we just concentrate on retrieving the doctor now? How much farther?"

"Just up ahead."

★   ★   ★

Dr. Shepherd took a deep breath and let it out slowly. He did it. He had purchased his plane ticket and entered the line for the security checkpoint. It was long but moving quickly. He still stood a chance to get out of the United States.

He moved through the line, stop and go. Thinking of his last minutes with Josie. The years lost. The moments that never were. But he thought of the years spent together, too. And those warmed his heart. And he smiled.

He was just a few feet from the checkpoint now. Five people were in front of him. That's when he heard a disturbance from behind. The glass door to the nearest entryway opened, and a dozen federal agents came storming in. The FBI. A wave of shouts and jeers washed through the crowded terminal.

Most of the agents wore their blue raid jackets embellished with bold yellow lettering, while others wore well-appointed suits and aviator-style sunglasses. True to them both, they wore their bulletproof vests.

They immediately began directing personnel, pointing in the general direction of the security checkpoint. They were scanning the crowd, searching for him. But they hadn't made him out yet.

Dr. Shepherd slipped back one space, allowing an elderly gentleman to cut in front of him. Then he started pushing farther back, staying close to the roping, keeping the other travelers between him and the FBI's line of sight. He slipped under the ropes twice. And he made it to the back corner and out of the line before the FBI spotted him.

"There he is!" one of the men in suits said, pointing right at him. "Stop him!"

The jig was up. Dr. Shepherd slipped under the last rope and took off running, back toward the main entrance. He was in such a hurry he ran past the first exit, frantically pushing his way through the throngs of people. They were mindless cattle, pushing and shoving, oblivious to the carnage around them.

Dr. Shepherd pushed blindly ahead, ignoring the expressions of surprise and outright annoyance on their faces. He was running through them, splitting the crowd on either side of him like he was Moses parting the Red Sea. Until he stumbled upon a dark-haired Latina woman, wearing faded jeans and a denim jacket, standing right in his path. Their eyes met, and instantly her expression changed from startled to clear recognition. That unsettled the doctor.

He spun around—realized he had passed yet another exit—and began running back toward the armed federal agents. He could just make them out amidst the swarms of people—who were just now realizing there was any sort of problem. A problem that threatened their very lives. Screams ensued, and people began running for cover. It was pandemonium.

Again, Dr. Shepherd stopped. He'd never reach the exit. The FBI was still pushing through the crowds, heading toward him.

He turned, frantically looking for a way out. The dark-haired woman was standing there, her outstretched hand reaching for him, her eyes pleading for him to follow. She had no visible weapon. No handcuffs, nor bulky bulletproof vest crammed beneath her jacket. She wasn't law enforcement. She mouthed the words, "This way! Follow me!" That was enough for Dr. Shepherd. He ran toward her.

She smiled in relief. She was just beginning to spin away, her arm still reaching back to him, when the report of a gunshot echoed across the airport.

★　　★　　★

Micaela had just grabbed the doctor's hand when she felt him go limp and fall, taking her down with him. It was only then, after he fell, that she heard the crack of the gunshot. Its harsh report clapped in the distance, followed by a cold and metallic echo. It slowly faded before disappearing altogether.

She was in shock. A vacuum. And all around her was silence. She crawled over to the doctor, cradling him in her arms. "No! No!" she screamed. "Dr. Shepherd!" But she couldn't hear her own words. There was a look of wide-eyed shock on the man's face. A look of disbelief. Disappointment.

"Oh my God! No!" They had shot him in the back—a sniper shot from a ceiling outcrop fifty yards away. Red bloomed on the front of his shirt like rose petals warming in the sun. He was bleeding out. Suddenly, the sounds of people screaming and crying, calling for help, overwhelmed her senses as her focus returned to the here and now. It was jarring. Disorienting.

The doctor looked up at her, his eyes having trouble focusing on her. "Who are you?"

"I'm Micaela Mendoza. I used to be the handler for NT-Zero. Cypher. But I quit—like you. I've been trying to help save him from the DCS."

Dr. Shepherd's eyes flickered. Brain cells firing. Memories returning. "Cypher. Yes. Is he all right? Did he escape?" He coughed. A fine spray of blood splattered his chin.

Micaela's face crumpled. Tears spilled down her cheeks, unencumbered, one after another. "Yes. He's alive. He sent me to warn you. To bring you back with me."

Dr. Shepherd's face pinched, a sharp pain taking hold of him.

"He wanted to protect you. But he couldn't come himself without putting Eliana Bautista's life at risk. The DCS still wants her dead."

His eyes drifted, becoming unfocused.

"The call girl? She was Cypher's mark three nights ago. But you did something to him. Remember? You broke him. He couldn't go through with it. He's been trying to save her life ever since."

Blood spilled from his mouth, heavier now. Frothy. He was having trouble breathing. He was looking at her face, but there was little recognition in his eyes. "Break him? No…no…I did nothing. I did nothing so that he *could* be free." He coughed again, still struggling for breath. "I tried to save him." His voice trailed off, sounding distant and weak. "In truth…he saved me."

Dr. Shepherd's head fell limply to the side. His eyes remained open but were now dark, void of all life.

The federal agents shoved their way through the stampede of people, forcing their way against the tide to reach the spot where the fugitive was last seen. Despite the sheer chaos of a panicked crowd, Sniper Two had a clean shot on the target and took him clean.

At first, the sniper watched the target run away from him amidst all the chaos. But suddenly the man stopped and changed direction. He went with the flow of the crowd for a few steps and then changed his mind once more. It was then, as the man turned to run, that the sniper was given a "go" to take the shot. The target collapsed like a trophy buck.

He glimpsed what looked like a woman reaching out to him, trying to save him. But when he attempted to reacquire her in the scope, she wasn't there.

A few minutes later, a half dozen or so federal agents pushed their way through the fleeing crowd and reached the doctor, who lay prostrate and lifeless in a pool of blood.

There was no woman there.

Denver, Colorado

Savage closed his eyes and took a deep breath. There was a snap to the air reminiscent of fall. But it smelled of diesel exhaust and jet fuel, like any other airport in the world. Denver International was no exception.

On the phone, Mendoza said, "Did you hear me? Dr. Shepherd is dead." Her voice quivered, trying to choke down her emotions. "I tried, Savage. I really, really tried. But the bastards shot him in the back. A sniper, I think."

A sniper. The words hung heavy in the air, taut, and strung around Savage's neck like a hangman's noose. He had been no better than that at one time.

"There was nothing else you could do, Agent Mendoza," he said finally. "Nobody could have saved him. Not even me." He tried to pass it off as reluctant acceptance. But the truth of the matter was it hurt. Something deep inside of him ached. A sadness he couldn't put into words.

She was quiet for a moment. Finally, she said, "Are you going to go through with it?"

"Yeah. I don't have a choice."

"It's suicide."

"Eliana needs me. I have to try."

"I know. If one thing is true in this world, it's you. That's just who you are. You'll never give up."

The sun was setting. Savage glanced at his watch. Seven twenty-nine. "They'll be calling me any minute."

"I wish you would change your mind, but I know you won't. Remember what I told you. The DCS's secret headquarters is impenetrable. It's an underground bunker. It's as deep underground as a skyscraper is tall. Their security is world class. And once they bring you in, there won't be any escape. It will become your tomb."

"I wouldn't count me out just yet."

"I never do." He heard her sniffle. "Is there anything else you need from me?"

"No. Newberg received the information you sent him. Building schematics. Security protocols. Everything."

"And are you going in unarmed?"

"They *told* me to come unarmed."

"That's not what I asked you."

Silence. Finally, Savage said, "I'll meet you on the other side. I'll call you when we get out."

"And if you don't?"

"Then keep running and never look back. Oh. And Mendoza?"

"Yeah?"

"If I don't get the chance to tell you later, I just wanted to say thank you. Thanks for everything."

"Yeah. You can tell me later. And Cypher? I'm going to hold you to that."

★   ★   ★

They called him on time. Right down to the second. "*Buenas noches*, Cypher."

Savage said nothing. He just walked into the airport's main terminal and waited for further instructions.

The Ghost chuckled, but it was without conviction. Overlaid like a laugh track. In his thick Cuban accent, he said, "I trust you have come unarmed and will follow my instructions to the letter. I would hate to have to kill the woman before you and I even get the chance to meet."

Savage balled his hands into fists, spoke through clenched teeth. "Maybe we would if you would stop fucking jawing all night."

At first, the Ghost didn't reply. There was nothing but silence. And it lingered, looming ominously over the phone. Then he said, "I agree, *pendejo*. Let us begin before you're late for the party. No?"

It was go time.

Savage had barely walked ten steps into the airport when he was "bumped" into by a preoccupied traveler. That stranger surreptitiously slipped an ID card into his back pocket.

When Savage retrieved it, the Ghost said, "Good. Now you have a government-issued ID."

He's watching. Savage swept the terminal with his eyes and spotted several security cameras. He knew there were many, many more.

"Now follow my instructions, and I will get you past the TSA security checkpoint."

Savage did as he was told, and following his instructions to the letter, he walked to an alternate staff-only access point. He never lifted the cell phone from his ear. He surrendered his security pass to the officer manning the entrance and was promptly sent on through. *This isn't an unusual occurrence. This is commonplace.*

After clearing the security checkpoint, Savage stayed put and waited for further instructions. Nothing. "Hello?"

"Patience, *vaquero*. What's your hurry?" the Ghost asked. Then he laughed. Again, it sounded flat. Without emotion. "Afraid we're going to start the party without you? Don't worry. We'll leave some of her to play with afterward."

Savage didn't respond. Not right away. He knew he was being provoked—knew they wanted to unsettle him. But knowing this did little to squelch his burning anger. He finally said, "Maybe you're just delaying the inevitable."

"Oh? And what's that?"

"Me cutting your fucking heart out."

This time, it was the Ghost who didn't respond. After a few seconds, he gave him more instructions. He had him go down the escalator to the lower level to find an employee-only access door. After entering, he walked down a long corridor. Then took a couple of turns. Left. Right. And right again. He finally came to a lone elevator. Again, employee access only. He entered and was told to insert the key into the slot. "What key, asshole?"

"Did you lose it already?"

Savage felt around his pants pockets and found a single brass key—apparently planted on him while he was given the security pass. He inserted the key. Then turned it. Next, the Ghost provided him with explicit instructions on the precise sequence of elevator buttons he needed to press.

It immediately began its long drop into the abyss. The floors ticked on by, each number representing another ten feet below ground. Five. Ten. Fifteen...

It seemed to go on forever. Each floor was just another reminder of how far away Eliana truly was. How alone she must have felt. The elevator creaked and groaned in its descent. Twenty. Twenty-five! It stopped with a jolt. The DCS's secret HQ was over two hundred and fifty feet below ground! Mendoza was right. This was a tomb.

The doors opened, and Savage was immediately taken into custody by two agents in suits. They escorted him through three more security doors, each with their own set of armed agents. Each door required a security code, retinal imaging, and a thermal palm scan.

At the end of the hall, they turned right and continued for another fifty feet. They stopped at a room with a nameplate that read *Security and Detention Center*. How benign. It sounded like a place you would send a high school student for cutting class.

They unlocked the door, ushered him into the room, and locked it behind them.

The room wasn't a security room. It looked to be nothing more than a seldom-used storage room. Maintenance perhaps? It had cinder block walls painted pale yellow, with exposed plumbing, conduit, and a plethora of maintenance tools mounted on the wall. There were two more doors leading to other rooms. The two DCS agents prodded Savage ahead, maintaining their positions behind him and flanking him. Agent Fenech on the left. Female. Five foot seven. Athletic build. With that resting bitch face that most men avoided like the plague. Agent Lavoy on the right. Male. Six foot even. Stout. Wearing a smug smirk on his face, as if he were James Bond himself.

In the center of the room, sitting behind a desk lamp at a folding table, was a smallish man. His hair was chestnut brown and receding, and he had narrow eyes set too close together. His lips were noodle thin and all but disappeared when he spoke. "You must be Cypher."

Savage instantly recognized the high-pitched, nasal voice. "And you must be Spearman."

His face betrayed his confusion, and he shook his head as if trying to shake something loose. "And how do you know that?"

"I'd recognize that whiny little voice anywhere."

His amusement turned to agitation in an instant. "Well, you're pretty mouthy for somebody at the very mercy of my goodwill." He stood up, loosened his necktie, and opened his collar. "I'd love to say something gracious, like how it's a pleasure to finally meet you. But, of course, that would be complete bullshit. You've been nothing but a pain in my ass, Cypher."

"I would say the feeling is mutual. The only difference is I'm here to put an end to it."

Spearman ignored that. He swept his arm around the room as if to invite him to take a look around. "I'd like to apologize for the accommodations. But I won't. Because I don't give a fuck. Besides, we're an intelligence agency. Not a military base. We're not equipped for such bullshit."

"It's as good a place as any."

"As good a place for what?"

"To kill you."

Spearman leaned on the table, shook his head in disbelief, and laughed. "The size of the balls you must have on you!" He gestured to

Agents Fenech and Lavoy as if seeking confirmation from them. They just smirked and nodded to each other.

The door opened from the side room, and a tall man with a buzz cut and light bronze skin strolled in like he owned the place. He was lean, well-built, and was wearing some type of form-fitting body armor. He wore a patch over one eye, the other smoky gray and burning with serious hate.

The Ghost.

"Can you believe this guy?" Spearman asked him.

The man said nothing. He tossed his cell phone on the table, now done with it, and never took his eye off Cypher. "He's all talk," he said in heavily accented English. A slow smile crept across his face.

Savage raised an eyebrow. "And I'd say there's been enough talk already. Where's Eliana? I told you I'd only come here of my own accord if you promised to let her go."

Spearman stood and threw up his hands. "Well…about that. I lied. You see…I can't let her go. She might blab about everything. And—"

"Where is she?" he interrupted, not even trying to sound compliant.

Spearman looked at the Ghost. Nodded to him.

The assassin turned and walked back into the other room. A moment later, he returned, pushing a metal chair across the floor with Eliana zip-tied to it, her mouth gagged. He pushed her to the center of the far wall and used handcuffs to fasten the chair to an exposed two-inch metal pipe. She had a cut across her cheek where the Ghost had apparently cuffed her. The blood was already beginning to dry.

She looked at Savage, trying to speak, but the gag mangled her words. He expected to see fear in her eyes. But it wasn't there. It was the look of defeat.

"Are you OK?" he asked.

Again, she tried to speak but couldn't.

Spearman nodded to the Ghost, and he complied, lowering the gag from her mouth. The moment he did, Eliana spit in his face.

The Ghost responded with a backhand to her face, reopening the cut on her cheek. "*Perra!*" Bitch!

Savage lunged at him, prepared to leap across the table, but the instant he moved, Fenech and Lavoy pulled their guns, each of them pointed at opposite sides of his head.

Savage froze.

Spearman laughed and slapped the wooden top of the folding table. "You're fearless. I'll give you that. Or maybe just plain stupid. Just where do you think you're going to go? You're a gazillion feet below ground, unarmed and surrounded by an army of special agents."

"I don't plan on going anywhere. And neither will you." Savage carefully used his left hand to expose his unfastened jacket, revealing the plastic explosives strapped to his chest. What Spearman didn't know—couldn't know—was that it was an experimental plastic explosive developed by the United States military. Savage was wearing enough of the CX14 to take out an entire city block. And tucked neatly in his right hand was a dead man's switch.

"Fuck me!"

Savage tilted his head.

Spearman's forehead began showing signs of sweat, its slick sheen reflecting the fluorescent lighting from above. "Jesus Christ! Are you crazy? You're going to commit suicide now?"

"If it means taking you with me."

Nobody moved, though the Ghost straightened. Took a step closer.

"Stay where you are." Savage raised the dead man's switch, showing he was serious.

"OK. OK. Let's not get excited," said Spearman. "There's no need for all this. I don't even want to kill you. I just want you back in the fold."

Savage's eyes narrowed.

"No shit. It's true! You're far too valuable for me to just kill you. You're broken. I get that. But we can fix it! I just have to make one phone call to Dr. Misra, and she'll fix you up as good as new. There's nothing here that can't be fixed, Cypher."

"He's bluffing," the Ghost said. "*El no tiene las pelotas.*" *He doesn't have the balls.*

"I'm not afraid to die."

"No. But you're afraid of *her* dying." The Ghost drew his .22 and stuck the barrel to the temple of Eliana's head. She closed her eyes, then said a quick prayer. Tears were streaming down her face.

Savage didn't move. He didn't dare. He was looking at Eliana when she opened her eyes. She shook her head, barely perceptible. "Don't," she said, her raspy voice sounding tired, scarcely a whisper. "Don't let them win. Not for me. You know you have to stop them."

Savage shook his head, exhaled audibly. He looked to Spearman. "OK. Fine. You win."

"No! Savage, don't!"

But he had already decided. He locked the plunger into place with the flip of a clamp and then slowly removed the jacket and suicide vest.

The Ghost pressed the gun harder into Eliana's temple, coercing a pain-filled cry from her.

Savage set the vest down and then kicked it across the floor toward Spearman and the Ghost. Fenech and Lavoy took the opportunity to re-grip their pistols, their extended arms becoming tired.

In a move too fast to see, Savage lunged for Fenech's left arm and pulled her toward him, falling in behind her as she tumbled past. Lavoy—startled—fired reflexively and shot her center mass twice. Savage tore the gun from her slackened grip and shot Lavoy once in the head. It was over in an instant, and when the sound of the gunshots faded, Savage had his gun pointing at the Ghost. "Put it down."

The Ghost smiled. "*No creo.*" *I don't think so.*

"Then you'll die."

"Then we'll both die." He turned the gun on Savage.

"Stop! Jesus Christ! What are you doing?" Spearman's eyes were practically bugging out of his head.

"I'm done playing games. It's time for this *nadie* to die."

"No! That's not what I want," Spearman said. "Now put the gun away! He's not going anywhere."

But the Ghost ignored him and took one step closer. His gun never wavered.

"Do you hear me? Put the goddamned gun down! That's an order."

"No," a voice announced from the open door on the other side of the room. "Actually…I give the orders here."

It was Victor Blackburn.

CHAPTER SEVENTY-THREE

The Ghost punched Spearman in the face with the full force of his body behind the blow. The slight man crumpled to the ground, his nose broken. A shower of blood splattered against the wall. Then he grabbed him by the shirt, lifted him off the floor, and punched him in the face again. Harder. Then he did it one more time for good measure, knocking one of his front teeth out. He dropped him to the floor, stood up, and finished by giving him a kick to the ribs.

"That's enough for now," Blackburn said. He slipped around the Ghost and walked over to the dead body of Agent Lavoy. He grabbed his set of cuffs. Tossed them back to the Ghost before retrieving the agent's gun as well. Blackburn made sure he kept at a favorable distance from Cypher.

Blackburn, in his full "Class A" service uniform, straightened his jacket, snugged his tie. Then he walked back over to where Spearman was. The Ghost had propped him up on the remaining folding chair, half-conscious and struggling to breathe through a busted nose. He then zip-tied his hands behind his back and cuffed the chair to a thick brass pipe.

Savage kept the Glock 19 he'd swiped from Fenech trained on the Ghost. That was where the danger lay. The political power struggle between Blackburn and Spearman didn't interest him.

Blackburn looked at Savage with mock interest. He pointed to Spearman. "Do you want to kill him? He's been quite the pain in your ass, so I understand. He's been a royal pain in my ass, too. But be my guest."

When Savage didn't respond, he continued. "He FUBARed the hell out of this mission, starting with fucking up the whole assassination thing. Or you did." He shrugged. "But how do you fuck up sniping a stupid call girl? With a super-assassin, no less!"

Eliana said, "Go fuck yourself, asshole."

Blackburn just laughed. "I'd have to, honey. I couldn't afford you."

Savage clenched his jaw. Glared at him with the fire of a thousand suns. But he refused to lower his weapon. Unlike the DCS agents, he didn't build up lactic acid in his muscles. He could hold the gun for hours without tiring.

"Do you know I specifically chose you for this job?" He smiled and turned his attention back to Savage. "It's true. Only I had no idea that Dr. Shepherd was going to fuck up the whole damn thing. That was a real special piece of work."

Spearman lifted his chin off his chest, blood dripping across his mouth and down onto his ripped dress shirt. His eyes widened. "It was you! It was you who ordered the NT for this hit!"

He chuckled and shook his head as he looked down at the deputy director. "Damn straight I did. Couldn't afford to have this one fucked up. The doctor saw to that, though, didn't he? Son of a bitch. And you!" He pointed at Spearman. "You had to spend half our resources tracking him down, trying to capture him instead of just making it easier on yourself and killing him."

"He was still a valuable resource for this operation. He was a brilliant—"

"Stop. You're embarrassing yourself. He was dead weight. But then again, you never knew when to cut your losses, Theo." Blackburn then pointed to Savage. "And you're trying to make the same mistake again with this asshole. And for what? Because we spent millions of dollars to create the perfect weapon? Please! The doctor made him worthless in the blink of an eye, didn't he? Hell, I think the only thing you did right during this entire mission was to activate NT-8 here."

Eliana shook her head, squinted in disgust. *"Crist!* Neither of you cares about anyone or anything but yourselves, do you?" Her accent had become so thick in her anger that her words were nearly unrecognizable as English.

Spearman spat a glob of blood out of his mouth, then tried to talk despite his broken nose. "I'm just doing my job. And it was me who's been trying to fix all of this. Trying to make it all work!"

"Oh, but it has worked," said Blackburn. "I've ensured that when this whole thing blows up—and it inevitably will—all the incriminating evidence will blow right back on you. You'll be the one left holding the bag when the hammer comes down."

Spearman's eyes flew open, his eyebrows reaching for the ceiling. "Fuck you! I was just following orders!"

"We're all following orders, Theo. Even me." Blackburn took two steps back and pointed the gun at Spearman's head. "Don't take it personally. We all get what's coming to us in the end."

"How's that?" Savage said, raising an eyebrow. He'd been listening to it all. Absorbing. Deciphering.

"Well, in a few short minutes, all three of you will be dead. They'll find that Theo here was killed by your hands after he shot the whore. And poor ol' defenseless me? I had to shoot the crazed rogue assassin in the name of self-preservation when he tried to murder me. And alas, tragically, the entire place burned down in a freak accident. The fire will burn so hot there will be nothing left to identify you. Not even your bones."

"Ah. And the Ghost?"

"He doesn't even exist."

"OK. What about you then? You're no saint. And just what do you have coming to you?"

Blackburn flashed a smug grin that only someone of supreme confidence could pull off. "Why—I'm the hero, of course! I'll be the man who uncovered all the corruption in this black-on-black program. For my service and dedication to this great country, the President will name me as the new director of the NSA. Well, with the current director notwithstanding, of course."

"You've thought of almost everything. Everything except having proof." Savage lowered his gun to his side.

Blackburn laughed out loud, sounding genuinely amused. "Proof? There is no proof. Even if there were, it would be buried so fucking deep they would never find it."

"As I said, you've thought of almost everything."

Blackburn walked over to Spearman and placed the gun to his temple. "Enough talk."

"Except you forgot one thing…"

Blackburn paused and turned to look at Savage, puzzlement on his face.

"I'm the perfect weapon." Savage raised his gun and shot Victor Blackburn right between the eyes.

CHAPTER SEVENTY-FOUR

The assassination of Victor Blackburn took the Ghost entirely by surprise. But whatever tactical advantage Savage gained by the unexpected move disappeared in an instant. Both men stood there facing each other, their guns aimed at the other's head.

They stared, their eyes communicating without words. Cold. Hard. Void of all emotion. But a thousand thoughts ran through Savage's head. They were sizing each other up, and the tension in the room grew heavy, suffocating, as if they were a thousand feet beneath the ocean.

"We could stand here staring at each other all day," Savage said. "Or just shoot each other. Not much of a tactical advantage for either of us if we're dead, though. Is there?"

The Ghost bobbed his head toward Eliana, just a short distance away, still tied to the chair. "Or I could just shoot her."

Eliana didn't react. But Savage could see the fear in her eyes, watched her breath turn shallow. Accelerate.

Savage shook his head. "No. The instant your gun moves, I'll kill you."

The Ghost conceded the point with a nod. "Then what do you suggest?"

"I'll put my gun down. You do the same."

He scoffed. "What game are you playing, John-Wayne-cowboy?"

"I'm more like The Man with No Name. But you got the general idea. So...no games. No tricks."

"What's stopping you from shooting me the moment I do?"

"Nothing. So I'll put my gun down first."

He laughed out loud. "Then I'd shoot you dead where you stand."

"No. You won't."

The Ghost angled his head slightly, improving his field of view with his one good eye. "What makes you so sure, *vaquero*?"

"Because I took something from you. I took your eye. And now you would like nothing more than to get even with me. By the way, what do you see when you look at yourself in the mirror? A monster?"

The Ghost's expression never changed. It was ice cold. "No. I will have an artificial eye soon enough. A cybernetic implant. Far superior to my old one."

Savage smiled. He had directed this conversation precisely to this moment. "Superior? I don't think so."

"You know nothing. I am superior to you in every way."

Savage flipped the gun in his hand, holding it up for the Ghost to see, and slowly reached across his body, placing the Glock on the table. "That's yet to be seen."

A slow, slithery smile stretched across the Ghost's lips. He nodded and followed suit, carefully laying his gun on the table. "Gun or no. You won't leave this room alive."

Savage didn't hesitate. He charged the Ghost at full speed, lowered his shoulder, and tried to drive the entirety of his weight right through him. But he never connected. The Ghost sidestepped Savage at the last moment, allowing his momentum to carry him through, before grabbing and throwing him across the room. He struck the block wall ten feet away, the wind driven from his lungs. He collapsed to the floor, trying to catch his breath.

The Ghost wouldn't allow it. He took two long strides, picked him up like a bag of dirty laundry, and threw him across the room again. This time, he landed on the folding table, crushing it and sending the lamp, guns, and suicide jacket crashing to the floor. Savage struck his head in the fall. Tried to shake it off. *Damn, he's strong!*

He tried to get back up on his feet, but as he gathered himself, the Ghost marched over and went to pick him up again. This time, Savage caught him by surprise and kicked him square in the face. The Ghost staggered backward, momentarily stunned. A trickle of blood seeped from his nose.

Savage took the reprieve to kip up, landing on his feet with ease. He immediately closed the distance to the Ghost and launched a flurry of quick strikes to his head. Left jab. Left jab. Right haymaker. The Ghost handily blocked each punch, his open palm slapping them away like pesky mosquitoes. The speed of each response was blindingly fast. Nearly impossible for the naked eye to follow.

Savage tried to catch him off guard with a left uppercut, but the Ghost merely ducked back, causing him to miss entirely. *Too fast!* Savage continued to throw lightning-quick punches, each of them easily parried. He tried again, surprising him with an open-palm strike to the chin, but the Ghost was too quick and caught Savage's hand with the left, stopping its momentum dead in its tracks. He then twisted his wrist, forcing Savage to succumb to the leverage and fall away or break a bone trying to resist. Savage collapsed to his knees. And the Ghost kicked him in the face, sending him sprawling onto his back, dazed. Unresponsive.

"No!" Eliana screamed. "Savage! Get up! Get up!"

Somewhere in the clouded fog of his brain, Savage responded to the cries of Eliana's voice. He shook the cobwebs free and finally struggled to his feet. The taste of warm copper flooded his mouth. He had a split lip, and his nose was bleeding.

"You can't beat me. I'm too strong for you. Too fast. I'm going to hurt you so bad you will beg me to kill you."

Savage didn't doubt it. Not anymore. He'd mistakenly thought the Ghost's form-fitting suit was body armor. But it wasn't. It was a bionic exoskeleton. A smart suit that used hydraulics and robotic joints to assist a human's natural physiology, increasing his strength and improving his speed. He knew that the Centurian Program was developing such technology. But how they managed to incorporate it into a body suit or solve the power demands of the microprocessor and servo motors completely escaped Savage. But he now understood why he'd never stood a chance at catching the Ghost last night. Worse, this was a fight he couldn't win.

But Savage would never surrender. He would protect Eliana if he had to die trying.

Savage charged him, and just before he reached him, he planted his feet and launched into a jump spinning hook kick. The height of his jump was amazing. The velocity of the spin unparalleled. But it was the synchronicity between the two that created its incredible power. None of it mattered. The Ghost snatched his foot midair with one hand, leaving all of Savage's momentum with nowhere to go but in the opposite direction. He fell back, landing hard beneath the utility sink, taking the full force of the fall on his left shoulder. The Ghost still had his foot in his hand, his leg lifted off the ground. Without hesitation, he drove his elbow into his thigh. Savage cried out in agony. Then the nanobots swarmed to the nerve centers of both his shoulder and leg, and the excruciating pain was immediately brought under control.

The Ghost walked over to Savage. He stood over him, the hint of a smile playing on his lips. "Such a disappointment. I had hoped for so much more."

Savage lay there, looking up at him, breathing hard. He thought he might have a broken rib.

The Ghost looked around, spotted a ten-pound steel hammer hanging on the wall, and grabbed it. "Perfect." He swung it down at Savage's left knee, but Savage rolled to the side just in time. The hammer pinged off the floor. The Ghost let loose a string of expletives, then knelt on one leg and swung the hammer again, this time toward his head. Instead, it clipped the side of the sink and bounced off a water pipe before it continued through and hit the ground. It had just missed Savage by inches.

But the galvanized pipe had broken off at the T-Joint, and an explosion of water blasted the Ghost in the face. It struck him in the eyes, causing his patch to become skewed and jet the water into his empty eye socket. He howled and staggered to his feet.

Savage seized the moment and kicked the Ghost in the leg, hitting just a few inches beneath the knee. Too low to destroy the joint, but it knocked him off his feet, and the hammer bounced away harmlessly across the floor. There was just enough time for Savage to climb back to his feet before the Ghost regained his bearings.

The Ghost reached behind his back and pulled out his Gerber Mark II knife. Deadly. A combat knife with a sturdy handle and a fixed six-and-a-half-inch serrated blade designed to pierce. It wouldn't be a fair fight. The Cuban assassin smiled.

Eliana screamed. "Savage!"

Spearman looked at her and shook his head, resigned to their fate. "He can't win."

"He can! And he will—Savage!"

The Ghost slashed the knife in front of him in wide, arcing strikes, pressing into Savage's space, forcing him to retreat. He continued to advance, swinging the knife with several more quick, violent slashes until there was no more room for Savage to retreat. He tried reaching behind him for the steel pry bar hanging on the wall to ward off the Ghost's attacks, but it was too late. There wasn't enough time. Not enough room. The Ghost thrust the knife toward his chest and tried to drive it home. But Savage grabbed hold of his arm and stopped it just in time.

Savage was unable to move his left arm. He had dislocated his shoulder when he fell on it earlier, and now he only had the use of his right arm to fend off the advancing knife. He was losing ground. Rapidly.

Savage pushed back with all his might, groaning under the duress. His genetic modifications offered him greater strength than most people could imagine. But it was no match for the Ghost's bionic-assisted power. The knife steadily made its way to his chest. The Ghost's face was mere inches away from him now, the gaping bloody socket of his eye winking lifelessly into his.

Savage's arm shook, his strength fading.

Then the Ghost said, "I will take good care of your woman…before I kill her. Who knows? Maybe she'll enjoy it."

Savage screamed. An angry, primal rage, fueling the last ounce of strength he had in him. It was desperate. Futile. His arm gave way, and the blade plunged into his chest. He let out a groan, staggered briefly, then collapsed. His body splashed down into the puddle of water at his feet. It grew deeper now, its icy tendrils spreading further across the floor.

Then a last breath of air expelled from his body, and his head fell to the wayside. He moved no more.

Eliana let out a scream. An ear-piercing shriek of grief. "No! Please, no! Savage!"

Spearman turned away, unable to look at her. Maybe he couldn't stand watching her cry and fall apart. Maybe he couldn't stomach having to hear her soul being ripped from her body. Eliana didn't care. Couldn't help it. She had never known such grief. "Savage!" she screamed again, her voice growing angrier. "Don't you do it! Don't you *dare* leave me! Please…"

The Ghost straightened. Readjusted his eyepatch. He then turned his attention back to the remaining prisoners. He walked over to Spearman first, glared at him. Scoffed. A pathetic excuse for a man. *"No recibo órdenes de nadie." I take orders from anyone.* But the Spanish was lost on Spearman. He never learned the language. And now he never would.

The Ghost turned to Eliana. "You see, my little whore? Your boyfriend was no match for me. I'm sure that will be true in many, many ways." He reached out, lifted her chin, looked at her. Her cheeks were red, streaked with tears. Then her face crumpled, transforming into the ugly mask of grief. But in her eyes…he saw raw hate. And they burned with a desire to kill him.

He looked her over carefully. Admired her beautiful brown eyes. The smoothness of her light bronze skin, her exposed shoulder. Took delight in the shape of her full lips. Even her dress, with a torn sleeve and tattered hem, accentuated her natural curves. He tsked. "That is a nasty cut you have. And your eye is starting to bruise. Shame, really," he said as if somehow he wasn't responsible. "Who knows? You might even have been able to please me. But tonight? I don't have time for such nonsense."

The Ghost walked over to the shelves on the wall, limping slightly as he dragged his foot through an inch of water. He looked down at the puddle, annoyed that his feet were getting wet, but ignored it. It took just a minute to find what he was looking for: flammable solvents. In this case, some turpentine and lacquer thinner.

"What the fuck do you plan on doing with that?" Spearman asked, his voice jumping an octave.

"I'm going to set this room on fire. Burn it to the ground. And you with it."

The blood drained from Spearman's face. Then he threw up.

CHAPTER SEVENTY-FIVE

Savage first felt the water lick at the side of his face before the sound of water pouring out of the broken pipe dragged him forcefully back to the present. He could still feel the heavy weight of the knife in his chest, but he was numb to the pain. He fumbled for the blade's handle, trying to determine how deep it was and what damage it may have caused. It had missed his heart. That much was obvious.

"Savage!"

He blinked. It was Eliana's voice. Angry. He tried to move. But he was so damn tired. If he could just lie there for a little longer…perhaps…

"Don't you do it! Don't you *dare* leave me! Please…"

Savage felt a sudden bolt of energy explode through his body. His blood felt suddenly alive. On fire. His eyes flew open. *Eliana!* She was in trouble.

Savage grabbed hold of the knife's handle and yanked the blade free of his chest. There was a brief wet sucking noise, followed by a gush of warm liquid rolling down his chest. There was no pain. And almost immediately the nanobots went to work to repair the open wound. The bleeding slowed, then stopped.

Savage rolled onto his stomach, then pushed himself up to turn around. His arms shook, strained to hold him up, but he was somehow able to turn around. He began sliding across the floor toward the sound of Eliana's voice. Then he heard her scream. Wail in despair. It was the most dreadful, soul-crushing sound he had ever heard. And it ripped his heart out.

He began pulling himself harder. Dragged himself through the deepening puddle of dirty water. He felt a strange source of energy begin pouring into him, and he was gaining strength. He climbed back onto all fours and started crawling.

He had closed half the distance to where the Ghost was standing. He was taunting Eliana. Threatening her. Then he stopped, straightened. He turned and began rummaging through items stored on the shelf. Savage felt like his heart would stop. Surely he would spot him now. But somehow he went unnoticed.

He heard another voice speaking. A man's voice. Spearman? He couldn't make out the conversation. He heard the words *fire* and *burn*. Though he couldn't quite make out the entire conversation, he had pieced enough of it together to understand the Ghost's intent.

Savage had to do something. He was too far away to reach the assassin. Not strong enough yet to stand and rush him. He looked around, trying to find something—*anything*—he could use to stop the Ghost. And there it was. The table lamp. It was broken. Its lampshade was torn off, its base cracked. The bulb had shattered. But it still rested on the overturned table, precariously perched on its edge, ready to tumble into the water. It was still plugged in! He smiled.

Savage knew what he had to do. He didn't even give it a second thought. He knew he would die. But so would the Ghost. It was the only way.

Savage screamed for Eliana to lift her feet off the ground. *Now!*

The Ghost whipped around, startled by the voice behind him. At first, his brain couldn't process what his eye was seeing. Savage alive? It was an impossibility. But there he was. And now he finally realized just what he intended to do. He screamed. "Stop!"

Savage plunged the exposed end of the lamp socket into the water. There was a brilliant spark, followed almost instantaneously by the crack of a corona discharge. Then there was darkness.

CHAPTER SEVENTY-SIX

Untold minutes passed. The smell of ozone drifted aimlessly in the dank, stagnant air, with nowhere to escape. A veil of darkness covered the farthest reaches of the room like a death shroud. The only sound was water pouring through a broken pipe, echoing faintly in the room's emptiness. And crying…

Savage gasped and sucked precious oxygen into his lungs. It was raw. Burned like an open wound. He opened his eyes and found himself staring at the ceiling. His mind was still in a fog. *Where am I?* Then he remembered. He knew where he was. He knew why he was on his back, lying in water. But for how long, he couldn't hazard a guess.

The emergency lights were on, apparently kicking in when the breaker tripped. Again, he heard Eliana. Crying. Sobbing. He let out a sigh of relief. She had made it; the rubber leg caps on the folding chairs had insulated her from electrocution.

Savage went to sit up but a sharp pain shot through his body, reminding him of how badly injured he was. *Pain?* That was new.

"He moved! Jesus Christ! Did you see that? He fucking moved!" A man's voice. High. Overly excited. Spearman. He must have made it, too.

"Savage! Oh, Savage! Thank God!"

He clenched his teeth and struggled to a sitting position.

"Oh, Savage! Sweetheart! You're alive!" She was breathing so fast, her words slurred together.

Savage squinted. Got his bearings. Then he saw the Ghost move. He was waking up, too.

"Watch out!" screamed Eliana. She tried to break free of the zip ties that bound her to the chair, but this only caused them to bite deeper into the soft flesh of her wrists. She ignored the pain and continued to thrash about. Screaming until her lungs ached for air.

The Ghost coughed, then sat up, having as much difficulty as Savage was. Their eyes met. And for a moment, neither said a word. Neither moved. Both of their minds racing to figure out what to do next.

Savage pushed himself up, using his thighs to steady himself, and then forced himself to a standing position. He wobbled, feeling faint, but stayed on his feet.

The Ghost tried to stand as well. He struggled just as mightily. Far more than anticipated. He appeared to be moving in slow motion. And if it weren't for the exertion on his face, Savage would have figured it to be some sort of trick.

He didn't wait to find out. He slogged over to the Ghost, dragging his right leg behind him, his left shoulder hanging limply at his side. But in his right hand, he still had a firm grip on the Ghost's Mark II knife. By the time he reached the assassin, he was on his feet, too. It had been a monumental feat for him. He was unsteady. Shaky. He tried to lift his arms, tried to attack Savage. But he was unable to move.

Then Savage realized something. Now it all made sense. When the Ghost was electrocuted, it fried his microprocessors—burned out his servo motors' delicate sensors. In short, the bionic exoskeleton was no longer helping him move faster. It was hindering it.

Savage slid closer. Stood face to face with the Ghost, their noses practically touching. The Ghost was sweating from the exertion. Beads of sweat popped out on his forehead. He gasped for breath.

"I can't move," he said through gritted teeth.

"I know. Your suit is fried."

He paused for a moment. Thinking. Then he said, "You won't kill me."

"No?"

"No. Not while I'm helpless. You are weak that way."

"Like Eliana and Spearman weren't helpless when you were going to burn them alive—while tied to their chairs?"

The Ghost shook his head, a slow smile pulling neatly into place.

Savage's eyes narrowed, his stare unflinching. "Remember when I told you I would cut your heart out?"

The Ghost smiled. Smug as ever. His belief absolute. "I remember. So?"

"Well, about that...I just wanted to let you know something."

"What is that?"

"I never lie." In one devastating move, Savage plunged the knife into the Ghost's heart. Watched his expression turn to shock. Then fear.

Savage twisted the knife. Hard. In a singular, violent move. Then there was nothing.

CHAPTER SEVENTY-SEVEN

Savage retrieved the knife, wiped the blood off the blade, and stood back up. He felt the blood rush from his head, teetered, and then caught himself before toppling over. He took a deep, lung-expanding breath and winced in pain. *Damn. I think I broke some ribs.*

Savage looked over at Eliana. Her face was still wet with tears. But she wore a smile that burned through the darkness like a shooting star. "Oh, God! Savage! Is it really you?"

He staggered over to Eliana and cut away her zip ties. She leaped up from the chair, knocking it over in her excitement. She began smothering him with kisses, her hands clutching his face, pulling herself into him. "I thought I lost you!" She kept repeating it over and over, clutching at him, desperate to keep him from ever leaving her again. She held him like that for a long time, though it seemed all too brief. He finally pulled back and took a good look at her. A little roughed up, but she would be all right. Unfortunately, she couldn't say the same about him.

"Oh my God! He stabbed you. I'm sorry! I...I forgot! I was just so happy to see you—"

"I know. It's all right," he said. Then he shifted his weight, walked gingerly over to the toppled table, and began rummaging through the wreckage. He retrieved both guns. Slipped the suicide vest over his good shoulder.

Eliana watched him hobble across the room and saw his arm swing uselessly at his side. "Savage—*oh, merda!* Are you OK? Wait. Of course you are! I keep forgetting! You have the nanobots!"

Savage made his way back to Eliana. When he reached her, his knees buckled, and he fell into her arms. She caught him at the last second, keeping him from falling. "Well…about that," he said, coughing. "I think I fried the nanobots."

Her eyes widened, and her mouth fell open, though she tried hiding it with her hand. "But you're not bleeding anymore. Are you?"

He shook his head. "No. They may have stanched the bleeding before I burned them to a crisp. My genetic modifications will still help me heal a bit—but as far as the nanobots go? I think I'm on my own."

"No. Never. I'll help you."

Savage smiled at her. Delicately brushed her cheek with adoration. Tenderness. "I know you will."

He then shuffled over to Spearman. Stood over him. He had one gun tucked in the back of his pants, the other resting at his side. Spearman knew what was going to happen.

"Fuck! No! No! I was just following orders!"

"Yeah. Well…that's the thing about orders…you don't have to follow them. You had a choice."

Spearman tried to speak. Tried to come back with something witty. Something that would absolve him of any accountability for his actions. But he was at a loss for words.

Savage remained silent as he studied the man. He watched his eyes, his body posture. Gave a disapproving shake of his head.

Spearman prepared for the inevitable. His normally alabaster skin flushed, then paled again, as all blood drained from his face. "Just get it over with." He clamped his eyes shut and started hyperventilating.

"No. I won't kill you."

Eliana locked eyes with him. "Savage? You know he's been trying to kill us this whole time, right? God knows how many people he's responsible for killing."

"I know. But you could say the same thing about me. Maybe I didn't have a choice back then. I was brainwashed. Programmed to follow orders. But I have a choice *now*. And I choose not to be a weapon." Savage tucked the other gun into the waistband of his pants. He pulled out the tactical knife and cut him free.

Spearman was stunned. Unsure of what to say or do. "You're going to let me go? Just like that?"

Savage shook his head. "No. Not exactly. We need your help."

Spearman laughed, sounding relieved, if not a little maniacal. "OK. Fine. Anything. What do you need me to do?"

"First of all, you'll walk away from all this. You're going to stop putting hits on innocent people. And if I ever hear of you doing so—well. There's nowhere you can go—no place you can hide—to keep me from finding you. Do we understand each other?"

"Yeah. Of course! I understand. No problem."

"Second thing you can do for us: if anybody asks about Eliana and me, tell them we're dead. Tell them we were killed in a firefight with Victor Blackburn and the assassin known as the Ghost. I'm going to burn this place down to the ground. And there'll be nothing left for them to find. If they find anything at all, it would be the unidentifiable bodies of Blackburn, the Ghost, and these two agents here. They'll pass for Eliana and me. Nobody can know that we survived. Ever!"

"Jesus." He made a face. "OK. But Blackburn—he fucking set me up. He planted all sorts of evidence to implicate me!"

Savage raised a finger. Then slipped the suicide vest off, fumbled around in a side pocket, and pulled out an earpiece. He plugged it into his ear. "Newberg? Did you get all that?"

"Copy that."

"Can you scan for any records that implicate Spearman? Make changes, and put the blame back on Blackburn, where it belongs."

"OK. Sure. But that's going to take time. It will delay me from transmitting the other information you requested."

"That's fine. I need you to wait until we're clear. Wait for my signal."

"Copy that. Are you ready for go?"

"Negative. Stand by." He turned to Spearman, raising his eyebrows. "You good?"

"Yeah. But you know that this doesn't end with Blackburn, right? He answered directly to the President."

"I know. But for once the President is going to pay for the crimes he's committed."

Spearman shook his head, then rolled his eyes in disbelief. "Wow. You really believe that, don't you? You're crazier than I thought."

"Yeah, so I've been told. Now get the hell out of here."

★ ★ ★

Savage doused the walls and all its shelves with a combination of turpentine and lacquer thinner. Then he handed Eliana one of the guns. "Remind me to show you how to use one of these things one day."

She started to protest, but then laughed. Nodded. "OK. Deal."

Next, he gave Eliana a name tag identifying her as Junior Agent Fenech with the corresponding information. He had swiped Agent Lavoy's tag and was already wearing it. "I was going to have us change into their clothes to complete the disguise, but..." He gestured to the mutilated dead bodies lying in a pool of blood, their clothes completely ruined.

"Oh! Yeah. That's not good."

"We'll just have to deal with it." Savage tapped a button on his earpiece. "We have a go."

At his command, the security panel flashed a series of green LED lights, and the door popped open. Savage flipped his lighter open and tossed it onto the pile of rags he placed along the storage shelves. They flared immediately and began climbing the walls to the ceiling. It ignited and raced across the room. "Let's go."

He placed his arm around Eliana, allowing her to assist him down the hall. He was straining. Struggling. He didn't want to burden her with his full weight. But there was little choice.

They continued, with Savage leaning on her, wincing every step of the way. They walked about fifty feet down the hall, then turned right and continued down another long corridor. Eventually, they reached the first of three locked doors. As expected, two agents were guarding it.

"Stop. Identify yourselves," one of them said, unsnapping the strap on his gun holster and taking hold of its grip. The other agent followed suit.

This wasn't going to go well. Eliana, a supposed DCS agent, wore a torn, tattered sundress. Savage was sporting a blood-drenched shirt and looked like he had just gone twelve rounds with a gorilla. Name tags be damned.

"Out of our way, Agent. Per Deputy Director Spearman, this wing will be shut down and sealed off. There's been an incident."

Both agents looked at each other and then back at Savage. They weren't convinced. "Deputy Spearman went through here no more than ten minutes ago. He said nothing about shutting this wing down."

The other agent chimed in. "It looked like somebody beat the shit out of him. He was bloodied all to hell." He unclipped his holster as well and placed his hand on his sidearm, ready to pull it immediately.

Savage didn't appreciate the irony. The agents had no idea just how bloody this was about to get.

Then an alarm sounded. A wailing Klaxon so loud it hurt their ears. It was the fire alarm. Emergency lighting kicked on while strobe lights flashed above the door, marking the exit. The two DCS agents jumped. Flustered.

"What the hell?"

"Fire alarm."

"What do we do? We can't abandon the post…can we?"

"Let me call it in…"

Just then, the green LED lights flickered on the security panel behind them, and the door swung open.

They looked back at the exit, trying to figure out what to do next.

Savage looked at Eliana. She seemed just as confused as they were but trusted Savage enough to follow his lead. She shrugged.

Savage offered her a boyish, lopsided smile, then said, "What are you two—stupid? There's a fire!" He swung his arm over Eliana, leaned on her for support, and urged her forward, pushing through the men.

"Get the hell out of here! This place is going to blow. Warn everybody you see! Tell them to evacuate immediately!"

"What about you two? You going to be able to make it out OK?"

Too easy. "Don't worry about us. We have to make sure there aren't others left behind. Now run!" Just who the "others" were, Savage didn't say. Nor did the agents ask. They were too busy hightailing it down the hall, running for their lives.

Eliana shook her head in disbelief. "*Maleïda!* I can't believe that worked!"

Savage fussed with his earpiece, adjusting the fit in his ear. "Was that you?"

Newberg's voice chirped back, "Of course. Did you doubt me?"

"Well, there's a first time for everything." He swung his arm back over Eliana's shoulder again and began walking as best he could. Then he said, "Thanks."

"All security doors have been unlocked. They're programmed to open automatically during a fire."

"Great thinking, Newberg. Now, can you get us to the command center? We need to get to Control. As fast as…" He winced. Tried to push through the pain in his side. "Make that as efficiently as possible."

"Copy. Working on it."

Moments later, Newberg had tapped into the original building schematics and gave them directions. He took them through a maze of corridors. Then he unlocked the access codes to the elevator when they arrived. It was slow going.

They had ascended five floors when the elevator stopped, and the doors opened. "This is your floor, Cypher. Head left down the corridor, and take the first hall to your right. There'll be a small set of stairs—sorry about that. It can't be helped. But that will lead you straight to the command center."

"Copy." Savage felt faint, his breaths shallow and more frequent now. He was having difficulty supporting any of his weight. But the stairs were almost his undoing. He tried pulling himself up using the handrail, but it was no good. Then Eliana tried. She used the handrail for balance while she supported his weight. Her legs nearly buckled. But she kept trying, pushing herself. Finally, they made it.

When they reached the command center, Eliana was drenched in sweat, gasping for air. She looked like she had run a marathon, her legs barely able to support her weight, much less his.

They entered Control, and it stood virtually empty. There were a few people left, running about, gathering their belongings, and heading for the exit. And much to Savage's surprise, Spearman was at their side, yelling at them, ordering them to clear out.

As the last of the staff evacuated the room, Spearman followed after them. Reaching the exit, he stopped and looked at Savage. Then Eliana. He said nothing. His face was battered. Bloody. His left eye swollen shut. Still, he showed no emotion. He pursed his lips, then nodded at them both before walking out of the room.

Savage had Eliana sit down in one of the console chairs. Told her to rest. He then slid off the suicide vest and began making some modifications to it.

Eliana watched him work, her eyes wide. "Won't that blow us up, too?" she asked.

"No, I have a secondary switch that will bypass the dead man's trigger. I have it set on a timer."

"How much time do we have?"

"Once I flip it on? Five minutes."

"Five minutes? That's not a lot of time, Savage."

He shrugged. "I didn't plan on being injured. Besides, the vest was only supposed to be used as a last resort. You know…in case I didn't succeed."

She swallowed. Bit her lip. "You mean…if you were unable to save me."

"Yeah."

Eliana noticed she was holding her breath and let it out slowly. "Can you adjust the time on it?"

"Afraid not."

Savage left the vest near the center of the room and activated the timer. They wasted no time getting back to the main elevator. Then again, they had so little of that to spare. Savage checked his watch. Over three minutes had already elapsed.

"Newberg…how much time before this crate reaches the top?"

"Just a sec…calculating. OK. It looks like the elevator is traveling about a hundred and fifty feet per minute."

Savage did some quick calculations in his head. "Newberg! That's not enough time."

"It's going to be close."

Eliana was resting her head against the elevator, still trying to catch her breath. "*Déu meu.* Just how big is this explosion going to be?"

"Hard to say. Depends on the construction and the building materials. Which I'd guess is probably robust, considering this is a bunker designed to withstand nuclear blasts…"

"Savage!"

"OK! Enough to take out a city block."

"*Oh, merda!* What about the people in the airport?"

He shook his head. "They'll be fine. The airport will be fine. But they're going to feel this!"

Savage looked up at the floor number, silently urging it to hurry. Each floor ticked down at a snail's pace. Fifteen. Twelve. Nine…

He glanced at his digital watch. It didn't look good. Even if the elevator reached ground level, they still had to wait for the doors to open. "Come on! Hurry!"

Six. Four. Two…

Eliana took a deep breath. Cast a glance in his direction. "We're not going to make it, are we?"

He shook his head.

One…

There was a thunderous explosion beneath them, followed by a deep, earth-shattering rumble. The imminent shock wave roared through the elevator shaft like a volcano about to blow. The doors opened just as the shock wave struck the elevator car, damaging its frame and destroying the hydraulic lift system. The car dropped a few feet, then stopped almost immediately, knocking them to the floor. Their hearts lurched into their throats. The elevator car was now dangling precariously from a solitary cable halfway between floors like a pendant swinging at the end of a chain.

Savage scrambled to his feet and helped Eliana up. "Move! Move! We need to get out of here! Now!"

"I don't think I can! The next floor is too high. I don't have the strength to pull myself up!"

"You can! I'll help you!" Savage stooped down. He pushed through the pain as he got onto all fours. "Climb on my back. Use it like a step stool."

"OK!" Eliana grabbed hold of the floor above to steady herself, then used Savage's back to get a boost. He screamed in agony, his bad leg having to support more than it was capable of. But Eliana pulled her upper body onto the floor above, then wiggled the rest of the way out of the elevator.

Now it was his turn. With great effort, Savage pushed himself off the floor and stood again. He stared at the opening and knew instantly he wouldn't be able to make it. His right leg couldn't help support him. His left arm was useless, so he couldn't pull himself up. Worse still, Eliana wasn't strong enough to pull him out alone.

"Give me your hand!"

"It won't work. You're not strong enough. *I'm* not strong enough!"

"You are! Give me your hand!"

Savage didn't move. He looked into her eyes. Saw their intensity. Understood her determination. But he didn't want to fail her.

"Damn it, Savage! You can't always be the hero! It's time to let somebody else help you for a damn change! Now grab my hand!" Eliana sat on the floor above. She braced her legs on either side of the doorjambs and offered him both hands.

Savage reached up with his right hand, and she grabbed it—pulled with all her might. She lifted him about six inches off the floor before she lost her grip, and he slipped back down.

"Again! Give me your hand!"

Savage looked away. Shook his head.

"Savage! Please!"

He took several rapid breaths and steeled himself to try again. "Fine. We've got one more shot at this. It's all I have left in me." Savage gritted his teeth and leaped up to grab her hands. She clutched his hand with one of hers. "Give me your other hand. I need both of them."

Savage closed his eyes. Cleared his mind. He knew this was going to hurt like hell. He reached up with his bad arm and grabbed her other hand. The searing pain was unbearable, but he refused to let go.

Neither did Eliana. She screamed and pulled on him with all her might. Then suddenly there was a pop, and Savage's dislocated shoulder slipped back into place. The pain was horrific, and he cried out in agony. He began to slip.

Eliana reached down deep inside herself, found a strength she didn't even know she had, and pulled one last time. Finally, she lifted him until he could hook his leg on the floor and pull himself out the rest of the way.

From inside the elevator shaft, there was an agonizing groan: death throes from the steel cable supporting the weight of the elevator. Then it snapped, and the elevator car plummeted from sight, falling some two hundred and fifty feet below before imploding into a thousand shards of mangled steel.

Savage lay on top of Eliana, his face inches from hers. Both of them gasping for breath. Both of them exhausted. She smiled. Elated.

Then they kissed. Softly at first. Then with need.

The sound of Newberg's voice in his earpiece broke the silence. "Hey…Cypher? You guys OK?"

Savage pulled back from the kiss, looking as annoyed as he felt, and pointed to his ear. "We're on our way."

Eliana rolled her eyes. Sighed in frustration. "Well, we *were* on our way."

"Well, you two better get a move on," said Newberg. "Full-on panic has already begun. People are running for the exits, convinced there's been a terrorist attack."

Savage and Eliana got up and made their way through the employee access tunnel, opened the exit door to the terminal, and joined the thousands of people screaming, pushing, and shoving their way to the exits. The police were on scene, barking out orders and trying to keep people calm.

Outside, sirens blared. Firetrucks were on their way. News crews were setting up equipment. Traffic jams ensued. It was nothing short of chaos. And that was when Brent Savage and Eliana Bautista slipped into the fleeing crowds of people and made their escape.

They would never be seen or heard from again.

CHAPTER SEVENTY-EIGHT

Philadelphia, Pennsylvania

Philadelphia International Airport, Atlantic Aviation

Following an underground explosion that rocked Denver International Airport five weeks ago, officials have announced that all terminals and gates are open as of this morning. Long suspected of being an act of terrorism, the NSA, in cooperation with the FBI, is reminding people that this is an ongoing investigation and it may take weeks, if not months, before any conclusions can be drawn. Meanwhile, airport officials are reminding travelers to plan for delays, as the backlog of flights in and out of Denver will continue to affect other airports throughout the country.

In other news, just five weeks after an anonymous whistleblower sent out mass unsolicited emails to news outlets nationwide, more damaging information has recently come to light, connecting President Turner to Operation Darkwater. The attached files contained details on alleged 'black ops' missions where the United States government targeted foreign nationals and, occasionally, its own citizens for assassination. The files were distributed to over three thousand news outlets, spanning newspapers, television, radio, and internet media. This has resulted in the most extensive investigation of a sitting U.S. president to date.

Today, just two days before the impeachment hearings begin in the Senate, House Speaker Claris Gammon has requested that Vice President Robert Haydon invoke Section 4 of the 25th Amendment to assume the role of acting president within twenty-four hours. It remains uncertain whether a House resolution could be introduced and voted on with such short notice. However, with Republican minority leader Travis

Rothman calling on other House Republicans to vote their conscience and uphold the Constitution, Democratic leaders say they have the votes to pass the resolution to invoke the 25th Amendment.

There has been speculation that even if there is a failure to convict President Turner on impeachment charges, he may still face charges of atrocity crimes in the International Criminal Court.

Meanwhile, despite his approval ratings at home plummeting nearly twenty-one points in the last month, President Turner continues his travels across Asia today, meeting with Chinese President Xiang Wei to discuss a new free trade agreement. This is the third such visit for President Turner this week, after stops in Korea and Japan. Critics at home have attributed these trips as just another ploy…

Savage got up and moved to the other side of the boarding area, away from the TV. He found a comfortable seat next to the fireplace. It was far more tranquil. And, right now, he needed that.

Micaela returned from the open kitchen with her coffee and cream cheese bagel in hand. She sat beside Savage, slipped the lid off the cup, and began blowing on the coffee. "It's all set. They'll be ready to board in just a few minutes. Eliana said she'll be back in a second. She had to freshen up."

Savage acknowledged he heard her with a nod. But he wasn't really listening. He took a sip from his cup of coffee. The soft light from the fireplace flickered across his face.

"Hey…you feeling OK?"

"Yeah. I feel pretty good now," he said, looking down at his arms and legs. "Even my ribs have healed."

When he electrocuted himself, he thought he had destroyed the nanobots. But what he didn't know at the time was their circuits had just become overloaded, causing them to shut down. Eventually, they simply rebooted. Or regenerated. Or some other nonsense. He wasn't sure. But he knew his body was right again.

Micaela tried to smile, but it lacked conviction. She found herself shaking her head instead. "No, Savage. I meant how are you *feeling*? You seem quiet today." She hesitated, not sure if she should continue. "Are you OK with all of this? I mean…you know…with Eliana moving to France. With you two going your separate ways?"

Savage made a face, then plopped his paper cup down. Coffee spilled down its sides and made a mess on the table. "No. I'm not OK with all of this," he said, frustrated. Crestfallen. "I feel like shit. Do you think I want to do this? Jesus, Mendoza…I'm just trying to do what's best for her."

"Ah. I see. Well, are you sure about that? Have you asked her about how she feels?"

"Of course."

"And?"

"She hates it. She doesn't want to go. But we don't have much of a choice. It's far too dangerous to stay with me. They're going to come looking for me someday. Maybe not right away. Destroying the DCS headquarters bought me a little time—it threw a monkey wrench into their machinery. But they'll eventually figure it out. And they're going to come after me. And God help anybody who's even remotely close to me. I can't have that. I *won't* have that!"

Micaela looked down at her coffee and sighed heavily. "Yeah. I know. I get why you're doing this. You want to protect her."

Savage nodded. "I do. She deserves a better life than I can provide for her. If she stays away from me, there's a chance she'll be safe." Savage choked on his words as he swallowed. "And happy."

"Men." Micaela slapped her hand down on the chair and rolled her eyes. "You think everything is so black and white!"

"What?"

"Happy? Damn, Savage. How happy do you think she'll be without you in her life? I *know* you aren't that dimwitted. She's in love with you!"

Savage couldn't meet her withering stare. He just looked at the tired fire, searching for answers that weren't there in its dying light. "She'll get over it." It sounded as hollow to him as it did to Micaela.

"Oh, right…just like that!" She snapped her fingers. "So you're one of those tough-as-nails-nothing-hurts-me kind of guys? Well…Tough Guy. How about you? Are you going to get over it?"

This time, Savage fixed his attention on the table next to him. He dabbed at the spilled coffee with his napkin. Anything to not have to look at her. But then he wiped away a tear with his thumb and finally screwed up enough courage to answer her. "No…never."

"And why is that?"

"Because I'm in love with her, too. OK?"

Micaela's face relaxed, her anger melting away. She placed her hand on his shoulder. "Does she know? Have you told her how you feel?"

"No. I don't want her to have to carry that burden around with her. Not knowing will be less painful and easier for her in the long run."

Micaela tossed her hands in the air, at a loss for words. "Men! Whatever, Tough Guy. I guess that cold detachment still runs pretty deep. Look. Here she comes now. Tell her. Don't tell her. The choice is yours. But I think she just might be the best part of you—the best part of you that will *ever* be."

Savage stood up and straightened his leather coat. "Yeah…I know. She *is* the best part of me, and I will never feel complete again. I'm certain of it. But that burden—that pain—will stay with me, not her. She deserves better than that."

He started to walk away, hesitated, then turned to look at her. "Thanks, Mendoza. Thank you for everything. Thanks for always being there."

Savage walked over to Eliana, meeting her halfway. He clasped her hands in his own and gazed into her eyes. She flashed a smile at him and casually brushed the left side of her hair up behind her ear. She was so beautiful. It took his breath away.

"I just met Micaela's army buddy who will fly me to Paris. It's really awesome of her to help arrange all this. Did you know he flies celebrities all around the world? He even met Denzel Washington! Can you believe that?" She had a big toothy grin, excited like a little kid at Christmas.

"Yeah, Mendoza told me. And it is great of her to help."

"I'm glad I got to meet her. She's so nice. You know…we couldn't have made it without her. Or Freeman. Or Newberg! And I didn't even have time to say goodbye to him! Is he still going to go through with it?"

"He's already done it. He's changed his entire identity. His family's, too. They moved away to someplace unknown." He glanced out the window and watched the crew loading her luggage onto the plane. "Just like you and I are doing now."

Eliana looked down, squeezed his hands a little harder. She started caressing them with her thumbs. She was no longer smiling.

"Hey, you OK?" He leaned down to get a better look at her. He raised her chin.

Her eyes were glistening with tears, sparkling like diamonds ready to fall. "No. Not really. I was trying to put on a brave face for you. Guess I didn't do a very good job of it. I didn't want you to see me crying. I didn't want you to know I was sad."

"It's OK. It's all right to be sad. I am, too."

"Then why are we doing this? I don't want to leave you!"

"Look…I know. I hate it as much as you do. But we talked about this. We agreed this is what's best—"

"I know we did! And I'll do whatever you say. Because I…I believe in you."

Savage averted his eyes. Looked down at his feet. "I wish it didn't have to be this way."

"Then why are you making me do this? Can't you see this is killing me?" She swiped a tear from her cheek. Sniffed.

"It will get better. I know it's not Catalonia. But if the government ever finds out you're still alive, home is the first place they'd look for you."

"Home," she said, devoid of emotion. "Catalonia isn't my home. It's just a place I grew up. And I don't belong there. I belong with you."

The door opened to the tarmac, and one of the ground crew announced that the luggage was loaded. It was time to board.

Eliana acknowledged him. Told him she would be right there. She turned to look at Savage. "I guess it's time."

"I guess so. I've already wired the money. Do you have all your papers with you? New ID? Your passport?"

She pulled the items from her purse, flipped open the passport, and looked at it one last time. "Eloise Marseau." She sighed.

The man from the ground crew was still standing at the door. Waiting.

"I guess this is goodbye."

Eliana gazed into his eyes, struggling to hold back her tears. "No. I won't say goodbye. Because when I board that plane and fly away, my heart will remain right here with you." She snuggled up to him. Placed her hands on his chest and raised her chin so their lips were just inches apart.

Savage could feel the warmth of her breath on his. A gentle reminder of what could have been. Their eyes locked, each taking the other in and joining in a way their bodies never could.

Eliana slid her arms around Savage's neck and met his lips with hers. It was slow. Gentle, like a warm tropical breeze. Their tongues danced the perfect Samba. Tentative at first, but in perfect harmony. Touching. Caressing. Both trying to satisfy a longing that could never be fulfilled. To feel as one. For one last time.

They parted, spent and out of breath, their dance complete.

They held each other's gaze, suddenly afraid to break the spell. Waiting for the bell to toll.

Savage took a shallow breath, his mouth falling open to speak. But the words never came.

Eliana inhaled, held it for a beat, then slowly let it out. She resigned herself to what she already knew in her heart. And through a cold veil of tears, she found an ember of warmth still burning somewhere safe deep within her. Then she smiled and said, "I love you…too."

Savage returned the smile, then squeezed her hand. It slipped away as she stepped back. Looked at him one last time.

"I will never forget you, Brent Savage. Not as long as I live. And I will never stop believing in us." She paused. Her wishful eyes studied him as if trying to take in every last detail. "I will never give up hope you will return to me one day. And wherever I go, I will leave a light on for you. A guiding light for you to find your way back. A reminder that my love still burns bright for you."

She turned and walked away. And just like that, she was out of his life.

Marches de Pierre, France

The clouds of woolen gray hung over the surrounding hills like an old, dusty blanket waiting out the cold. The snow was falling, lazy and unhurried, the cobblestone streets white and smeary. By afternoon, the snow would be deep enough for many shop owners to close up and head home for an early start to the holiday.

And despite it being the day before Christmas, Eliana began her morning like any other day. She cooked her favorite breakfast. Eggs over easy, with a side of bacon, cooked extra crispy in her oversized iron skillet. A mug of coffee, dark and robust, to wash it all down.

She cleaned up the kitchen, then dressed in her winter coat and woolen hat before heading to the market in town. She had a few things to get before the holiday, a few staples she was running low on.

The wintry weather was new for her. Having grown up in Catalonia, and then later moving to Miami in the States, she had never experienced the snow. The cold. She didn't like it. Admittedly, its white dreamscape was beautiful. Romantic even. But that, of all things, made her sad.

It was a long walk to town, mostly downhill, but she enjoyed her time away from the cottage. It offered her a chance to exercise and breathe some fresh air.

The small village of Marches de Pierre was quaint. Familiar. And old world. This time of year, the medieval buildings were tastefully decorated in their holiday fare. Wreaths adorned their brightly colored doors, while pine swags hung neatly above the narrow streets like party streamers.

Her first stop was *la boulangerie*, or the bakery. She was greeted by a singsong bell over the door and the heavenly aroma of sweet bread baking in the ovens. A moment later, Liane Blanchett appeared from the back room, wearing a white apron and a dab of flour on her generous cheeks.

"Bonjour, Madame Blanchett," Eliana said cheerily.

Liane knew very little English, and Eliana was still struggling with her French, so their communication was broken at best. But Eliana knew enough to understand her meaning, even when she didn't catch every word.

"Ah! Merry Christmas, Eloise! I'm so happy you stopped by today. I made something special for you. Something to take home for Christmas."

Eliana had a hard time hearing her fictitious name. It hadn't taken, and she wasn't sure it ever would. But, like most things in her life, she somehow managed to push through it. "You didn't have to do that!"

"Oh, sweet dear. It's my pleasure. Just a moment." Liane was more round than tall and a bit knock-kneed. But she was back in no time with a freshly baked bundt cake in her hands. She boxed it up and said, "I hope you like kougelhopf, dear."

"It's my favorite! How did you know?"

"A little birdy told me." She gave her a wide, horse-toothed grin, her cheeks forming two crater-like dimples.

"Thank you!"

"So what brings you in today?"

"Oh, yes. I need two baguettes, please."

Liane slipped the loaves of bread into a brown paper bag and promptly rang her up. After making change, she handed Eliana her order.

Eliana wished her a Merry Christmas and had turned to leave when Liane caught her by the arm.

"Oh! I heard you singing at the *Sanglier Bleu* last night," she said. "You were wonderful. I didn't know you played piano!"

"I dabble a little bit. Did you really like it?"

Liane clapped her hand across her bosom and looked up at the ceiling as if swearing an oath. "Oh, my heavens! You have the voice of an angel, dear."

Eliana couldn't help but smile at that and found herself blushing. "I'm glad you enjoyed it."

Liane had been smiling freely, but then her face sagged into something more serious. "Tell me, dear. You have such a lovely voice…why must you sing such sad, sad songs? Why not something more cheerful? No?"

Eliana shrugged, but kept her smile locked in place. "I guess I just sing what I feel. It's the only way I know how to sing. From the heart."

"Oh. Oh, honey." Liane looked at her, eyes drooping like a hound dog. "That can't be true. That's the sound of a lonely heart breaking. And you're such a lovely girl."

Eliana nodded and looked at the door like it was time to be on her way.

"Don't worry, Eloise. Chin up!" She threw her a wink. "One day, your prince will come."

"No," she said, scrunching her mouth to one side. Considering. "He was never a prince. He was my knight."

Eliana thanked her for the cake one last time and then walked back out into the snow. After enduring the bakery's oppressive heat, the sting of the cold felt like a slap to the face.

She snugged the collar of her coat tighter and continued down the main street. She had more shopping to do.

For the next couple of hours, she made stops at several more stores. She needed some cured ham, butter, and a quart of milk from the market. She also bought a couple of pine-scented candles for her kitchen table at the boutique next door. Next, she made her way to *la fromagerie* and bought some Cantal cheese. And finally, before heading home, she picked up a bottle of Languedoc red wine from a darling little wine shop off Rue du Moulin.

She made the long slog back home, which was mostly uphill now. As promised, the snow fell harder in the afternoon, and there was now a good four or five inches on the ground, making it much harder to walk on the slippery cobblestone streets.

She made it back to her cottage before dark, which came early during this time of year.

Her small cottage was half-timber and half-stone, with two stories and a steeply pitched roof. It had weathered wood shutters and colonial-style muntins on the windows. The chimney was built with smooth river rock and was soot-stained from centuries of good use. Even now, a ropy curl of smoke climbed into the sky, its sweet, earthy aroma both pleasing and inviting.

Inside, the rooms were dressed in simple fare. A large kitchen dominated the main floor, appointed with dated but functional appliances. The only other rooms were the sparsely furnished living area and a closet-sized pantry. The focal point, as was true of all medieval homes, was the stone hearth. Upstairs were the two bedrooms and bath.

Eliana knocked the snow off her boots before entering the house and promptly hung her coat to dry by the door. She took the time to put her groceries away, then stoked the fire to take the nip out of the air.

As the night settled in, she took great care in arranging the two candles on the oak table and lit them with a long wooden match. She then fixed herself a snack of cheese and ham and enjoyed a couple of glasses of wine. She sat quietly by the hearth, lost in thought, watching the fire dance to the songs of aged hardwood, crackling and popping as it burned.

As the hours grew heavy, Eliana went upstairs and drew a hot bath, soaking the tiredness from her back and legs and washing the smell of smoke from her hair. She looked at herself in the mirror as she towel-dried her tangles of wet hair and was reminded of her time with Savage at the Echo Bay motel in Miami. She cried. And was angry at herself for doing so.

She brushed her teeth and then slipped into her wool pajamas. She went to the spare room, which also doubled as her sitting room. Its only furniture was an antique rocking chair, a small dusty bookshelf, and an old upright piano. She'd just had it tuned as it offered her the one respite from her daily drudgery and loneliness. She let her fingers glide over the keys for a minute, her thoughts again drifting to another place and time. Her fingers finally found the melody and started to play "Have Yourself a Merry Little Christmas." She sang it as well as she ever had, perfect in pitch and with a genuine sadness that could only come from the heart. When she wept again, she stopped, closed the lid, and called it a night.

Eliana walked down the small hallway to her bedroom. It was cold, and the windowpane was frosted with winter's breath. She drew down the covers and slid into bed, snuggling beneath the weight of the heavy blue comforter. She lay staring at the ceiling, unblinking, unmoving, for what seemed like hours. Yet only minutes had passed. Her stomach hurt, and she was tired of crying. She finally rolled onto her side and tucked her folded hands beneath her head.

She stared at the table lamp for a long time. She lay still again. Her breathing was slow, rhythmic. Finally, she reached over and turned out the light.

Outside, across from the cozy Tudor-style cottage, leaning against a century-old oak tree, Savage watched the snowfall. The flakes were huge, billowy, and floated lazily to the ground like soft, downy feathers—a picturesque postcard on a cold winter's night.

He had come to the cottage earlier in the day. Knew it stood empty, as there was just a solitary track of footprints leading away in the light skiff of snow. He didn't stay. Instead, he canvased Marches de Pierre, a small town with little more than a thousand people, careful to remain inconspicuous. There were no strangers. No new arrivals in the town. No recent home purchases or rentals. The town remained innocuous.

More importantly, Eliana seemed well. Safe. At least as much as possible in this crazy world.

He returned hours later to find new tracks in the snow, this time leading back to the small cottage. Lights in the kitchen burned bright, inviting and warm.

Savage remained vigilant. Steadfast. And despite the cold, he remained beneath the tree, shivering, keeping watch. A small reassurance that she would be all right.

But the truth of the matter was he missed her. And there was nothing in this world that could fill that void. The best part of him—as Mendoza so succinctly pointed out—was slipping away forever.

He watched the lights turn off downstairs. Then a new one appeared upstairs. At first there was an indistinct glow, suggesting it originated from somewhere other than the two rooms on the second level. But then another light appeared in the room on the right. Soon, the soft tinkle of a piano found its way through the stone and plastered walls of the cottage. Then she began to sing, and Savage thought his heart would stop. It was beautiful. Angelic. And it broke his heart.

She sang only one song—not even finishing it—before she turned out the light. There was a brief pause before the light in the other room flipped on. Then Eliana passed by the window, her silhouette offering Savage a momentary glimpse of his heart's desire—a reminder of what could have been.

The light remained on in the room for a long time. And Savage thought back to their last time together at the airport. She swore she would never forget him, and she would leave a light on to guide him home. And the thought brought a smile to his face. But the pleasant thought was short-lived.

The light turned off. And the room fell dark. And it remained so.

Savage felt like a rug had just been pulled out from under him. His stomach twisted and turned, and his chest drew tight—ached in a way he couldn't fathom. He sighed. And then he knew.

After a few minutes, Savage brushed off the snow that had collected on his coat and started to walk away. But at that very moment, the bedroom light turned back on. And there it remained, steady, burning bright. A beacon of hope. And, for Savage, his guiding light. This he knew. And he smiled.

ABOUT THE AUTHOR

Matt Ryland was born in Ohio, but after spending a lifetime moving from one city to another—six times before he turned eleven—he considers himself a hometown orphan. He studied English and creative writing at the University of Wyoming, helping fuel his passion for great stories, and instilling a lifelong love for the Rocky Mountain West. *Cypher* is the first book in a planned series of action-thrillers featuring Brent Savage. When not traveling (or moving), Matt loves to hike, enjoys landscape photography, and is a self-proclaimed computer geek. Matt lives with his family in Northeast Ohio…for now.